HANS ANDERSEN'S FAIRY TALES

HANS ANDERSEN'S
FAIRY TALES

Abridged Edition

PRINTED IN GREAT BRITAIN
DEAN & SON Ltd.
41/43 Ludgate Hill LONDON EC4

MADE AND PRINTED IN GREAT BRITAIN BY PURNELL AND SONS, LTD.
PAULTON (SOMERSET) AND LONDON

603 03039 4

CONTENTS

THE STORKS

ON the last house in a village was a stork's nest. The stork-mother sat in the nest with her four little ones, which stretched out their heads with the little black beaks, for they had not yet become red. A little way off, on the ridge of the roof, stood the stork-father, quite stiff and rigid, with one leg drawn up under him, so that, at any rate, he might have some trouble in standing as he kept watch. It seemed almost as if he were carved in wood, he stood so still. "It must certainly look quite grand that my wife should have a guard near the nest," he thought, "for no one can know that I am her husband, but they will surely think that I have been ordered to stand here. It looks well!" and he continued to stand on one leg.

In the street below a troop of children were playing; and when they saw the storks, first one of the boldest of them, and afterwards altogether, sang the old rhyme about the storks, but they sang it just as it came into the first singer's head : —

> "Stork, stork, fly home, I beg,
>   And don't stay idling on one leg.
> There's your wife sits in her nest,
> Rocking all her young to rest;
> The first he will be hung,
> The second roasted young,
> They'll come and shoot the third,
> And stab the fourth, I've heard."

"Just listen to what the boys are singing," said the little storks; "they say we shall be hanged and roasted."

"You need not mind that!" said the mother; "don't listen to them, and it matters not what they say."

But the boys went on singing, and made game of the storks, pointing at them with their fingers; only one of them, whose name was Peter, said it was wrong to laugh at the poor things, and he himself would not join in. The stork-mother, in the meantime, consoled her young ones, saying, "Do not mind them; just look how unconcerned your father stands there, and on one leg too."

"We are so afraid!" said the young ones, and they drew back their heads into the nest.

On the following day, when the children met together again to play, and saw the storks, they sang their rhyme,—

"The first he will be hung,
The second roasted young."

"Must we be hanged and roasted?" the young storks asked.

"No, certainly not!" said the mother; "you shall learn to fly, which I'll teach you, and then we'll fly out into the meadows and pay the frogs a visit as they sing 'croak, croak!'; then we'll eat them up, and that will be fun."

"And what next?" asked the little ones.

"Then all the storks of the whole country will meet together, and the autumn manœuvring begins, when you must be able to fly well. That is of the greatest importance; for whichever of you does not fly properly, the general will pierce through with his beak, and kill;—so take care that you attend to the exercising when it begins."

"So we shall be stabbed after all, as the boy said; and there! listen!—they are singing it again."

"Attend to me, and not to them," said the stork-mother: "after the grand manœuvre we fly away to a warmer country, far, far from here, over mountains and forests. To Egypt we fly, where there are three-cornered stone houses which rise up into a point above the clouds; these are called pyramids, and are older than a stork has any notion of. In that country is a river, which, overflowing its banks, turns the whole land into slime, and all one has to do is to pick up the frogs."

"Oh, how nice!" cried all the young ones.

"Yes, that is a glorious life! One has nothing to do all day but to eat; and during the time we are living there in such luxury, in this country there is not a single green leaf on the trees; it is so cold here that the clouds freeze, and break to pieces in white flakes." She meant snow, but did not know how to express it better.

"Do the naughty boys, then, freeze and break into pieces too?" the young storks asked.

"No, they do not break into pieces, but are very cold and miserable, and have to huddle together in their dark rooms, whereas you can fly about in a foreign country, where there are flowers, and where the sun gives warmth."

Some time had now passed by, and the young ones had grown so big that they could stand up in the nest, and watch their father from afar, as he brought them beautiful frogs and small snakes, and suchlike delicacies. Then what fun it was to watch his tricks! His head he would bend right back, laying it upon his tail, and with his beak he made a noise like a rattle, and told them besides such stories all about the swamps.

"Listen to me; you must now learn to fly," said the stork-mother one day; and then all the four young ones had to get out of the nest on to the ridge of the roof. Oh, how they waddled, how they balanced themselves with their wings, and yet were near falling down.

"Now watch me," said their mother, "this is the way you must hold your head, and place your feet thus! One, two; one, two; that's the way to get on in the world." Then she flew a little way, and the young ones gave an awkward jump, when, plump, down they went, for their bodies were too heavy.

"I'll not fly," said one of them, and crept back into the nest; "what do I care about going into a warmer country?"

"Do you wish to freeze to death when winter comes? And shall the boys come to hang and to roast you? Well, then, I'll call them."

"No, no!" cried the young stork, and hopped out of the nest again to the others.

On the third day they began to be able to fly a little, and then thought they could float in the air; but, when they tried that, over they went, and were obliged to move their wings again pretty quickly. Then came the boys again, down below in the street, and sang,—

"Stork, stork, fly home, I beg."

"Shall we not fly down and peck out their eyes?" said the young storks.

"No, leave that alone," said the mother. "Attend to me, which is much more important. One, two, three; now we'll fly to the right. One, two, three; and now to the left, round the chimney. Now, that was very well done, particularly the last turn, so that to-morrow you may be allowed to fly with me to the marsh. There we shall find several nice stork families; and mind you show that my children are the best. You may strut about as proudly as you like, for that creates respect."

"But are we not to be revenged on the naughty boys?" they asked.

"Let them say what they like; you'll fly up into the clouds, and go to the land of the pyramids, whilst they are freezing here, and haven't a green leaf nor a sweet apple."

"We'll be revenged for all that," said they to each other, and then they went on with their exercising again.

Of all the boys in the street, not one was worse with the mocking than just he who had begun the rhyme, and he was quite a little fellow, not more, perhaps, than six years old. The young storks, indeed, thought he must be a hundred years old, for he was so much bigger than their father or mother: and what should they know of the age of human beings, old or young? All their revenge should fall upon this one, for it was he who had begun. The young storks were much enraged, and as they grew bigger the less they could bear it, so that at last their mother was obliged to promise that they should be revenged, but not till the last day of their being in the country.

"We must first see how you get on at the great manœuvre. If you come off badly, so that the general runs you through with his beak, then the boys are right, at least in one respect. Now let us see how you get on."

"Yes, that you shall," they answered, and took particular pains. They practised so diligently every day, and flew so straight and lightly, that it was a pleasure to look at them.

Now came autumn; and the storks began to meet together, preparatory to migrating to a warmer climate during our winter. Then there was a grand manœuvre. They had to fly over forests and villages, in order to see how they got on, for it was a serious journey that was before them. The young storks managed so well that they received a reward of a frog and snake, which they lost no time in eating.

"Now we ought to take our revenge," said they.

"Yes, certainly," said their mother; "and what I have planned is just the very best thing to do. I know where the pond is, in which the children lie till the stork comes and takes them to their parents. The dear little children sleep, and have such delightful dreams as they never have in after-life. All parents are anxious to have such a child, and all children wish to have a brother or a sister. Now, we will fly off to the pond, and fetch a child for each of those that did not sing that naughty song about the storks."

"But what are we to do to him,—to that bad, ugly boy, who began the song?" cried out the young ones.

"In the pond there lies a dead child, which has dreamed itself to death. That one we will fetch for him, and then he will have to cry, because we have brought him a dead brother; but for the good boy, whom I hope you have not forgotten,—the one who said it was wrong to make game of the birds—for him we will fetch a brother and a sister; and as his name is Peter, so shall all storks be called Peter."

What she said was done, and all storks were called Peter, as they are up to this day.

THE GARDEN OF PARADISE

THERE was once a King's son, who had so many and such beautiful books as no one ever had before, and in these he could read of all that had happened in this world, and admire the beautiful pictures illustrating the various events. Of every nation and of every country he could gain information, but where the Garden of Paradise was to be found, of that there was not a word in his books, and it was just this he thought most of.

His grandmother had told him, when he was still quite little but about to go to school, that each flower in the Garden of Paradise was the sweetest of cakes, and had its stamens filled with the most delicious of wines; that on one were written lessons in history, and on another geography, or multiplication-tables, so that to learn one's lessons nothing was required but to eat cake, and the more one ate the more history, geography, and multiplication, was learned.

He believed that then, but when he had grown a bigger boy, had learnt more and was wiser, he understood that the splendour and delights of the Garden of Paradise must be something far different.

"Oh, why did Eve pluck the fruit from the tree of knowledge? and why did Adam taste of it? If it had been I, all this would not have happened, and never would sin have come into the world."

This he said when a little boy, and still said the same when seventeen years old. The Garden of Paradise engrossed all his thought.

One day he was walking in the forest, and was walking alone, for that was his greatest delight.

Evening approached, and the clouds having gathered together, it came on to rain as if heaven were one great flood-gate from which the waters rushed; it was as dark as it can possibly be at night in the deepest well. Now he slipped in the wet grass, and then fell over the rough stones which projected from the rocky ground. All dripped with water, and there was not a dry thread upon the poor Prince. He had to climb huge blocks of stone, the water oozing out from the thick moss, and he was near fainting, when he heard an extraordinary rushing sound, and saw before him a large illuminated cavern. In the middle of the cavern was a large fire, at which a whole stag could be roasted, and this, indeed, was being done, for the most magnificent stag, with its high antlers, was turning round slowly, fixed between two fir-trees. An elderly woman, big and strong, as if she were a disguised man, sat by the fire, on to which she threw one log of wood after another.

"Come nearer," she said, "and seat yourself by the fire, so that your clothes may get dried."

"There is a nasty draught here," said the Prince, as he seated himself on the ground.

"It will be still worse when my sons come home," the woman answered, "for you are here in the Cavern of the Winds, and my sons are the four winds of the universe. Can you understand that?"

"Where are your sons?" the Prince asked.

"It is difficult to answer when one is asked a foolish question," she said. "My sons act on their own account, and are playing at foot-ball with the clouds,—up there"; and she pointed above her with her finger.

"Oh, that's it," said the Prince; "and you yourself are somewhat harsh, and do not talk over civilly and softly, like the women I have been accustomed to have about me."

"They have nothing else to do, but I must be harsh if I wish to keep my boys in order, which I can do, stiff-necked as they are. Do you see those four sacks hanging against the wall? those they fear as much as you once feared the rod behind the looking-glass. I can bend them to my will, I tell you; they must go into the sack, for I stand no nonsense. There they sit, and dare not stir till I allow them to get out and wander about. But here is one of them."

It was the North Wind who came in with icy coldness. Large hailstones bounded about the floor, and snow-flakes floated in the air. He was clad in bear's skin, with a sealskin cap, which hung down over his ears; long icicles hung down from his beard, and one hailstone after another rolled down from underneath his jacket.

"Do not go too suddenly to the fire," the Prince said, "for fear your hands and feet should be frost-bitten."

"Frost!" the North Wind said, and burst out laughing; "why, it's just frost I most delight in. And pray, what spooney are you? and how do you get here into the Cavern of the Winds?"

"He is my guest," the old woman said; "and if you are not satisfied with that explanation, you may go into the sack. Do you understand me?"

Well, that had the desired effect, and the North Wind narrated whence he came, and where he had been nearly a whole month.

"I come from the Polar Sea," he said. "I was on the Island of the Bears with the Russian whale-fishers. I sat and slept at the helm when they started on their expedition, and when I did wake up for a minute the stormy petrel flew round my legs. That is a curious bird, it gives one strong flap with its wings, and then stretching them out keeps them motionless, and this is enough to carry it on."

"Well, you need not be too minute," said the mother of the Winds. "And so you were on the Island of the Bears?"

"It's delightful there. That's the floor for dancing on! flat and smooth as a plate, all half-thawed snow, with a little moss. There were sharp stones and skeletons of whales and polar bears, green with mould. One would think the sun never shone there. I blew a little into the fog so that the huts might be seen. They were built with the wood of wrecks, covered over with whale-skins; on the roof of one sat a living polar bear and growled. I went to the shore and looked after the birds' nests; saw the unfledged young ones, and blowing down their open throats, taught them to shut their beaks."

"You talk well, my son," said the mother. "It makes my mouth water to listen to you."

"Then came the fishing. The harpoon was struck into the whale's breast so that the streaming blood spouted forth like a fountain. Then I thought of my own game, and bestirring myself blew the icebergs before me, till the boats were hemmed in. Then there was a shouting and howling, but I howled louder still. The dead whales, boxes and cordage had to be thrown on to the ice, and covering all up with snow, I drove them towards the south, there to taste salt water. They will never come back to the Island of the Bears."

"So you have done mischief," the mother of the Winds said.

"Let others tell the good I have done," he said; "but here comes my brother from the west. Him I like best of all, for he has a smack of the sea and brings a delightful coolness with him."

"Is that the little Zephyr?" the Prince asked.

"It is Zephyr sure enough, but he is not so very little. In olden times he was a beautiful boy, but that is past."

He looked like a wild man, but wore a slouched hat to protect him. In his hand he carried a mahogany club, cut in the American mahogany forests, and that was no trifle.

"Where do you come from?" his mother asked.

"I come from the wilds of the forest," he said, "where the thorny bushes form thick hedges between the trees, where the water-snake lies in the wet grass, and where man seems unwonted."

"What were you doing there?"

"I looked down into the deep rivers, watched the waters as they fell from cliff to cliff, became dust and flew up towards heaven, to bear the rainbow. I saw the buffalo swimming in the river, but, carried away by the stream to the waterfall, amidst a swarm of wild ducks, which flew up into the air, it was dashed down. This pleased me, and I blew up a storm so that the oldest trees tottered and were splintered to pieces."

"And have you done nothing else?" the old woman asked.

"I have stroked the wild horses, and have shaken the cocoa-nuts from the lofty trees. I have played many a prank. Yes, yes, I have many a story to tell, but one must not tell everything that one knows. You know that well enough, you old one," and he kissed his mother so boisterously that she almost fell backwards. He was, indeed, a wild fellow.

Now came the South Wind, wearing a turban and a flowing Bedouin mantle.

"It is wretchedly cold here," he said, throwing more wood on the fire; "one can easily feel that the North Wind arrived first."

"It is so hot here, that one might roast a polar bear," the North Wind said.

"You are a polar bear yourself," the South Wind answered.

"Do you wish to be put in the sack?" the old woman asked. "There, seat yourself on yonder stone and tell us where you have been."

"In Africa, my mother," he answered. "I joined a party of Hottentots in a lion-hunt. Oh! what grass grows there in the plains, green as an olive. There the ostrich ran a race with me, but I am the fleeter-footed. I went to the sandy desert, which is like the bottom of the sea, and there I came up with a caravan, just as they were killing their last camel for the sake of the water, but it was little they got. The sun burnt from above and the sand scorched from below. There was no end to the vast desert. Then I crept under the fine loose sand, and whirled it up in huge pillars. You should have seen how lost the dromedary stood there, and the merchant, drawing his kaftan over his head, prostrated himself before me, as before Allah, his God. Now they are buried, and there stands over them a pyramid of sand; when I blow that away, the sun will bleach their bones, and travellers will see that human beings have been there before them, which, in the desert, it is difficult to imagine."

"So you have done nothing but evil," said the mother; "into the sack with you!" and before he was prepared for anything of the sort, she had caught the South Wind round the body, and thrust him into the sack. He rolled about on the floor, but she seated herself upon him and he was forced to lie quiet.

"Those are lively boys of yours," the Prince said.

"Yes, indeed they are," she answered, "and I can correct them when necessary : but here is the fourth."

This was the East Wind, dressed like a Chinese. "Well, and do you come from the Garden of Paradise?" the old woman said.

"I go there to-morrow," the East Wind answered. "To-morrow it will be a hundred years since I was there. I now come from China, where I was playing round the Porcelain Tower, till all the bells rang. Below, in the street, the various officers of state, from the first to the ninth degree, were being chastised, and the cane was split across their shoulders. They cried, 'Many thanks, my parental benefactor,' but they meant nothing by it, and I rang the bells, singing, tsing, tsang, tsu."

"You are wanton," said the old woman. "It is well that to-morrow you go to the Garden of Paradise, for that always adds to your improvement. Take a good draught from the spring of Wisdom, and bring home a bottle full of it for me."

"I'll not forget that," the East Wind said. "But why have you put my brother from the South into the sack? Out with him, as I want him to tell me all about the bird, Phœnix, for the Princess in the Garden of Paradise always wishes to hear of him, when every hundredth year I pay her my customary visit. Open the sack, and you shall be my sweetest of mothers, and I will give you two pockets full of tea, so fresh and green, just as I gathered it on the spot itself."

"Well, for the sake of the tea, and because you are my own dear boy, I will open the sack." She did so, and the South Wind crept out, quite humbled, because the strange Prince had been a witness of his punishment.

"There is a palm-leaf for the Princess," he said. "This leaf, the old Phœnix, the only one in the world, gave me himself. With his bill he has scratched the whole history of his hundred years' life upon it. She can there read how the Phœnix himself set fire to his nest, sitting in it and burning, like the wife of a Hindoo. How the dry twigs crackled, and then there was a smoke and a smell. At length all broke out into a flame, and the old Phœnix was burnt to ashes, but its egg lay red-hot in the nest, which burst with a loud explosion, and the young bird flew out, to be the Regent of all birds, and the only Phœnix in the world. He bit a hole in the palm-leaf, which I gave you, and that is his greeting to the Princess."

"Now let us have something to eat," the mother of the Winds said, whereupon they all drew round the roasted stag, and as the Prince sat by the side of the East Wind, they soon became friends.

"I wish you would tell me," the Prince said, "who the Princess is of whom there has been so much talk, and where the Garden of Paradise is situated."

"No, no!" the East Wind cried. "If you want to go there, fly off with me to-morrow, but one thing I must tell you, that no human being has been there since Adam and Eve. I suppose you know them from your Bible?"

"Of course I do," the Prince answered.

The East Wind continued, "When they were driven from Paradise, the garden sank down into the earth, but it retained its warm sunshine, its balmy air, and all its splendour. The Fairy Queen lives there, and there is the Island of Bliss, where death never comes. Seat yourself on my back to-morrow, and I will take you with me. I think it can be done, but now you must speak no more, for I want to sleep."

And they all slept.

Early in the morning the Prince awoke, and was not a little taken aback to find himself high above the clouds. He was seated upon the back of the East Wind, where he was as comfortable and safe as possible, though they were so high up in the air that the scene below, with the forests and fields, rivers and lakes, looked like an illuminated map.

"Good morning!" said the East Wind; "though you might as well have slept a little longer, for the country is so flat that there is not much to see, unless you have a fancy for counting the churches, which looks like so many spots dotted down at random upon the map."

"It was ill-behaved of me not to say good-bye to your mother and brothers," the Prince observed.

"Being asleep was excuse enough," the East Wind said; and hereupon they flew on more swiftly than ever, as might be seen by the trees, for as they passed over, the branches and leaves rustled, and it might be seen in the lakes and seas, for as they swept on the waves rose higher and the large ships dipped down into the water like swimming swans.

Towards evening, when it got dark, the great towns produced a most curious effect, for the lights seemed to disappear and appear again, now here, now there, like the sparks in a burnt piece of paper, which children call coming out of school; and the Prince was so amused that he clapped his hands but the East Wind told him he had as well leave that alone, and hold fast rather, or he might fall down and find himself hanging to the steeple of some church.

The eagle in the dark forest flew swiftly, but the East Wind more swiftly still, and the Cossack on his little horse swept across the plain, but very differently the East Wind sped on.

"Now you can see the Himalaya, which is the highest mountain in Asia," the East Wind said, "and now we shall soon be in the Garden of Paradise." They turned more towards the south, and soon the delicious scent of flowers and fruits reached them. Figs and pomegranates grew wild, and the vines bore black and white grapes. Here they descended and stretched themselves in the soft grass where the flowers, nodding to the Wind, seemed to say, "Welcome back here."

"Are we now in the Garden of Paradise?" the Prince asked.

"No, no," the East Wind answered; "but we shall soon be there. Do you see yonder high rock, and the cavern where the vine hangs like a green curtain? Through that we shall get to it; but wrap your cloak well around you, for, though the sun here is scorching hot, a few steps farther and it is icy cold. The bird that is now flying past the cavern has one wing in the warm summer, and the other in the cold winter."

"And that, then, is the way to the Garden of Paradise?" the Prince said.

They now went into the cavern, and bitterly cold it was there, but did not last long. The East Wind spread out wings, which shone like the brightest fire; and, oh! what a cavern it was! The huge blocks of stone, from which the water dripped, hung over them in the most fantastic shapes; and in some places the cavern was so low that they had to creep on their hands and knees, whilst in others it was so high and wide, as if they were in the open air. It looked like a large chapel, pervaded by the solemnity of death, with petrified organs and silent pipes.

The Prince said, "It seems we have to pass through the Valley of Death to reach the Garden of Paradise." But the East Wind did not answer a syllable, pointing only before him; and the most beautiful blue light streamed towards them. The blocks of stone above them became more and more as a mist, and at last clear as white clouds in moonshine. They were now in the most delightful balmy air, fresh as on the mountains, but soft and sweet as amongst roses in the valley. There was a river, clear as the air itself, and the fish were as gold and silver; purple-coloured eels, which at every movement emitted sparks of fire, played at the bottom of the water; and the broad leaves of the water-lilies shone with all the colours of the rainbow, whilst the flower itself was an orange-coloured flame, which was nourished by the water, as oil keeps up the life of a lamp. A firm, marble bridge, which, however, was of such skilful workmanship that it looked like lace-work and pearls, led across the river to the Island of Bliss, in which was the Garden of Paradise.

The East Wind took the Prince in his arms, carrying him across; and then the flowers and leaves began to sing the most delightful songs of his youth, but so full and soft as no human voice could imitate.

Were those palm-trees, or gigantic water-plants, that grew there? Such large trees, and so full of sap, the Prince had never before seen. The most wonderful creepers hung in large festoons, as you only find painted in gold and bright colours in the margins of illuminated missals, or winding through the initial letters. It was the strangest mixture of birds, flowers, and flourishes. Close by, in the grass, stood a swarm of peacocks with outspread, radiant tails. It seemed reality; but no, when the Prince touched them he found they were not birds, but only plants; they were the large burdock-leaves, which there shone like the beautiful tail of the peacock.

Lions and tigers were springing about like playful cats between the scented hedges, and they were tame. The wood-pigeon, shining like the purest pearl, struck the lion's mane with its wings, and the antelope, generally so wild, stood and nodded with its head as if it wished to join the game.

Now the Fairy of Paradise appeared, her dress shining like the sun, and her countenance was mild, like that of a happy mother rejoicing in her child. She was young and beautiful; and the prettiest girls, each with a bright star in her hair, followed. The East Wind gave her the Phœnix's manuscript, and her eyes beamed with pleasure. She took the Prince by the hand and led him into her palace, where the walls shone with colours, like unto the most beautiful tulip-leaf held between the eye and the sun; whilst the roof was as a bright flower, and the more you looked up into it the deeper its calyx appeared. The Prince walked up to the window, and through one of the panes he saw the tree of knowledge of good and evil, with the snake and Adam and Eve standing by the side. "Are they not banished?" he asked. And the Fairy, smiling, explained that time had engraved on each pane the events as they passed, but not like ordinary pictures—no, it was life itself, for the leaves of the trees moved, and the persons went and came. He looked through another pane, and there saw Jacob's dream, the angels ascending and descending the ladder with their wings spread out. All that had happened in this world was here represented on the panes of glass, and such pictures Time alone could paint.

The Fairy smiled, and led him into a large and lofty room, the walls of which appeared transparent. There were portraits, the one face more beautiful than the other—millions of happy beings smiling and singing, so as to form one delightful melody, the upper ones being no larger than dots drawn with the pencil. In the middle of the room stood a tree, with luxuriant hanging branches, on which golden apples, large and small, appeared amongst the green leaves. This was the tree of knowledge of good and evil, of the fruit of which Adam and Eve had eaten. From each leaf dripped a bright red dew-drop, as if the tree were shedding tears of blood.

"Let us now enter the boat," the Fairy said; "and there, on the cool waters, partake of some refreshment. The boat rocks, though it does not move from the spot; and yet all the lands of the world glide past us."

So, indeed, it was, for the whole coast was in motion. Now passed the high, snow-capped Alps, partially covered with clouds and the black fir whilst the horn sounded sorrowfully, and the shepherds sang merrily, in the valley. Now the banana-tree bent its long drooping branches down over the boat; coal-black swans swam past, and the most extraordinary creatures and flowers appeared on the banks of the river. This was Australia, the fifth division of the world. One might hear the song of the priests, and see the dance of the savages to their barbarous music. The pyramids of Egypt, rising up above the clouds, overthrown columns and sphinxes, half buried in sand, sailed past. The aurora borealis shot up streams of light, like fireworks, that no one can imitate. The Prince was in ecstasies, for he saw a hundred more wonderful things than we can here describe.

"And can I always remain here?" he asked.

"That depends upon yourself," the Fairy answered. "If you do not, like Adam, allow yourself to lust after what is forbidden, you may always remain here."

"I shall not touch the apples of the tree of knowledge," the Prince said. "There are thousands of other fruits, just as beautiful as that."

"Examine yourself, and if you are not strong enough, return with the East Wind, who brought you; he now flies back, and will not appear here again for a hundred years, though that time will seem to you as if it were only a hundred hours, but it is a long time to resist temptation and sin. Every evening, when I part from you, I must call to you, 'Come with me,' and must beckon you with my hand, but remain where you are. Do not follow me, for with every step your desires will become more ungovernable; you will come into the room where the tree of knowledge of good and evil grows; I shall sleep under its fragrant hanging branches, and you will bend over me, when I must smile. If then you kiss my lips, the Garden of Paradise will sink deep into the earth, and to you it will be lost. A cutting wind will howl round you, and a cold rain will drip from your hair. Sorrow and distress will be your portion."

"I will remain," the Prince said, and the East Wind, kissing him on the forehead, said, "Be strong and then we shall meet again here, after a hundred years. Farewell! Farewell!" The East Wind then spread out his enormous wings, which shone like lightning at harvest time, or the aurora in cold winter.

"Farewell! farewell!" resounded from the flowers and the trees. The storks and the pelicans flying in a line, like fluttering ribbons, accompanied him as far as the limits of the garden.

"Now we will begin our dance," the Fairy said, "and at its close when the sun is setting you will see that I wink to you, and hear me call to you to follow, but do not do so. For a hundred years must I repeat the same every evening, and every time that you resist the temptation, you will gain strength, till at length resistance will be no longer an effort. This evening I make the beginning, and now I have warned you."

Now the Fairy led him into a large hall filled with white, transparent lilies, the yellow stamens in each forming a small, golden harp, which gave forth the sound of the harp and the flute. The loveliest girls, slim and graceful, dressed in transparent gauze, seemed to float in the air as they danced, and they sang how delightful life was, that they should never die, and that the Garden of Paradise would flourish in its splendour to all eternity.

The sun now went down, tinting the sky with the colour of gold, which gave the lilies the appearance of the most beautiful roses, and the Prince drank the sparkling wine which the girls handed him, feeling a happiness he had never before experienced. He saw how the farther end of the hall opened, and the tree of knowledge shone with such splendour that his eyes were dazzled. The sounds that came from thence were soft and sweet, like the voice of his mother, and it seemed as if she sang, "My child, my dearest child."

Then the Fairy nodded to him and said so lovingly, "Come with me, come with me," that he flew towards her, forgetting his promise the very first night, and she nodded and smiled. The fragrant exhalations from the plants grew stronger, and the harps sounded more lovely, and it seemed as if the millions of smiling heads nodded and sang, "Man is the lord of the creation, he must know everything." They were no longer tears of blood that fell from the leaves of the tree of knowledge of good and evil, but they appeared to be shining stars. "Come, come," sounded from all sides, and at every step the Prince's cheeks burned warmer, and his blood rushed more quickly through his veins. "I must," he said; "it is not—it cannot be a sin. Why should I not follow where pleasure and beauty call me?"

The Fairy threw off her sparkling ornaments, bent back the branches of the tree, and the next moment she was hidden amongst them.

The Prince drew the branches on one side. She was already asleep, and lovely as only the Fairy of the Garden of Paradise can be. She was smiling in her sleep, but as he leant over her he saw a tear on her beautiful long eyelashes.

"Are you crying on my account?" he said. "Do not cry, most

excellent of women! I now begin to understand what happiness is in this place. I feel it in my blood and in my thoughts. I feel the strength of eternal life in this temporal body. Even if eternal night is to be my lot, a minute such as this is bliss enough." And he kissed the tears from her eyes. His lips pressed hers.

Then there was a clap of thunder, so loud and awful that no one has ever heard the like, and all sank together. The lovely Fairy, the beautiful garden; they sank so deep that the Prince saw them disappear in black night till only a small star shone in the distance. The coldness of death crept over his whole body—his eyes closed and he lay for a long time as if dead.

The cold rain beat in his face, and a cutting wind whistled around him, when his senses returned. "What have I done?" he sighed. "I have sinned like Adam—sinned, so that the Garden of Paradise has sunk into the earth." He opened his eyes—the star he still saw—it was the morning star.

He roused himself up, and found he was in the depth of the forest, close to the Cavern of the Winds, and the mother of the Winds sat by his side. She looked angry, and raising her arm said:—

"The very first evening! Well, it is just as I expected; if you were my son, you would soon be in the sack."

"And into it he shall go," Death said. He was a strong old man with a scythe in his hand, and with large black wings. "In the grave he shall be laid, but not yet; I will let him wander about the world for a time, to atone for his sin and become better, but I shall return. When he least expects it, I shall return; place him in the black coffin, and taking it on my head fly up towards the stars. There, too, is a Garden of Paradise, and if he is good he will be admitted; but if his thoughts are bad and his heart still full of sin, then he will sink with the coffin, deeper than the Garden of Paradise sank, and only every thousandth year shall I fetch him, that he may sink still deeper, or reach to that star—that shining star above."

LITTLE THUMB

THERE was once a woman who was very lonely, and had a very strong desire to have a little child for a companion, but did not at all know how it was to be managed, and therefore went to an old witch, to whom she said, "I do so heartily desire to have a little, little child; will you not tell me how I am to come by one?"

"Yes, that is easily done," the witch said; "there is a barley-corn, in no way like what the farmers sow, or is given to chickens to eat; set that in a flower pot, and then you shall see what you shall see."

"I thank you," the woman said, and giving her a shilling, went home, where she set the barley-corn, and immediately there sprang up a magnificent, large flower, which looked like a tulip, but the leaves of the flower were closed as if it were only in bud.

"That is a pretty flower," the woman said, and kissed the red and yellow leaves, but just as she did so the flower opened with an explosion. It was a real tulip, as now could easily be seen, but seated in the middle of the flower was a quiet little girl. She was so pretty and delicate, and not being above the length of one's thumb, she was called Little Thumb.

She had a neat lackered walnut-shell for a cradle, blue violet leaves were her mattress, and a roseleaf her covering. There she slept at nights, but during the day she played on the table, on which the woman placed a plateful of water, with flowers all round the edge, and a lily-leaf floating in the middle. On this Little Thumb could sit and row herself from one side to the other, which looked very pretty. She could sing too, and so sweetly that the like had never been heard.

One night, as she was lying in her beautiful bed, an ugly toad came hopping through the window, one of the panes of glass being broken. The toad was a big, wet, and frightfully ugly creature, and happened just to hop on to the table on which Little Thumb was asleep, under her roseleaf.

"That would be a charming wife for my son," the toad said, and taking up the walnut-shell, in which Little Thumb was lying, hopped with it through the broken window, down into the garden.

There flowed a broad river, the banks of which were muddy and marshy, and it was here the toad lived with her son. Oh dear! how ugly and disgusting he was too, exactly like his mother. "Koar, koar, croak, croak!" was all that he could say when he saw the pretty little girl in the walnut-shell.

"Do not speak so loud, or she may wake up," the old toad said, "and might escape us, for she is as light as swansdown. We will put her on one of the water-lily leaves out in the river, for, to her, who is so light, that will just be like an island, and from there she cannot get away, whilst we are busy preparing the state-room under the marsh where you are to live."

In the water grew a quantity of water-lilies, with their broad green leaves, which seemed to be floating on the top of the water, and the one which was the farthest out from the banks was also the largest. To this the old toad swam, and placed Little Thumb, with her walnut-shell, upon it.

The little thing awoke early in the morning, and when she saw where she was, she began to cry bitterly, for there was water on all sides of the large green leaf, and there was no reaching the land.

The old toad was busy, down in the marsh, decorating her room with rushes and yellow flowers, for she wanted all to be very smart for her new daughter-in-law; and when she had finished she swam, with her ugly son, out to the leaf, where Little Thumb stood, for she wanted to fetch the pretty bed, to place it in the bridal-chamber. The old toad bowed low to her and said, "Here you see my son, who is to be your husband, and you will live splendidly together, below under the marsh."

"Koar, koar, croak, croak," was all the son could say.

Then they took the pretty little bed and swam away with it, but Little Thumb sat all alone on the green leaf and cried, for she could not bear the idea of living with the ugly old toad, or of having her ugly son for a husband. The little fish that swam about in the water had seen the toad and heard all she said, so they popped up their heads to see the little girl, and finding her so pretty, they grieved to think that she should have to live with the ugly toads. "No, that must never be." So they assembled together, round the green stalk of the leaf on which Little Thumb stood, and bit it through, so that the leaf floated down the river, far away, where the toads could not reach it.

Little Thumb floated past many cities, and the little birds, as they sat in the bushes, saw her and sang, "What a lovely little girl!" The leaf swam on with her, further and further, and they got into another country.

A pretty little white butterfly fluttered round her constantly, and at last settled down on the leaf, for Little Thumb pleased him. She was very happy, for the toad could not now reach her, and it was very beautiful all around, the sun shining on the water so that it glittered like the brightest gold. She now took her girdle, tied one end of it round the butterfly, whilst she fastened the other to the leaf, which glided on much faster, and she as well, for she was standing upon it.

Then came a large cockchafer, and seeing her, instantly caught hold of her slender body with its claws, and flew with her into a tree. The green leaf swam on down the river, and the butterfly too, for it was tied to it and could not get away.

Oh! how frightened poor Little Thumb was when she found herself carried away by the cockchafer, but she felt still more sad, on account of the beautiful white butterfly, which she had fastened to the leaf, for it could not get away and must starve. But the cockchafer did not care a pin about that. He seated himself with her upon the largest leaf of the tree, gave her honey out of the flowers to eat, and said that she was very pretty, though not a bit like a cockchafer. Later, all the other cockchafers that lived in the tree came to visit her, and the young ladies, turning up their feelers, said, "What can any one see to admire in her! Why, she has only two legs, how ridiculous that looks!" "She has no feelers," another said, "and how small she is in the waist. Oh my, she is like a human being!" "And how ugly she is!" all the young ladies joined in. Now Little Thumb was exceedingly pretty, which the cockchafer that had carried her off knew well enough; but as all the others said she was ugly, he began to believe it himself at last, and would have nothing to do with her, so he carried her down from the tree, and placed her on a daisy. There she sat and cried, because she was so ugly that even the cockchafers would have nothing to do with her, and yet she was the prettiest and most delightful girl that can be imagined, as clear and blooming as the most beautiful roseleaf.

During the whole summer poor Little Thumb lived all alone in a large forest. She plaited herself a bed of grass, and hung it up under a burdock leaf, where she was sheltered from the rain. She ate the honey out of the flowers and drank the dew that lay every morning upon the leaves. In this manner passed summer and autumn, but now came winter—the cold, long winter. The birds that had sung so sweetly to her flew away; the flowers died and the trees lost their leaves; the large burdock leaf, under which her dwelling was, rolled up, and nothing remained but a yellow, withered stalk, and she was dreadfully cold, for her clothes were worn out, so that she was nearly frozen to death. It began to snow, and each flake that fell upon her was as if a whole shovelful were thrown upon one of us, for she was so little, not more than an inch in height. She wrapped herself up in a dry leaf, but that did not warm her, and she shook with cold.

She wandered out of the forest with difficulty, and came to a cornfield, but the corn had long gone, and only the short dry stubble stood out of the frozen earth, which to her was like another forest. Oh! how she shook with cold. At length she reached the door of the dwelling of a field-mouse. There the mouse lived warm and well, having a whole room full of corn and every comfort. Poor Little Thumb stood inside the door, just like any other poor beggar-girl, and begged for a small piece of a barley-corn, for she had not eaten a morsel of anything for two days.

"You poor little being," the field-mouse said, for at heart she was a good old field-mouse; "come into my warm room and dine with me."

Now as Little Thumb pleased her much, she said, "You may remain with me here all the winter, but you must keep my room tidy and clean as well as tell me stories, of which I am very fond"; and Little Thumb did what the good old field-mouse desired, and in return was made uncommonly comfortable.

"We shall now soon have a visitor," the field-mouse said; "my neighbour is in the habit of visiting me once a week. He is still better off than I, has large rooms, and wears the most beautiful black fur coat. If you could only get him for a husband, you would be well provided for, but he cannot see. You must tell him the very prettiest stories that you know."

But Little Thumb was not at all anxious to see the neighbour, for he was a mole.

He came, however, and paid his visit in his black fur coat. The field-mouse said he was so clever and so rich; that his house was more than twenty times larger than hers, and that his learning was very great, but the sun and the beautiful flowers he could not bear, and had little to say of them, for he had never seen them.

Little Thumb had to sing to him. She sang, "Ladybird, ladybird, fly away home," and, "Sir frog he would a-wooing go," and he fell in love with her on account of her sweet voice, but he said nothing, for he was a very prudent man.

He had lately dug himself a walk underground, from his own house to the field-mouse's, in which she and Little Thumb received permission to walk as much as they liked, but he warned them not to be frightened at the dead bird which lay there, in the walk he had made, for it was a perfect bird with feathers and beak and all, which could only lately have died and got buried there.

Then the mole took a piece of rotten wood in its mouth, for that shines in the dark like fire, and went on in front to light them in the long dark passage. When they came to the place where the dead bird was, the mole, thrusting its broad nose into the roof of the passage, began throwing up the earth till it had worked a large hole, through which the light shone. In the middle of the walk lay a dead swallow, with its beautiful wings pressed close to its sides, and its feet drawn in under the feathers. The poor bird had evidently died of cold. That grieved Little Thumb so much, for she was very fond of all little birds, they having chirped and sung so beautifully to her all the summer; but the mole pushed it on one side with its short legs and said, "He'll sing no more; how miserable it must be to be born a bird! Thank goodness that will not happen to any of my children. What has a bird but its twittering and chirping, and in winter it dies of hunger!"

"Yes, a sensible man like you may well say so," the field-mouse said; "what does a bird get by all its twittering when the winter comes? It must die of cold and hunger; yet how proud they are!"

Little Thumb said nothing, but as soon as the other two had turned their backs upon the bird, she bent down, and dividing the feathers that covered the head, kissed it on the closed eyes.

"Perhaps it was he who sang so beautifully to me in the summer," she thought. "What pleasure has he not caused me, the dear, beautiful bird!"

The mole now filled up the hole which let in the light, and accompanied the two ladies home. But that night Little Thumb could not sleep, so, getting up, she plaited a beautiful large mat with hay, which she carried with her, and covered up the bird, laying some soft wool, which she had found in the mouse's room, at both sides so that it might lie warm in the cold earth.

"Farewell, you beautiful little bird," she said; "farewell, and many thanks for the delightful songs during the summer, when the trees were green, and the sun shone warm, down upon us." She then laid her head upon the bird's breast, but was frightened, for it was just as if there were some noise within. It was the bird's heart beating, for he was not dead, but only benumbed by the cold, and being now warmed, had come to life again.

In autumn all the swallows fly away to warmer countries; but if one remains by chance till it is too cold, it falls down like dead, and lies there, where it fell, till the cold snow covers it.

Little Thumb trembled violently, she had been so frightened, for the bird was big, very big compared to her, who was only an inch in height, but she mustered courage, and laid the wool still closer to the bird's sides, fetching, besides, the mint-leaf which had served her as a bed-covering, and laid it over the bird's head.

The next night she stole away to him again, and found him quite alive, but very weak, so that he could only for a moment open his eyes and look at Little Thumb, who stood before him with a piece of rotten wood in her hand, for that was the only lantern she had.

"I thank you, my pretty little girl," the invalid said; "you have warmed me so nicely that I shall soon get my strength back, and shall then be able to fly about again, outside in the warm sunshine."

"Alas!" she said, "it is very cold, it snows and freezes; so you must still remain in your warm bed, and I will nurse you."

She then brought some water in the leaf of a flower, and the swallow drank, and told her how it had wounded one of its wings in a thorn-bush, so that it could not fly so well as the others, which had gone off to a warmer country, and that at last it had fallen to the ground, when it could remember no more, and did not know at all how it had got there, where it was.

The whole winter the swallow remained underground, and Little Thumb attended to it with the utmost care, without the mole or the field-mouse knowing anything about it, for they could not bear the swallow.

As soon as spring came and warmed the earth, the swallow said farewell to Little Thumb, who opened the hole which the mole had made above. The sun shone so beautifully down upon them, and the swallow asked, "Will you not go with me, for you can sit on my back, and we will fly far away into the green woods?" But Little Thumb knew that the old field-mouse would feel much hurt if she left in that manner, so she said,—

"No, I cannot go with you."

"Farewell, then, farewell, you good, charming girl," the swallow said and flew out into the sunshine. Little Thumb looked after it, and the tears came into her eyes, for she was very fond of the swallow.

"Quiwit, quiwit," the bird sang, as it flew away into the wood, and Little Thumb was very sorrowful. The poor little thing could get no permission to go out at all into the warm sunshine, though all was so beautiful; and the corn, which grew over the field-mouse's house, had shot up so high, that it was quite like a forest of tall trees to her who was only an inch high.

"Now, in the summer you must work at your wedding outfit," the field-mouse said to her, for their neighbour, the tedious old mole, with the black fur coat, had proposed for her. "You must have a good stock of woollen, as well as linen clothes, for there must not be anything wanting when you are the mole's wife."

Little Thumb had to work at her spindle, and the field-mouse hired four spiders as well to spin and weave day and night for her. Every evening the mole visited her, and his constant theme was, that, when the summer should be over, the sun, which now baked the earth as hard as a stone, would not be nearly so hot, and that then they would be married. The prospect of this did not afford Little Thumb much pleasure, for she could not bear this tedious mole. Each morning, when the sun rose, and each evening when it set, she stole outside the door; and when the wind separated the ears of corn so that she could see the blue sky, she thought how light and beautiful it was out there, and wished with all her heart that she could see the dear swallow again; but it did not come back, and was, no doubt, far away in the beautiful green wood.

When autumn came, Little Thumb's wedding outfit was all ready.

"In four weeks' time your wedding will take place," the field-mouse said to her. But Little Thumb cried, and said that she would not have the tedious mole.

"Fiddlededee," the old mouse said. "Don't be perverse, or I'll bite you with my white teeth. Your future husband is a handsome man, and the queen herself has not such a fur coat. His kitchen and cellar are well stored, so, bless your stars that you make such a match."

The time for the wedding had now come. The mole had arrived to fetch away Little Thumb to live with him deep underground and never to come up to the warm sunshine, which he was not at all fond of. The poor child was very sad, for she was now to bid the beautiful sun good-bye, which she had had permission to look at from the door at any rate, whilst living with the field-mouse.

"Farewell, you bright sun!" she said, raising up her hand towards it, and she went a few steps outside the door, for the corn was carried, and there was now only the dry stubble. "Farewell! farewell!" she again said, and flung her arms round a little red flower which stood there. "Remember me to the little swallow, when you happen to see it."

"Quiwit, quiwit!" sounded at that moment from above, and when she looked up she saw the little swallow just flying over her head. When it perceived Little Thumb, it was much rejoiced: and she told her story, how unwillingly she was about to marry the ugly mole, when she would have to live underground, where the sun never shone, and she could not help crying.

"The cold winter is now coming," the swallow said, "and I am

B

about to fly off to a warmer country. Will you go with me? You can sit on my back; only tie yourself fast with your girdle, and we will fly away from the ugly mole and his dark room, far, far away to a warmer country, where the sun shines more brightly than here; where it is always summer, and there are the most beautiful flowers. Come with me, you dear little girl, you who saved my life, when I lay frozen and buried."

"Yes, I will go with you," Little Thumb said, and seating herself on the bird's back, she tied herself fast with her girdle to one of the strongest feathers, when the swallow flew up high into the air, over forests and seas; high up over mountains that are always covered with snow, and she shivered in the cold air, but she crept under the bird's warm feathers, only having her head out, that she might admire the wonders and beauties below.

They at length reached a warmer country, where the sun shines much more brightly than here, where the sky is twice as deep a blue, and where the most beautiful grapes grow in the hedges. There were forests of orange and citron trees, and the air was sweet with the scent of myrtles and mint, whilst on the roads there were charming children, playing with the most beautifully painted butterflies. The swallow, however, flew on still further, and it grew more beautiful and more beautiful, till they came to a delightful blue lake, where there stood a marble palace, from olden times surrounded by sweet-scented trees. The vine wound round the high columns, and at the top there were many swallows' nests, one of which belonged to Little Thumb's companion.

"This is my house," the swallow said; "but if you choose yourself one of the most beautiful of the flowers that grow there below, I will place you in it, and you may be as happy as the day is long."

"That will be delightful," she cried and clapped her little hands with joy.

There lay a large white marble column, which had fallen to the ground and broken into three pieces, and from between these grew up the most beautiful large white flowers. The swallow flew down with Little Thumb, and placed her upon a broad leaf of one of these, but how astonished she was when in the flower she saw a little man sitting, so white and transparent, as if he were of glass. He wore a beautiful gold crown upon his head, and had the most lovely gauzy wings, being scarcely bigger in body than Little Thumb himself. This was the Spirit of the Flowers. In each flower there lived a like little man or woman, but this was the king of them all.

"Oh, how beautiful he is!" Little Thumb whispered to the swallow.

The little Prince was greatly frightened at the swallow, for compared to him it was a monstrous bird; but, when he saw Little Thumb, he was as much rejoiced, for she was the most beautiful girl he had ever seen. He took off his crown, and placed it upon her head, asking at the same time what her name was, and if she would marry him, when she should be queen over all the flowers? This was, indeed, a very different being from the toad's son and the mole with his fur coat; so she answered "Yes" to the delightful Prince; and immediately there came a little man or woman from the different flowers, all so charming that it was quite a pleasure to look at them, and each brought her a present, the best of which was a beautiful pair of wings, taken from a large white fly. These were fastened to her shoulders, so that now she could fly from flower to flower; and all was happiness. The little swallow sat above in its nest, and sang its best to them, but at heart it was sad, for it loved Little Thumb, and wished never to be parted from her.

"You shall not be called Little Thumb," the king of the flowers said, "for that is an ugly name, and you are so beautiful. Your name shall be Maga."

"Farewell, farewell!" the little swallow said, and flew away from the warm country again back to Denmark. There it had a nest, above the window of the man who tells stories, and there it sang, "Quiwit, quiwit!" and that is how we know the whole story.

THE TINDER-BOX

A SOLDIER came marching along the highroad,—left, right! left, right! He had his knapsack at his back and his sword at his side, for he had been in the wars, and was now going home.

He fell in with an old witch on the road,—oh, she was so frightful! for her under-lip hung down right upon her breast. "Good day, soldier," she said; "what a beautiful sword and large knapsack you have! You are a real soldier, and shall have as much money as you can possibly wish for."

"Thank you, old witch!" the soldier said.

"Do you see that large tree there?" the witch said, pointing to one which stood by the side of the road. "It is quite hollow, and if you climb to the top you will see a hole, through which you can let yourself down, right to the bottom of it. I will tie a rope round your body, so as to pull you up when you call to me."

"And what am I to do down there, inside the tree?" the soldier asked.

"Fetch money," the witch said. "For you must know, that when you reach the bottom of the tree, you will find yourself in a large hall, lighted by more than a hundred lamps. Then you will see three doors, which you can open, for the keys are in the locks. If you go into the first room, you will see, in the middle of the floor, a large box on which a dog is seated; it has eyes like big teacups but you need not mind it. I will give you my blue check apron, which you must spread out upon the floor, then walk straight up to the dog, lay hold of it, and place it upon my apron, when you can take out as many pennies as you like. It is all copper money; but if you would rather have silver you must go into the next room. There sits a dog with eyes as large as the wheels of a water-mill, but do not let that trouble you, for if you place it on my apron you can take the money. If, however, you prefer gold, you can have that too, and as much of it as you like to carry, by going into the third room. But the dog that is seated on the money-box has two eyes, each one as big as the Round Tower of Copenhagen. That is a dog! but never mind him, only put him upon my apron, when he will not hurt you, and you can take as much gold out of the box as you like."

"That is not so bad," the soldier said; "but what must I give you, you old witch, for of course you want something?"

"No," the witch said, "not a single penny do I want. For me you need only bring an old tinder-box, which my grandmother forgot the last time she was in there."

"Well, then, tie the rope round me at once," the soldier said.

"Here it is," the witch said; "and here, too, is my blue check apron."

Then the soldier climbed up the tree, let himself slip down through the hole, and found himself, as the witch had said, down below in the large hall where the many hundred lamps were burning.

Now he opened the first door, and sure enough, there sat the dog with eyes like big cups, staring at him.

"Well, you are a pretty fellow," the soldier said, placed him upon the apron, and filled his pockets with pence, after which he locked the box, and having put the dog back upon it, went into the next room, where he found the dog with eyes like mill-wheels.

"Now, you shouldn't look at me in that way, for it may strain your eyes and injure your sight," the soldier said. He then seated the dog upon the apron; and no sooner did he see all the silver in the box than he threw away the copper money he had, and filled his pockets and knapsack with the more valuable metal. He then went into the third room, and it was an ugly beast he saw there. The dog's eyes were, indeed, as large as the Round Tower, and kept turning round in its head exactly like mill-wheels.

"Good-day to you," the soldier said, touching his cap, for such a dog he had never seen in all his life, but after examining him for a time, he thought that was enough, so he took him down and opened the box. Good gracious! what a quantity of gold was there! With that he could buy the whole of Copenhagen, and all the gingerbread horses, all the tin soldiers, whips, and rocking-horses in the whole world. There was a quantity of gold! He now threw out all the silver with which he had filled his pockets and knapsack, and replaced it by gold. Yes, his pockets, the knapsack, his cap, and even his boots, were filled with it so that he could scarcely walk. He was now rich, so he put the dog back on the box, shut the door, and called out to the old witch—

"Now pull me up."

"And have you got the tinder-box?" the old witch asked.

"Well, to be sure, that I had clean forgotten," the soldier said, so he went back and fetched it. The witch pulled him up, and there he stood again on the highroad, but with his pockets, his knapsack, cap, and boots filled with gold.

"And what do you intend to do with the tinder-box?" he asked.

"That is no business of yours," the witch said. "You have got your gold, so give me my tinder-box."

"What does this mean?" the soldier cried; "tell me at once what you want to do with the tinder-box, or I'll draw my sword and cut off your head."

"No," the witch said.

So the soldier cut off her head, and there she lay. But he tied up all his gold in her apron, slung it across his shoulder, and thrusting the tinder-box into his pocket, walked on, straight to the town.

That was a beautiful town, and he turned into the very grandest hotel, where he bespoke the best rooms, and ordered his favourite dishes, for he was rich now that he had so much money.

It certainly struck the servant, as he cleaned his boots, that they were most wretched things to belong to so rich a gentleman, for he had not yet bought any new ones, but the next day he got good boots and fine clothes. Now the soldier had become a gentleman of rank, and he was told of all the wonders that were to be seen in the town, of the King, and what a pretty princess his daughter was.

"How can one get to see her?" the soldier asked.

"She is not to be seen at all," they all said, "for she lives in a brass castle surrounded by many walls and towers. No one but the King himself can go in and out there, it having been prophesied that she will be married to a common soldier, to which the King cannot consent."

"I should like to see her," the soldier thought, but nowhow could he gain permission to do so.

Now he led a merry life, drove about in the King's garden, and gave a great deal of money to the poor, which was very good of him; but he recollected from former times how miserable it is not to possess a penny. He was now rich, had beautiful clothes and many friends, who all said that he was a first-rate fellow and a real gentleman, which the soldier liked to hear. But as he spent money every day and never received any, it happened after a while that he only had a shilling left; so he was obliged to give up his splendid rooms, where he had lived, and go into a small garret under the tiles, and clean and mend his own boots; and no more of his friends came to see him, for there were so many stairs to mount.

It had grown quite dark and he could not even buy a candle, but then he bethought himself that there was a small taper in the tinder-box which he had got out of the hollow tree. He got the flint and steel out of the box, and no sooner had he struck a few sparks, than the dog which had eyes as big as a teacup and which he had seen in the tree, stood before him, and said, "What are your commands, sir?"

"How is this?" he said. "That is a good sort of tinder-box, if I can so easily get all by means of it. Procure me some money," he said to the dog. In an instant it was gone, and almost at the same moment was back again, with a purse of money in its jaws.

Now the soldier knew what a valuable tinder-box it was. If he struck the flint once the dog that sat on the box containing the copper money appeared; if twice, that which had care of the silver; and if three times, there came the dog that guarded the gold. The soldier now moved back to his splendid rooms, and reappeared in fine clothes, when all his friends immediately recognised him again, and made much of him.

It occurred to him once that it was something very extraordinary there was no seeing the Princess. By all accounts it appeared she was very beautiful, but what was the good of that if she was always to be shut up in the brazen castle with the many towers? "Cannot I get to see her anyhow?" he said; "where is my tinder-box?" He struck fire, and on the instant the dog with eyes like a tea-cup appeared.

"It is true it is in the middle of the night," the soldier said, "but I should so very much like to see the Princess, only for a moment."

The dog was gone in an instant, and before the soldier thought it possible was back again with the Princess. She was lying asleep on its back, and so lovely, that every one could see at once she was a real princess. The soldier could not possibly resist kissing her, for he was a true soldier.

Then the dog ran back with the Princess, but the next morning when the King and Queen were taking their breakfast with her, she said she had had a most extraordinary dream of a dog and a soldier. That she had ridden on the dog, and the soldier had kissed her.

"That is a pretty story indeed!" the Queen said.

It was now settled that the next night one of the old ladies of the court should sit up by the Princess's bed-side, in order to see whether it was really a dream, or how it might be.

The soldier had an irresistible desire to see the Princess again, so the dog came in the night, took her up, and ran off as fast as possible, but the old lady immediately put on a pair of magic boots and followed quite as quickly, and when she saw that they disappeared in a large house, she thought, "Now I'll know where it is," so made a large cross on the door, with a piece of chalk. She then went home to bed, and the dog returned with the Princess. But the dog had seen that a cross was chalked on the door of the house where the soldier lived, so he took a piece of chalk too, and made a cross on all the doors of the town, which was cleverly done, for now the old lady could not find the proper door, as there were crosses on them all.

Early the next morning, the King and Queen, the old lady and all the officers of the court, came to see where the Princess had been.

"Here it is," the King said, when he saw the first door with the cross upon it.

"No, there it is, my dear husband," the Queen said, seeing the second door with the cross.

"But here is one, and there is one," they all said, for whichever way they looked, there was a cross on the doors, so they saw well that their looking would be of no avail.

The Queen, however, was a very clever woman, and could do more things than drive in her carriage, so she took her large golden scissors, cut up a large piece of silk, and made a pretty little bag, which she filled with buck-wheat meal and tied it round the Princess's neck. When this was done, she cut a small hole in the bag, so that the meal falling out would strew the road the whole way the Princess might take.

In the night the dog came again, took the Princess on his back, and carried her to the soldier, who loved her dearly, and wished so much he were a prince that he might marry her.

The dog did not notice how the meal strewed the whole of the way from the castle to the soldier's window, where he ran up the wall with the Princess. The following morning the King and Queen saw plainly where their daughter had been, so they had the soldier taken and put in prison.

There he was, and oh! how dark and frightful it was there, nor was it cheering when he was told, "To-morrow you are to be hanged." It was not pleasant to hear, and his tinder-box he had left behind him at the hotel. In the morning he could see, through the bars of his prison window, how the people were hurrying to the place of execution to see him hanged. He heard the drum, and saw the soldiers marching. All were running to get out of the town in time, and amongst the rest a shoemaker's boy with his apron on, and in slippers, one of which flew off as he ran along right against the wall, where the soldier was looking out through the prison window.

"Here, you shoemaker's boy," the soldier said to him, "you need not hurry so, for there will be nothing to see till I come; but if you will run to where I lived, and fetch me my tinder-box, you shall have a shilling. But you must make good use of your legs." The boy was willing enough to earn the shilling, so he ran and fetched the tinder-box, which he gave to the soldier, and—— Yes, now it comes!

Outside the town a high gallows was erected, and all round it stood soldiers, besides several hundred thousand people. The King and Queen sat upon a beautiful throne, and opposite to them the judges and all the council.

The soldier stood already on the top of the ladder, but when they were about to put the rope round his neck, he said that the condemned were always granted any innocent desire before undergoing their punishment. He wished so much to smoke one pipe of tobacco, the last he should get in this world.

This the King did not like to refuse, so the soldier took out his tinder-box and struck fire. One—two—three, and immediately the three dogs stood before him, the one with eyes like a tea-cup, that with eyes like a mill-wheel, and the one with eyes like the Round Tower of Copenhagen.

"Help me now, that I may not be hanged," the soldier said; and the dogs fell at once upon the judges and the council, catching one by the legs and another by the nose, and threw them up so high in the air that when they fell down they were all smashed to pieces.

"You must not touch me," the King said, but the biggest of the dogs caught hold of him as well as the Queen, and threw them after the others. Then the soldiers were frightened, and all the people cried, "Good soldier, you shall be our king, and marry the beautiful Princess."

They then seated him in the King's carriage and the dogs sprang on in front, crying, "Hurrah!" The boys whistled with their fingers, and the soldiers presented arms. The Princess came out of the brazen tower, and was elected Queen, which pleased her well enough. The marriage-feast lasted a whole week, and the dogs sat at table with the others, staring with amazement.

THE ANGEL

"WHENEVER a good child dies, an angel comes down from heaven, takes the dead child in its arms, and, spreading out its large white wings, visits all the places that had been particularly dear to the child, where it gathers a handful of flowers, flying up again to heaven with them, and there they bloom more beautifully than on earth; but that flower which it loves most receives a voice, so that it can join in the universal chorus of thanksgiving and praise."

Thus spoke an angel whilst carrying a dead child up to heaven;

and the child listened as in a dream; and they visited the places
that had been most dear to the child whilst alive, and where it had
played, passing through gardens full of the most beautiful flowers.

"Which flowers shall we take with us to plant in heaven?" the
angel asked.

Now there stood a solitary rose-tree of extraordinary beauty, but
a mischievous hand had wantonly broken the stem, so that all the
branches, recently of such a beautiful green, laden with half-
opened buds, hung down, withered and sad upon the mossy turf
below.

"Oh, that dear little tree!" the child sighed. "Pray take that with
you, so that in heaven it may again come to life."

The angel took it, kissing the child at the same time, and the
little thing half opened its eyes. They gathered of the beautiful
plants, the perfume and colours of which delight mankind; but
the despised buttercup, and the wild pansy, they also took with
them.

"Now we have flowers," the child said; and the angel nodded.
But still they did not fly up to heaven. It was night, and all was
quiet; but yet they remained in the large town, hovering over one
of the narrowest streets, where there were heaps of straw, ashes,
and all manner of rubbish, for it was quarter-day when many
people change their lodgings. There lay broken plates, pieces of
plaster, the crowns of old hats, and rags of all sorts—in short, a
mass of things in no way pleasing to the eye.

The angel pointed down amongst all this rubbish to some pieces
of a broken flower-pot and a lump of earth which had fallen out
of it, held together by the roots of a large dried-up wild-flower,
which had been thrown into the street as useless.

"That we will take with us," the angel said: "I will tell you why
as we fly on."

And the angel spoke thus:—

"There, below, in that narrow street in a cellar, lived a poor, sick
boy, who from his earliest years had been bedridden. When at his
best, he could manage to walk round the little room a couple of
times on his crutches, and that was all. On some few days during
the summer, the sun's rays shone upon the floor of the cellar for
half an hour; and when the poor boy sat there warming himself in
the sun, and wondering at the red blood which he saw through his
thin fingers as he held them up to his face, it was said, 'To-day he
has been out.' He only knew of the green forest by the son of a
neighbour bringing him the first branch of a beech-tree that was

out in leaf, which he held over his head, fancying that he was in the forest under the beech-trees, with the sun shining and birds singing. One day in spring the neighbour's son brought him some wild-flowers, amongst which there happened to be one that had its roots, and it was therefore set in a pot and placed near his bed. The flower flourished, sending forth new shoots, and blossomed every year, so that it became the sick boy's flower garden, his greatest comfort and treasure here on earth. He watered and watched it, taking care that it had even to the last ray of the sun which glided through the low window. The flower became identified with his dreams, for it was for him alone it blossomed, delighting him by its scent and its beautiful colours, and to it he turned in death. It is now a year he has been in heaven, and for a year the flower has stood, forgotten and dried up in the window, till, during the moving, it was thrown out into the street. And that is the flower, the poor withered flower, which we have placed in our nosegay, for it has given more pleasure than the most beautiful flower in the garden of a queen."

"And how do you know all this?" the child asked.

"I know it," the angel answered, "because I myself was that poor sick boy who walked on crutches. I know my flower well."

The child now thoroughly opened its eyes, and looked up into the angel's beautiful face, which beamed with happiness, and at the same moment they were in heaven, where joy and bliss reigned. The dead child received wings like the other angel, with whom he flew about hand in hand. The flowers received renewed life; but the poor withered wild-flower received a voice, and sang with the angels, with whom the whole space of the heavens was filled, in circles, one row behind the other, further and further back, and so on to infinity, all being equally happy.

All sang praises and thanksgivings,—the child just received into heaven, and the poor wild-flower, which had been thrown out amongst the rubbish in the narrow, dark street.

LITTLE IDA'S FLOWERS

"My poor flowers are quite withered," little Ida said. "They were so beautiful yesterday evening, and now the leaves are all dead. What is the reason?" she asked the student, who was sitting on the sofa, for she was very fond of him, as he told her all manner of pretty stories and cut out the most amusing pictures for her,—hearts with little ladies dancing inside; flowers, and castles of which the doors opened. He was a lively young man. "Why do the flowers look so wretched to-day?" she asked him again, showing him a nosegay, which was quite dead.

"Why, don't you know what's the matter with them?" the student said. "The flowers were at a ball last night, and that's why they hang their heads."

"But how can that be, for the flowers cannot dance," little Ida said.

"And why not?" the student answered. "As soon as it gets dark, and we are all asleep, they jump about merrily enough; almost every night they have a dance."

"Are there no children at the balls?"

"Oh yes," the student said, "there are quite little daisies and may-blossoms."

"And where do the most beautiful flowers dance?" little Ida asked.

"Have you not often been outside the city gates, to the palace, where the King lives in summer, and where there is the beautiful garden with such quantities of flowers? You know the swans which swim up to you when you feed them with bread-crumbs. Depend upon it, there are large balls there."

"I was in the garden yesterday with my mother," Ida said, "but all the leaves were off the trees, and there were no flowers whatever. Where are they all? In summer I saw such quantities."

"They are inside the palace," the student said. "You must know that as soon as the King and all the courtiers move into the town, the flowers run off, at once, out of the garden into the palace, and there make merry. You should see that. The two most beautiful of the roses seat themselves upon the throne, and they are then king and queen. The red cockscombs stand bowing on either side, and they are the pages. Then come the prettiest flowers, which represent the maids of honour, and there is a grand ball. The blue violets are midshipmen, and they dance with hyacinths and crocuses, whom they call milady. The tulips and the great tiger-lilies are old ladies who watch that the dancing is good, and that all goes on with propriety."

"And does no one interfere with the flowers going into the palace?" little Ida asked.

"No one knows really anything about it," the student said. "It's true that sometimes the old steward, who has to see that all is right, comes in of an evening, but no sooner do the flowers hear the jingling of his big bunch of keys than they are quite quiet, and hide themselves behind the curtains. 'I smell that there are flowers here,' he says, but he cannot see them."

"Oh, what fun that is!" little Ida said, clapping her hands. "And should I not be able to see the flowers either?"

"Yes," the student answered, "and remember the next time you go out there, that you look through the window, and you will see them plainly enough. I did so to-day, and there lay a long yellow lily stretched upon the sofa. That was one of the ladies in waiting."

"And are the flowers from the botanical garden there? can they get as far?"

"To be sure they can," the student answered, "for if necessary they can fly. Have you noticed many beautiful butterflies, red, yellow, and white, that look almost like flowers, which indeed they have been? They have broken off from their stems, flying up in the air, beating about with their leaves as if they were wings; and as they behaved well, they received permission to fly about, and not be obliged to sit quietly fastened down to their stems, till at length the leaves became real wings. All this you may have seen yourself. However, it may be that the flowers from the botanical garden have never been in the King's palace, or even that they do not know what sport goes on there at nights. And now I'll tell you something, how you can astonish the professor of botany, who lives here close by. You know him, do you not? When next you go into his garden, you must tell one of the flowers that there is dancing at the palace every night. That one will tell the others, and away they'll fly. Then when the professor goes into the garden, he will not find a single flower, and he will be nicely puzzled to think what has become of them all."

"But how can the flower tell the others? for flowers cannot speak."

"That is true enough," the student said, "but then they make signs. Have you not noticed that when the wind blows a little the flowers bend down, and all the green leaves move? That is as plain as if they spoke."

"And can the professor understand them?"

"Certainly he can. One morning he went into the garden and saw a stinging nettle making signs to a red carnation, which signs meant, You are very pretty and I love you. Now the professor cannot bear anything of that sort, so he gave the stinging-nettle a slap on its leaves, for those are its fingers, but he stung himself, and since then he had not ventured to touch a stinging nettle."

"Oh, what fun!" little Ida said, and laughed out loud.

"How can any one talk such nonsense to a child!" the tedious chancery counsellor said, who, having called to pay a visit, was sitting on the sofa. He did not much like the student, and always began to growl when he saw him cutting out the funny pictures: first it was a man hanging on the gallows with a heart in his hand, for he was a robber of hearts, and then an old witch riding on a broom, and carrying her husband on her nose. That sort of thing annoyed the counsellor, and he would then say, "How can any one put such foolish notions into a child's head!"

But what the student told little Ida about her flowers appeared very funny to her, and she thought much of it. The flowers hung their heads, because they were tired, after dancing all the night, and no doubt they felt ill. Then she carried them to her other playthings, which were on a nice little table, the drawer of which, also, was full of pretty things. In the doll's bed lay the doll Sophy, sleeping, but little Ida said to her, "You must really get up, Sophy and be satisfied with passing this night in the drawer, for the poor flowers are ill, and must sleep in your bed, which will perhaps put them right again." She then took the doll out of its bed, and it looked quite fretful, but did not say a word, for it was sulky at having to give up its bed.

Ida laid the flowers in the doll's bed, and covering them up with the clothes, said they must lie quite quiet, and she would make them some tea, so that they might be quite well by the following day and be able to get up; and she then drew the curtains of the little bed that the sun might not shine in their eyes.

The whole evening she could not help thinking of what the student had told her; and when it was time for her to go to bed she must needs first look under the curtain that hung at the window, where her mother's beautiful flowers, hyacinths as well as tulips, stood, and she whispered quite low, "I know that you are going to the ball to-night"; but the flowers pretended not to understand her, and did not move a leaf; however, little Ida knew what she knew, for all that.

When she was in bed she lay awake a long time thinking how pretty it must be to see all the beautiful flowers dancing in the King's palace. "I wonder whether my flowers were really there?" She then went to sleep, but woke again in the night, having dreamed of the flowers, the student, and the chancery counsellor, who said he was putting foolish fancies into her head. All was quiet in the bedroom where Ida lay; the night-lamp burned on the table, and her father and mother were asleep.

"I wonder whether my flowers are still lying in Sophy's bed," she thought. "I should much like to know." She raised herself up a little in the bed and looked towards the door, which stood ajar. In the next room lay her flowers and all her playthings, and as she listened it seemed to her as if she heard the piano being played, but quite softly and so beautifully as she had never heard before.

"No doubt all the flowers are now dancing in there," she said. "Oh, dear, how much I should like to see them"; but she could not venture to get up for fear of waking her father or mother.

"If they would but come in here," she said. But the flowers did not come in, and as the music continued playing she could resist no longer, for it was much too pretty; so she crept out of her little bed gently to the door and looked into the next room. Oh, how beautiful it was, what she there saw!

There was no night-lamp burning, but yet it was quite light, for the moon was shining through the window right into the middle of the room, and it was almost like day. All the hyacinths and tulips stood in two rows along the room, so that there were none left in the window. The flower-pots stood there empty, whilst flowers were dancing so prettily on the floor of the room, round each other, forming a regular ladies' chain, and holding each other by the long green leaves as they whirled round. At the piano sat a large yellow lily, which Ida must certainly have seen during the summer, for she remembered quite well that the student had said, "How exactly it is like Miss Line." Every one laughed at him then, but it really seemed to little Ida now, that the long tall yellow flower was indeed like that young lady, and it had the same ways too at the piano. Now it leaned its long yellow face to one side, now to the other, whilst it nodded the time to the beautiful music. Little Ida was not noticed, and she now saw a large blue crocus jump on to the table on which the playthings were, go straight up to the doll's bed and draw the curtains. There lay the sick flowers, but they got up at once and nodded to the others, as much as to say that they would dance too. The old shepherd, who had lost his under-lip, stood up and bowed to the beautiful flowers, which did not appear at all sick now, for they jumped down to join the others and were as merry as possible.

It sounded as if something fell, and when Ida looked round she saw that it was the little three-legged stool that had jumped down from the table, seeming to think it belonged to the flowers. It was a neat little stool, and on it there sat a little wax doll, with just such another broad-brimmed hat on its head as the chancery counsellor was in the habit of wearing. The stool hopped about on its three legs, stamping heavily, for it was dancing the Mazurka, which the flowers could not dance, for they were too light to stamp.

The wax doll on the stool became, all at once, quite big, and cried out, "How can any one talk such nonsense to a child!" and then it was exactly like the counsellor, looking quite as yellow and fretful. Then it became a little wax doll again, and all this was so droll that Ida could not restrain her laughter. The three-legged stool continued to dance, and the chancery counsellor had to dance with it, whether he would or no, whether he made himself big, or remained the little wax doll with the large black hat. There was now a knocking in the drawer, where Ida's doll, Sophy, was lying with the other playthings; and the old shepherd, jumping on to the table, lay flat down, and crept as near as possible to the edge, when he was able to pull the drawer out a little. Then Sophy got up and looked around her, quite astonished. "Why, here is a dance!" she said. "Why did no one tell me that?"

"Will you dance with me?" the shepherd said.

"Oh, yes; you are a pretty fellow to dance," she said, and turned her back upon him. She then seated herself upon the table, expecting that one of the flowers would come and engage her, but none came, and then she coughed, "Hem, hem, hem!" but none came, for all that. The shepherd danced all by himself and not so badly either.

Now, as not one of the flowers appeared to see Sophy, she let herself fall from the table on to the floor, with a great noise, which brought all the flowers about her, and they asked her whether she had not hurt herself. They were all so kind and polite to her, particularly those that had lain in her bed. But she had not hurt herself at all. Ida's flowers thanked her for the beautiful bed, were very attentive to her, and leading her into the middle of the room, where the moon shone, they danced with her. Sophy was delighted, and said they might keep her bed, for she did not at all mind sleeping in the drawer.

But the flowers said, "We thank you from our hearts, but we cannot live so long, for to-morrow we shall be quite dead. Then tell little Ida to bury us where the canary lies, and we shall grow again next summer, when we shall be more beautiful than now."

"No, you must not die," Sophy said, kissing them, and just then a quantity of the most beautiful flowers came dancing in through the door. Ida could not at all imagine where they came from, unless from the King's palace. In front were two beautiful roses, wearing little crowns of gold; these were king and queen. Then followed the prettiest gilly-flowers and pinks, bowing on all sides. They had music of their own, large poppies and peonies blowing away on pea-shells till they were quite red in the face. The snow-drops and bluebells were ringing, exactly as if they had metal bells, so that altogether it was most extraordinary music. Then came quantities of other flowers, the blue violets and the red amaranths, daisies and mayflowers, and all danced together, and kissed each other, so that it was delightful to look at them.

At length all the flowers wished each other good-night, and then little Ida crept back to her bed, where she dreamed of all she had seen.

As soon as she got up the next morning she went to the little table to see whether the flowers were still there. She drew aside the curtains of the little bed; yes, there they lay, but quite withered, a great deal more so than the day before. Sophy was lying in the drawer, where she had laid her, and she looked very sleepy.

"Do you remember what you were to tell me?" Ida asked, but Sophy looked quite stupid, and did not answer one single word.

"You are not at all good," Ida said, "when all of them danced with you too." She then took a little paper box, on which the most beautiful birds were painted, and having opened it, laid the dead flowers in it. "That shall be your pretty coffin," she said; "and when my cousins come, they shall help me to bury you in the garden, so that you may grow again next summer, and be more beautiful than ever."

The two cousins were two lively boys whose names were John and Adolphus. Their father had given each of them a crossbow, which they had brought with them to show Ida. She told them of the poor flowers which had died the day before, and invited them to be present at the funeral. The two boys walked on in front, with their crossbows on their shoulders, and little Ida followed with the dead flowers in the pretty box. They dug a small grave in the garden, and Ida, first having kissed the flowers, placed them with the box in the earth, and the cousins fired their crossbows over the grave, for they had neither guns nor cannon.

THE PRINCESS ON THE BEAN

THERE was once a Prince who wished to marry a Princess, but it must be a real Princess. So he travelled about the whole world to find such an one, but everywhere there was something in the way. Princesses there were plenty, but whether they were real Princesses he could not satisfy himself, for there was always something that did not seem quite right. He, therefore, came home again and was quite sad, for he wished so very much to have a real Princess.

One night a terrific storm came on; it thundered and lightened, and the rain poured down, till it was quite dreadful. There was then a knocking at the gate of the town, and the old King went to open it.

It was a Princess who stood outside at the gate. And, oh dear! what a state she was in. The water ran down from her hair and her clothes, in at the toes of her shoes and out at the heels, but she said she was a real Princess.

"Well, that we'll soon find out," the old Queen thought. She said nothing, however, but went into the bed-room and having taken all the things off the bed, laid a small bean upon the slabs, upon which she heaped twenty mattresses, and then twenty eider-down beds upon the mattresses.

There the Princess was to lie that night.

In the morning she was asked how she had slept.

"Oh, abominably badly!" she answered. "I have scarcely closed my eyes the whole night. Heaven knows what there may have been in the bed! but I lay upon something hard, so that I am black and blue all over my body. It is quite dreadful."

It was evident, then, that she was a real Princess, since she had felt the bean through the twenty mattresses and the twenty eider-down beds. No one could have so very fine a sense of feeling but a real Princess.

So the Prince married her, for he knew that now he had a real Princess; and the bean was placed in the royal museum, where it may still be seen if no one has taken it.

THE EMPEROR'S NEW CLOTHES

MANY years ago there lived an Emperor who was so excessively fond of new clothes that he spent all his money in order to be well dressed. He did not care about his soldiers, nor did he care for the theatre, neither was he fond of driving out, excepting for the sake of showing his new clothes. He had a different coat for every hour of the day, and just as one says of a King, "He is in the council," so it was here always said, "The Emperor is in his dressing-room."

In the large city where he lived, it was very gay, for every day fresh visitors arrived; and one day there came amongst others two impostors, who pretended to be weavers, and that they had the secret of weaving the most beautiful fabrics that could be imagined. Not only were the colours and designs pretended to be uncommonly beautiful, but that the fabric possessed the wonderful peculiarity of being invisible to every one who was either unfit for his situation, or unpardonably stupid.

"Clothes made of that material would be inestimable," the Emperor thought. "If I had such on, I could discover which men in my empire are unfit for the offices they hold, and could at once distinguish the clever from the stupid. That stuff must be at once woven for me." So he gave an order to the two impostors, and a large sum of money, in order that they might begin their work at once.

They set up two looms, and did as if they were working, but there was nothing at all on the looms. Straightway they required the finest silk, and the most beautiful gold thread to work into their stuffs, which they put into their pockets, and worked away at the bare looms till late at night.

"I should like to know how they have got on with the stuff," the Emperor thought; but at the same time he was greatly embarrassed when he thought of it, that he who was stupid or ill-fitted for his situation could not see it. Now he had no doubts about himself, but yet he thought it as well, first to send some one else, to see how it was getting on. Every one in the city knew the peculiarity of the fabric, and every one was anxious to see how unfit for his situation, or how stupid his neighbour was.

"I will send my old, honest minister to the weavers," the Emperor thought. "He will be best able to judge how the fabric succeeds, for he has sense, and no one is better fitted for his office than he."

So the good old minister went to the room where the two impostors were working at the bare looms. "Heaven preserve me!" the old minister thought, and he opened his eyes wide. "Why, I cannot see anything." But that he did not say.

Both impostors begged of him to step nearer, and they asked whether he did not think the design pretty and the colours beautiful? They then pointed to the bare loom, and the poor old minister opened his eyes still wider, but yet he could see nothing, for there was not anything to see. "Can it be possible," he thought, "that I am stupid? That I would never have believed, and no one must know it. Or is it that I am not fit for my office? It will never do to tell that I cannot see the stuff!"

"Well, you say nothing of our work," one of the weavers said.

"Oh, it is very pretty! quite beautiful!" the old minister said, looking through his spectacles. "The design and the colours—— Yes, I shall not fail to tell the Emperor that it pleases me very much."

"We are delighted to hear it," both the weavers said; and then they mentioned all the different colours, and explained the curious design. The old minister paid great attention, that he might use the same words when he returned to the Emperor: and he did so.

The impostors now applied for more money, more silk, and more gold, to be used in their weaving, which they put in their pockets, for not a single thread was put upon the looms, though they continued their pretended work as heretofore.

The Emperor soon after sent another able statesman to see how the weaving got on, and whether the stuff would soon be ready. With him it was exactly as with the other, he looked and looked, but as there was nothing besides the bare loom he could see nothing.

"Well, is not that beautiful stuff?" the two impostors asked; and they explained the magnificent design which did not exist.

"I am not stupid," the man thought, "so it must be my good appointment that I am unfit for. That would be funny enough, but it must never be suspected." So he praised the fabric which he did not see, and assured them he was highly pleased with the beautiful design and colours. "Oh, it is lovely," he said to the Emperor.

Every one in the city spoke of the magnificent fabric.

The Emperor was now desirous of seeing it himself, whilst still on the loom, so with a host of chosen followers, amongst whom were also the two honest statesmen who had been before, he went to the two artful impostors, who now worked away with all their might, though without a fibre or thread.

"Is that not magnificent?" the two honest statesmen asked. "Will not your Majesty look more closely into it and examine the design and beautiful colours?" and they pointed to the bare loom, for, they thought, the others could see the fabric.

"How is this?" the Emperor thought. "Why, I see nothing at all, it is quite dreadful. Can it be that I am stupid, or am I not fit to be Emperor? That would be the most dreadful thing that could happen to me. Yes, it is very beautiful!" he said. "It has my highest approbation"; and he nodded with apparent satisfaction at the bare loom, for he would not confess that he did not see anything. All his followers looked and looked, seeing no more than the others, but they said the same as the Emperor. "Yes, it is very beautiful!" and they advised him to wear the clothes of that magnificent fabric at the approaching grand procession. "It is delightful, charming, excellent!" passed from mouth to mouth, and all seemed really delighted. The Emperor decreed an order to each of the impostors to wear in their buttonholes, with the title of Court weaver.

The whole night before the day on which the procession was to take place, the impostors were up, and had more than twenty lights burning. Every one could see that they were busy getting the Emperor's new clothes ready. They made appear as if they took the stuff off the loom, cut away in the air with large shears, and sewed with needles without thread, and said at length, "See, now the clothes are ready."

The Emperor himself came with his chief nobility, and both impostors raised one arm, exactly as if they were holding something up, and said, "These are trunk-hose; this is the vest; here is the mantle," and so on, "all as light as a cobweb, that one might think one had nothing on; but just in that consists the beauty."

"Yes," all the nobility said; but they saw nothing, for there was nothing.

"If your Imperial Majesty will please to take off your clothes," the impostors said, "we will put the new ones on for you here, before the looking-glass."

The Emperor took off all his clothes; and the impostors pretended to help him on with one article after another of the new garments; and the Emperor bent and turned his body about before the looking-glass.

"Oh, how becoming they are! how beautifully they fit!" all said. "The pattern and colours are perfect; that is a magnificent costume."

The chief usher said, "The canopy, which is to be carried over your Majesty in the procession is waiting for your Majesty without."

"Well, I am ready," the Emperor said. "Do not the things fit well?" And then he turned again to the looking-glass, for he wished it to appear as if he were examining his attire carefully.

The pages, who were to carry the train, stooped, and pretended to lay hold of something on the ground, as if they were raising the train, which they then pretended to hold up, for they would not have it appear that they could not see anything.

So the Emperor walked in the procession, under the magnificent canopy; and all the people in the street and in the windows said, "The Emperor's clothes are not to be equalled, and what a magnificent train he has!" No one would let it appear that he did not see anything, for if so, he would have been unfit for his situation, or very stupid. No clothes of the Emperor's had ever had so much success as these.

"But he has nothing on," said at length a little child.

"Just listen to the innocent little thing!" its father said. And one whispered to the other what the child had uttered.

"But he has nothing on!" all the people cried at last.

This perplexed the Emperor, for it appeared to him that they were right; but he said to himself, "Now that I have begun it I must see it through and go on with the procession." And the pages continued to carry the train which had no existence.

THE LITTLE MERMAID

FAR out in the sea the water is as blue as the most beautiful cornflower, and as transparent as the clearest glass; but it is very deep,—deeper than any ship's cable can reach, and many church-spires would have to be placed one on the top of the other to reach from the bottom above the surface of the water. There below lived the people of the sea.

Now it must not be imagined that the bottom is merely bare white sand; no, the most curious trees and plants grow there, the stems and leaves of which are so pliant, that the slightest agitation of the water moves them, just as if they were alive. All the fish, large and small, slip through the branches like the birds here, in the air above. In the very deepest part lies the Sea-King's palace, the walls of which are of coral, the long, pointed windows being of the purest amber, and the roof is formed of mussel-shells, that open and shut according to the flowing of the waters, and have a very beautiful appearance, for in each lie the glistening pearls, any one of which would be the chief ornament in the crown of a queen.

The Sea-King there below had been a widower for many years, and his old mother conducted his household for him. She was a clever woman, but very proud of her birth, on which account she wore twelve oysters on her tail, whereas the highest of the nobles were allowed to wear only six. In other respects she deserved the highest praise, particularly for her great care of her grand-daughters. These were six beautiful children. But the youngest was the most beautiful of all; her skin was as clear and smooth as the leaf of a rose, and her eyes as blue as the deepest sea; but, like her sisters, she had no feet, her body ending in the tail of a fish.

The whole day they could play in the large halls of the palace, where living flowers grew out of the walls. When the amber windows were thrown open, the fish swam in, as with us the swallows fly into the room; but the fish swam straight up to the Princesses, eating out of their hands, and allowing themselves to be stroked by them.

In front of the palace was a large garden, with deep red and dark blue trees, the fruit of which shone like gold, and the flowers were like the brightest fire, the stems and leaves being in perpetual movement. The ground was the finest sand, but blue, like the flame of burning sulphur, and indeed a peculiar blue tint pervaded everything, so that one would have thought one was high up in the air, with sky above and below, rather than at the bottom of the sea.

During very calm weather the sun could be seen, looking like a purple flower, from the calyx of which streamed all the light.

Each Princess had a little piece of ground in the garden, where she could dig and plant as best pleased her. The one gave her garden the form of a whale, whilst another preferred hers looking like a mermaid; but the youngest made hers round, like the sun, and planted it only with flowers of the same colour as the sun. She was a strange child, quiet and thoughtful; and whilst her sisters delighted in all the beautiful things they got from wrecked vessels, she, besides her flowers that were like the sun, cared only for a beautiful statue of a boy, of pure white marble, which had fallen down from some vessel to the bottom of the sea. She planted a rose-coloured weeping willow by the side of her statue, which it covered with its branches, hanging down towards the blue sand, where they cast violet shadows, in constant movement like the branches themselves. It had the appearance as if the top of the tree and the roots were playing, and wished to kiss each other.

Nothing gave her so much pleasure as to hear about the world above, and her old grandmother had to tell all she knew of ships, cities, men and beasts: but of all things it seemed to her most delightful, that the flowers on the earth had scent, which those of the sea had not; that the woods were green; and that the fish, which were there seen amongst the trees, sang so loud and beautifully that it was a pleasure to listen to them. These were the birds, which the grandmother called fish, for otherwise they would not have understood her, as they had never yet seen a bird.

"When you have reached your fifteenth year," the grandmother said, "you will be allowed to rise up to the top of the sea, where, seated on a rock in the moonlight, you will see the large ships sail past, and also see cities and forests." The following year the eldest sister would be fifteen, and as there was a year's difference in all their ages, the youngest would consequently have five full years to wait before being allowed to come up from the bottom of the sea, and see how all looked with us. But the eldest promised to tell the others what she should see, and find the most beautiful on the first day, for their grandmother did not tell them near enough, and there remained much they wished to know about.

Not one had such a strong desire after this knowledge as the youngest, just the one that had the longest to wait, and who was so quiet and thoughtful. Many a night she stood at the open window watching the fish, how they moved their fins and tails about in the water. She could see the moon, and stars, which certainly appeared paler than with us, but through the water they seemed much larger than appears to our eyes; and when anything dark, like a cloud, passed between them and her, she knew that it must be either a whale-fish, or a ship full of human beings, into whose heads it certainly did not enter that a pretty young mermaid was standing below, raising up her white hands towards them.

The eldest Princess was now fifteen years old, and might rise up to the surface of the sea.

On her return she had a hundred different things to tell, but the most beautiful of all, she said, had been lying on a sandbank in the calm sea, with the moon shining, and looking at a large city on the coast close by, where the light glittered like hundreds of stars; to hear the music, and the noise made by the men and the conveyances of different sorts; to see the church-spires, and to listen to the ringing of the bells, and she felt the greater longing for all these, just because she could not get there.

Oh, how attentively the youngest sister listened, and as she, later in the evening, stood at the open window looking up through the dark water, she thought of the large city and the noise, and then she thought she heard the ringing of the bells.

The following year, the second sister's turn came to rise up through the water, and to swim whither she felt inclined. She rose to the top just as the sun was going down, and this sight she thought the most beautiful. The whole sky looked like gold, she said, and the beauty of the clouds she could not describe, as they sailed over her head, red and violet-coloured, but still faster than these flew a flock of wild swans, across the water towards where the sun was. She herself swam in the same direction, but the sun went down, and the rose-coloured tint faded from the water and the clouds.

The next year the third sister rose to the surface of the water, and she was the boldest of them, for she swam up a broad river which flowed into the sea. She saw beautiful green hills covered with vines; she saw castles and farmhouses appearing from amongst magnificent forests; and heard how the birds sang, the sun shining so hot that she often had to dive under the water, in order to cool her burning face. In a little creek she came upon a number of children, who were splashing about in the water quite naked. She wished to play with them, but they ran away frightened, and a little black animal, namely a dog, came and barked so fiercely at her, that she was quite afraid and sought the open sea again. She could never forget the magnificent forests, the green hills, and the pretty children that could swim, although they had no fishes' tails.

The fourth sister was not so bold, remaining out in the middle of the vast sea, and she maintained that just there it was the most beautiful, for one could see for miles around, with the sky above like a glass bell. She had seen ships, but only far off in the distance, looking like little dark specks, and the funny dolphins turning somersets, and the large whales throwing up the water through their nostrils, so that it looked like hundreds of fountains.

Now the fifth sister's turn came, and as her birthday happened to be in winter, she saw what the others had not seen the first time. The sea looked quite green, and round about large icebergs were floating, which, she said, looked like pearls, but were much larger than the church-steeples that men build. They were of the most extraordinary forms and sparkled like diamonds. She had seated herself upon one of the largest, the wind playing with her long hair, and towards evening the sky became overcast; it thundered and lightened, whilst the black sea raised the large blocks of ice high up, and they glittered with the reflection of the lightning. On all the vessels the sails were taken in, and there was fear and trembling, as they sought to steer clear of the huge masses of ice, but she sat calmly watching the lightning passing zigzag through the air, till lost in the sea.

The first time that each of the sisters came up to the top of the water, she was delighted with the beauty and novelty of all she saw, but now, as grown-up girls, they could rise up when they chose, it became indifferent to them, and after the lapse of a month they said that down below it was most beautiful, as there they felt at home.

Often of an evening the five sisters, arm in arm, rose to the surface of the water. They had beautiful voices, far more beautiful than any human being; and when a storm was coming on, and they might expect the ships to be wrecked, they swam before them, singing so delightfully how beautiful it was at the bottom of the sea, and begging the sailors not to fear going down: but these could not understand their words, thinking it was the storm, nor did they ever see the splendour there below, for when the ship sank they were drowned, and as dead bodies only reached the Sea-King's palace.

When the sisters rose thus, arm in arm, from their dwelling below, the little sister stood alone watching them, and she felt as if she must cry, but a mermaid has no tears, and therefore she suffers far more.

"Oh, were I but fifteen!" she would say. "I know that I shall love the world above, and the beings that inhabit it, with all my heart."

At length she was fifteen.

"Well, now you are grown up," her grandmother, the old

widowed Queen said, "come that I may decorate you like your sisters"; and she placed a wreath of lilies on her head, of which each leaf was the half of a pearl, and let eight large oysters stick fast on the Princess's tail, in order to show her rank.

"Oh, how it hurts!" the Little Mermaid said.

"Yes, rank has its inconveniences," the old Queen answered.

She would so gladly have thrown off all this magnificence, for the red flowers of her garden would have become her better, but she could not help herself. "Farewell!" she cried, and rose up in the water, as light as a bladder.

The sun had just gone down, as her head appeared above the water, but the clouds still glittered like roses and gold, and in the midst of the light red sky the evening star sparkled so bright and beautiful, the air was mild and the sea quite calm. There lay a large ship with three masts; she had all her sails spread, for scarcely a breath of air was stirring, and the sailors sat about in the rigging. On board there was music and singing, and as the evening grew darker hundreds of variegated lamps were lighted which looked like the flags of all nations waving in the air. The Little Mermaid swam right up to the cabin window, and each time that she rose with a wave, she could look into the room, where there were several richly dressed men, but by far the handsomest of all was a young Prince, with large black eyes. He could not be more than sixteen years old, and this being his birthday was the cause of all the splendour. The sailors were dancing, and when the young Prince appeared on deck, more than a hundred rockets rose up in the air, which threw light around like day, so that the mermaid was very much frightened and dived down under the water; but her head soon appeared again, and it was just as if all the stars of heaven were falling down upon her. She had never seen any fireworks before. Splendid suns whirled round, and serpents of fire rose up in the air, all being reflected in the clear calm sea. On the vessel itself it was so light that one could see every rope, much more the men. Oh! how handsome the young Prince was, and smilingly he pressed the sailors' hands whilst the music sounded through the clear night.

It was growing late, but the Little Mermaid could not turn her eyes away from the ship and the handsome Prince. The lamps were put out, no more rockets rose up in the air, nor did the cannon sound any longer; but deep down in the sea there was a rumbling and rolling noise, whilst she was rocked up and down on the waves, so that she could see into the cabin window. The ship began to make more way, one sail after the other was unfurled, the waves rose higher, and black clouds began to appear, whilst it lightened in the distance. It threatened to be bad weather, and the sailors therefore again furled the sails. The large ship rocked to and fro in its rapid course on the wild sea, and the water rose like black mountains, threatening to overwhelm it, but it dived down like a swan between the high waves, appearing again on the heaped-up waters. The Little Mermaid thought this most delightful, but it did not seem so to the sailors, for momentarily the ship's distress increased. The thick planks began to yield to the pressure of the waves, and the water burst into the vessel, the mast now snapped in two as if it were only a reed, and the ship lay entirely at the mercy of the waves. The Little Mermaid now saw that they were in danger, and she had to be on her guard against beams and pieces of the ship which were floating on the water. One moment it was so pitch-dark that she could see nothing, but when it lightened it became so light again that she could recognise all on board the vessel. In particular she sought the young Prince, and she saw him, as the ship disappeared, sink into the depth of the sea. Her first feeling was that of delight, for he would now come down to her, but then she bethought herself that human beings could not live in the water, and that he would not reach her father's palace otherwise than dead. Die he must not, and therefore she swam between beams and planks which were floating on the sea without a thought that she might be crushed by them, dived down deep under the water, rising again between the waves, and thus at length reached the spot where the Prince with difficulty kept himself afloat. He was nearly exhausted, his beautiful eyes closing, and he must have died had not the Little Mermaid come to his assistance. She held his head above the water, and allowed herself to be borne along with him at the will of the waves.

In the morning the storm had subsided, but of the ship not a splinter was to be seen; the sun rose red and bright, and it appeared as if life returned to the Prince's cheeks, but his eyes remained closed. The mermaid kissed his beautiful high forehead, stroking back his wet hair, and it seemed to her that he resembled the marble statue down below in her little garden. She kissed him, and wished he might come to life again.

She now saw land before her with high blue mountains, on the tops of which lay the snow as if it were swan's down. Below on the coast were beautiful green woods, and in front stood a church or convent, she did not know exactly which, but it was a building, at any rate. In the garden there grew lemon and orange-trees, and before the gates stood high palm-trees. The sea here formed a little creek, where the water was calm but very deep, and under the cliffs were firm white sands. To these she swam with the handsome Prince, and laid him in the sand, taking care that his head lay high in the warm sunshine.

Now the bells began to ring in the large white building, and many young girls came through the garden, when the Little Mermaid swam further out behind some rocks that rose from the water, and she laid some of the foam of the sea on her hair and her breast, so that she might not be noticed. Then she watched to see who would come to the poor Prince.

Not long after a young girl came to the spot where he lay. At first she seemed frightened, but only for a moment, when she called several others, and the mermaid saw that the Prince came to life, smiling on all around him, but on her out in the sea he did not smile, for how should he know that it was she who had saved him? She felt quite sorrowful, and when he was led into the large building, she dived down under the water, in sadness returning to her father's palace.

She had always been quiet and thoughtful, but she was now much more so. Her sisters asked her what she had seen, but she did not answer them.

Many an evening and morning she returned to where she had left the Prince. She saw how the fruit of the garden ripened and was gathered, she saw how the snow on the high mountains melted, but the Prince she did not see, and sadder and sadder she returned home. It was now her only consolation to sit in her little garden, with her arms around the beautiful marble statue, but her flowers she did not attend to, so that they grew wild across the paths, winding amongst the branches of the trees till it was quite dark there.

At length she could bear it no longer, and told one of her sisters, when the others knew it too, but none besides these and a couple of other mermaids, who spread it no further than amongst their intimate friends. One of them knew who the Prince was; she had seen the rejoicing on board the vessel, and told whence he came and where his kingdom lay.

"Come, little sister," the other Princesses said, and arm in arm they rose with her, swimming to where they knew the Prince's palace stood.

This was built of a light yellow sparkling stone, with large marble steps, which ran down into the sea. Splendid gilt domes rose above the roof, and between the pillars, which quite surrounded the building, were marble statues, which looked as if they were alive. Through the clear glass in the high windows the most magnificent rooms could be seen, with costly silk curtains, and the walls all hung with beautiful paintings which were delightful to behold. In the middle of the largest room a fountain threw up its sparkling waters to the glass dome in the roof, through which the sun shone upon the water and the beautiful plants which grew in the basin.

She now knew where he lived, and there she was on the water many an evening and many a night; she swam much nearer the land than any of the others had ventured to do, and even made her way along the whole length of the canal, up to the magnificent marble terrace, which threw a long shadow over the water. Here she sat and watched the young Prince, who thought himself quite alone in the clear moonlight.

She saw him many an evening sailing with music in his beautiful boat; she listened from amidst the green reeds, and when any one saw her long silvery veil, waving in the air, he thought it was a swan spreading out its wings.

At night when the fishermen were out by torchlight, she heard them say so much in praise of the young Prince that she felt delighted she had saved his life when half dead he could no longer struggle with the waves, and she thought how his head had rested on her bosom, and how she had kissed him, but of that he knew nothing, and could not even dream of her.

She began to love the human race more and more, and more and more she wished she could dwell amongst them, for their world appeared much larger to her than hers. They could cross the seas in ships, and they could climb the mountains high above the clouds, and the territory they possessed with forest and fields stretched further than her eye could reach. There were so many things she wished to know, but her sisters could not answer all her questions, and therefore she had to ask her grandmother, who knew the upper world well, and called it the lands above the sea.

"If men are not drowned," the Little Mermaid asked, "do they live for ever? do they not die, as we here below in the sea?"

"Yes," the old grandmother answered, "They must die, too; and their life is even shorter than ours. We may live for three hundred years; but then, when we cease to exist, we only turn to foam on the water, and have not even a grave here below amongst those we love. We have no immortal soul, we never come to life again; we are like the green reeds, which, if once broken, can never become green again; whereas men have a soul which lives for ever,—lives after the body has turned to dust. It takes its flight through the clear air up to the shining stars, and the same as we rise to beautiful, unknown places, which we shall never see."

"Why did we not receive an immortal soul?" the Little Mermaid said, sadly; "I would gladly give my hundreds of years that I have to live to be a man for only one day, and have part in the heavenly kingdom."

"You must not think of that," the old grandmother said; "we feel much happier and are better than the men above."

"I must die, then, and become foam on the top of the water, and not hear the music of the waves, nor see the beautiful flowers and the red sun. Can I do nothing to gain an immortal soul?"

"No," was the answer; "only if a man were to love you so that you would be more to him than father or mother; if he clung to you with all his thoughts and all his love, and let the priest lay his right hand in yours, with the promise of fidelity now and to all eternity, then his soul would flow into your body, and you would have part in the felicity of mankind. He would give you a soul, and still keep his own. But that can never be. Just that which is a beauty here in the sea, namely, your fish's tail, is thought ugly on earth. They know no better; and to be beautiful one must have two sturdy props, which they call legs."

Then the Little Mermaid sighed, and looked down sadly upon her fish's tail.

"Let us be happy," the old grandmother said. "We will jump and dance during the three hundred years we have to live, which is long enough in all conscience, and then we shall rest all the better. To-night there is a state ball."

There was splendour, such as is never seen on earth. The walls and ceiling of the large dancing-hall were of thick but clear crystal. Several hundred colossal mussel-shells, red and green, stood in rows on either side, with a blue burning flame, which lighted up the hall, and shone through the walls, so that the whole sea around was bright. Innumerable shoals of fish, large and small, were seen swimming about, the scales of some being scarlet, and of others silver and gold. In the middle, through the hall, flowed a broad stream, and in this the mermaids and men danced to their own lovely singing. The beings on earth have not such beautiful voices. The Little Mermaid sang more beautifully than any of them, so that she was very much applauded, and for a moment she experienced a feeling of pleasure, for she knew that she had the most beautiful voice of all on earth or in the sea. But soon again she thought of the world above her. She could not forget the handsome Prince, and her sorrow at not possessing an immortal soul. Then she stole out of her father's palace, and whilst all within was merriment and happiness, she sat in deep sorrow in her little garden. She now heard a horn sound through the water, and she thought, "That is no doubt the Prince sailing there above, he for whom all my desires centre, and in whose hands I would trust my life's happiness. I will venture everything to gain him and an immortal soul. Whilst my sisters are dancing in my father's palace I will go to the Water-witch, of whom I have always been so afraid; but she can, perhaps, advise and help me."

Now the Little Mermaid left her garden, and went to the roaring whirlpool, beyond which the Water-witch dwelled. She had never been that way before. No flowers grew there,—no sea-grass—only the naked grey sand stretched towards the whirlpool, where the water whirls round like boisterous water-wheels, dragging everything it lays hold of down into depths below. Through the middle of this all-destroying whirlpool she had to pass in order to reach the domains of the Water-witch; and part of the way she had to cross hot bubbling slime; this the witch called her peat-bog. Behind this lay her house, in the midst of a most extraordinary forest. All the trees and bushes were polypi,—half-animal and half-plant—which looked like hundred-headed snakes growing out of the earth. All the branches were long slimy arms with fingers like plant worms, and every limb from the root to the highest point moved. Everything in the sea that they could catch they laid hold of and never let it go again. The Little Mermaid was quite frightened; her heart beat with fear, and she nearly turned back again; but then she thought of the Prince and of the human soul, which gave her fresh courage. Her long, flowing hair she fastened up tight round her head, that the polypi might not catch her by it; and, with her hands crossed over her bosom, she swam swiftly between the hateful polypi, which stretched out their pliant arms after her. She saw how each of them held something, or other, that it had caught, with hundreds of little arms like strong iron bands. Human beings, that had been drowned and sunk deep down in the sea, remained as skeletons in the arms of the polypi. They held boxes and rudders of ships, and the skeletons of animals, besides a little mermaid which they had caught and smothered; and this was to her the most horrible sight of all.

Now she came to a large swampy spot in the forest, where huge fat water-snakes twisted and twirled about; and in the middle of this spot was a house built of the bones of wrecked human beings, and there sat the witch, feeding a toad out of her mouth, just as we give a canary sugar, and the snakes hung round her neck.

"I know already what you want," the witch said; "it is foolish enough of you, but you shall have your wish, since it will bring you to misery, my pretty Princess. You want to get rid of your fish's tail and have two legs instead, like a man, so that the young Prince may fall in love with you, and you may gain him and an immortal soul." Saying this the witch laughed so loud and repulsively that the toad and the snakes fell to the ground, where they rolled together. "You come just in time," she continued, "for tomorrow, after the rising of the sun, I could not have helped you for another year. I will prepare you a draught with which, before the sun rises, you must swim to the land and there drink it. Then your tail will disappear, shrinking into what men call legs, but it will give you pain, just as if a sword were being thrust through you. All who see you will say you are the most beautiful being they have seen, you will retain a floating gait, such as no dancer can equal, but every step you take will be as if you trod on sharp knives, and as if your blood must flow. If you consent to suffer all this I will help you."

"Yes," the Little Mermaid answered quickly, and she thought of the Prince and of an immortal soul.

"But consider," the witch continued, "after you have once assumed the human form you can never become a mermaid again. You can never return to your sisters or to your father's palace; and if you do not gain the Prince's love, so that for you he forgets father and mother, clinging to you with body and soul, and if the priest does not join your hands together so that you are man and wife, you will not gain an immortal soul. The first morning after his marriage with another, your heart will break and you will turn to foam on the water."

"I agree," the little Mermaid said, and she was as pale as death.

"But I must be paid," the witch resumed, "and it is not little I require. You have the most beautiful voice of any here at the bottom of the sea; with that you trust to fascinating him, but that

c

voice you must give me. The best you possess I require for my invaluable draught, for it is some of my own blood I must give you, so that I may be sharp like a two-edged sword."

"But if you take my voice what have I left?" the Little Mermaid said.

"Your beautiful person, your floating gait, and your speaking eyes and these are enough to gain any heart. Well, have you lost your courage? Come, put out your little tongue, which I will cut off in payment for the powerful draught."

"So be it," the Little Mermaid said, and the witch put her kettle on the fire to boil the magic draught. "Cleanliness is a good thing," she said, as she scoured out the kettle with the snakes, which she tied in a knot. She then cut open her breast, and let the black blood drop into the kettle, the stream of which formed such extraordinary figures, enough to frighten any one. Each moment she threw fresh things into the kettle, and when it boiled thoroughly it was like the crying of a crocodile. At length it was ready and looked like the clearest water.

"There it is," the witch said, and cut off the Little Mermaid's tongue, so that she was now dumb, and could neither sing nor speak.

"If the polypi should lay hold of you as you pass through my forest," the witch continued, "throw only one drop of this draught upon them and their arms and fingers will break into a thousand pieces." But that was not necessary, for they drew back frightened when they saw the sparkling draught, which shone like a star, so she passed quickly through the forest, the bog, and the roaring whirlpool.

She could see her father's palace. The lights were extinguished, and no doubt all were long past asleep, but she dared not go to them now that she was dumb, and on the point of leaving them for ever. She felt as if her heart would break with grief. She stole into the garden, took a flower from each of her sisters' beds, and kissing her hand, she rose up through the dark blue sea.

The sun had not yet risen when she reached the Prince's palace, and the moon was still shining brightly. She drank the magic draught, and it felt as if a two-edged sword were cutting through her tender body, so that she fainted and lay there as dead. When the sun shone upon the sea she awoke, feeling a cutting pain, but immediately before her stood the handsome young Prince, who fixed his coal-black eyes upon her, so that she cast hers down, and then she perceived that her fish's tail had disappeared, in the place of which she had the prettiest little white legs that any girl can have. The Prince asked who she was and how she came there, and she looked at him mildly, yet at the same time so sadly, with her dark blue eyes, but speak she could not. He then took her by the hand and led her into the palace. Every step she took was, as the witch had foretold, as if she were walking on the edge of sharp knives, but she bore it willingly, and led by the Prince she mounted the steps so lightly that he and every one marvelled at her lovely, floating gait.

She had now costly clothes of silk and muslin, and was the most beautiful of all in the palace, but she was dumb and could neither speak nor sing. Beautiful female slaves, dressed in silk and gold, sang before the Prince and his royal parents, and one sang so much more delightfully than all the others, that the Prince clapped his hands and smiled, which made the Little Mermaid quite sad, for she knew that she had sung much better, and she thought, "Oh, did he but know that in order to be near him I have sacrificed my voice for ever."

The slaves now danced to beautiful music, and the Little Mermaid rose, stood on the points of her toes, and then floated across the boards so that none had danced like her, her beauty becoming more striking at every moment; and her eyes spoke more touchingly to the heart than the singing of the slaves.

All were delighted with her, particularly the Prince, who called her his little foundling, and she danced more and more, though each time she put her foot to the ground it was as if she trod on knives. The Prince said that she should always remain with him, and she received permission to sleep on a velvet cushion at his door.

He had man's clothes made for her so that she might accompany him on horseback, and they rode together through the fragrant groves where the green boughs touched their shoulders and the little birds sang behind the fresh leaves. She climbed with the Prince up the highest mountains, and though her tender feet bled so that he could see it, she only laughed, and still followed him till they saw the clouds floating beneath them, like a swarm of birds flying to another country.

At night, when the others slept, she would go down the broad marble stairs and cool her burning feet in the cold sea, and her thoughts then flew back to those below in the deep.

One night her sisters came arm in arm, and they sang so sadly as they floated on the water. She made signs to them, and when they recognised her they told her into what grief she had plunged them all. After that they came every night, and once she saw, far out in the sea, her old grandmother, who for many years had not risen to the surface of the water, as also the Sea-King with the crown upon his head. They stretched out their hands towards her, yet they did not venture so far inland as her sisters.

She daily became dearer to the Prince, who loved her as one loves a good, dear child, but to make her his queen never once entered his head; and unless she became his wife, she would not receive an immortal soul, but the morning after his marriage with another must become foam upon the sea.

"Do you love me more than them all?" the Little Mermaid's eyes seemed to say, when he took her in his arms and kissed her beautiful forehead.

"Yes, you are the dearest to me," the Prince said, "for you have the best heart and are the most devoted to me; besides that you are like a young girl whom I saw once, but shall never see again. I was on board a ship that was wrecked when the waves cast me on land near a holy temple, which was tended by several young girls, of whom the youngest found me on the shore and saved my life. I saw her only twice, and she is the only one in the world whom I could really love, but you are like her and have nearly driven her image from my heart. She belongs to the holy temple, and therefore my good fortune has sent you to me, and we will never more be parted." "Oh, he does not know that it was I who saved his life, carrying him through the sea to where the temple stands!" the Little Mermaid thought. "I sat behind the foam, watching till some one should come, and I saw the pretty girl whom he loves more than me. The girl belongs to the temple, he has said, so they can never meet, whereas I am with him, and see him daily. I will tend him, love him and sacrifice my life for him."

"The Prince is about to marry our neighbouring King's beautiful daughter, and therefore so magnificent a ship is got ready," was said on all sides. "It is announced that he is going to travel, but it is in reality to see the King's daughter, and a large retinue is to accompany him." The Little Mermaid smiled, for she knew the Prince's thoughts better than they. "I must travel," he had told her. "My parents desire that I should see the beautiful Princess, but they will not force me to marry her. I can never love her, for she is not like that beautiful girl in the temple whom you resemble, and if I must ever choose a wife it would be you rather, my dumb foundling with the speaking eyes"; and he kissed her rosy lips, played with her long hair, and laid his head on her heart, so that it dreamed of human happiness and of an immortal soul.

"You are not afraid of the sea, my dumb child?" he asked, as they stood together on the deck of the magnificent vessel which was to carry him to the neighbouring King's country; and he told her of storms and calms, of the curious fish in the deep, and of what the divers had seen below. She smiled at what he told her, for she knew better than all what it was like at the bottom of the sea.

In the moonlight night, when all, even the pilot who stood at the rudder, were asleep, she sat at the side of the vessel staring down into the clear water, and she thought she saw her father's palace, with her grandmother looking up towards her. Then her sisters appeared above the water, and looking at her sadly, wrung their white hands. She nodded to them, and, smiling, wished to tell them that all was going well and happily for her, but the cabin-boy came near, so that her sisters dived down, and he thought what he had seen was the foam of the waves.

The next morning the ship entered the harbour of the neighbouring King's splendid city. All the church-bells rang, the trumpets sounded from the high towers, and the soldiers presented arms. There was some new fête every day. Balls and parties followed one upon the other, but the Princess was not yet there. She was far away, it was said, being educated in a holy temple where she was learning all royal virtues. At length she arrived.

The Little Mermaid was very anxious to see her, and was obliged to acknowledge her beauty, for a more lovely apparition she had never beheld. Her skin was so clear and transparent, and from beneath the long dark lashes smiled the most honest eyes of a deep blue.

"It is you," the Prince said,—"you, who saved me when I lay as dead on the shore"; and he pressed his blushing bride to his breast. "Oh, I am too happy!" he said to the Little Mermaid. "My fondest hopes are realised. You will rejoice in my happiness, for you take more interest in me than any of them." The Little Mermaid kissed his hand, and began to feel already as if her heart was breaking. Was not the morning after his marriage to bring death to her and to change her into foam on the sea?

All the church-bells rang, and heralds rode about the streets announcing the betrothal. On all the altars sweet-scented oil was burning in beautiful silver lamps. The priests swang the censers, and the bride and bridegroom received the bishop's blessing. The

Little Mermaid stood there, clothed in silk and gold, holding the bride's train, but she did not hear the beautiful music, nor did she see the holy ceremony, she only thought of her death and of all she had lost in this world.

The same evening the bride and bridegroom went on board the vessel. The cannon thundered, the flags were flying, and in the middle of the ship's deck a magnificent tent of purple and gold was erected, furnished with the most beautiful cushions, and there the newly-married couple were to pass the night.

The sails swelled with the wind and the ship glided smoothly through the calm sea.

When it grew dark lamps of all colours were lighted, and the sailors danced merrily on the deck. The Little Mermaid could not help thinking of the first time she rose to the surface of the sea, when she witnessed the same magnificence and rejoicing, and she whirled round in the dance so that all applauded her, for she had never danced so beautifully. It was as if sharp knives were cutting into her tender feet, but she did not feel it, for her heart was cut still more painfully. She knew it was the last night she would see him for whom she had left her home and relations, for whom she had sacrificed her lovely voice and had suffered daily tortures, and of all this he knew nothing. It was the last night that she should breathe the same air with him, or behold the sea and the sky studded with stars. An eternal night without thoughts or dreams awaited her, who had no soul, and could not gain one. All was joy and merriment till long past midnight, and she laughed and danced with death in her heart. The Prince kissed his beautiful bride, whilst she played with his black hair, and hand in hand they retired to rest in their magnificent tent.

All was silent and quiet on board, only the pilot stood at the helm, when the Little Mermaid laid her white arms on the side of the vessel looking towards the east, for she knew that the first rays of the sun would kill her. She now saw her sisters rise from the waves as pale as herself. Their beautiful long hair did not now float in the air, it was cut off.

"We have given it to the witch to purchase help for you," they said, "so that you may not die this night, and she has given us a knife,—here it is,—see how sharp it is. Before the rising of the sun you must bury it in the Prince's heart, and when the warm blood falls upon your feet, they will turn into a fish's tail, and you will again be a mermaid. You can then return to us and live your three hundred years, before you become the dead salt sea-foam. Make haste, for he or you must die before the sun rises. Your old grandmother has fretted so that her white hair has fallen off, like ours has fallen by the witch's scissors. Kill the Prince and return to us, but make haste, for do you not see the red streak in the sky? In but a few minutes the sun will rise and you must then die." They heaved a heavy sigh and disappeared in the waves.

The Little Mermaid drew back the curtain from the tent and saw the beautiful bride resting with her head on the Prince's breast. She bent down and kissed him on the forehead, then looked at the sky which was becoming redder and redder. She examined the sharp pointed knife, and again fixed her eyes on the Prince, who in his dreams murmured his bride's name. She only was in his thoughts. The knife trembled in the Little Mermaid's hand, but then she threw it far out into the sea, which shone red where it fell, as if drops of blood bubbled up from the water. Once more she looked upon the Prince with dying eyes, then threw herself from the vessel into the sea, and felt her body dissolving into foam.

The sun now rose above the water, the rays falling warmly upon the cold sea-foam, and the Little Mermaid felt nothing of death. She saw the bright sun, and just above her floated hundreds of transparent, beautiful beings, through whom she could see the white sails of the ship and the red clouds in the sky. Their voices were delightful melody, but so spiritual that no human ear could hear them, nor could the eye of man perceive them, and they were so light that they floated in the air without wings. The Little Mermaid saw that she had a body like these, which rose higher and higher out of the foam.

"To whom am I carried?" she asked, and her voice sounded like that of the other beings, so spiritual that no earthly music could imitate it.

"To the daughters of the air," the others answered. "Mermaids have no immortal soul, and can never have one unless they gain a man's love, so that their future existence depends upon another power. The daughters of the air have no immortal soul either, but by good acts they can gain one for themselves. We fly to the warm countries where the plague is in the burning air, and there we fan coolness, we impregnate the air with the scent of flowers, and give relief and health. When we have striven for three hundred years to accomplish all the good we can, we then receive an immortal soul, and share in the eternal bliss of mankind. You, poor Little Mermaid, have had the same lofty aspirations, you have suffered and endured, and thus raised yourself to the equal of the spirits of the air, so that you can now, after three hundred years of good works, earn an immortal soul."

The Little Mermaid raised her hands towards the glorious sun, and now for the first time refreshing tears filled her eyes. On the vessel there was again life and bustle, and she saw the Prince with his beautiful bride looking for her. Sadly they looked down upon the waves as if they knew that she had thrown herself into the water, when, invisible, she kissed the bride's forehead, smiled upon her and rose with the other children of the air upon the red cloud into the ethereal regions.

"After three hundred years we shall thus glide into heaven."

"And we may even get there earlier," one of the daughters of the air whispered. "Invisibly we glide into the dwellings of man, where there are children, and for each day on which we find a good child that pleases its parents and deserves their love, the Lord shortens the time of our probation. The child does not know that we pass through the room, but if it draws from us a smile of pleasure, one year is taken off the three hundred; but if, on the contrary, we have to shed tears of sorrow over a bad child, each tear adds one day to the time of our probation."

LITTLE CLAUS AND BIG CLAUS

IN a village there lived two men of the same name, both being called Claus, but one had four horses, whereas the other only possessed one; and to distinguish them from each other, the one that had four horses was called Big Claus, and he who had only one horse, Little Claus.

The whole week through Little Claus had to plough for Big Claus, and lend him his single horse, for which Big Claus in return helped him with his four horses, but only once a week. How Little Claus clacked with his whip over the five horses, for they were as good as his on that one day! Now when the people saw Little Claus ploughing with the five horses, he was highly delighted, and again clacking his whip, cried, "Gee, woh! all my horses!"

"You must not say that," Big Claus said, "for only one of the horses is yours."

But when the next person passed, Little Claus forgot that he was not to say it, and again cried, "Gee woh! all my horses!"

"Now I'll trouble you not to try that again," Big Claus said, "for if I hear it once more, I'll knock your horse on the head, and there'll be an end of that."

"Well, now, indeed it shall not escape me again," Little Claus said, but no sooner did another come by and wish him good day, than he thought how grand he looked ploughing his field with five horses, and then he clacked his whip, crying, "Gee woh! all my horses!"

"Oh, it is to be, then?" Big Claus said: and taking up a large stone struck Little Claus' horse on the head, so that it fell over and was quite dead.

"Oh dear, now I have no horse at all," Little Claus said, and began to cry. He then took the skin off his dead horse, and after it had thoroughly dried in the wind, packed it in a sack, which he slung over his shoulder, and started off to the town to sell it there.

He had far to go, besides having to pass through a great dark forest, and the weather came on very bad. He now quite lost his way, and before he found it again it was growing dark, and he was too far off from the town or his home to be able to reach either before night thoroughly set in.

Close by the road-side there stood a large farm-house, and though the shutters were closed, the light could still be seen shining above them. "There I shall no doubt obtain permission to pass the night," Little Claus thought, so he went and knocked at the door.

The farmer's wife opened it, but when she heard what he wanted, she said he might trudge on, for her husband was not at home, and she could not admit any strangers.

"Well, then, I suppose I must stop outside," Little Claus said, and the woman slammed the door in his face.

Close by there was a large hay-stack, and between that and the house a small shed with a flat straw roof.

"I can lie up there," Little Claus said, when he saw the roof, "and a first-rate bed it will be, but I hope the stork won't come down and bite my legs." For on the roof of the house there stood a stork, which had its nest there.

Little Claus now climbed up on to the shed, where he turned and turned till he made himself comfortable, and it so happened that just as he lay he could see right into the room of the farm-house, for the wooden shutters did not close at the top.

He saw a large table laid with wine and roast meat, besides a magnificent fish, the farmer's wife and the sexton sitting there all alone, and she filled his glass whilst he stuck his fork into the fish, for that was his favourite dish.

"If I could but have some of that," Little Claus thought, and he stretched out his neck to see further into the room. There was also a beautiful cake. That was, indeed, a feast.

Just then he heard some one come riding along the road towards the house, which was the farmer coming home.

He was the very best-natured man, but had one peculiarity—he could not bear to see the sexton at his house. If he even met a sexton he at once got into a rage. That was the reason why the sexton had gone in to wish the woman a good evening, knowing her husband was from home, and she in gratitude had put all that good cheer before him; but when she heard her husband, she was frightened and begged the sexton to get into a large empty box that stood in the room, as she well knew her poor husband would be in a great rage if he saw him. The woman hastily hid all the eatables as well as the wine in the oven, for if her husband had seen them he would certainly have asked the reason for all those preparations.

"Oh, dear!" Little Claus sighed from the top of his shed when he saw all the good things disappear.

"Is any one up there?" the farmer asked, looking up. "Why are you lying there? it will be better to go into the house with me."

Little Claus then told him how he had lost his way, and begged for a night's lodging.

"Certainly," the farmer answered; "but the first thing to do will be to get something to eat."

The wife received them cheerfully, laid the cloth for them, and brought a large bowl of oatmeal porridge. The farmer was hungry and ate with a right good appetite, but Little Claus could not help thinking of all the delicacies which he knew to be in the oven.

Under the table at his feet, he had thrown the sack with the horse's skin, to sell which he had come out, as we already know.

The porridge was not at all to his taste, so he pressed his foot upon the sack, and the dry skin made a loud crackling noise.

"Be quiet, there!" Little Claus said to his sack, but as he pressed his foot more heavily upon it at the same time, it crackled louder than before.

"What have you got in your sack?" the farmer asked.

"Oh, it's a magician," Little Claus answered; "and he says we should not be eating porridge, for that by his witchcraft he has filled the oven with roast meat, fish, and cake."

"Bless me, can it be possible?" the farmer exclaimed, and opening the oven, he discovered all the dainties his wife had hidden there, but which he believed the magician in the sack had provided for them. His wife dared not say anything, so she placed all on the table, and they ate of the fish, meat, and cake. Little Claus trod again upon the sack till it crackled.

"What does he say now?" the farmer asked.

"He says," Little Claus answered, "that there are three bottles of wine for us in the oven." The farmer's wife was obliged to fetch the wine, and her husband drank and grew as merry as possible. Such a magician as Little Claus had in his sack he would give anything to possess.

"Can he call up the evil one?" he asked, "for I am right merry now and should like to see him."

"Yes, my magician can do all I ask him. Can't you?" he said, pressing his foot upon the sack, and when it crackled he continued, "Don't you hear? he says the evil one is so ugly that we had better not see him."

"Oh, I am not at all afraid! I wonder what he looks like!"

"Why, he looks exactly like a sexton."

"Whew!" the farmer cried, "that is ugly; for you must know that of all things, I hate a sexton. But it doesn't matter, for I shall know it is only the evil one, and shall be the better able to bear the sight. Now I have courage for it; but he must not come too near me."

"Well, I'll ask my magician," Little Claus said, and, treading on the sack, held down his ear.

"What does he say?"

"He says you may go and open the box that stands there in the corner, and you will see him huddled up in it; but you must not raise the lid too high, or he'll escape."

"Pray help me to hold it," the farmer begged; and he went to the box where the real sexton was hidden, who sat there in a great fright.

The farmer opened the lid a little, and looked in. "Whew!" he cried, and sprang back. "Now I've seen him, and he's exactly like our sexton. That was dreadful."

After that they must have another glass, so they went on till late in the night.

"You must sell me the magician," the farmer said. "Ask whatever you like. I'll give you a whole bushel of money."

"No, I can't sell him," Little Claus said, "for just consider the great use he is to me."

"I should so much like to have him," the farmer said, and he went on importuning him.

"Well," Little Claus at length said, "since you have been so good as to give me shelter this night, I consent, and you shall have the magician for a bushel of money, but I must have the bushel heaped up."

"That you shall," the farmer said; "but you must take yonder box as well, for I won't keep it a minute longer in the house. How should I know, perhaps he is therein still?"

Little Claus gave the farmer his sack with the dry skin, and received a bushel heaped up with money in return. The farmer besides made him a present of a large wheelbarrow to carry his money and the box.

"Good-bye," Little Claus said, and he wheeled off his money and the box, in which the sexton was still huddled up.

On the other side of the forest was a broad, deep river, which ran so rapidly that it was scarcely possible to swim against the stream, and over this river a new bridge had been built, in the middle of which Little Claus stopped, saying out loud, so that the sexton in the box might hear him: —

"What am I to do, I wonder, with this stupid box? It is as heavy as if it were full of stones, and I'm only tiring myself to death by wheeling it along with me. I'll throw it into the river, and if it floats on to my house, well and good, and if it does not, it is no great matter."

He then laid hold of the box with one hand, and lifted it up a little, just as if he were going to throw it over the side of the bridge.

"Don't do that!" the sexton cried from inside the box. "Let me get out first."

"Whew!" Little Claus cried, pretending to be frightened; "he is in it still. I must be quick and throw him into the river, so that he may be drowned."

"No, no!" the sexton screamed. "I'll give you a whole bushel of money if you let me out."

"Well, that's quite another thing," Little Claus said, and opened the box. The sexton made haste to get out, pushed the empty box into the river, and went home, where he gave Little Claus a bushel of money, so that, with the one he had already received, he now had his barrow full.

"I am not badly paid for my horse," he said to himself, when he had got back to his room and heaped the money up in a pyramid in the middle of the floor. "What a rage Big Claus will be in when he hears how rich I have become through my single horse, but I'll not tell him all at once!"

He then sent a boy to Big Claus to borrow a bushel measure.

"What can he want with it?" Big Claus thought; and he smeared some tar at the bottom of the bushel, so that some of whatever was measured might stick to it, which indeed happened, for when he got the bushel measure back, he found three new shilling pieces sticking to the bottom.

"How is this?" Big Claus cried, and ran immediately to the little one. "How did you come by all that quantity of money?"

"Oh, that I got for my horse's skin, which I sold yesterday evening."

"That was well paid," Big Claus said; and, having run home quickly, he took an axe, knocked all his four horses on the head, and having taken their skins off, drove with them to the town.

"Hides! hides! who will buy hides?" he cried through the streets.

All the shoemakers and tanners came running, and asked how much he wanted for them.

"A bushel of money for each," Big Claus said.

"Are you mad?" all the people cried. "Do you think that we have money by the bushel?"

"Hides! hides! who will buy hides?" he cried again. And to all those who asked the price of them, he answered, "A bushel of money for each."

"He is making fools of us," the people cried. And the shoemakers took up their thongs, and the tanners their leather aprons, and set to thrashing Big Claus with them. "Hides! hides! Yes, we'll tan your hide for you," all cried after him. "Out of the town with you as quickly as possible!" And Big Claus had to hurry his best. He had never been so thrashed in his life before.

"Wait a bit," he said, when he got home. "Little Claus shall pay for this, for I'll certainly kill him."

Now Little Claus' old grandmother was just dead, and though she had always been cross and malicious he was quite sad, and taking the dead body he laid it in his warm bed to see whether that would restore life. There she should lie the whole night, whilst he sat in the corner and slept in a chair as he had often done before.

As he sat there in the night, the door opened and Big Claus came in with his axe. He knew well where Little Claus' bed stood, so he went straight up to it, and knocked the old grandmother on the head, thinking that it was Little Claus.

"Now we'll see," he said, "whether you'll make a fool of me again," and he went home.

"Well, that is a bad man," Little Claus said, "for he intended to kill me; it was well for my old grandmother that she was already dead, or he certainly would have taken her life."

He then dressed his dead grandmother in her Sunday's best, borrowed a horse from his neighbour, which he put to the cart, and seated her upon the back seat so that she could not fall. Having arranged all this they rolled off through the forest, and by the time the sun rose had reached a large inn where Little Claus stopped and went in to get some refreshment.

The landlord had a great, great quantity of money, and was a very good man, but so hot, as if he had been made up of pepper and tobacco.

"Good morning," he said to Little Claus. "Why, you are early on the stir."

"Yes," Little Claus answered, "I am going to the town with my old grandmother, who is outside in the cart. I wish you would take her out a glass of mead, for she will not come in, but you must speak very loud, as she is rather deaf."

"Most willingly," the landlord answered, and having poured out a glass of mead, took it to the dead woman, who was seated upright in the cart.

"Here is a glass of mead from your grandson," the landlord said; but the dead woman did not answer a word, sitting perfectly quiet.

"Do you not hear?" he cried as loud as he could. "Here is a glass of mead from your grandson."

Once more he shouted the same words, and then again, but as she did not take the slightest notice nor stir in the least, he got in a passion and threw the glass in her face, so that the mead trickled down her nose, and she fell back into the cart, for she was only seated upright but not bound.

"What is this?" Little Claus cried, and, rushing out, seized the landlord by the throat. "You have killed my grandmother. Do you not see there is a great hole in her forehead?"

"Oh, what a misfortune!" the landlord cried, wringing his hands. "That comes of my hot temper. My dear Little Claus, I will give you a bushel of money, and have your grandmother buried as if she were my own mother, but do not say a word about it, or I shall lose my head, which would be too bad."

So Little Claus got a bushel of money, and the landlord buried his grandmother just as if she were his own mother.

As soon as Little Claus reached home with all that quantity of money, he sent to Big Claus again to borrow a bushel measure.

"How is this?" Big Claus said. "Have I not killed him? Then I must go myself and see how that is"; so he went himself to Little Claus with the bushel measure.

"Why, where did you get all that money?" he asked, opening his eyes wide at the sight of the addition to his treasure.

"You killed my grandmother and not me," Little Claus said, "so I sold her body for a bushel of money."

"That was a good price," Big Claus said, and hurrying home he took an axe, with which he killed his old grandmother, and laying her in a cart drove to the town where the apothecary lived, whom he asked whether he would buy a dead body.

"Who is it, and where did you get it?" the apothecary asked.

"It is my grandmother," Big Claus said, "and I killed her in order to get a bushel of money for her body."

"The Lord forbid!" the apothecary said. "Surely you are rambling. Don't talk that way or you'll lose your head." He then told him what a sinful act it was, and what a bad man he must be, threatening him besides with punishment, so that Big Claus was frightened, and jumping at once into his cart, he lashed the horses and drove home as fast as possible. The apothecary and all the people thought he was mad, and therefore let him go his way.

"You shall pay for this," Big Claus said, on his road home. "Yes, Little Claus, dearly you shall pay"; and as soon as he reached home he took the largest sack he had, and going with it to Little Claus' house said, "You have made a fool of me a second time. First I knocked my horses on the head, and now I have killed my grandmother. This is all your fault, but you shall not make a fool of me a third time." Thereupon he seized Little Claus round the body, and having put him into the sack threw it across his shoulder, saying, "Now I am going to drown you."

He had a long way to go before reaching the river, and Little

Claus was not so light a weight to carry. He had to pass close by a church in which the organ sounded, and the people were singing so beautifully that Big Claus thought he might as well go in and hear a hymn before going further, so he put down the sack, with Little Claus in it, by the side of the church-door, and went in. He knew well that Little Claus could not get out, and as all the people were in church there was no one to help him.

"Oh, dear me! oh, goodness me!" Little Claus sighed, as he turned and twisted in the sack, but it was impossible to undo the rope that tied the mouth of it, when an old drover, with snow-white hair, and a long staff in his hand, came that way. He was following a drove of cows and oxen, which ran up against the sack in which Little Claus was, so that it was upset.

"Oh, dear me!" Little Claus sighed, "I am still so young to be bound for the kingdom of heaven."

"And I, poor wretch," the drover said, "am so old and yet cannot get there."

"Open the sack, then," Little Claus cried, "and get into it instead of me, and you will soon be there."

"That I will do, with pleasure," the old man said, and no sooner had he unfastened the sack than Little Claus jumped out.

"Will you take care of the cattle for me?" the old man asked, as he crept into the sack, and Little Claus having fastened it, went on with all the cows and the oxen.

Soon after Big Claus came out of church and took up the sack, which appeared to have grown much lighter, for the old drover was not more than half the weight of Little Claus. "How light it has grown! That comes of having heard a hymn," he said, and went on to the river, which was both wide and deep. He then threw the sack with the drover in it into the water, and called out, "Now I think you will not make a fool of me again."

After this he returned towards home, and when he got to where the roads crossed he met Little Claus driving his cattle along.

"How is this?" Big Claus said. "Did I not drown you?"

"Yes," Little Claus answered, "it's scarcely half an hour since you threw me into the river."

"But how came you by all that beautiful cattle?" Big Claus asked.

"It is sea cattle," Little Claus answered. "I will tell you the whole story, and must thank you for having drowned me, for now I am up in the world and am really rich. I was so frightened in the sack, and the wind whistled through my ears when you threw me off the bridge into the cold water. I sank to the bottom immediately, but I was not hurt, for the most beautiful grass grows down there. On that I fell and immediately the sack was opened, when a most lovely girl, dressed in snow-white garments, with a green wreath round her wet hair, took me by the hand, saying 'Are you there, Little Claus? For the present, here are a few head of cattle for you, but about a mile further on the road you will see a whole drove which I give you.' Then I perceived that the river formed a large road for the people of the sea. Down below they were walking and driving straight from the sea as far inland as the river runs. There were such lovely flowers and such beautiful fresh grass grew by the side of the road, and the fish swimming about in the water shot past my ears like the birds here in the air. What beautiful people they are, and, oh, what magnificent cattle!"

"But why did you come up again to us so soon?" Big Claus asked. "I would not have done so, if it is as beautiful down there as you say."

"Well, you shall see how politic that was on my part," Little Claus said, "for as I told you, the girl said that about a mile further on the road there is a whole drove of cattle for me, and by the road she of course meant the river, for she can walk on no other. Now I know what turns the river takes, first here and then there, so that it is a long way round, and it is much shorter to cut across the dry land here and get to the river again. By that I save at least half a mile, and shall all the sooner come into the possession of my cattle."

"Oh, you are a lucky man," Big Claus said. "And do you think I should get some sea cattle too, if I were down there at the bottom of the river?"

"No doubt about it," Little Claus answered: "but I cannot carry you in the sack as far as the river; you are too heavy for me. If you like to walk there and then get into the sack, I will throw you in with the greatest pleasure imaginable."

"Thank you," Big Claus said. "But if I do not get any cattle when I am down there, take my word for it, I will cudgel you well."

"Oh no, you won't use me so ill as that." With this they walked towards the river, and as soon as the cattle, which were very thirsty, saw the water they ran as fast as they could to get some to drink, and Little Claus continued, "Just look, what a hurry they are in to get to the bottom again!"

"Yes, I see," Big Claus said, "but you had better make haste and help me, or you'll feel my stick," and he got into the sack which lay across the back of one of the oxen.

"Put a stone in as well," Big Claus said, "or I fear I may not sink."

"It will do as it is," Little Claus said: but for all that he put a large stone in the sack, secured the mouth well, and then pushed it in. Plump! into the water went Big Claus, and sank at once to the bottom.

"I'm afraid he won't find the cattle," Little Claus said, and he went home with that which he had.

THE TRAVELLING COMPANION

POOR John was very sad, for his father was so dangerously ill that there were no hopes of his recovery. Besides those two there was no one in the little room, where the lamp on the table was near going out, as it had grown late.

"You have always been a good son, John!" his sick father said, "and the Lord will help you on in the world." He looked at him with mild, earnest eyes, and drawing a deep breath died. It was just as if he were asleep. John cried, for now he had no one in the whole world, neither father nor mother, brother nor sister. Poor John! He knelt by the bedside and kissed his dead father's hand, crying many bitter tears, but at last his eyes closed, and he fell asleep with his head resting on the edge of the bed.

He then had a curious dream: it was as if the sun and moon bowed down before him, and he saw his father brisk and well, and heard him laugh as he always laughed when he was particularly joyous. A beautiful girl with a golden crown on her shining hair held out her hand to him, and his father said, "See what a beautiful bride you have. She is the most beautiful in the whole world." He awoke, and all the splendour was gone, his father lay dead and cold in the bed and there was no one with them. Poor John!

The next week the dead body was buried; John followed close behind the coffin, and in this world never again was he to see his good father who had loved him so much. He heard how they threw the earth down upon the coffin, he still saw one corner of it: but the next spadeful that was thrown down, that too disappeared, and he felt as if his heart would break, he was so wretched. All around hymns were being sung which sounded so beautiful, and the tears came into his eyes: he cried, and that lightened his sorrow. The sun shone brightly on the green trees, as if to say, "You must not be sad, John! see how beautifully blue the sky is, and your father is now up there in heaven praying to God that all may go well with you."

"I will always be good," John said, "and then I shall go to heaven to my father. What delight it will be when we see each other again, and how much I shall have to tell him, and he will show me so many things, instructing me in all the splendour of heaven, exactly as he taught me here on earth. Oh, how delightful that will be!"

All this assumed such reality in his thoughts that he smiled whilst the tears still ran down his cheeks. The little birds sat above in the chestnut-trees and twittered "Quiwit! quiwit!" They were so joyous, though they had been present at the funeral, but they knew that the dead man was now in heaven and had wings, larger and more beautiful than theirs, that he was now happy because he had been good on earth, and at this they rejoiced. John saw how they flew away from the green trees far into the world, and he longed to go there too, but first he made a large wooden cross to place upon his father's grave, and when in the evening he took it there, the grave was decorated with sand and flowers. Strangers had done that, for all thought so highly of his dear father who was now dead.

Early the next morning John packed his small bundle, and secured his inheritance, consisting of ten pounds and a couple of pence, in his girdle; and with this he was about to wander forth into the world, but first he went to the churchyard, to his father's grave, where he prayed and said, "Farewell, my dear father. I will always be good, and therefore you may beg of the Lord that it may go well with me."

Out in the fields, where he now went, the flowers stood so fresh and beautiful in the warm sunshine, and they nodded in the wind, just as if they meant to say, "Welcome out here in the green fields! Is it not beautiful?" But John turned once more to look at the old church, where, as a little child, he had been christened, and where he had gone every Sunday with his father to divine service. High up in the tower he saw the church sprite standing at one of the openings with his pointed red cap on, and with his bent arm shading his eyes from the sun. John nodded him a farewell, and the little sprite waved his red cap, and, with one hand on his heart, kissed the other to him, to show how well he wished him, and that he might have a happy journey.

John thought how many beautiful things he should see in the large magnificent world, and he went on and further on,—further than he had ever been. The places through which he passed he did not know at all, nor the people whom he met.

The first night he had to sleep on a haycock in the open field, for he had no other bed; but just that he thought delightful. No king could be better off. The field with the river, the haycock, and the blue sky above, was a splendid bedroom. The green grass, with the little red and white flowers, was the carpet; the elder-trees and the rose-bushes were nosegays, and his wash-basin was the river, with the clear, fresh water, in which the rushes nodded him a good night and good morning. The moon was a large lamp, high up in the ceiling, which would not set fire to the curtains. He might sleep in perfect security, which he did, and did not wake till the sun rose, and the little birds all around sang, "Good morning! good morning! Are you not up yet?"

The bells rang for church, for it was Sunday, and the people went to hear the clergyman. John followed them, sang a hymn, and listened to the word of God, and it seemed to him exactly as if he were in the church where he had been christened, and where he had sung hymns with his father.

In the churchyard were many graves, some of them covered with high grass, and he thought of his father's grave, which would some day become like one of these, now that he could not weed and attend to it. He therefore seated himself and pulled up the grass, raised the crosses that had fallen, and put back the wreaths which the wind had blown off the graves, thinking, "Perhaps some one will attend in like manner to my father's grave now that I cannot do it."

Outside the church-door there stood an old beggar, supporting himself on his crutches, to whom John gave the pence which he had, and then went on happy and cheerful.

Towards evening a storm was blowing up, so that he hurried on to get under cover, and as it grew quite dark he reached a small church that stood by itself on a slight eminence, the door of which standing fortunately open, he slipped in, intending to remain till the storm should have passed over.

"I will seat myself here in a corner, for I am tired and need rest," he said; and, folding his hands, he repeated his evening prayer, but before he knew it he was asleep and dreaming, whilst it thundered and lightened without.

When he awoke it was the middle of the night, but the storm was over, and the moon shone in through the window. He now saw an open coffin, with a dead man in it, standing in the middle of the church, but he was not in the least frightened, for he had a good conscience, and he knew that the dead never do any injury to any one; it is the living bad people who do harm. Two such evil-disposed persons stood close by the side of the dead man, who had been placed here in the church previous to being buried. It was their intention to take the poor dead man out of his coffin and throw him outside the church-door.

"Why would you do that?" John asked. "That is a bad act. Let him rest."

"Oh, stuff and nonsense!" the two wicked men said. "He has cheated us. He owed us money, which he could not pay, and now he must needs die, so that we shall not get a penny; but we will have our revenge, for he shall lie outside the church-door like a dead dog."

"I have only ten pounds," John said; "that is my whole inheritance, but that I will give you with pleasure if you promise me faithfully to leave the poor dead man in rest. I shall no doubt get on without the money. I have strong limbs, and God will at all times help me."

"Well," the two wicked creatures said, "if you pay his debt we will not do anything to him, you may rely upon that"; and they took the money which John offered them, laughing at him for his good nature, and they went away. John now put the dead man in order in his coffin again, folding his hands, then took his departure, and wandered contentedly through the forest that lay before him.

On all sides, where the moon could shine through the trees, he saw the prettiest little elves playing merrily; and they did not allow themselves to be disturbed, for they knew that he was a good, innocent fellow, and it is only the wicked who can never see the elves. Some of these were no bigger than the breadth of a finger, and they had their long, yellow hair fastened up with golden combs. Two and two they were rocking on the large dew-drops which hung to the leaves and the high grass. Occasionally one of the drops would burst, and they then fell down amongst the grass, which caused laughter and confusion amongst the other little beings. It was delightful to watch them. They sang; and

John recognised all the pretty songs which he had learnt as a little boy. Large speckled spiders, with silver crowns on their heads, spun hanging bridges from one hedge to another, which looked like shining glass in the clear moonlight, as the fine dew fell upon them. This continued till the sun rose, when the little elves crept into the flower-buds, and the wind seizing their bridges and palaces swept them through the air.

John had now left the forest, when a man's voice called after him, "Hallo, comrade! where are you going to?"

"Out into the wide world," John answered. "I have neither father nor mother, and am a poor lad; but the Lord will help me."

"I am going into the wide world, too," the stranger said, "so let us go together."

"With all my heart," John said. So they went on in company, and soon grew friends, for they were both good fellows. John very soon found out that his companion was by far more clever than he, for he had travelled nearly all over the world, and knew something of everything.

The sun was already high up, when they seated themselves under a large tree to have their breakfast, and just then an old woman came by. Oh, she was so old that she walked quite double, supporting herself with a stick, and on her back she carried a bundle of wood, which she had gathered in the forest. Her apron was tucked up, and John saw that she had three large fern-leaves in it. When she had got close up to them her foot slipped, and she fell, uttering a loud cry, for she had broken her leg,—the poor old woman!

John proposed at once that they should carry her home; but the stranger opened his knapsack, and, taking out a small jar, said that he had a salve in it which would immediately set her leg, making it as strong as if it had never been broken, so that she could walk home alone. For this, however, he required that she should give him the three fern-leaves which she had in her apron.

"That will be paying somewhat dear," the old woman said, nodding her head in a peculiar manner, and she did not seem at all inclined to part with the leaves; but then it was not agreeable to lie there with a broken leg, so she gave them to him; and as soon as he had applied the salve to her leg she got up and walked better than she had done before. Such were the effects of the salve; but that was not to be bought at an apothecary's.

"What do you want with the fern-leaves?" John asked his travelling companion.

"They will make capital brooms," he answered, "which I am very fond of, for I am a queer fellow."

Then they went on a considerable distance further.

"How overcast the sky is becoming!" John said, pointing before him; "those are immensely heavy clouds."

"No," his companion said, "those are not clouds but mountains. Oh, the beautiful high mountains! at the top of those one is high above the clouds, in the purest air. That is delightful, and by tomorrow we shall be there."

They were not as near as appeared, and had a whole day to walk before they reached the mountains, which were partly overgrown with black forests, and there were rocks as large as a town.

It threatened to be hard work to get over these, and therefore John and his companion went into the inn to have a good rest and gather strength for the next day's walk.

Down below, in the public room of the inn, were a great many people assembled, for there was a man there who performed plays with dolls. He had just erected his little theatre, and the people sat all around to see the play, but right in front, in the very best place, was a big butcher with a large bulldog,—oh, what an ugly beast!—seated by his side, and staring before it just like all the others.

Now the play began, and a very pretty play it was, with a King and Queen sitting on a beautiful throne, with gold crowns on their heads and with long trains; for why should they not? The very prettiest wooden dolls with glass eyes and large mustachios stood at all the doors, opening and shutting them to let fresh air into the room. It was the prettiest possible play, and not at all doleful; but no sooner did the Queen rise and walk across the room, when no one knows what the great bulldog could have been thinking of, but as the butcher did not hold it, it made a spring right on to the stage and seized the Queen round her slender waist, so that it went "krick, krack!" How dreadful it was to hear!

The poor man who owned the dolls was quite frightened and sad, for the Queen was the very prettiest of all his dolls, and now the ugly bulldog had bitten off her head; but when all the people had gone the stranger who had come with John said he would put her to rights again. Hereupon he took out his jar and rubbed the Queen with the salve with which he had cured the old woman when she broke her leg. As soon as the doll was salved it was not only whole again, but it could move all its limbs of its own accord; there was no longer any necessity for pulling a string. Indeed the doll was a living human being in everything, excepting that it could not speak. The master of the dolls was delighted, for now he had not to touch this one at all, but she danced of her own accord, which none of the others could do.

Now, late at night, when all were in bed in the inn, there was some one sighing so dreadfully, and for so long a time, that all got up to see who it could be. The man who had performed the play went to his little theatre, for from there the sighing came, and he found all the dolls lying about, the King with all his vassals, and they were all sighing so piteously, and staring with their glass eyes, for they too wanted to be salved a little, the same as the Queen, so that they might move as she. The Queen kneeled down, and, holding up her beautiful crown, prayed, "Take this from me, but salve my husband and all my court." The poor man could not help crying, for he sincerely pitied them, and he promised the stranger all the receipts from the next performance if he would only salve four or five of the prettiest dolls; but the stranger would accept nothing but the large sword which the man wore at his side, and no sooner had he received this than he rubbed six of the dolls with his salve, and they immediately began to dance so prettily that all the girls,—the live girls,—danced with them. The coachman and the cook danced, the waiter and the housemaid, and all the strangers danced, as did likewise the fire-shovel and the tongs, but they fell over the very first step they took—that was a merry night.

The next morning, John and his companion went away from them all, up the high mountain and through the large pine-forests. They mounted so high that at last the church-roofs below looked like little red berries amongst all the green, and they could see so for many, many miles, where they had never been. So many beauties of nature John had never before beheld at once, and he heard amongst the mountains the huntsman's horn blown so delightfully, that tears of pleasure came into his eyes, and he exclaimed, "Oh God, how grateful we ought to be for all Thy goodness, and for all the beauties in this world!"

His companion stood there also, with folded hands, looking down upon the forest and the towns, and just then there was a delightfully sweet sound above their heads. They looked up and saw a large white swan floating in the air and singing so, as they had never heard a bird sing before; but the sounds became fainter and fainter, and the beautiful bird, drooping its head, sank slowly down at their feet, where it lay quite dead.

"Two such beautiful wings," the travelling companion said, "so large and so white, are worth any money, and I must take them with me. Now you see how useful the sword is"; and with one stroke he cut off the two wings of the dead bird, which he carried with them.

They travelled many, many miles further, over the mountains, till at last they saw a large city before them, with more than a hundred towers, which sparkled like silver in the bright sunshine; and in the middle of the city there stood a magnificent marble palace with a roof of pure gold, and there the King lived.

John and his companion would not enter the town at once, but remained in an inn outside, for they wished to smarten themselves up before appearing in the streets. The innkeeper told them that the King was a very good man, who would never hurt any one, but that his daughter was, oh, such a wicked Princess! Beauty she had enough, for there was no one to compare to her; but what use was that, for she was a wicked, cruel witch, and was the cause of so many excellent young Princes losing their lives. She gave permission to all to woo her, be it Prince or beggar, it was all the same to her, and he need only guess three thoughts of hers, at the time of her asking them. If he could do this she would marry him, and he should be King of the whole country after her father's death, but if he could not guess them, she then had him hanged or beheaded. All this made the old King, her father, very sad, but he could not interfere, for he had once said that he would have nothing to do with her lovers; that she might do as she liked. Now each time a Prince came and she asked him her thoughts, he could not guess them, so that he was hanged or beheaded, for he had been warned of the consequences and might have left the wooing alone. The King was in such deep sorrow on account of all this mourning and misery, that for one whole day in the year he lay on his knees, with all his soldiers, praying that the Princess might be less wicked, but she would not alter. The old women who drank brandy coloured it black before drinking it. That was their way of mourning, and what more could they possibly do?

"The hateful Princess!" John said, "she ought to be whipped, which would do her good. If I were but the old King she should smart!"

They then heard the people without shouting "Hurrah!" The Princess was passing, and she was so beautiful that all forgot how wicked she was, and therefore they shouted "Hurrah!" Twelve beautiful maidens, all dressed in white silk, holding a golden tulip in their hands, rode by her side, mounted on coal-black horses. The Princess herself rode a snow-white horse, decorated with diamonds and rubies, and her riding-dress was of pure gold, whilst the whip she had in her hand was like a ray of the sun. The golden crown on her head looked like stars from the heavens above, and her mantle was made of more than a thousand butter-flies' wings, but for all that she was much handsomer than all her clothes.

When John saw her he turned as red as a drop of blood, and he could scarcely utter a word. The Princess was exactly like the beautiful girl with the gold crown of whom he had dreamed the night of his father's death. She was so beautiful that he could not help loving her. "It cannot possibly be true," he said to himself, "that she is a wicked witch, who has the people hanged or be-headed if they cannot guess what she asks them. Every one is allowed to woo her, even the poorest beggar, and I will therefore go to the palace, for I cannot help it." Every one advised him not to do so, for he would be sure to share the fate of all the others. His travelling companion also tried to dissuade him, but John said all would be right, and having brushed his boots and coat, washed his face and hands, and combed his beautiful yellow hair, he went into the town, all alone, straight to the palace.

"Come in," the old King said, when John knocked at the door, and as he opened it came to meet him in his dressing-gown, and with worsted-work slippers on his feet. He had his gold crown on his head, his sceptre in one hand, and the imperial globe in the other. "Wait a minute," he said, and he put the globe under his arm, so that he might be able to give John his hand, but when he heard the object of his visit, he began to cry so that the sceptre and the globe fell on the floor, and he had to dry his eyes with the corner of his dressing-gown. The poor old King!

"Have nothing to do with her," he said; "you will come to grief, like all the others. But come and see." He then led John out into the Princess's pleasure-garden, and it was horrible what he saw there. Up aloft in each tree were hanging three or four sons of kings, who had wooed the Princess, but had not been able to guess her thoughts. At every breeze the skeletons rattled and frightened the little birds so that they never ventured into the garden again. The flowers were tied to human bones instead of sticks, and in the flower-pots were grinning skulls. That was certainly an extraordin-ary garden for a Princess.

"Here you see," the old King said, "and you will fare just the same as all the others whose bones you behold here. Do not persist, therefore. Indeed, you make me quite unhappy, for I take it so to heart."

John kissed the good King's hand and said it would all be right, for he was quite enchanted with the beautiful Princess.

She just then came riding into the court-yard with all her ladies, so they went out to meet her and wished her a good morning. She was so lovely, and when she shook hands with John, he loved her more than ever. It was quite impossible she should be the wicked witch all the people said she was. They then went up into the drawing-room, where little pages handed them preserves and gingerbread nuts, but the old King was so sad that he could not eat anything, and the gingerbread nuts were besides too hard for his old teeth.

It was settled that John should come to the palace again the following morning, when the judges and the whole council would be present to hear how he succeeded with his guessing. If he answered correctly he would have to come twice more, but no one yet had got over the first visit.

John felt in no way troubled about how he should succeed but was in high spirits, thinking only of the beautiful Princess. He firmly believed that he would be helped, but how he did not know and would rather not think at all about it.

He seemed never to grow tired of talking about the Princess, how kindly she had behaved to him, and how beautiful she was, and he longed for the following day, that he might see her again and try his fortune at the guessing.

But his travelling companion shook his head and was quite depressed. "I have grown so fond of you," he said, "and we might still have remained a long while together, but now I am to lose you. My poor, dear John, I could cry, but I will not trouble the last evening very likely that we are to spend together. Let us be merry, right merry, and to-morrow morning, when you are gone, I can cry quite undisturbed."

It was known all over the city that a new pretender to the Princess's hand had arrived, and sorrow reigned everywhere, for it was not likely John would succeed better than others had done. The theatre remained closed, the old cake-women tied crape round their gingerbread, and the King with all the priests remained on their knees in the churches all day long.

Towards evening the travelling companion prepared a large bowl of punch, saying, "Now we will be very merry and drink the

Princess's health!" but when John had drunk two glasses he became so sleepy that it was quite impossible to keep his eyes open, and he sank into a sound sleep. His companion then took him gently off his chair and put him to bed, and as soon as it had grown dark he took the two large wings which he had cut off the dead swan, and fastened them to his shoulders. He also took the largest of the fern-leaves he had received from the old woman who fell and broke her leg; he put it into his pocket and flew out of the window, over the city, straight to the palace where he seated himself in a corner above the window of the Princess's bedroom.

All was quiet in the city, and it had just struck a quarter to twelve when the window opened, and the Princess in a long white cloak and with black wings, flew away to a large mountain. The travelling companion made himself invisible and flew after her, whipping her with the fern-leaf till the blood came. Oh, that was a flight through the air! the wind seizing her cloak, which spread itself out, like a large sail, and the moon shining all the while.

"How it hails! Oh, how it does hail!" the Princess cried at every stroke from the fern-leaf, but she got to the mountain where she knocked. There was a rolling noise like thunder as the mountain opened, and the Princess went in, John's companion following her, for no one could see him, as he was invisible. They went along a wide passage, the sides of which glittered in a very peculiar manner, owing to thousands of spiders running up and down the walls, and they shone like fire. They now came to a large hall, built of silver and gold; and red and blue flowers, as large as sunflowers, grew out of the walls, but no one could pluck them, for the stalks were ugly, poisonous snakes, and the flowers were fire coming out of their throats. The whole ceiling was covered with glow-worms and sky-blue bats, constantly fluttering their wings, which had a very extraordinary effect. In the middle of the floor stood a throne supported by four skeletons of horses with harness made of the red fiery spiders. The throne itself was of milk-white glass, and the cushions were little black mice holding each other by the tail. Above the throne was a covering of rose-coloured cobweb, spotted with the prettiest little green flies which shone like jewels. On the throne sat an old magician with a crown on his ugly head, and a sceptre in his hand. He kissed the Princess on the forehead, made her sit by his side on the splendid throne, and then the music began. Large black grasshoppers played the Jew's harp, and the owl struck itself on the stomach, for it had no drum, so that it was a strange concert, during which little black goblins with will-o'-the-wisps in their caps danced about the hall. No one could see John's companion, who had taken his station immediately behind the throne, where he heard and saw everything.

The courtiers who now entered were very fine and grand, but whoever examined them closely could see at once that they were only broom-handles with cabbages for heads to which the Magician had given life and embroidered clothes. But that did not matter as they were only used for show.

After the dancing the Princess told the Magician that there was a new pretender to her hand, and consulted him about what she should think of, so that she might ask him when he came to the palace the following morning.

"Attend," the Magician said, "and I will tell you. You must choose something very easy, and then he is sure not to hit upon it. Think of one of your shoes, and that he will never guess. Then have his head cut off, and do not forget, when you come to-morrow night, to bring me his eyes, for those I will eat."

The Princess bowed low and said that she would not forget the eyes, whereupon the Magician opened the mountain, and she flew back home, her follower whipping her so hard all the time that she sighed heavily over the violent hail, and hastened as much as possible to get through the window into her bedroom. The travelling companion then flew back to the inn where John was still asleep, took off his wings and went to bed too, for he might well be tired.

It was quite early morning when John awoke, and his companion, who got up at the same time, told him that he had a most strange dream about the Princess and her shoe, wherefore he begged him to ask her whether it was not of her shoe she was thinking.

"I may as well ask that as anything else," John said. "It may be all right what you dreamed, for I put my trust in God, who will help me. I will, however, say good-bye to you, for if I guess wrong I shall never see you again."

They then embraced each other, and John went to the palace. The whole hall was full of people, the judges sitting in their arm-chairs with eiderdown pillows behind their heads, for they had so much to think of. The old King got up and dried his tears with a white pocket-handkerchief, and just then the Princess entered. She was more lovely than the day before, and saluted all so kindly, but to John she gave her hand wishing him a good morning.

The time had come for John to guess what she was thinking of, and oh, goodness! how lovingly she looked at him, but as soon as she heard him pronounce the one word "shoe," she turned as white as a sheet, and her whole frame trembled; but that was of no use, for he had guessed right.

Oh, how delighted the old King was; he capered about so, that it was a pleasure to see him, and all the people applauded both him and John, who had guessed right the first time.

His companion was pleased also when he heard how well all had gone off, but John folded his hands and thanked God, in whom he put his trust, to help him the other times as well. The next day he was to guess again.

That evening passed the same as the evening before, and when John was asleep, his travelling companion flew after the Princess to the mountain, whipping her harder than the first time, for he had now two of the leaves. No one saw him, and he heard everything. The Princess was to think of her glove, and that he told John, as if he had dreamed it, so that there was no difficulty in guessing right, and there was rejoicing all through the palace. The whole court turned head over heels, just as they had seen the King do it the day before; but the Princess lay on the sofa and would not utter a syllable. It was now the question whether John would guess correctly the third time. If he succeeded he was to have the beautiful Princess, and after the old King's death inherit the whole kingdom, but if he guessed wrong he was to lose his life, and the Magician would eat his beautiful blue eyes.

That night John went to bed betimes, said his prayers and slept soundly, whilst his companion fastened on the wings, hung the sword at his side, and taking the three fern-leaves flew off to the palace.

The night was as dark as pitch, and the wind blew so that the tiles from the roofs flew in all directions, and the trees in the garden where the skeletons hung were bent like reeds in a storm. It lightened every moment, and the thunder rolled as if it were one clap that lasted the whole night. The window was now thrown open and the Princess flew out. She was as pale as death, but she laughed at the bad weather, saying that it might as well blow a little harder. Her white cloak was whirled about in the air, whilst the travelling companion whipped her with the three leaves till the blood dripped down upon the earth and she could scarcely fly, but she reached the mountain at last.

"It hails and blows," she said. "I have never before been out in such weather."

"One may have too much, even of a good thing," the Magician said. She then told him that John had again guessed right, and that if he should do so for the third time on the morrow, he would then have won, and she could never again come to the mountain or practise magic as during the past, and that she was therefore quite sorrowful.

"But he shall not guess it," the Magician said. "I will set him something that he will never think of, or he must be a greater magician than I am. Now let us be merry"; and taking the Princess by both hands they danced about with all the little goblins, whilst the red spiders ran up and down the wall so quickly that it seemed to be on fire. The owl beat the drum, the crickets whistled, and the black grasshoppers played the Jew's harp. It was a merry ball!

When they had danced long enough the Princess had to go home, for fear she might be missed, and the Magician said he would accompany her, so that they might be as long together as possible. They flew off through the storm, and the travelling companion broke his three rods upon their backs; never had the Magician been out in such hail. When they reached the palace he said good-bye to the Princess, whispering to her, "Think of my head"; but the travelling companion heard it, and at the very moment that the Princess entered her bedroom window, and the Magician turned to go home, he caught him by his long black beard and with the sword cut his ugly head off his shoulders, without the Magician once seeing him. His body he threw into the sea to the fish, but the head he only dipped in the water, and tying it up in his silk pocket-handkerchief he carried it to the inn with him and went to bed.

The next morning he gave John the handkerchief, and told him that he must not undo it till the Princess should ask him what her thought was.

There were so many people in the great hall at the palace that they were packed as closely together as radishes tied up in a bundle. The judges sat in their arm-chairs with the soft pillows, and the old King had new clothes on, and his crown and sceptre had been polished up, so that he was quite smart, but the Princess was very pale and wore a black dress as if she were going to a funeral.

"What is my thought?" she asked John, who immediately untied the handkerchief, and was himself quite frightened when he saw the hateful head. All shuddered, for it was frightful to look at, but the Princess sat there exactly like a statue and could not speak a word. At length, however, she got up and gave John her hand, for he had guessed right. She looked neither to the right nor to the left, but sighed heavily and said, "You are now my master, and this evening our marriage shall take place."

"Well, that's right," the old King said, "and just as it should be." All the people shouted "Hurrah!" the royal guard played on their instruments, and the cake-women took the crape off their gingerbread, for joy now reigned. Three whole oxen, stuffed with chickens and ducks, were roasted in the market-place, and every one might cut himself a piece off; the fountains ran with wine; and whoever bought a penny loaf at the baker's received six buns as well, with plums in them, too.

At night the whole town was illuminated, and the soldiers fired off the cannon, whilst the boys did the same with crackers, and there was eating, drinking, and dancing everywhere.

But the Princess was still a witch and could not bear her husband John, which his travelling companion happening to think of, he gave him three feathers out of the swan's wings with a bottle containing three drops, and told him to have a large tub of water placed by the side of the Princess's bed, and that just as she was getting in he should give her a little push, so that she might fall into the water, in which he was previously to put the three feathers and the drops out of the bottle; he was then to dip her down three times, when she would lose her witchcraft and love him dearly.

John did everything just as his travelling companion advised him, and the Princess screamed when he dipped her under the water. As she struggled in his hands she appeared as a black swan with flaming eyes, but when she rose the second time above the water the swan was white, with only a black ring round its neck.

When the water for the third time covered the bird, it was changed into the most beautiful Princess. She was more lovely than before, and with tears in her delightful eyes thanked him for having disenchanted her.

The next morning the old King came with his whole court and the congratulations lasted till late in the day. John's travelling companion came also, with his stick in his hand and his knapsack on his back. John embraced him over and over again, and said that he must not go, but stay with him, for he was the cause of his good fortune. But his companion shook his head, saying in a mild and friendly voice, "No, now my time is up. I have only paid my debt. Do you remember the dead body which the wicked men were going to throw out of its coffin? You gave all you possessed that he might have rest in his grave. I am that dead man."

And at the same moment he disappeared.

The marriage festivities lasted a whole month, John and the Princess loving each other with all their hearts; and the old King lived to enjoy many a happy day, letting his grandchildren ride on his knees and play with his sceptre, but John ruled over the whole kingdom.

THE NIGHTINGALE

IN China, you know, the Emperor is a Chinese, and the people whom he has around him are all Chinese. It is many years ago since the events of my story took place, but on that very account they deserve the more to be listened to, before they are forgotten.

The Emperor's palace was, with good reason, considered the most magnificent in the whole world, for it was built entirely of the finest porcelain, so costly, but at the same time so fragile, and so dangerous to be touched, that one could not be sufficiently on one's guard with it.

In the garden there were the scarcest flowers, the most beautiful of which had silver bells hanging to them, and these rang melodiously, of their own accord, so that no one might pass them without duly admiring such wonders from the vegetable kingdom.

Everything was of the most extraordinary kind in the Emperor's garden, which was of such extent, that even the gardener did not know exactly where it ended. If, however, one walked straight on, one came at last to a beautiful forest, with high trees and deep lakes. This forest bordered immediately on the most picturesque shore of infinite extent, which the bottomless sea sprinkled with its snow-white foam. Large ships could sail in close under the branches of the trees, and here, amongst the shady foliage, lived a Nightingale, which sang so sweetly that even the poor fisherman, who must not neglect a single minute, if, in the Celestial Empire, he would, by the most untiring industry, gain the merest pittance on which to subsist, was accustomed to rest there for a moment to listen with delight as soon as the Nightingale sang, when he was out at night drawing in his nets. "Oh, how beautiful it is!" he often involuntarily exclaimed.

D

But more than one instant he must not indulge in such delights, for his hard work had to be done, and during the labours of the days he forgot the bird in the grove; but the next night, when the Nightingale sang, and the fisherman, as usual, came to that part, he again exclaimed, "Dear me how beautiful it is!"

From all countries travellers flocked to the Imperial city, and in amazement admired it, as well as the palace and the garden; but when they heard the Nightingale, they all with one voice exclaimed, "The Chinese magic bird is the most wonderful of all."

When the travellers returned to their countries, they narrated all they had seen, and the learned wrote many thick books describing the city, the palace, and the garden. Neither did they forget the Nightingale, which indeed was made most of; and those who could write poetry coupled the most ingenious verses together, in praise of the feathered wonder of the Chinese forest by the side of the deep sea.

By degrees these books and verses got spread over the world, and fate, which has a hand in everything, carried some of them even to the Emperor of China. The ruler of the "Celestial Empire" sat reading in his arm-chair of gold, and every two or three minutes nodded his head, for it gave him unbounded pleasure to read the pompous descriptions of his city, palace and garden, as he most condescendingly turned over the leaves. "But the Nightingale is best." This he found written in several places.

"What can that mean?" the Emperor said. "The Nightingale I do not know at all. Can it be possible that there is such a bird in my empire, and that, too, in my garden? The like is only learnt by reading."

He now ordered his cavalier, or gentleman-usher, before him, who was so high a personage that when any one who was beneath him in rank ventured to address him or ask him a question, he need give no other answer than "Ph!" and that means nothing at all.

"There is said to be here a most extraordinary bird called the Nightingale," the Emperor uttered, with much gravity. "It is said that this little creature is the most remarkable curiosity in the whole of my unbounded states. Why have I never been told anything whatever about it?"

"May your Majesty please to excuse me, but never before have I heard such a creature mentioned," the cavalier answered. "Such a person, at least, has never been presented at court," he added.

"It is my will that she appears to-night, and sings before me.

Here, all the world knows what I possess, and I myself know nothing of it."

"I have never, till now, heard the name," the cavalier humbly assured his Imperial Majesty. "But I will seek the person, and will find her."

But where was the wonderful songstress to be found? The cavalier ran up and down the stairs, rushed through halls and passages, but none of those whom he met had heard speak of the Nightingale. So the cavalier ran back to the Emperor, and said that it certainly must be one of the many fables that are frequently found in books.

"Your Majesty must not believe everything that is printed or written," he said, touching the earth with his forehead. "This is a mere invention, such as is called the black art."

"But the book in which I have read it," the Emperor said, "has been sent to me by the mighty Emperor of Japan, so there can be nothing that is untrue in it. In short, I am determined to hear the Nightingale. She must be here this evening, for it is my intention to show her my utmost favour. And if she does not appear at the proper time in my palace, then, at supper-time, the whole court shall receive a sound bastinadoing on their empty stomachs."

"Tsing-tza!" the cavalier groaned, as he again rushed up and down the stairs, through the halls and passages; and half the court ran with him, for the good people were most anxious to spare themselves the threatened bastinadoing on an empty stomach. There was a seeking and inquiring after the Nightingale, which all the world, excepting the people at the Imperial court, knew so well.

At last, in the kitchen, they fell upon a poor little girl, the daughter of one of the lowest of the cooks. She exclaimed, "Oh, dear me! yes, the Nightingale I know well. Oh, how she sings! Every evening I have permission to carry home a little of the remains from the table, to my sick mother, who lives down on the shore, and when returning tired, I rest in the forest, I hear the dear Nightingale sing. Tears then come into my eyes; yes, I feel just as if my good mother were kissing me."

"Little kitchen wench," the cavalier said, "I will obtain you a permanent appointment in the kitchen, besides the permission to see the Emperor sup, if you lead us to the Nightingale, for she is invited here this evening."

Then they all wandered together into the forest, where the Nightingale was in the habit of singing. Half the court, at the very least, were present, and when they had got about half-way, a cow began to low.

"Oh," said the chief page, "now we have her! It is certainly a remarkable power of voice for so small a creature. But it strikes me that I have heard this sound before, somewhere or another."

"No, those are the cows lowing," the little girl said. "We are still far from the place."

The frogs then croaked in the pond.

"Delightful! truly delightful!" the commander of the body-guard said: "now I hear her, the celebrated singer. It sounds like church bells, only subdued."

"No!" the little girl again said, "those are the frogs; but I think we shall now soon hear her."

Immediately after the Nightingale struck up with a long, long shake.

"This is she," the little girl whispered, pointing with her finger to a little ash-grey bird sitting high up amongst the branches. "Listen, listen! And there, you can see her!"

"Can it be possible?" the cavalier said. "I should never have imagined her like that. How plain she is! No doubt she has lost her colour, seeing so many noble persons before her."

"Little Nightingale," the girl cried out, quite loud, "our most gracious Emperor desires so much that you will sing before him."

"With the greatest pleasure," the Nightingale answered, and sang so sweetly, that it was real delight to listen to her.

"It is exactly as if a number of glass bells were ringing harmoniously together. Upon my honour, like harmoniously tuned glass bells," the cavalier asserted. "And how her little throat works. It is strange, indeed, that we never heard her before. For certain she will have great success at court."

"Shall I sing any more to the Emperor?" the Nightingale said, under the impression that the Emperor was present.

"My most esteemed little lady," the cavalier said, "I have the— to me so flattering—commission, to invite you this evening to a party at court, where you will delight our most gracious Emperor with your charming singing."

"It sounds better in the open air," the Nightingale said. She, however, went willingly with them, as she understood that the Emperor wished it.

The palace was set off to the greatest advantage; the walls and floors, which were both of more or less transparent porcelain, glittered with the reflection of many thousand golden lamps, like the sparkling stars of the milky way, the rarest flowers, which failed not to use their bells, stood in rows, ranged along the ante-room. There was much running backwards and forwards, and a strong draft; but the bells rang all the more melodiously, so that people could scarcely hear even themselves talk.

Across the middle of the great hall, where the Emperor sat, there might be seen a golden rod, which was to be the Nightin-gale's seat of honour. The whole court was present, even the little kitchen wench, who had received permission to stand behind the door, now that she held the appointment of a court cook. All were dressed out to the best, and every one looked with curiosity at the little unsightly grey bird, to which the Emperor nodded most graciously.

The Nightingale sang so sweetly and affectingly that large tears came into the Emperor's eyes. The tears rolled down his cheeks, and the Nightingale sang more and more enchantingly. Did it touch his heart, I wonder? Yes, the Emperor was so affected that he said the Nightingale should wear his golden slipper round its neck. But the Nightingale thanked him modestly, and declined the great honour, as she felt herself sufficiently rewarded by the Emperor's approbation.

"I have seen tears in the Emperor's eyes; those are the most valuable treasures. The tears of a monarch possess a wonderful virtue; heaven knows, I am rewarded enough." And now she sang again, with her sweet, enchanting voice.

"It is the most delightful accomplishment that I know of," each of the ladies said, as they sat around in a circle, and each took water in her mouth, that she might warble when spoken to, and then they thought that they were nightingales also. What will not female vanity do, particularly when supported by the imagina-tion! Even the footmen and maids expressed their satisfaction; which is a great thing, for to do anything to please them rightly is the most difficult of all tasks. The Nightingale had, indeed, won-derful success.

She was now to pass her life at court, was to have a cage of her own, with liberty to take an airing twice in the day, and once at night. Twelve servants, however, were to accompany her, each holding her by a silken string, fastened round her slender leg. These excursions afforded no particular pleasure, as they reminded her too much of the restricted walks of a state-prisoner.

The whole town, in the meantime, spoke with its many hundred thousand tongues of the hitherto unknown wonderful bird; and

when two people met in the street the one said, "Night," the other,
"In," when they understood each other without the "Gale." Even
eleven children of the highest families, boys and girls, were named
after the feathered songstress, but not one of them could ever
sing.

One day a large parcel with "The Nightingale" written on the
outside, was delivered to the Emperor.

"Here we have another book about our celebrated bird," the
Emperor said. It was, however, no book, but an automaton of
inexpressible value, a costly little plaything, which lay securely
packed, in a neat box. It was a Nightingale of most ingenious
mechanism, resembling the real bird, in every respect, excepting
that it was nearly weighed down by a covering of diamonds,
rubies, and sapphires. When this bird was wound up like a watch,
it sang one of the real Nightingale's songs, imitating the shakes
most accurately; and then its tail wagged up and down sparkling
with gold and silver. Round its neck was a scarlet ribbon with
these words embroidered, symbolic of the flowery manner of
speech of those countries,—"The Nightingale of the Emperor of
Japan is poor compared to that of the Emperor of China."

"That is splendid!" the ladies and gentlemen said, and the
bearer of the bird received his patent in a sealed letter, with the
title of "First Imperial Nightingale bearer."

"Now they must sing together. Oh, what a duet that will be!"

This was done, but they did not get on well together, for the
real Nightingale sang in its own peculiar manner, whereas the
other sang methodically, and the practised ear of a musician
might easily have detected a grating sound of the machinery. But
the reader must recollect that they were only Chinese.

The leader of the Imperial band assured them all, "The noble
lady in the box keeps perfect time, and is quite of my school."

The artificial bird was then made to sing alone, and had equal
success to the real one. With what splendour, too, it presented
itself, glittering like diadems, necklaces, and bracelets of precious
stones! Thirty-three times it sang off the same piece as accurately
as clockwork and yet it was not tired. The people would gladly
have heard it once more from the beginning, but the Emperor
thought that for a change the real Nightingale should be heard a
little. However, she was nowhere to be found. No one had noticed
how, taking advantage of being unobserved, she had flown out of
the open window, away into the green forest, where the sea-breeze
blew.

"What is the meaning of this?" the Emperor grumbled, offended at the unceremonious departure of the grey lady. All the courtiers scolded, and were of opinion that the Nightingale was a most ungrateful creature, utterly unworthy of having basked in the sunshine of the Imperial favour.

"However, the better bird remains with us," they said, and the artificial bird had to sing again. This was the thirty-fourth time that, as taken out of the box, the bird sang the same piece to them, but did not yet know the end of it, it was so difficult. The leader of the Imperial band bestowed unbounded praise upon the bird, and assured them, on his honour as a musician, that it was better than the little grey lady herself, not only with respect to outward appearance, on account of the many beautiful diamonds, but also as to its inner worth.

"For note, my lords and ladies, your Majesty in particular, that with the real Nightingale one can never calculate as to her song, neither how it will begin, continue, nor end; whereas, all in the artificial bird goes by rule: so it will be, and no otherwise. One can with certainty tell beforehand how every part will be; and indeed the mechanism will prove how one part must necessarily follow another, as clearly as a correctly worked arithmetical sum."

"That is exactly how I think," each said at the same time; and the leader of the band had permission to exhibit the bird to the public on the following Sunday, for the good Emperor said, "Why should I not give my poor subjects a treat, particularly as it will cost me nothing?" So all heard the glittering bird, and were as delighted as if they had intoxicated themselves with drinking tea, which is the custom in China, and all cried out, "Oh!" at the same time holding up one finger, nodding and wagging their heads from side to side. But the poor fisherman, who had heard the real Nightingale in the forest, shook his head and said to himself, "That sounds pretty enough, it is true, and is very like, but there is something wanting, I don't know rightly what."

The real Nightingale was for ever banished from the Imperial states, but she troubled herself little about that, keeping quietly in her shady grove.

The artificial bird had its place on a satin cushion by the side of the Emperor's bed; all the presents that were made it, ornaments and jewels, were spread around it: in title it had risen to "Imperial Nightingale Singer," and in rank to "Number One on the Left Side," for the Emperor considered the left side noblest, where the heart is, and an Emperor's heart is on the left side, the same as other people's. The worthy leader of the band wrote twenty-five volumes full, respecting the bird. They were so learned and far-fetched, and so lavishly interlarded with the most difficult Chinese words, that all at once said they had read, and understood them too, for if not they would be stupid, and the bastinado on a full stomach was the punishment for proved stupidity.

So matters went on for a whole year. His Majesty, the court, and all other Chinese knew every shake, however insignificant, in the song of the noble jewelled lady by heart, and just for that reason they liked the bird all the better, for they could now join in, which they did not fail to do. The boys in the streets sang "Pipipi, gluck—gluck—gluck!" and the Emperor sang the same, though, perhaps, in a different tone of voice. Now what could be more delightful?

One evening, however, when the bird had been singing its very best, and the Emperor lay in bed listening, it went "Kur-r-r" inside the bird. Something had snapped, the wheels whirled round, and there was an end to the music.

The Emperor jumped out of bed in an instant, and had the court surgeon called, but what good could he do in such a case? The court watchmaker was next called, who, after long considera-tion and examination, at last succeeded in putting it to rights, in a certain measure; but he said at the same time that the greatest possible care must be taken of it in future, for that, from constant use, many parts of the works were very much worn, and that these could not be put in new without destroying the harmony of the whole. This misfortune caused great sorrow, as may be imagined; and henceforth the now half-pensioned-off, after-dinner, imperial singer was allowed to sing only once a year, and then only with great risk and precautions; but the leader of the band then delivered a short and most incomprehensible address, proving that, with respect to the singer's celebrity, there could be no possible difference between past and present, and that the bird was therefore as good as ever.

Five years had now passed over, when the whole land was unexpectedly thrown into the deepest distress by the startling news that the old Emperor was so seriously ill that his death might momentarily be expected, for all were sincerely attached to their magnanimous monarch, by whose decease they would in fact gain nothing, but might be much worse off under his successors. A new Emperor was already chosen, and a countless mass of people thronged the streets of the capital, but more particularly the large court of the palace. From all corners the poor, fagged cavalier was overwhelmed with the thousand-times-repeated question, "How is our Emperor?"

"Ph!" he said, and shrugged his shoulders.

Cold and pale the Emperor lay in his large, magnificent bed; the whole court thought him dead, and all hastened to pay their humble respects to his successor. The footmen ran out to chat about it out-of-doors; and the maids had large tea-parties within. In all parts, in the passages and the halls, matting had been laid down, so that no footstep might be heard, and it was therefore doubly quiet. But the old Emperor had still a little life in him, though he certainly lay there, stiff and pale in his splendid bed, with the long satin curtains and the heavy gold tassels. There stood a window open, and the moon shone in, as if in pity, upon the sick Emperor and the artificial bird.

The poor Emperor could scarcely breathe, he felt as if some weight lay on his chest. With difficulty he opened his eyes, and saw with horror that Death had made his oppressed chest its throne. On its bare skull it had placed the golden crown, in one hand holding the Emperor's sword of state, and in the other his magnificent flag; and on all sides, out of the folds of the full satin bed-curtains, peeped the most extraordinary heads, some very ugly, but others, on the contrary, most lovely and mild. These were the bad and good actions of the Emperor which, now that Death had possession of him, were looking deep into his heart, like stern unbending judges.

"Do you remember?" sounded from one side. "Do you remember?" sounded from another, and drops of cold perspiration stood upon his forehead.

"That I never knew!" groaned the tortured Chinese Emperor. "Music, music, the large drum!" he cried in despair, "so that I may not hear all these dreadful sayings."

They, however, continued, and Death nodded each time that anything new was said, like a real Chinese.

"Music, music!" the Emperor cried; "sing, you delightful little jewelled bird! sing, sing! I have given you gold and precious stones, and I, myself, have hung my golden slipper round your neck, so sing, pray sing!"

But the bird stood immovable, for there was no one present to wind it up, and without that it could not sing, Death in the meantime staring at the Emperor with its hollow eye-sockets, and all was still—so fearfully still.

All of a sudden, close to the window, there sounded the most delightful song. It was the little live Nightingale, sitting on a branch without, for she had heard of her Emperor's distress, and had come to sing him hope and consolation; and as she sang the spectral visions became fainter and fainter, the stagnant blood began to flow again through the weak limbs of the gradually reviving body, and Death itself listened with astonishment, saying, "Go on, go on, little Nightingale, go on!"

"Yes, if you will give me the beautiful golden sword, if you will give me the rich flag and the Emperor's crown."

Death gave up each bauble for a song, and still the Nightingale went on. She sang louder and louder and more irresistibly; she sang of the quiet burial-ground, where the white roses grow, where sweet marjoram scents the air, and where the grass is bedewed with the tears of mourners. Death was seized with an irresistible longing for his garden, and, like a cold white mist, floated out at the window.

"Thanks, thanks," the Emperor sighed, breathing more freely. "I know you well, you heavenly bird. I, fool, banished you from my empire and yet you have drowned the frightful voices around my bed, and have driven death from my heart! How can I reward you?"

"I have received my reward, above my deserts, beforehand," the Nightingale answered, "for, the first time I sang I drew tears into my Emperor's eyes, which I shall never forget. These are the jewels a singer's heart delights in. Now go to sleep and awaken refreshed and well! In the meanwhile I will continue to sing to you."

The sun was shining through the stained window, when he awoke refreshed and strengthened. As yet none of the servants had returned, for they thought him dead, but the Nightingale was at her post singing.

"You must remain with me for ever," the Emperor said. "You shall sing only when you feel inclined, and the artificial jewelled bird I will break into a thousand pieces."

"No, do not do that," the Nightingale said, "for it has done as much as it could. Keep it the same as ever. Besides, I cannot live in the palace, but let me come when I am inclined, and then of an evening I will sit in the branches, there at the window, and sing my best, so that you shall be happy, and at the same time thoughtful. I shall sing of those that are happy, and of those that suffer but bear their troubles with patience; in fact, I shall sing of the good and the evil, which unfortunately is but too often un-

known to you. The little bird flies far around, to the poor fisherman, to the peasants' thatched huts, to all who are far away from
you and your court. I love your heart more than your crown,
although the crown has a certain almost sacred halo around it. I
will come, then, from time to time, and sing to you as much as
you wish, but one thing you must promise me."

"Everything!" the Emperor cried, and standing there in his
imperial splendour with which he had clad himself, unaided, he
held the point of his heavy gold sword to his heart, in confirma-
tion of his promise.

"One thing I beg of you. Tell no living soul that you have a
little bird that tells you everything, and all will go on well."

Therewith the Nightingale flew away.

THE YOUNG SWINEHERD

THERE was once a Prince who was poor, for his kingdom was very
small, but still it was large enough for him to think of getting
married, and think of it he did.

It was certainly rather bold of him to venture to say to the
Emperor's daughter, "Will you have me?" But he ventured, for all
that, for his name was celebrated far and near, and there were
hundreds of Princesses who would readily have said "Yes," but did
she say so?

We shall hear.

On the grave of the Prince's father there grew a rose-tree,—oh,
such a beautiful rose-tree!—for, though it blossomed only every
fifth year, and then bore but one rose, that was a rose, with such a
delicious scent, that whoever smelt it forgot all care and trouble.
He also had a nightingale, which sang as if all the most beautiful
melodies were congregated in its little throat. This rose and this
nightingale the Princess was to have, and they were therefore put
in silver boxes and sent to her.

The Emperor had them carried before him into the great hall,
where the Princess was playing at "Puss-in-the-corner" with her
ladies in waiting, and when she saw the large boxes with the
presents she clapped her hands with delight.

"I hope it's a little kitten," she said; but the rose tree with the
beautiful rose appeared.

"Oh, how prettily it is done!" all the ladies cried.

"It is more than pretty; it is beautiful," the Emperor said.

"Fie, papa!" the Princess cried, "it is not artificial, it is natural."

"Fie!" all the ladies cried, "it is natural."

"Let us first see what is in the other box before we grow angry," the Emperor said; and then the nightingale made its appearance, singing so beautifully that nothing could be said against it.

"*Superbe, charmant!*" all the ladies cried, for they all jabbered French, some worse than others.

"How the bird reminds me of the musical box of the late Empress," an old courtier said. "It is exactly the same tone, the same execution."

"Yes," the Emperor said, and he cried like a little child.

"I hope that at least is not natural," the Princess said.

"Yes, it is a natural bird," those who brought it answered.

"Then let the bird fly," the Princess resumed; and she would by no means listen to the Prince's coming.

But he came for all that. He painted his face with brown and black, pulled his cap down over his eyes, and knocked at the gate.

"Good day, Emperor," he said. "Can I not meet with some employment here in the palace?"

"Yes, certainly," the Emperor answered. "I want some one to look after the pigs, for we have a great many."

So the Prince was appointed imperial swineherd. He had a miserable little room down below, near the pigsty, and there had to live; but the whole day he sat working, and when night came he had made a pretty little iron pot, with bells all round, and as soon as the pot boiled they rang so prettily and played the old tune, "Home, sweet home." But the most curious part was, that by holding one's finger in the steam of the boiling pot, one could immediately smell what food was being prepared in every house in the town. Now, that was a very different thing from the rose.

The next time the Princess went out with her ladies she heard the beautiful melody, and was quite delighted, for she, too, could play "Home, sweet home,"—it was the only thing she could play, and that she played with one finger.

"That is the very same tune that I play," she said; "and he must be a very well-educated swineherd. Just go down, one of you, and ask him the price of the instrument."

So one of the ladies had to go down, but she put on wooden clogs.

"What do you want for the iron pot?" the lady asked.

"I must have ten kisses from the Princess," the swineherd answered.

"Good gracious!" the lady cried.

"I cannot take less," he replied.

"He is a rude fellow," the Princess said, and she went on, but had not gone many steps when the bells sounded so prettily, "Home, sweet home."

"Go again, and ask him whether ten kisses from my ladies will not do."

"I am very much obliged," he answered, "they must be ten kisses from the Princess herself, or I keep my instrument."

"What rubbish all this is!" the Princess said. "Now you must all stand round me, so that no one may see it."

Then the ladies stood round her, spreading out their dresses; and the swineherd got the ten kisses, and the Princess the iron pot.

Never did anything give so much pleasure. The whole evening, and the whole of the following day, the iron pot had to keep boiling, so that there was not a single hearth in the whole town that they did not know what had been cooked on it—at the Prime Minister's as well as at the shoemaker's. The ladies danced about, clapping their hands.

"We know who will have sweet soup and omelettes for dinner, and who will have broth and sausages. Oh, how interesting that is!"

"Yes; but you must not blab, for I am the Emperor's daughter."

"Oh, no!" they all cried.

The swineherd, that is, the Prince,—but no one knew he was anything more than a real swineherd—did not pass his time idly. He had now made a rattle, which, when swung round, played all the waltzes and quadrilles that had been heard from the beginning of the world.

"Oh, that is superb!" the Princess said as she passed. "I have never heard a more beautiful composition. Go and ask him how much the instrument costs; but I will not kiss again."

"He asks a hundred kisses from the Princess," the lady said who went in to ask.

"I believe he is mad," the Princess said, and she went on, but had not got many yards when she stopped. "The arts must be encouraged," she continued; "and am I not the Emperor's daughter? Go and tell him that he shall have ten kisses from me, the same as the last time, and the rest he can have from my ladies."

"Oh, but we are very unwilling!" the ladies cried.

"What rubbish that is!" the Princess said. "If I can kiss him I should think you can, too; remember that I feed you and pay you wages."

So what could they do but go again?

"A hundred kisses from the Princess," he said, "or let each keep his own."

"Stand there," she said. The ladies stood round her, and the kissing began.

"What is all that commotion at the pigsty?" the Emperor cried, as he stepped out on the balcony. He rubbed his eyes, and put on his spectacles. "Why, it is the court ladies, who are up to some of their tricks! I suppose I must go and look after them." So he pulled his slippers up at the heel, for they were shoes the heels of which he had trodden down.

What haste he did make, to be sure!

When he reached the yard he walked quite softly, and the ladies were so busily engaged counting the kisses, to make sure all was fair, that they did not notice him. He stood on tiptoe.

"What's this?" he cried, when he saw them kissing, and he hit them on the head with his slipper, just as the swineherd was receiving the eighty-sixth kiss.

"Get out with you!" he said, for he was very angry; and the Princess, as well as the swineherd, was banished the Empire.

There she now stood, crying; the swineherd grumbled, and the rain came pouring down.

"Oh, miserable wretch!" the Princess cried. "Had I but accepted the handsome Prince! Oh, dear, how unhappy I am!"

The swineherd now went behind a tree, washed the black and brown from his face, threw off the shabby clothes, and appeared in his Prince's costume so handsome that the Princess courtesied to him.

"I only despise you konw," he said. "You refused an honest Prince, and did not understand the value of the rose and the nightingale, but were ready enough to kiss the swineherd for a plaything. Now you see what you get for it all."

He then went into his kingdom, and shut the door in her face. So she was left outside to sing, "Home, sweet home."

THE LITTLE LOVERS

A WHIPPING-TOP and a Ball lay next to each other in a drawer, amongst a quantity of other playthings, and the Whipping-top said to the Ball, "Why should we not be lovers, since we are lying together in the same drawer?" But the Ball, which was made of satin, and thought as much of itself as any pretty girl, deigned no answer.

The following day, the little boy, to whom the playthings belonged, went to the drawer, and painted the Top red and yellow, quite smart, and drove a bright brass-headed nail through the middle of it. It looked quite magnificent as the Top turned round and round, with the velocity of a whirlwind.

"Look at me attentively, I pray," he said to the Ball, with a self-satisfied air. "Why should we not be engaged as well as others? We are admirably suited to each other, for you jump and I dance. We should be as happy as the day is long."

"What are you thinking of?" the fine little lady, the Ball, answered pertly. "Perhaps you do not know that my father and my mother were real satin slippers, and that I have a ball of Spanish cork in my body."

"Yes, but then I am of mahogany wood," the Top answered, "and the town-clerk himself turned me, for he has his own turning-lathe, and the work gave him the greatest possible pleasure."

"Well, but may I confidently trust to that?" the Ball said, incredulously.

"May I never be whipped again if I tell a falsehood," the Top said, impressively.

"There is no denying that you speak well," the Ball replied; "but still I cannot say yes, for, in fact, I am half engaged, and that to a most charming Swallow. Every time that I fly up in the air, he thrusts his head out of his nest, and whispers 'Will you?' And now I have fully made up my mind, which is nearly the same as an engagement. However, I promise that I will never forget you."

"That is a pretty consolation to me," the Top grumbled, and they spoke no more together.

Some days later the Ball was taken out of the drawer. The Top saw with astonishment how, like a lively bird, she flew high up in the air, until the eye could scarcely reach her, but soon returned from the upper regions, and when she touched the ground always gave a high jump. This was either from buoyancy of spirits, or because she had a cork in her body. But the ninth time the Ball did not return at all. The boy looked and looked, but it was gone.

"I know well where the charming creature is," the Top sighed. "She is in the Swallow's nest, and has married him."

The more the Top thought of it, the more strongly he felt himself attracted by the lost Ball. Just because he could not gain the object of his love, his consuming passion increased tenfold, and her marriage with another only added fuel to the fire, constantly increasing the flame.

As formerly, the Top danced round and round, but his thoughts were perpetually with the Ball, who, waking or dreaming, appeared to him constantly in a new light of increased perfection.

Thus many years passed over till by degrees it became an old love.

Neither was the Top young any longer, and therefore he was one day gilt all over, so that he had never before seen himself, nor had any one else seen him, in such splendour. He was now a golden Top, and sprang doubly high. It can be imagined that the dancing went well; but once he jumped too high, and was gone.

Where was he? Guess who can.

Quite unintentionally he had sprung into the dust-bin, where all manner of useless things had been thrown, and lay heaped together, forming a strange medley enough. There were old cabbage-stalks, potato-peelings, lettuce-leaves, bits of dirty rag and dust, together with sand, lime, and small stones which had fallen off the roof.

"Well, I have got into nice quarters," he moralised, pretty loud. "Here I shall soon lose my gilding. And what tag-rag I have fallen amongst!" he grumbled, as he looked with contempt upon a long cabbage-stalk with a vestige of leaf, which had not even the grace to be ashamed of its disgusting nakedness. His eyes then rested upon a most extraordinary round thing, which, from its appearance, looked like a half-rotten, shrivelled old apple. It was, however, not an apple, but an old, soaked through, torn ball which lay for several years in the roof-gutter, till at length it had been washed down by a heavy fall of rain.

"Thank goodness that a decent being has come, with whom one can have a little talk!" the Ball said, looking with admiration at the gilt Top. "The fact is, I am made of satin," the now no longer pretty little lady continued after a while; "I was sewn by delicate maiden hands, and have a ball of real Spanish cork in my body, though no one would guess it to look at me now. I was on the point of being married to a swallow, when I fell into the roof-gutter, where I lay, unfortunately, a whole eternity of five years without pleasure, indeed, without a covering, exposed to bad weather and dampness, whilst my best years were flying past. Believe me, such a hard fate was not promised me in my cradle."

But the Top made no answer. He thought of his old love, and the more he heard the more evident it became that this was she and no one else.

Then the cook came to empty something into the bin.

"Well, I never! if this is not Master Rudolph's gold Top," she cried.

And the Top appeared again in the drawing-room, where it was held in great honour and esteem; but of the Ball nothing more was heard, neither did the Top talk at all about his old love. What love, indeed, would bear an eternity of five years' lying in a wet, dirty gutter, exposed to all weathers and all sorts of mishaps? Why, no one would recognise the object of his deepest veneration if met with in a dust bin.

THE FLYING TRUNK

THERE lived once, in a certain town, which you would now look for in vain on a map, a merchant, who was so rich that he could have paved the whole street in which his house stood with silver money, and perhaps the little street that ran into it as well; but he did nothing of the sort, for he knew how to make better use of his money. If he parted with a shilling it came back to him a pound; that is the sort of merchant he was. But at last he died.

Now, his son inherited all this money, and he led a merry life, going every night to masquerades, and making kites with bank-notes, besides amusing himself with throwing ducks and drakes on the glassy surface of the lake, just below his window, with gold pieces instead of stones. By such means the money might well disappear; and so it did, till at last he possessed no more than four shillings, and had no other clothing but a pair of slippers and an old dressing-gown. His friends now naturally took no notice of him, since they could no longer walk in the streets together; but one of them, who was particularly good-natured, sent him an old trunk, with the well-meant advice, "To pack up as soon as possible." That was all very well; but the poor spendthrift had nothing to pack up, so he put himself in the trunk.

A most curious piece of furniture it was. When the lock was pressed the trunk could fly. So it happened, to the no slight astonishment of the young man, who now flew up the chimney, high above the clouds, as if in a balloon. Further and further he flew, the bottom of the box giving an occasional crack, as if it would break in pieces; and the venturesome traveller was dreadfully frightened, for in that case he would have a pretty fall. That, however, did not happen, and at length he reached the country of the Turks. The trunk he carefully hid in the forest, under some dry leaves, and went straightway to the city, near to the gates of which he had arrived in so extraordinary a manner. There was no impropriety whatever in this, for the Turks all go about in slippers and dressing-gowns, like himself. On his way he met a nurse with a little Turkish child in her arms.

"Listen to me, you Turkish woman," he said, "what castle is this, close to the city, with the high windows?"

"The king's daughter lives there," she answered. "It has been prophesied that a lover will cause her much heartache, and therefore no one is allowed to go near her, unless accompanied by the king and queen."

"Many thanks," said the merchant's son, and hastened back into the forest, seated himself in his trunk, and flew up on to the roof of the castle, whence he crept through a window into the room where the Princess was.

She was lying on a sofa asleep, and she was so wonderfully beautiful, that the young man could not resist kissing her on the instant. She awoke quite frightened, but he said he was a Turkish god, who had flown through the air down to her, to honour her with his company, and to this she had nothing to object.

So they sat side by side, in confidential conversation, and he told her stories of her eyes, how they were the most beautiful dark lakes, in which the thoughts swam about like alluring mermaids: he told her stories of her forehead, how it was a proud mountain of snow with magnificent chambers and paintings; and he told her of the storks, how they brought the pretty little children.

These were, indeed, delightful stories! and then, in well-chosen words, he besought the Princess to marry him, to which she immediately said yes.

"But you must come again next Saturday evening," she said. "Exactly at six o'clock the king and queen are here to tea, and they will certainly feel highly flattered to have a Turkish god for a son-in-law. But be prepared, my friend, to tell us a really pretty story, for my parents dote on such. For my mother, it must be moral and exalted, but to suit my father it must be merry—something very laughable."

"Well, I will bring a story, and that will be my only wedding present," he answered, embracing her. Herewith they parted, the Princess having buckled a magnificent sabre round his loins, the sheath of which was adorned with gold coins, and gold coins were particularly useful to him.

He now flew away, bought himself a new dressing-gown, and a few hours later was seated in the forest composing a story to be ready by Saturday, which was no such easy matter.

After much thought and consideration it seemed to be in a fair way, and was ready on Saturday exactly at six o'clock.

The king, the queen, and the whole court were waiting for their tea at the Princess's, and they received the strange suitor most civilly.

After tea the queen begged he would tell them a story. "I pray," she said, "let it be very profound and instructive."

"But let us have a good hearty laugh, too," the king put in.

"Most certainly," the stranger assured them, and he began after a-hemming only three times.

Now listen attentively.

"There was once a bundle of Matches, and they scarcely knew what to do with themselves for very pride, for they considered themselves of remarkably high descent. The head of the family, that is a mighty pine-tree, of which they were small splinters, had been formerly a large old tree in a northern forest. The Matches were now lying on a rather bare hearth in the kitchen, between a Tinder-box and an old Iron-pot, to whom they were telling the most remarkable events of their youth. 'You may believe us,' they said, 'whilst we were still a green branch—we were, in fact, a green branch—every morning and evening we had diamond tea,' that was the dew, 'and the whole day we had sunshine, when the sun shone, and all the little birds had to sing to us, or amuse us with interesting stories. We could plainly see that we were rich, for the other trees had decent clothing only during the summer, whereas our whole family wore, even during the hardest winter, a beautiful green dress, which neither wind nor frost could rob us of. At last, however, in the midst of this pleasant life, the wood cutters came—that was the dreadful revolution that cut up our family. The head of the family was appointed to the post of main-mast on a magnificent ship, which could sail round the world if it would. The branches were otherwise disposed of, and it is our tedious, though undoubtedly honourable, employment to give light to the lower orders, on which account we are banished here into the kitchen, away from the society of the great.'

" 'Well, it has been different with me,' said the Iron-pot, next to which the Matches lay. 'From the very beginning of my life I have been first put on the fire, and then scoured. The solids are my care, and I am, in fact, the first person in the house. My only pleasure is after dinner to stand neat and clean upon the shelf, and have some sensible conversation with my comrades. With the exception of the Pail, which sometimes gets out into the yard, we, however, lead a more secluded life here than in a convent. Our only news-purveyor is the Market-basket; but he talks too freely of the government and of the people. Why, it was only yesterday, I think, that an old jug fell off the shelf from sheer fright, and broke into pieces.'

" 'You chatter too much,' the Tinder-box interrupted her, and the flint and steel came in such violent contact that sparks followed. 'Let us now have a merry evening of it.'

" 'Let us discuss which of us is of the noblest birth,' the Matches said.

" 'No, I do not like talking about myself,' a Dish said. 'Let us rather have a general friendly conversation. I will make a begin-ning, and tell things such as every one has experienced, for then one can enter so thoroughly into the story, and it becomes really amusing. Well, on the coast of the German Ocean, under the shade of the Danish beech forests——'

" 'What a delightful beginning!' the Plates exclaimed with one voice. 'That will certainly be a story after our own hearts!'

" 'Well, there I spent my youth in a quiet family. Each piece of furniture was dazzlingly bright, that one might see oneself in it. Every morning the floor of hard, white wood, most tastefully laid down in a pattern, was scoured clean, and regularly every fort-night clean curtains were put up.'

" 'My gracious! how interestingly you do tell the story!' the Broom interrupted. 'One can see at once it is a lady who is talking, for there is something so neat and tidy in it all.'

" 'Yes, indeed, one feels that without a doubt,' the Pail asserted;

and it gave a little hop of delight, that it went splash on the floor.

"The Dish now went on with its story, and the end was in no way inferior to the so much promising beginning.

"All the Plates rattled with delight, whilst the Broom fetched some dry flowers out of the dust-hole and crowned the Dish with a wreath, for she knew it would vex the others; and she said to herself, 'If I crown her to-day she will crown me to-morrow.'

" 'Now I'll dance,' the Tongs said, and she did dance. Oh dear, how she lifted up one leg in the air, nearly as high and much more gracefully than Mademoiselle Elsler! The old chair-cover in the corner split with staring at her.

" 'Am I not to be crowned too?' the Tongs asked, and she was crowned.

" 'They are only low people,' the Matches thought.

"Now the Tea-urn was asked to sing, but she excused herself, saying she was cold, and could only sing when very hot, which, however, was her pride, for she would only sing when she was grand, standing on the drawing-room table.

"In the left hand corner of the window there lay an old Pen the cook was in the habit of writing with, and in which there was nothing particularly remarkable, excepting that it had gone down too deeply in the inkstand, but just this it was proud of. 'If the Tea-urn won't sing,' it said, 'she is quite welcome to leave it alone. Outside, in a cage, there is a Nightingale, who is a little musical too. It is true that she hasn't a note of school-learning, but this evening we will be particularly lenient.'

" 'Well, I think it highly improper that a stranger should be heard,' the Tea-kettle said, who was the kitchen-singer, and half-brother to the Urn. 'Is that patriotic? I appeal to the Market-basket, who is a man of experience; let him decide.' 'What a rage it puts me in to hear all this nonsense,' the grumbling old Market-basket said; 'would it not be more sensible to turn the house topsy-turvy, and then, perhaps, some of us would get into our proper places? That would be another sort of fun.'

" 'Yes, let us have a regular row,' all cried together; but at that very moment the door opened and the servant came in, when all were immediately as quiet as mice. Not a syllable was uttered, but there was not one of them, the smallest or the meanest, that did not feel what he or she could do. 'Yes, if I had wished,' they thought, 'it would certainly have been a merry night.'

"The servant lighted the Matches. Oh, how they fizzed, and with what a blue flame they burned!

"'Now,' they thought, 'every blockhead amongst them can see that we are the first. What splendour! what a light!' and then all was over, for they were burned out."

"That was a delightful story," the Queen said. "I felt exactly as if I were in the kitchen with the Matches. You shall certainly have my daughter."

"That, as a matter of course," the King said, nodding approval. "Monday next you shall have our daughter; so, now, my friend, you may consider yourself one of the family."

The wedding-day was fixed, and the night before the whole city was illuminated. Biscuits and cracknels were showered down upon the eager crowd, the boys climbed into the trees, shouting "Hurrah!" and whistling through their fingers, so that altogether it was a scene of splendour.

"Well, I must see whether I cannot do something to add to the general festivity," the merchant's son thought, so he bought some rockets, wheels, and serpents, not forgetting a good supply of squibs and crackers. In short, he provided all that belongs to the most splendid fireworks, and, having laid all in his trunk, he ascended into the air.

What a cracking and whizzing there was!

The Turks all sprang up in the air with excitement at the enchanting sight, till their slippers flew about their ears. Such an aerial spectacle they had never witnessed. There could not now be the shadow of a doubt that it was a Turkish god himself who was to have the Princess.

As soon as the merchant's son had got back into the forest with his trunk, he thought, "I must go into the city just to ascertain what effect it produced!" Was it not perfectly natural that he should have this fancy?

And what wonders he heard!

"I saw the Turk himself," one said, "and he had eyes like sparkling stars, and a beard like the foaming sea."

"He floated on a fiery mantle," another asserted, "and the heads of blessed cherubs peeped forth from the folds."

All these accounts he received from the enthusiastic people, and the next day his marriage was to take place.

He now hurried back into the forest, to seat himself in his trunk; but what had become of it? The trunk was burned. A spark from the fireworks had, through his carelessness, remained in it, so that the dry wood took fire, and the trunk lay there in ashes. The poor lover could no longer fly, and therefore could not get to his future bride.

She stood the whole day on the roof waiting for him. She is waiting still, whilst he wanders homeless about the world telling stories, which, however, are nothing like as good as the story of the Matches.

THE DAISY

Now listen.

In the country, close by the road-side, stands a beautiful villa, built in the pure Italian style. You have no doubt seen it yourself. In front of the house is a garden which, though not large, is exceedingly pretty with all sorts of flowers, enclosed by a neat freshly-painted railing. Close to it, at the edge of a ditch, in the midst of the most beautiful green grass, there grew a little Daisy, which the sun shone on as warmly and refreshingly as on all the luxuriant, splendid flowers in the garden, and in consequence it grew stronger from hour to hour. One morning it appeared quite in bloom, with its tender, dazzlingly white little leaves, like rays from the yellow sun which they surrounded. It did not think at all about it, that here, in the high grass, no one would notice it, nor that it was only a poor despised flower. It felt so thoroughly happy, for it might turn its pretty little face towards the glorious sun, looking up at it without any opposition, and could besides listen to the lark as, high up in the blue air, it sang its melodious songs, the harbingers of spring.

The poor little Daisy felt as happy as if it were a high festive day, though it was no more than a commonplace Monday.

The children were all being taught at school, and whilst they sat on their benches, deep in study, the little flower sat on its slender green stalk, learning also, for the dear sun and all around taught it how good God is, and it seemed as if the little lark sang plainly and prettily all its own sensations, though it could not express them. And the little Daisy looked up, with a sort of veneration, at the happy bird which could sing and fly, though not sad that it could not do so itself. "Can I not see and hear?" it thought. "The sun shines upon me, and the wind kisses me. Oh, how favoured I am!"

Within the railing there stood many stuck-up, grand flowers; the less scent they had, the more proudly they held themselves. The Peonies, puffed with pride, tried all they could to look larger than a rose, but what has the size, more or less, to do with it? The Tulips were of the most splendid colours, and they knew it well enough, for they held themselves stock upright that they might attract the eye.

And yet they did not pay the slightest attention to the modest little Daisy, but the Daisy looked at them with admiration and thought, "How rich and beautiful they are, and to visit them, no doubt, the charming bird will come down. How glad I am that I am so near, for I shall be able to see their happy meeting!" Just then there sounded from above "Quivit." The lark came down in its rash flight, but its visit was not to the Tulips and Peonies in the villa-garden, but to the poor little flower in the green grass, which was so frightened with sheer delight, that it did not know at all what to think.

The merry little bird danced round it and sang, "Oh, what beautiful soft grass, and what a sweet little flower with its golden heart and silver dress!" The yellow centre of the Daisy looked indeed like gold, and the surrounding leaves were of a silvery white.

The surprise and delight of the Daisy at this greeting can in no way be described, and the bird kissed it with its beak and sang to it in the most beautifully soft tones, when it again flew up into the blue spring air. It was, at the very least, a full quarter of an hour before the flower recovered itself. Half ashamed, yet inexpressibly delighted, she glanced across at her courtly sisters in the garden, who had been involuntary spectators of the honour that had been done her, and who would surely share her pleasure, but the Tulips looked more stiff than ever, and their faces were so sharp and so red, that it was evident they were in a rage. As for the thick-headed Peonies, they seemed ready to burst with rage, and looked only the more stupid.

It was fortunate that they could not speak, or they would have well exercised their poisonous tongues upon the timid little Daisy. The poor flower saw plainly that they were in a bad humour, and she was much grieved at it. At that very moment a girl came into the garden from the house; a large, sharp knife glittered in her hand, and hurrying straight to where the tulips stood, she cut one after the other. "Oh, dear!" the Daisy sighed, "how dreadful that was, and now it is all over with them." After this the cruel girl went away with the tulips. Now, had not the Daisy every reason to be grateful that it stood without, in the green grass, and that it was only a little unpretending field flower? It felt, too, a flow of the warmest gratitude, and when the sun went down it folded its leaves as if in prayer, slept softly, and dreamed the whole night through of the sun and of the charming bird.

The next morning, when the little flower stretched out its white leaves, like longing little arms, to the air and light, it heard the bird's voice, but what it sang sounded quite melancholy. The poor Lark had but too good a reason for losing its cheerfulness, for it had been caught, and was now in a cage hanging close by the open window. It sang how delightful it was to fly about freely and joyously through the wide expanse of smiling nature. It sang of the young, green corn in the fields, and of its past delightful flights. The so-much-to-be-pitied bird greatly missed the soft elasticity of the air, in which it had been accustomed to rock itself, as also its lost freedom—the choicest of treasures, to be able to resign itself patiently to its fate. Imprisoned it sat there, behind the brass bars, and bitterly bemoaned its misfortune.

The tender, good-natured Daisy wished so much to be of assistance; but how to set about it? That was a difficult problem. She forgot entirely how beautiful all around her the vast creation was; forgot how warm the sun was, and how white her own leaves were. Her thoughts were constantly with the imprisoned bird, whom, as much as she wished it, she could not help.

Just then two little boys came running out of the garden, one of whom held a knife, large and sharp, like that with which the girl had cut the flowers. They ran directly towards the spot where, sad and silent, the little Daisy, with drooping head, gave way to her thoughts, little dreaming what their intentions were.

"Here we can cut a beautiful piece of turf for our Lark," one of the boys said; and he began to cut a square, deeply into the earth around the Daisy, so that it stood pretty near in the middle of the piece of turf.

"Pluck that flower," the one boy said; and the Daisy trembled with fear, for to be plucked was to lose its life, and just now it particularly wished to live, for it was to go into the cage to the Lark.

"No, let it remain," the other said, "for it makes it look pretty." So it remained, and was put into the cage to the Lark.

Loudly the poor bird lamented its lost freedom, striking its prison bars with its wings, and the little Daisy could not speak.

Not a word could it utter, as much as it wished to console the poor prisoner. Thus passed the whole morning. "No water," the Lark complained. "They are all gone out, and have forgotten me. They have not given me a single drop to drink. My throat is parched and burning. It is as if I were all ice and fire; and the air is so oppressive. I shall die, and must part for ever from the warm sun, from the fresh green, and from all the beauties God has created." And in despair it bored its little beak deep into the cool turf. Its eyes then fell upon the Daisy, to which the bird nodded, and, kissing it, whispered, "You, too, must wither here, you poor, innocent flower! They have given you and the little clod of grass to me instead of the whole world, which I possessed. Each blade of grass shall be a green tree to me, and each of your white leaves a sweet-smelling flower. Oh, you only recall to me how much I have lost!"

"Oh, could I but console the charming singer!" the little Daisy thought. But it could not move a leaf. The scent, however, which the tender leaves exhaled was much stronger than is usual in this wild flower. The bird noticed this, too; for although it was dying of thirst, and in its sufferings bit off the blade of grass, it took care not to do the flower any injury.

It was evening, and still no one came to give the poor bird any water. It stretched out its beautiful wings, which shook convulsively. Its once joyous song was now only a melancholy "Pip-pip." Its head drooped down towards the flower, and the dear little bird's heart broke from longing and from want. The flower could not, as on the previous evening, fold its leaves and sleep quietly; no, it hung on a withered stalk, drooping to the earth.

The next morning only the boys appeared, and when they saw the bird lying dead in the cage they cried bitterly. They dug a grave under a rose-bush, and strewed it with the leaves of flowers, but the dead bird they put in a pink box, for it was to have a regal funeral. Whilst it was alive and sang they forgot it, and let it die shamefully of want in its close prison; but, now that it was dead, they thought to honour it with tears and pomp.

The clod of turf with the Daisy in it was thrown into the road in the dust, and no one thought of the modest, affectionate little flower, which, however, had felt most for the bird, and, not able to give consolation and relief, had died with it.

THE FIR TREE

ONCE upon a time there stood out in the forest such a pretty little fir-tree; it had a good place, for there was sun, plenty of air, and all around grew many larger comrades, spruce as well as larch, but the little tree thought of nothing but growing. It did not trouble itself about the sun or the fresh air, nor about the children who came into the forest to gather strawberries and raspberries. Often they seated themselves close to the little fir-tree; and then they would say, "How charmingly little that tree is!" which it did not at all like to hear.

The next year it was a long joint bigger, and the year following another; for with fir-trees one can always tell, by the number of joints, how many years they have been growing.

"Oh, were I but a large tree like the others!" the little thing said, plaintively, "for then I could stretch out my branches far around, and look out into the world. The birds would build nests in my branches, and when the wind blew I could nod as proudly as the others."

It took no pleasure in the sunshine, in the birds, and in the red clouds which sailed over it night and morning.

In winter, when the snow was lying all around so glitteringly white, a hare would frequently come running that way, and, without troubling itself to turn to the right or to the left, would jump over the little tree. Oh, how annoying that was! But two winters passed, and the third the tree was so tall that the hare had to run round it. Oh, to grow, to grow, to become big and old, was the only thing worth living for! the tree thought.

In autumn the woodcutters always came and cut down some of the largest trees. This happened every year, and the young Tree, which had considerably sprung up, shuddered at the sight, for the great magnificent trees fell with a crash to the ground, when their branches were cut off, and the trees looked so long and thin, that they could scarcely be recognised; but they were then laid upon carts, and horses dragged them away out of the forest.

Where were they going to? What awaited them?

In spring, when the Swallows and Storks came, the Tree asked them, "Do you not know where they are carried to? Have you not met them?"

The Swallows knew nothing, but the Stork looked thoughtful, nodded his head, and said, "Yes, I should think so; for we met many new ships when we left Egypt, and the ships had magnificent masts. We may suppose those were they, for they had a smell of turpentine, and they looked so fine, that I must congratulate you."

"Oh, were I but big enough to cross the sea too! But what is the sea really, and what does it look like?"

"That would take rather long to explain," the Stork said, and went its way.

"Rejoice in your youth!" the Sunbeams said; "rejoice in your power of growing, and in your young life."

And the Wind kissed the Tree, and the Dew shed tears over it, but the Fir-tree did not understand them.

Towards Christmas some quite young trees were cut down, many that were not even as big or old as this Fir-tree, that had neither peace nor rest, but was constantly longing to get away. These young trees—and they were just the most beautiful—always retained their branches, and thus put upon waggons, were drawn out of the forest.

"Where are they going to?" the Fir-tree asked. "They are no bigger than I; indeed, there was one considerably smaller; and why do they keep all their branches? Where can they be going to?"

"We know all about that," the Sparrows twittered. "Down there in the town we were looking through the windows of the houses, and we know where the young trees are carried to. Oh, the greatest splendour that can be imagined awaits them! When we looked through the windows we saw that they were stood up in the middle of the warm room, and adorned with the most beautiful things—gingerbread, gilt apples, playthings of all sorts, and hundreds of wax-tapers!"

"And then?" the Fir-tree asked, trembling all over; "and then? What happens then?"

"We did not see more, but that was incomparably beautiful."

"I wonder whether I am destined to enjoy all this splendour?" the Fir-tree thought. "That is better still than crossing the sea. Oh, I am consumed by an inward longing! Were it but Christmas-time! for I am now as tall and stretch out as far as those that were carried away last year. Oh, were I but on the waggon! were I but in the room with all the splendour! and then—yes, then something still better and more beautiful must come, or why should they adorn me so? Oh, yes, something by far better must follow. But what? Oh, how unsettled I feel! how I suffer! I do not know what is the matter with me!"

"Rejoice in us!" the Air and Light cried. "Rejoice in your youth, out in the open air!"

But it did not rejoice at all; it grew and grew; winter and summer it stood there equally green, and all who saw it said, "That is a beautiful tree!" When Christmas came, it was the very first to be cut down; and as the tree fell with a sigh, it felt a sharp pain—a feeling of faintness. It could not think of any happiness, for it was sad at having to leave the place of its birth, that it would never see its dear old comrades again, nor the little bushes nor the flowers that grew round about, nor perhaps even the birds. The start was anything but cheerful.

The Tree did not recover itself till it was being unpacked with others, and it heard a man say, "This is a magnificent one; we shall not want any other."

Two servants in grand livery then came out and carried the Fir-tree into a large and beautiful room. The walls all around were hung with pictures, and by the side of the stove stood two large Chinese vases, with lions on the lids. There were rocking-chairs, satin sofas, and large tables covered with picture-books, besides playthings, which cost large sums of money. The Fir-tree was put into a large tub filled with sand, but no one could see it was a tub, for it was covered with green cloth, and stood upon a gay carpet. Oh, how the Tree trembled! What was going to happen now? The servants, as well as the young ladies, helped to decorate it. They hung little baskets, cut out of coloured paper, upon the branches, and each basket was filled with sweets. Gilt apples and walnuts hung there, as if they had grown on the Tree; and more than a hundred little red, blue, and white tapers were fixed among the branches. Dolls, exactly like human beings, such as the Tree had never seen before, were swinging in the air, and at the very top of the Tree there was a star of gold tinsel. It was beautiful—truly beautiful!

"Won't it be bright to-night?" all said.

"Oh, were it but night," the Tree thought, "and the tapers lighted! And what will happen then, I wonder? Will the Trees come from the forest to see me, and the Sparrows fly against the panes of glass? I should like to know whether I shall grow here, and remain decorated like this summer and winter."

It thought and thought, till its back ached, and that is the same for a tree, and quite as bad as the headache with us.

The tapers were now lighted. What brilliancy and splendour! The branches of the Tree trembled, so that one of the lights set fire to the green leaves, and it burned up. "Good gracious!" the young ladies exclaimed, and hastily extinguished it.

After this the Tree suppressed its emotion, for it was so afraid of losing any of its splendour, but it felt quite giddy with all the glare. The folding doors were now thrown open, and a number of children rushed in, whilst the older people followed more steadily. For a moment the young ones stood still in admiration; but then their joy broke forth again, and they danced round the Tree.

"What are they doing, and what will happen now?" the Tree thought, as one present after the other was torn off. The tapers, too, began to burn down to the branches; and as they did so they were put out, when the children received permission to plunder the Tree. They fell upon it, so that all the branches cracked; and if the top with the gold star had not been fastened to the ceiling, the whole Tree would certainly have been thrown over.

The children danced about with their beautiful playthings, and no one looked at the Tree, excepting the nursery-maid, who only looked to see whether a fig or an apple had been forgotten.

"A story! a story!" the children cried, and they dragged a little fat man up to the Tree. He seated himself under it, "for now we are in the green," he said, "and what I tell you may be heard by the Tree. But I shall only tell you one story. Which will you have, the one about Ivede-Avede, or that about Humpty-Dumpty, who fell down the stairs, but was still exalted, and married the Princess?"

"Ivede-Avede!" some cried; "Humpty-Dumpty!" cried the others. Then there was a shouting and noise; only the Fir-tree was quiet, and thought, "Shall I not have anything more to do in the evening's amusement?"

The little man told the story of "Humpty-Dumpty, who fell down the stairs, but was still exalted, and married the Princess"; and the children clapped their hands, crying, "Go on! go on!" They wanted to have the story of Ivede-Avede as well, but got no more than Humpty-Dumpty. The Fir-tree stood perfectly quiet and thoughtful. The birds in the forest had never told such stories as that of how Humpty-Dumpty fell downstairs and yet married the Princess. "That is how things go on in the world," the Fir-tree thought, believing that the story was true, since so decent a man told it. "Who can tell? perhaps I may fall down-stairs and marry a Princess!" It rejoiced in the thought that the next night it would be adorned again with lights and playthings, fruits and gold.

"To-morrow I shall not tremble," it thought. "I will enjoy all my splendour thoroughly, and shall hear the story of Humpty-Dumpty again, and, perhaps, that of Ivede-Avede." The Tree stood in deep thought the whole night.

The next morning the servants came in.

"Now it's going to begin again," the Tree thought; but they carried it out of the room, upstairs to the loft, and there they put it in a dark corner, where the daylight never reached. "What can this mean?" the Tree thought. "What am I to do here, and what shall I hear, I wonder?" It leaned against the wall, and thought and thought, and for that it had plenty of time, for days and nights passed without any one coming up, and when at last some one did come, it was to bring up some large boxes to stand in the corner. The Tree was quite hidden, and it seemed as if it were forgotten as well.

"It is now winter!" the Tree thought. "The ground is hard and covered with snow, so that they cannot plant me; and therefore I am to be taken care of here till spring. How good and thoughtful men are! If it were but a little less dark and lonely here. Not even a hare. Oh, how beautiful it was out in the forest, when the snow lay on the ground, and the hare came running past, even when it jumped over me, though then I did not like it! It is dreadfully lonely up here!"

"Squeak! squeak!" a little Mouse said, cautiously coming forward. Then another came, and having sniffed at the tree, they crept between its branches.

"It is awfully cold here!" the little Mice said, "or else it would be well enough. Is it not true, you old Fir-tree?"

"I am by no means old!" the Fir-tree said. "There are many who are much older than I."

"Where do you come from?" the mice asked, "and what do you know?" They were so mighty inquisitive. "Tell us all about the most beautiful place in the world. Have you been there? Have you been in the store-room, where the cheeses lie on the shelf and the bacon hangs from the ceiling; where one runs about on candles, and into which one goes in thin and comes out fat?"

"I have not been there," the Tree answered; "but I know the forest, where the sun shines and the birds sing." And then it told them all about its youth; and the little mice, who had never heard anything of the sort before, listened with all their ears, and said, "What a deal you have seen! how happy you must have been!"

"Why happy?" the Fir-tree said, and thought over all it had been telling. "Yes, after all those were happy times"; but then it told them about Christmas-eve, when it was covered with cakes and tapers.

"Oh!" the little mice exclaimed. "How happy you have been, you old Fir-tree!"

"I am not at all old," the Tree answered. "It was only this winter I was brought from the forest, and I am just in the prime of life."

"How well you talk!" the little mice said; and the next night they came again with four others to listen to it; and the more it talked of the past, the more clearly it remembered all itself, and thought, "Yes, those were happy times, but they may come again —may come again! Humpty-Dumpty fell downstairs, and yet married the Princess, and so may I marry a Princess." The Tree then remembered a pretty little Birch-tree that grew in the forest, and that seemed a real Princess.

"Who is Humpty-Dumpty?" the little mice asked; and the Fir-tree told them the whole story, every word of which it remembered perfectly well; and the little mice were so delighted that they were ready to jump right into the top of the Tree. The following night still more mice came; and on Sunday even two rats, who did not think the story pretty, which vexed the little mice, and they now thought less of it themselves.

"Do you only know that one story?" the rats asked.

"Only that one," the Tree answered, "and that I heard the happiest night of my life; but then I did not properly feel how happy I was."

"It is a most miserable story," the rats said. "Do you not know any store-room story about bacon or tallow?"

"No," the Tree answered.

"We are very much obliged to you, then," they said, and went away.

After a time, the little mice did not come either, and the Tree sighed. "It was quite pretty as they sat round me and listened, and now that is over, too; but I will not forget to enjoy it thoroughly when I am again taken out from here."

But when was that to happen? Well, one morning people came and rummaged about in the loft. The boxes were taken away, and the Tree, too, was dragged out from the corner. It is true they threw it down rather roughly upon the floor; but one of them then dragged it to the stairs where it was light.

"Now life will begin again," the Tree thought. It felt the fresh air and the first rays of the sun, for it was now in the yard. There was so much to see all around, that the Tree quite forgot to look at itself. The yard adjoined a garden, where everything was beautiful and fresh. The roses smelt so delicious, and the lime-trees were in blossom, and the Swallows flew about, saying, "Quirre-virre-vit, my husband has come!" but it was not the Fir-tree they meant.

"Now I shall live!" the Tree cried, with delight, and it spread out its branches; but oh, dear! they were quite dry and yellow; and there it lay in the corner, amongst nettles and rubbish. The gold star was still fastened to the top of it, and glittered in the sun.

A couple of the merry children that had danced round the Fir-tree on Christmas-eve were playing in the yard, and one of them, seeing the star, ran and tore it off.

"Look here, what was left on the ugly old Fir-tree," he said, and trod upon the branches, so that they cracked under his boots.

The Tree looked on all the splendour of the flowers in the garden, and then, looking at itself, wished it were back again in its dark corner in the loft. It thought of its fresh youth in the forest, of the merry Christmas-eve, and of the little mice listening so attentively to the story of Humpty-Dumpty.

"All is over now!" the poor Tree said. "Oh, had I but enjoyed myself whilst I could. All is over!"

Then the servant came and chopped the Tree into pieces, which he laid in a heap. Brightly the fire was burning under the large kitchen kettle; and as one piece of wood after another was thrown in it sighed heavily, and each sigh was as the report of a small pistol. The children came running into the kitchen to listen, and, seating themselves before the fire, they cried, "Puff, puff!" but at each report, which was a sigh, the Wood thought of a bright summer's day in the forest, or of a winter's night, when the stars twinkled; it thought of the Christmas-eve and of Humpty-Dumpty, the only story it had ever heard or could tell—and then the Tree was consumed!

The children played in the garden again, and one of them had the gold star on his breast, which had been on the Tree the happiest night of its life. That was passed; with the Tree all was over too; and with the story it is over. So it must be with all stories.

E

THE BRAVE TIN-SOLDIER

THERE were once twenty-five Tin-soldiers, who were all brothers, for they were born of the same old tin-spoon. They looked straight before them, shouldering their muskets in military style, and their uniforms were blue and red, of the most splendid description. "Tin-soldiers" was the very first word they heard in this world, when the lid was taken off the box in which they lay. That was the exclamation of a little boy who had received them as a birthday present; he clapped his hands, and stood them up on the table. One soldier was the very image of the other, with the exception of one single one, who had only one leg, for he had been cast last, when there was not tin enough remaining; but he stood as firmly on his one leg as the others on their two; and it is just he whose adventures we have to relate.

On the table, on which they were placed, there were several other playthings; but that which attracted the eye the most was a pretty castle made of cardboard. One could see through the windows into the rooms, and in front there were several small trees, standing round a piece of looking-glass, which represented a lake, reflecting the wax swans that swam upon it. It was all pretty, but the prettiest of all was a little girl, who stood in the middle of the open door. She was also made of cardboard, but had a dress of the thinnest muslin, and a piece of blue ribbon across her shoulders for a scarf, fastened at the neck with a brooch quite as big as her whole face. The little girl held both her arms stretched out, for she was a dancer, and one leg was raised so high that the Tin-soldier could not discover it, so that he thought she, like himself, had only one leg.

"That would be just the wife for me," he thought; "but she is rather grand, living in a castle, whereas I have only a box, and that I have to share with twenty-four others. That is no place for her; but yet I must try to make acquaintance with her." So he laid himself down flat behind a snuff-box that was upon the table, from whence he could watch the pretty lady, who continued to stand on one leg without losing her balance.

At night all the other Tin-soldiers were put in their box, and the people of the house went to bed. Now the playthings began to play on their own account at all manner of games, and the Tin-soldiers made a commotion in their box, for they wanted to share the fun, but they could not raise the lid. The Nut-crackers turned somersaults, and the Pencil had fine sport on the slate, so that there was such a noise that the canary woke up, and began to join in. The only two that did not move from their places were the Tin-soldier and the little Dancer. She stood still on the tip of her toe, with her two arms stretched out, and he did not turn his eyes from her for one instant.

It now struck twelve, and all of a sudden the lid flew off the snuff-box, but it was not snuff that was in the box; no, it was a little black imp, such as children call a "Jack-in-the-box."

"Tin-soldier," the Imp said, "keep your eyes to yourself!"

But the Tin-soldier pretended not to hear him.

"Well, just wait till to-morrow," the Imp said.

The next morning, as soon as the children were up, the Tin-soldier was stood in the window, and it was either the black Imp's doing or the draught—anyhow, the window flew open, and the Soldier went over head and heels from the second storey down into the street. That was a dreadful fall, and he reached the ground head first, so that the bayonet stuck in the ground between two paving stones.

The servant and the little boy came running down immediately to look for it, but though they were near treading upon it, they could not find it. If the Soldier had cried out, "Here I am!" they would have found him, but he did not think it becoming to call out, as he was in uniform.

It now began to rain, and the drops fell faster and faster, till it came down in torrents.

When the rain was over, two boys came that way, and one of them exclaimed, "Look, here lies a Tin-soldier; he shall have a sail down the gutter."

So they made a boat of a piece of newspaper and put it, with the Soldier standing in the middle, into the water, which, after the heavy rain, rushed down the street. The paper-boat was tossed about, and occasionally whirled round and round, so that the Soldier quite shook, but yet he did not move a feature, looking straight before him and shouldering his musket, and the boys ran by the side clapping their hands.

All at once the gutter turned under the pavement, which thus formed a stone bridge, and here the Soldier was as utterly in darkness as if he were in his box.

"Where am I going to now?" he thought. "This is certainly

the black Imp's doing, but if only that dear little girl were
here in the boat with me, it might be twice as dark for aught I
care."

Now a large Water-rat suddenly appeared, for it lived under the
bridge.

"Have you a pass?" it cried. "Come, show your pass!"

But the Tin-soldier was silent, holding his gun still firmer.

The boat rushed on, and the Rat after it. Oh, how it showed its
teeth, and shouted to the wooden beams and to the pieces of
straw, "Stop him! stop him! for he has not paid toll; he has not
showed his pass."

The rushing of the water grew stronger and stronger, and
already the Soldier could see light at the further end, but at the
same time he heard a noise which might have frightened the
bravest man. Only imagine, where the bridge ended the gutter
emptied itself into a canal, a descent as dangerous to him as it
would be to us, were we carried down a high waterfall.

He was so near upon it that there was no help, and down the
boat rushed, the poor Soldier holding himself as steady as he
possibly could. No one should be able to say that he as much as
blinked his eyes! Four times the boat was whirled round and
round, and was filled with water nearly up to the top, so that it
was evident it must sink. The water already reached up to the
Soldier's shoulders, and momentarily the boat sank deeper and
deeper, and more and more the paper became unfastened. The
water was now over his head, and he thought of the pretty little
dancer, whom he should see no more. Then the paper tore, and he
fell through, but at the very moment he was swallowed by a large
fish.

Oh, how dark it was! worse than under the bridge, and there
was no room to move; but the Tin-soldier's courage did not
forsake him, and he lay there his full length with his musket in
his arm.

Soon after, the fish made the most frightful contortions and
struggling, and was then quite quiet. Suddenly light appeared, and
a voice exclaimed, "The Tin-soldier!" The fish had been caught,
and taken to the market, where it was bought and carried into the
kitchen, and the cook cut it open with a large knife. With two
fingers she laid hold of the Soldier round the body and carried
him into the room for all to see the extraordinary man who
had been swallowed by a fish, but the Soldier was not at all
proud. He was placed upon the table, and, wonder of wonders!

the Tin-soldier was in the same room he had been in before, where he saw the same children and the same playthings on the table. The beautiful castle was there, and the pretty little dancer!

Then one of the boys took the Soldier and threw him into the fire, without giving any reason for doing so, but no doubt the Jack-in-the-box had something to do with it.

The Tin-soldier stood there in the midst of flames, and the heat was something dreadful, but whether it was the heat of the fire or of his love he did not know. His colour had clean gone, but whether caused by his travels or by grief, no one could tell. He looked at the little girl, and she looked at him, when he felt that he was melting, but still he stood firmly with his musket at his shoulder. A door was then opened suddenly, and carried away by the draught, the little dancer flew like a sylph into the fire, to the Tin-soldier. She blazed up and was gone. The Soldier now melted down into a lump, and the next morning, when the servant cleared out the ashes, she found a tin heart. Of the little dancer nothing remained but the brooch, which was burnt quite black.

THE SNOW QUEEN

In Seven Stories

STORY THE FIRST

Which treats of a Looking-glass and the Broken Pieces

WELL, now we are going to begin, and when we have got to the end of the story we shall know more than we do now, for it is a wicked sorcerer, one of the very worst of sorcerers. One day he was in high glee, for he had made a looking-glass which possessed this peculiarity, that everything good or beautiful reflected in it dwindled down to almost nothing, but whatever was worthless and unsightly stood out boldly, and became still worse. The most beautiful landscapes, when seen in it, looked only like crooked spinach, and even handsome people became repulsive, or stood on their heads and looked ridiculous. The faces were so distorted that they could not be recognised, and if any one had a freckle, however small, it was sure to spread over nose and mouth. That was

highly amusing, the sorcerer said. When anything good or innocent entered a man's head, there was a grin on the face of the
looking-glass, and the sorcerer laughed heartily at his ingenious
invention. All who attended his school of magic related everywhere that a miracle had happened, and that now, for the first
time, one could see what man and the world really were. They ran
about everywhere with the looking glass, till at last there was no
man and no country that had not been distorted by it. Not satisfied
with this, they flew up towards heaven with it; but the looking-
glass shook so violently with its own grinning that it slipped out of
their hands; and having fallen down to the earth it broke into
hundreds of millions of billions of pieces, and still more, which
caused greater mischief than ever, for some of the pieces were no
larger than dust, and these flying about in the air, whoever got
them in his eyes saw the whole human race distorted, for each
particle, however small, retained the peculiarity of the whole
looking-glass. Some men even got a small piece of the glass in
their hearts, and that was dreadful, for the heart became like a
lump of ice. Some of the pieces were so large that they were used
for panes of window glass, but it would not do to look at one's
friends through them. Other pieces got made into spectacles, and
then indeed all went wrong, particularly when people put them on
in order to see right and to be just.

And some of the dust of the broken glass is still flying about in
the air, as is seen, unfortunately, every day.

STORY THE SECOND

A Little Boy and a Little Girl

IN a large city, where there were so many people and houses that
there was not room enough for all to have a little garden, and
where they were mostly, therefore, obliged to be satisfied with
flowers in flower-pots, there lived two poor children who had a
garden a little larger than a flower-pot. They were not brother and
sister, but were as fond of each other as if they had been so. Their
parents lived exactly opposite in two attics, for where the roof of
the one house would have joined the other, only that they were
separated by the gutter running between the two, there was in each
house a small window, and one had but to step across the gutter to
reach from the one to the other.

Outside each window was a large wooden box, in which grew some kitchen-herbs and a rose tree, flourishing equally well in the two. It occurred to the parents to place the boxes crossways over the gutter, so that they reached nearly from one window to the other, looking like two walls surmounted by the flowers. Peas hung down over the sides of the boxes, and the branches of the rose-trees bent forward towards each other, so that it looked almost like a triumphal arch of leaves and flowers. As the boxes were very high, and the children not allowed to climb upon them, they often received permission to get out of the windows, where, seated on their little stools under the rose-trees, they used to play together.

In winter there was an end to this amusement, for the windows were often frozen quite over, but then the children warmed half-pence on the stove, and laying the warm coin against the frozen glass made a beautiful peep-hole—so round; and behind each there shone a bright sparkling eye, that of the little girl and the little boy. His name was Kay, and hers Gerda. In summer, with one jump, they could be together, but in winter they had to run down the many stairs of the one house and up the others, whilst the snow was falling without.

"Those are the white bees swarming," the old grandmother said.

"Have they a queen too?" the little boy asked, for he knew there was such amongst the real bees.

"Yes, they have," the grandmother said. "She is flying there, where they are swarming the thickest; she is the largest of them all, and never rests quiet on the ground, but flies up again into the black cloud. Often during the winter nights she flies through the streets of the town and looks in through the windows, which are then covered with frost, in such strange forms as if they were so many flowers."

"Yes, I have seen that!" both children said, and they now knew that it was true.

"Can the Snow Queen come in here?" the little girl asked.

"Let her come," the boy said, "and I will put her on the stove, so that she will melt."

But the grandmother smoothed his hair and told them other stories.

That evening, when little Kay was at home and half undressed, he climbed into a chair by the side of the window and looked through the hole. Some flakes of snow were falling, and one amongst them, the very largest, remained lying on the rim of the

flower-box. It increased more and more, till at last it became
a woman, dressed in the finest white crape, as if formed by
millions of starlike flakes. She was so beautiful, but of ice—
dazzling, glistening ice; and yet she was alive. Her eyes sparkled
like two bright stars, but they were restless and unsteady. She
nodded toward the window and beckoned with her finger,
which frightened the little boy, so that he jumped down from
the chair; and just then it seemed as if a large bird flew past the
window.

The next day it was a clear frost. Then came spring; the sun
shone, the trees began to bud, the swallows built their nests, the
windows were opened, and the little children again sat in their
small garden, high up in the gutter of the roof.

The roses blossomed more beautifully than ever this summer,
and the little girl having learnt a hymn, in which there was
mention of roses, it reminded her of her own, and she sang the
hymn to the little boy, he joining in,—

> "The rose blooms but its glory past,
>   Christmas then approaches fast."

The little ones held each other by the hand, kissed the roses,
and stared up into the sky, into the clear sunshine.

What delightful summer-days those were! and how pleasant it
was to be out-of-doors near the fresh rose-trees, which seemed as if
they would never have done blossoming!

Kay and Gerda were seated, looking over a picture-book of
animals and birds, when, just as the church clock struck five, Kay
exclaimed, "Oh, something sharp has run into my heart! and now
something has flown into my eyes."

The little girl took him round the neck, and looked in his eyes,
but no, there was nothing to be seen.

"I think it has gone again," he said; but it was not gone. It was
just one of the pieces of the magic glass, which, we recollect, fell
and was broken—the hateful glass, that made everything great
and good reflected in it appear small and contemptible, but what
was bad and mean was made the most of, and the faults in
anything were very perceptible. Poor Kay had got one of those
pieces in his heart, and soon it will become a lump of ice. It no
longer hurt him, but it was there.

"Why are you crying?" he asked. "It makes you look so ugly,
and there is nothing whatever the matter with me." Then, all at

once, he exclaimed, "Look there, how nasty that rose is! it is all worm-eaten; and this one is quite out of shape. They are ugly flowers, like the box in which they grow," and he kicked the box, and tore off some of the roses.

"What are you about, Kay?" the little girl cried; and as he saw her fright he tore off another rose and clambered in through his window, running away from the dear little girl.

Now, when she came with the picture-book, he said it was only fit for babies; and when the old grandmother told stories, he would constantly interrupt her with a "but"; and when he could manage it, he got behind her, and putting a pair of spectacles on his nose, imitated her so exactly that all who saw him laughed. Soon he could mimic all the inhabitants of the whole street, taking off their peculiarities, and defects, so that people said, "That boy has a good head"; but it was only the glass that had got into his eyes, the glass that was in his heart, and that was the reason why he teased even little Gerda, who loved him with all her heart.

His play was now quite different from what it used to be, it was so sensible. One winter's day, when it was snowing, he came with a large magnifying glass, and holding out a corner of his blue coat let the snow-flakes fall upon it.

"Look through the glass, Gerda!" he said, and the snow-flakes appeared much larger, looking like beautiful flowers or ten-cornered stars; they were quite beautiful to look at. "Now, are not these more interesting than the real flowers?" Kay said. "See, there is not a single fault in them, they are all so accurate, if they could but remain without melting."

Soon after Kay appeared with large gloves on, carrying his sledge on his back, and he shouted in Gerda's ear, "I have got permission to go to the great square, where the other boys play!" and he was gone in an instant.

There, in the square, the boldest of the boys fastened their sledges behind the farmers' carts, and went a good way with them. All was life; and when they were at the height of their games there came a large sledge, painted all white, and in it sat a figure muffled up in shaggy white fur, with a white cap on. The sledge drove ten times round the square and Kay quickly fastened his little sledge to it. It drove faster and faster, and then turned into one of the streets that ran out of the square. The person driving turned round and nodded so friendly to Kay, just as if they knew each other; and each time he was on the point of unfastening his sledge the person nodded to him again, so that he remained as he was, and they drove out through the city gates. The snow began to fall so thick that the little boy could not see his hand before him, and then he undid the string with which he had fastened himself to the large sledge; but that was of no use, for his little sledge remained attached to the other, and on they flew as fast as the wind. He called out as loud as he could, but no one heard him, and the sledge seemed to drive over hedges and ditches. He now grew quite frightened, and tried to say his prayers, but could think of nothing but his multiplication-table.

The snow-flakes became larger and larger, till at last they appeared like white chickens, when of a sudden they turned on one side and the large sledge stopped. The person driving it stood up, and Kay now saw that it was a lady, tall and slim, and dazzlingly white. It was the Snow Queen.

"We have had a good drive," she said; "but how is it that you are cold? Come, creep under my bear's-skin"; and she seated him by her side in the sledge, covering him up with the skin, but it appeared to him as if he were sinking into a snowdrift.

"Are you still cold?" she asked, and kissed him on the forehead. Oh, that was colder than ice, and seemed to penetrate to his very heart, which was already half a lump of ice. He felt as if he were going to die, but only for a moment, after which he was particularly comfortable, and did not in the least feel the cold around him.

"My sledge! Do not forget my sledge!" Of that he thought first, and it was fastened to one of the white chickens, which now followed with the sledge on its back. The Snow Queen kissed Kay again, and he then forgot little Gerda, her grandmother, and all at home.

"You must now have no more kisses," she said, "or else I shall kiss you to death."

Kay looked at her, she was so beautiful, and a more intelligent, lovely face he could not imagine. She no longer appeared of ice like when she sat outside on the window-sill and beckoned to him. In his eyes she was perfection and he felt no fear; he told her that he could reckon in his head, and knew the number of square miles in the country as well as the number of its inhabitants, and she smiled at all he said. It then seemed to him as if he did not yet know enough, and he looked up into the vast expanse of air. She flew up with him, high, high, on to the black cloud; and the storm whistled and howled, as if it were singing old songs. They flew over forests and lakes, over seas and continents. Beneath them the cold wind whistled, the wolves howled, the snow sparkled; but high above them the moon shone brightly, and on this Kay's eyes were fixed the whole long winter night. During the day he slept at the feet of the Snow Queen.

STORY THE THIRD

The Flower Garden of the Enchantress

BUT how did little Gerda fare when Kay did not return? What could have become of him? No one knew, no one could give any information. The boys could only tell that they had seen him fasten his sledge to a magnificent large one, which had driven along the street and out of the city gates. No one could tell where he was; many tears were shed, and little Gerda cried more than all. It was then said he was dead, that he had fallen into the river which flowed past the town. Oh, what long, dreary winter days those were!

Now came spring and warmer sunshine.

"Kay is dead and gone!" little Gerda said.

"I do not think so," the Sunshine said in reply.

"Kay is dead and gone!" she said to the Swallows.

"We do not think so," these answered; and at last little Gerda did not think so either.

"I will put on my new red shoes," she said one morning, "those which Kay has never seen, and I will go down to the river and ask it about him."

It was still early. She kissed her old grandmother, who was not awake yet, and having put the red shoes on, she went all alone out at the city gates and down to the river.

"Is it true that you have taken my little playfellow? I will give you my red shoes if you restore him to me."

It seemed to her as if the waves nodded in a peculiar way, and she then took her red shoes, the things she liked best, and threw them both into the river; but they fell near the side, and were washed on land again. It was exactly as if the river would not take what was so dear to her, for it had not little Kay to give in return; but she thought she had not thrown the shoes out far enough, so she got into a boat, which was there amongst the rushes, and going to the farthest end of it she from there threw the shoes into the water again. Now the boat was not fastened, and the motion she caused in it drove it off from land. She noticed it and hastened to get back, but it was already more than a yard from land, and now drifted fast out into the river.

Then little Gerda was frightened and began to cry, but no one heard her excepting the Sparrows, and they could not carry her to land, but they flew along the banks singing, as if to console her, "Here we are! here we are!" The boat glided down the stream, and little Gerda sat there quite quiet, in her bare stockings, whilst her little red shoes floated after her, but they could not overtake the boat.

It was very pretty on both sides; there were beautiful flowers, old trees and meadows with sheep and cows, but not a human being was to be seen.

"Perhaps the river will carry me to little Kay," she thought; and then she grew more cheerful: she stood up, and for hours she admired the beautiful green banks. At length she came to a large orchard full of cherry-trees, in which there stood a little house with strange red and blue windows. It had a straw roof, and in front stood two wooden soldiers, which presented arms as Gerda passed.

She called to them, thinking they were alive; but they returned no answer, as was quite natural.

Gerda cried still louder, and then there came an old, a very old, woman out of the house, supporting herself on a hooked stick. She wore a large straw hat, painted all over with the most beautiful flowers.

"You poor little child!" the old woman said, "how did you get on to the rushing stream, thus carried out into the world!" and she walked right into the river, caught hold of the boat with the hook of her stick, and having drawn it to land, lifted little Gerda out.

Gerda was delighted to feel herself on dry land again, though a little bit frightened at the strange old woman.

"Come, and tell me who you are, and how you came here," she said.

And Gerda told her all. The old woman shook her head, mumbling "Hem! hem!" and when Gerda asked her whether she had seen little Kay, she said that he had not passed yet, but that he would be sure to come, and that therefore she must not be sad, but had better taste her cherries, and look at her flowers, which were more beautiful than any picture-book, and each could tell a story. She then took Gerda by the hand, and having led her into the house, locked the door.

The windows were up very high, and the panes of glass red, blue, and yellow, so that the light came in of various colours, which looked very strange. On the table were the most delicious cherries, of which Gerda ate as many as she felt inclined, for she had permission to do so. Whilst she was eating the old woman combed her hair with a golden comb, and the beautiful yellow hair shone so bright, and curled round her pretty, cheerful, little face, which was as round and blooming as a rose.

"I have always longed to have a dear little girl like you," the old woman said, "and you shall see how happily we get on together." As she combed Gerda's hair, the little girl more and more forgot her playfellow Kay, for the old woman practised magic, but she was not a wicked witch, and only conjured a little just for her own amusement, and she wished to keep Gerda with her. On this account she went into the garden, and touching all the rose-trees with her stick, they sank down into the black earth, so that there was no trace left of where they had stood. The old woman was afraid that when Gerda saw the rose-trees she might think of her own, and remembering little Kay, run away.

She then took Gerda into the flower-garden. Oh, what a perfume, and what splendour! There were all imaginable flowers of every season of the year, so that no picture-book could be more showy or prettier. Gerda jumped with delight and played till the sun went down behind the high cherry-trees, when she had a beautiful bed with red silk pillows, stuffed with violets, and she slept and dreamed as delightfully as any queen on her wedding day.

The next day she again played with the flowers in the warm sunshine, and thus many days passed by. Gerda knew every flower, but as many as there were, it seemed to her as if one were wanting, though she did not know which. Now, one day, she was sitting looking at the old woman's painted hat, and just the most beautiful of the flowers was a rose. The old woman had forgotten to blot that out when she banished the others into the earth, for so it is when one has not one's thoughts constantly about one.

"What!" Gerda cried; "are there no roses here?" She looked in all the beds, but none was to be found; and she then sat down and cried, when it so happened that her tears fell just on one of the spots where a rose-tree was buried, and as the warm tears watered the ground the tree sprang up in as full and beautiful blossom as it had ever been. Gerda threw her arms round it, kissed the roses, and thought of her own rose-tree at home, as well as of little Kay.

"Oh, how I have been delayed!" the little girl said. "I came to look for Kay. Do you know where he is?" she asked the flowers. "Do you think he is dead?"

"He is not dead," the Roses said; "for we have been in the earth, where all the dead are, but Kay was not there."

"Thank you," Gerda said, and she went to the other flowers, looked into their calyx and asked, "Can you not tell me where little Kay is?"

But each flower stood there in the sunshine, dreaming its own story, which Gerda had to listen to, but of Kay they knew nothing.

And what did the Tiger-lily say?

"Do you hear the drum?—drum! drum!—only two notes, always the same drum, drum! Listen to the funeral song of the women, to the call of the priests! The Hindoo-woman stands in her long red mantle on the funeral pile; the flames flicker around her and her dead husband; but the Hindoo-woman thinks of a living one there in the crowd, of him from whose eyes the fire burns hotter, and troubles her heart more than the flames which will soon burn her body to ashes. Will the flame of the heart be consumed in the flame of the funeral pile?"

"I do not understand a word of that," little Gerda said.

"That is my story," the Tiger-lily answered.

What says the Convolvulus?

"At the end of a footpath rises an old castle. The ivy climbs up the old red walls, thickly covering the terrace, and there stands a beautiful girl. She leans over the balustrade, looking eagerly down the path. No rose is fresher than she; no apple-blossom carried from the tree by the wind moves more gracefully. Now her magnificent satin dress rustles. Is he not coming yet?"

"Do you mean Kay?" little Gerda asked.

"I am speaking only of my story, my dream," the Convolvulus answered.

What says the Snow-drop?

"A board hangs on a rope fastened between two trees. That is a swing, and two pretty little girls, with dresses as white as snow, and long green ribbons fluttering from their hats, are seated on it swinging. Their brother, who is bigger than they, is standing in the swing, with one arm round the rope to keep himself up; for in one hand he holds a cup, and in the other a clay pipe: he is blowing soap-bladders. The swing is moving, and the bladders fly with beautiful constantly-changing colours; the last still hangs to the pipe, and is wavering in the wind. A little black dog is standing on its hind-legs, wanting to get into the swing too. The bladder flies, the dog falls and barks, for it is angry. The dog is teased, and the bladders burst. A swinging-board, and a bursting airy vision, are my song."

"I dare say your story is very pretty, but you tell it in such a melancholy voice and there is not a word of little Kay."

What do the Hyacinths say?

"There were three sisters, so lovely and fragile. The dress of the one was red, of the other blue, and of the third entirely white. Hand in hand they danced by the side of a lake in the bright moonshine. They were not fairies, but human beings. There was a sweet scent, and the girls disappeared in the forest. The scent became stronger, and three coffins, in which lay three beautiful girls, glided out of the forest, and floated across the lake, the glow-worms flying around them. Are the girls asleep, or are they dead? The scent from the flowers says they are dead, and the vesper-bell tolls for their funeral."

"You make me quite sad," Gerda said. "You have such a strong scent that I cannot help thinking of the dead girls. Can it be that Kay is really dead? The roses have been buried, and they say no."

"Ding, dong!" sounded the Hyacinth-bells. "We do not toll for little Kay—we do not know him; we only sing our song, the only one we know."

Gerda went to the Buttercup, which shone from amongst its glittering green leaves, and said, "You are a little clear sun. Tell me if you know whether I shall find my playfellow."

The Buttercup shone so beautifully, and looked at Gerda, but its song was not of Kay either.

"In a small yard the sun shone so warmly the first day of spring; the rays were reflected from the white wall of the house, and close by stood the first yellow flower, shining like gold in the sun. The old grandmother was sitting out-of-doors in her chair, and her grand-daughter, a poor, beautiful servant-girl, was parting from her, after a short visit. She kissed her grandmother. In that kiss there was a blessing. Well, that is my little story."

"My poor old grandmother!" Gerda sighed; "she is no doubt longing for me, and is sad about me, as she was about Kay. But I will soon be back home, and bring Kay with me. It is of no use my asking the flowers, for they only know their own song, and can give me no information." She then tucked up her dress, in order to be able to run faster; but, as she jumped over a white tulip, it struck her across the legs. So she stopped, looked at the long white flower, and said, "Perhaps you have something to tell me"; and she bent down her ear to the flower. Now what did the Tulip say?

"I see myself! I see myself! Oh, how beautiful I am! Up above, in a small attic, stands a little dancer, half dressed. She stands first on one leg, and then on two. She is nothing but a delusion. She is pouring water out of the tea-pot upon a piece of stuff, that is her bodice. Cleanliness is a good thing. And the white dress which hangs upon the nail has also been washed in the tea-pot and dried on the roof. She puts it on, and, tying a yellow handkerchief round her neck, makes the dress look whiter still. With one leg out, is she not standing on a stalk? I see myself! I see myself!"

"I care little about that," Gerda said. "You need not tell me that"; and she ran off to the end of the garden.

The door was locked; but she pressed heavily against the rusty hinges, and it sprang open, when out she ran in her bare feet, out into the wide world. She looked back three times, but there was no one following her. When she could run no longer she seated herself upon a large stone, and, looking round her, saw that the summer was gone; it was late in the autumn; but that could not be perceived in the beautiful garden, where the sun was always shining, and where there were flowers of all seasons.

"Oh, goodness, how long I have delayed!" little Gerda said. "Why, it has grown to autumn, and now there is no time to rest!" So she got up again to go on.

Oh, dear, how sore and tired her little feet were! and all around her it looked cold and comfortless. The long leaves of the willow were quite yellow, and the dew dripped from them. One leaf fell after the other, and only the sloe-tree bore fruit but that was so rough that it set the teeth on edge. How grey and depressing it was in the wide world!

STORY THE FOURTH

The Prince and the Princess

GERDA was obliged to rest again, where, just opposite the spot where she was sitting, a large Raven was hopping about on the snow. It had been watching her some time, shaking its head, and now it cried, "Caw! caw! how do? how do?" It could not express itself better, but meant kindly towards the little girl, and asked where she was going all alone into the wide world. Gerda felt how much there lay in that one word "alone," and then she told her whole story and fortunes, asking whether it had not seen Kay.

The Raven nodded quite knowingly, and said, "It may be, it may be!"

"What! you think you have seen him!" the little girl cried, and hugged the Raven so that she nearly squeezed it to death.

"Gently, gently!" the Raven said. "I think I know; I think it may have been little Kay; but, for certain, by now the Princess has driven you out of his thoughts."

"Does he live with a Princess?" Gerda asked.

"I understand what you say," the Raven replied, "but I find it difficult to express myself in your language. If you understand the Raven's language it will go better."

"No, I never learnt that," Gerda said; "but my grandmother knew it. Oh, had I but learnt it!"

"It does not matter," the Raven said, "I will tell the story as well as I can, though it will be badly done"; and then it related all it knew.

"In this kingdom in which we are now sitting, lives a Princess, who is so immoderately clever; but then she has read all the newspapers that are in the world, read and forgotten them again, so clever is she. Lately she was sitting on her throne, which is said not to be over-pleasant, when she began to sing, and the theme of her song was, 'Why should I not marry?' 'Well, there is something in that,' she said, and so she determined to get married; but she must have a husband who knew how to answer when spoken to, not one who could only stand there and look grand, for that is too stupid. She now had all her court ladies drummed together, and when they heard what her intention was they were much delighted. 'That would suit my fancy very well,' one said; and 'I have been thinking of that too,' said another. You may believe every word of what I tell you," the Raven said, "for I have a tame sweetheart who wanders at liberty all over the palace, and it is she has told me all."

The sweetheart was, as a matter of course, a raven too.

"The newspapers appeared with a border of hearts and the Princess's monogram. Therein might be read, that every good-looking young man was at liberty to go to the palace and converse with the Princess, and that she would marry him who spoke the best and who appeared to feel at home there. Yes, yes!" the Raven said, "you may believe what I say, for it is as true as that I sit here.

There was a fine stream of people, a crowding and pushing; but it did not succeed, either the first or second day. They could speak well enough out in the street, but when they got into the palace and saw the guards in silver, and the stairs lined with footmen in gold, and saw the splendid rooms, they were quite bewildered, so that when they stood before the throne on which the Princess sat, they could say nothing more than repeat the last word she had uttered, and that she did not particularly care about hearing again. It was exactly as if the good people had swallowed snuff and fallen asleep till they were in the street again, when they could talk fast enough. There was a string of people all the way from the city gates up to the palace, and I was there myself to see them," the Raven said. "They grew hungry as well as thirsty, but in the palace they did not get as much as a glass of water. Some, it is true, had prudently taken some bread and butter with them, but did not share it with their neighbour, for they thought, let him look hungry, and certainly the Princess will not have him."

"But Kay, little Kay!" Gerda asked, "When did he come? Was he amongst the crowd?"

"Patience, patience! for we are just coming to him. It was on the third day, there came a little person without horse or carriage, but walking merrily straight up to the palace. His eyes were bright like yours, and he had beautiful long hair, but he was poorly dressed."

"That was Kay!" Gerda shouted with delight. "At last I have found him!" and she clapped her little hands.

"He had a little knapsack on his back," the Raven continued.

"No, that must have been his sledge," Gerda said, "for he went away with his sledge on his back."

"That may be," the Raven replied, "for I did not pay particular attention to it; but this I know from my sweetheart, that, when he got inside the palace and saw the body-guard in silver, and the footman in gold on the stairs, he was not in the least abashed, but nodded and said to them, 'That must be tedious work to stand there on the stairs, so I will go in at once.' The rooms were splendidly lighted, and there were lords and excellencies walking about barefoot, whereas his boots creaked awfully, but he was not in the least concerned."

"That was certainly Kay," Gerda said, "for I know he had new boots on, and I heard them creak."

"Yes, creak they did," the Raven continued; "but merrily he walked straight up to the Princess, who was sitting on a pearl as large as a spinning wheel, and all the court ladies with their maids, and their maids' maids, and the courtiers with their servants and their servants' servants, who kept a boy in turn, were standing around, and the nearer they stood to the door the prouder they looked. The servant's servant's boy, who always wears slippers, stands so proudly in the door that one dare scarcely look at him."

"That must be horrible," little Gerda said; "but Kay has gained the Princess, for all that."

"If I had not been a raven I would have had her myself, for all I am engaged. My tame sweetheart says that he spoke as well as I speak, when I am talking the raven's language. He was gay and well-behaved, but had not come at all to pay court to the Princess, but only to hear how clever she was. He had every reason to be satisfied with her, and she no less so with him."

"Oh, for certain that was Kay," Gerda said, "for he was always so clever. Will you not introduce me into the palace?"

"Well, that is easily said," the Raven answered, "but how are we to manage it? I must talk it over with my tame sweetheart, and she will no doubt be able to advise us; for I must tell you, that a little girl like you will never obtain permission to enter in the ordinary way."

"Oh, yes, I shall," Gerda said, "for as soon as Kay hears that I am there, he will come out directly and fetch me."

"Wait for me there at the railing," the Raven said, wagging its head, and flew off.

The Raven did not return till late in the evening, when it said, "She sends you all sorts of kind messages, and here is a small loaf for you, which she took from the kitchen, where there is plenty of it, and no doubt you are hungry. It is impossible for you to be admitted into the palace, for you are barefooted. The guards in silver and the footmen in gold would never allow it; but do not cry, for get in you shall. My sweetheart knows a little back staircase, which leads up to the bedroom, and she knows where to find the key."

So they went into the garden, into the great avenue, where one leaf was falling off after the other; and when the lights in the palace were put out, one after the other, the Raven led Gerda to a back-door, which stood ajar.

Oh, how Gerda's heart beat with fear and anxiety! She felt exactly as if she were going to do something wrong, and yet she only wanted to know whether little Kay was there, and there he must be. So vividly she called to mind his clear eyes and long hair, and it seemed as if she saw him smiling, as he used to do when at home they sat together under the roses. He would surely be pleased to see her and to hear what a long way she had come for his sake, as also to know how they had all fretted at home at his not returning. Oh, what fear, and, at the same time, delight.

They were now on the stairs, where a small lamp was burning, and on the floor stood the tame Raven, turning her head first on one side and then on the other, looking at Gerda, who courtesied as her grandmother had taught her to do.

"My future husband has spoken to me so much in your praise, and your story, too, is very touching," the tame Raven said. "If you, my little lady, will please to take the lamp, I will lead the way. We are going the straight way, for there we shall not meet any one."

"It seems to me as if some one were coming just behind us," Gerda said, and then there was a rustling past them. It was like shadows on the wall, horses with flowing manes and thin legs, huntsmen, and ladies and gentlemen on horseback.

"Those are only dreams," the Raven said, "and come to carry the ladies' and gentlemen's thoughts off to the chase; which is well, for we can the better examine them in bed. But I hope that when you have risen to honour and dignity you will show a grateful heart."

"It is quite unnecessary to talk about that," the Raven from the forest said.

They now entered the first room, the walls of which were hung with rose-coloured silk and artificial flowers. Here the dreams rushed past them again, but went so fast that Gerda could not catch a sight of them. Each room was more splendid, as they passed from one to the other—almost enough to make one giddy; and now they reached the bedroom. That ceiling was like large palm-leaves made of the most beautiful glass, and from the centre were suspended by a golden branch, two beds in the form of lilies. The one was white, and in that lay the Princess; whilst the other was red, and in that Gerda was to look for little Kay. She bent one of the red leaves on one side and saw a brown neck. Oh, that was Kay! She called his name out loud holding the lamp towards him. The dreams rushed back out of the room; he awoke and turned his head round—it was not little Kay!

The Prince's neck only was like Kay's, but he was young and handsome. At the same time the Princess's face appeared from amongst the white lily leaves, and she asked what was the matter. Little Gerda then cried and told her whole story, and all that the Ravens had done for her.

"Poor child!" the Prince and Princess said, praising the Ravens for what they had done, and saying they were not at all angry, but that they must not repeat it. A reward was promised them.

"Will you go free?" the Princess asked, "or will you have a fixed appointment as court-ravens, with all the kitchen remains?"

The two Ravens made their bows and begged they might have a fixed appointment, for they thought of their old age, saying, "It is so nice to have something for the old age," as they called it.

The Prince then got out of his bed and let Gerda sleep in it; more he could not do. She folded her little hands and thought, "How good men and beasts are!" and then closing her eyes, she slept soundly. The dreams came flying back, and they looked like angels drawing a sledge, on which sat Kay and nodded. But the whole was only a dream, and was therefore all gone again as soon as she awoke.

The next day she was clothed from head to foot in silk and velvet, and she received the offer to remain at the palace and enjoy herself; but she only begged for a little carriage with a horse, and for a pair of boots, when she would go out again into the wide world and look for Kay.

And she not only got the boots but a muff; and when she wished to leave, a new coach of pure gold drew up at the door, with the Prince's and Princess's coat-of-arms upon it, like shining stars. The coachman, footmen, and outriders, for there were outriders too, wore golden crowns. The Prince and Princess themselves helped her into the carriage and wished her success. The Raven of the forest, who was now married, accompanied her the first ten miles, sitting by her side, for riding backwards disagreed with him, whilst the other Raven stood at the door flapping her wings. She could not go with them as she suffered from headache, since she had a fixed appointment at the palace and got too much to eat. The inside of the carriage was lined with cakes and sweets, and in the seat were fruits and gingerbread nuts.

"Farewell! farewell!" the Prince and Princess said, whilst little Gerda cried, and the Raven cried too. They went on for ten miles, and then the Raven had to say farewell, which was the saddest parting of all. He flew up into a tree and flapped his black wings as long as he could see the carriage, which shone like the sun.

Story the Fifth

The Little Robber-Girl

THEY drove through the dark forest, but the carriage gave light like a torch, which affected the robbers' eyes so that they could not bear it.

"That is gold! that is gold!" they cried, and rushing forward seized the horses, killed the little jockeys, coachman, and servants, and then dragged little Gerda out of the carriage.

"She is nice, she is fat, she has been fed upon nuts!" the old robber-woman said, who had a long bristly beard, and eyebrows which hung down over her eyes.

"Why, she is as good as a fat lamb! how nice she will taste!" and she then drew out her long knife, which shone so that it was horrible to look at.

"Oh!" the woman cried at the same time, for she was bitten in the ear by her own daughter, who was hanging at her back, and who was so wild and wicked that nothing could be done with her. "You hateful imp!" the mother cried, and now had not time to kill Gerda.

"She shall play with me," the little robber-girl said. "She shall give me her muff and her beautiful dress, and shall sleep with me in my bed"; and she then bit her mother again, so that the woman jumped and twisted herself about, and the robbers laughed, shouting, "See how she dances with her cub!"

"I will get into the carriage"; and she would have her own way, for she was so obstinate and spoiled, so she and Gerda sat in it, and were driven over stones and through holes deeper into the forest. The little robber-girl was as tall as Gerda, but stronger, with broader shoulders and a dark skin. Her eyes were black, and had rather a melancholy expression. She laid hold of Gerda round the waist and said, "They shall not kill you, as long as I am not angry with you! You are a Princess, I suppose?"

"No," Gerda said, and told her all she had undergone, and how much she loved little Kay.

The robber-girl looked at her quite seriously, nodded her head slightly, and said, "They shall not kill you, if even I am angry with you; but I'll do it myself then." She dried Gerda's eyes, and then put both her hands in the beautiful muff, which was so soft and warm.

The carriage now stopped, and they were in the yard of a robber's castle. It was all in ruins, and the ravens and crows flew out of the holes, and large bull-dogs, of which each looked as if it could devour a man, sprang towards them; but they did not bark, for that was forbidden.

In the large, old, smoke-coloured hall, in the middle of the stone floor, a huge fire was burning, and the smoke, rising to the roof, had to find itself an outlet. Soup was boiling in a caldron, and hares as well as rabbits were roasting on spits.

"To-night you shall sleep with me, with all my animals," the robber-girl said; and after they had had something to eat and drink they went into a corner, where there was straw and a piece of carpet. More than a hundred pigeons sat above upon laths and sticks, and they all seemed to be asleep, though they did turn round a little at the approach of the two little girls.

"They belong all to me," the robber-girl said; and catching hold of one of the nearest by the feet shook it till it flapped its wings. "Kiss her," she cried, and she struck Gerda in the face with it. "There, behind those bars, there are two that would fly away directly if they were not properly secured; and here stands my dear old Bae!" As she said this she pulled the horns of a reindeer, which was fastened by a bright copper ring it had round its neck. "We have to keep him a prisoner, too, or he would be off. Every evening I tickle his throat with my sharp knife, which frightens him dreadfully." The little girl drew a long knife out of a crack in the wall and let it glide across the reindeer's throat, which made the poor beast tremble and kick, and the little robber-girl, laughing, drew Gerda into the bed with her.

"Are you going to keep that knife in bed with you?" Gerda asked, and looked rather nervously at it.

"I always sleep with the knife," the robber-girl said; "one can never tell what may happen. But let me again hear what you said about little Kay, and why you came out into the wide world." And Gerda told all again from the beginning, and the wood-pigeons fluttered in their cage, but the others slept. The little robber-girl put one arm round Gerda's neck, holding the knife in the hand of the other, and soon fell asleep, but Gerda could not close her eyes; she did not know whether she was to live or whether death awaited her. The robbers sat round the fire, drinking and singing, whilst the robber-women turned somersets. It was quite horrible for the little girl to watch them.

The wood-pigeons said, "Coo! Coo! we have seen little Kay. A white chicken carried his sledge, and he sat in the Snow Queen's carriage, which drove close over the forest as we lay in our nest. She blew upon us young ones, and all excepting us two died. Coo! Coo!"

"What are you saying, up there?" Gerda asked. "Where was the Snow Queen going to? Do you know anything about it?"

"She was most likely going to Lapland, for there is always snow and ice there. Ask the Reindeer that is tied up there."

"There is ice and snow, and there it is delightful and healthy," the Reindeer said. "There one can jump and run about. There the Snow Queen has her summer tent, but her palace is up towards the North Pole, on the island which is called Spitzbergen."

"Oh, Kay! dear little Kay!" Gerda sighed.

"You must now lie quiet," the robber-girl said, "or I will run the knife into you."

The next morning Gerda told her all that the Wood-pigeons had said, and the little robber-girl looked quite serious, but nodding her head said, "It doesn't matter! it doesn't matter! Do you know where Lapland is?" she asked the Reindeer.

"Who should know better than I?" the animal answered, its eyes sparkling. "I was born and bred there, and there I have run about in the snow-field."

"Listen!" the robber-girl said to Gerda. "You see that all the men are gone; my mother, however, is still here, and she will remain; but about midday she drinks out of the great flask, and then sleeps a little. I will then do something for you." She now jumped out of bed, rushed to her mother, and pulling her beard, said, "My own beloved goat, good morning!" Her mother in return flipped her on the nose, so that it was red and blue; but that was from sheer love.

As soon as her mother was asleep, after having drunk out of the flask, the robber-girl went to the Reindeer, and said, "I might still have a good deal of fun, tickling you with the sharp knife, for then you are very old; but that doesn't matter. I will unfasten you, and let you out, so that you may run back to Lapland; but you must make good use of your legs, and carry this little girl to the Snow Queen's palace, where her playfellow is. You heard what she said, for she spoke loud enough, and you were listening."

The Reindeer jumped high up in the air with delight. The robber-girl lifted little Gerda on to its back, having taken the precaution to tie her fast, and even to give her a little cushion to sit upon. "It doesn't matter," she said. "There are your fur boots, for it will be cold; but the muff I shall keep, for it is too pretty. You shall not freeze, however, for you shall have my mother's large warm gloves, which will reach up to your elbow. There, put them on. Now, as to your hands, you look exactly like my ugly mother."

Gerda cried with joy.

"I won't have you blubbering," the little robber-girl said; "you ought now to look particularly happy. Here are two loaves and a ham, so you will not die of hunger." Both were fastened behind her; and the little robber-girl opened the door, having chained up all the big dogs, cut the rope with her sharp knife, and said to the Reindeer, "Now run; but take great care of the little girl."

Gerda stretched out her hands, with the large gloves on, towards the robber-girl, and cried, "Farewell!" And the Reindeer flew as fast as possible through the great forest, and over heaths and marshes. The wolves howled, and the birds of prey screamed "Atchue! atchue!" It sounded from the sky exactly like sneezing.

"There are my old friends the northern lights," the Reindeer said; "see how they shine!" and then it ran even faster than before. It ran day and night. The loaves were demolished, and the ham also, and then they were in Lapland.

Story the Sixth

The Lapland Woman and the Finland Woman

They stopped at a small house, and a miserable place it was. The roof reached to the ground, and the door was so low that the inmates had to crawl on their stomachs when they wanted to go in or out. There was no one at home, excepting an old woman, who was cooking fish by the light of a train-oil lamp; and to her the Reindeer told Gerda's whole story, but his own first, for this appeared to him by far the most important, and the cold had nipped Gerda, so that she could not speak.

"Oh, you poor creatures!" the old woman said, "you have far to run still. You must go more than a hundred miles into Finland, for there the Snow Queen lives. I will write a few words on a dried haberdine, for I have no paper, and that I will give you for the Finn up there, for she can give you more accurate information than I."

Now, as soon as Gerda was warm, and had got something to eat and drink, the old woman wrote a few words on a dried haberdine, begged Gerda to take great care of it, and, having tied her on the Reindeer again, off it started. "Atchue! atchue!" it sounded from above, in the air, and the whole night long the northern lights shone the most beautiful blue. They arrived in Finland, and knocked at the Finn's chimney, for she had no door at all.

There was such a heat within, that the woman had few garments on. She was little, and very dirty. She immediately undid Gerda's things, taking off her gloves and boots, for it would otherwise have been too hot for her; laid a lump of ice on the Reindeer's head; and then read what was written on the haberdine. She read it three times, when she knew it by heart, so put the fish in the soup-pot, for it was good to eat, and she never wasted anything.

The Reindeer then told, first its own story, and then Gerda's; and the little woman blinked with her clever eyes, but said nothing.

"You are so clever," the Reindeer said; "I know that you can bind all the winds of the world together with one piece of string, so that when the sailor unfastens the one knot, he has a fair wind; if he unties the other it blows freshly; but if the third or fourth, the wind rages so that it overthrows the trees of the forest. Won't you prepare the little girl a drink to give her the strength of twelve men, so that she may vanquish the Snow Queen?"

"The strength of twelve men!" the little woman said. "That would help her a great deal." And then she went to a cupboard, from which she took a large rolled-up skin. As she unrolled it there appeared strange letters written, and she read till the water dripped down from her forehead.

But the Reindeer begged again so hard for Gerda, and she looked at the little woman with such beseeching eyes full of tears, that she again began to blink her eyes, and, drawing the Reindeer into a corner, whispered to him, whilst she put fresh ice upon his head.

"Little Kay is still with the Snow Queen, and finds everything there to his taste, so that he thinks it is the best place in the world; but this is caused by his having a piece of broken glass in his heart, and another piece in his eyes. These must come out, or he will never be a man, and the Snow Queen will retain full power over him."

"But can you not give little Gerda something, so that she may obtain power over all?"

"I cannot give her greater power than she already possesses, and do you not see how great that is? Do you not see that men and beasts must serve her, and how, barefooted as she is, she has got on so well in the world? She cannot receive her power from us, that is in her own heart, and consists in her being a good, innocent child. If she cannot herself get into the Snow Queen's palace and free little Kay from the glass, we cannot help her. Ten miles from here the Snow Queen's garden begins, and there you must carry the little girl. Set her down at the large bush, which stands there in the snow, covered with red berries; and do not waste many words, but make haste back here." The little woman then placed Gerda upon the Reindeer, which ran off as fast as it could.

"Oh, I have not got my boots! I have not got my gloves!" little Gerda cried out, for this she noticed in the piercing cold; but the Reindeer could not venture to stop, and it ran on till it came to the bush with the red berries. It there put her down, kissed her on the mouth, and large clear tears ran down the animal's cheeks when it started off back again. There stood poor Gerda, without boots and without gloves, in the middle of that fearfully cold Finland.

She ran forward as fast as possible, and was soon met by a whole regiment of snow-flakes, which did not fall from heaven, for that was quite clear, but they ran straight along the ground, and the nearer they came the larger they grew. Gerda remembered how large and beautiful those looked which she saw through the magnifying glass; but these were much larger, and far different; they were living, and dreadful to look at—they were the Snow Queen's guards. They had the strangest shapes, some looking like frightful porcupines, others like knots of living snakes stretching out their heads, and others like fat little bears with bristly hair, but all were a glittering white—they were all living snow-flakes.

Little Gerda then prayed, and the cold was so great that she could see her own breath coming like smoke out of her mouth. The breath became denser and denser, at length assuming the forms of little angels, which grew larger and larger as they touched the ground. They all wore helmets on their heads, and held spears and shields in their hands, and their number was constantly increasing, so that, by the time Gerda had finished her prayer, she was surrounded by a whole legion. They thrust their spears into the frightful snow-flakes, breaking them into hundreds of pieces, and Gerda went on joyously and in safety. The angels kissed her hands and feet, so that she felt less how extremely cold it was; and quickly she hastened on to the Snow Queen's palace.

But now let us first see what Kay was doing. He was certainly not thinking of little Gerda, and, least of all, that she was then standing outside the palace.

STORY THE SEVENTH

Of the Snow Queen's Palace, and what happened in it

THE palace walls were of driven snow, and the doors and windows of the cutting winds. There were more than a hundred rooms, as the snow had formed them, the largest extending several miles, and all were lighted by the bright northern light. They were all so large, so empty, and so icy-cold and shining. There was never any amusement here, not even a bears' ball; for which the storm could have provided music, and the polar bears could have shown off their antics, walking on their hind feet. Never any card-parties, with tea and scandal, but empty, vast, and cold, were the rooms in the Snow Queen's palace. In the middle of the empty, immense snow-room there was a frozen lake, cracked into a thousand pieces, but each piece was so like the others that it appeared a masterwork of art, and in the middle of this sat the Snow Queen when she was at home. She used to say that she then sat in the mirror of reason, and that it was the only one in the world.

Little Kay was quite blue with cold—indeed almost black; but he did not know it, for she had kissed away the frost-shiver, and his heart was like a lump of ice. He was dragging some sharp-edged, flat pieces of ice about, and these he fitted together in all possible ways, just as we do small pieces of wood which we call the Chinese puzzle. Kay was also forming figures of the most wonderful description, and that was the ice-game of the understanding. In his eyes the figures were perfect, and of the highest importance, for the piece of broken glass which was in his eye made him think this. He formed whole words, but he could never succeed on the one word he wished to have—the word Eternity—for the Snow Queen had said to him, "If you can succeed in forming that one word you shall be your own master, and I will give you the whole world, together with a new pair of skates." But he could not.

"I am now going to pay a visit to the warmer countries," the Snow Queen said, "and intend giving a peep into the black caldrons": she meant the volcanoes Etna and Vesuvius. "I will cover them with white, which will also do good to the orange-trees and vines." The Snow Queen then flew away, and Kay was left alone in those vast empty rooms, staring at the pieces of ice, and thinking and thinking, till his brain almost cracked. He sat there quite stiff and still, so that it appeared as if he were frozen.

Just then little Gerda came through the large gate into the palace. Here were cutting winds, but she said her evening prayer, and the winds were lulled as if they wanted to go to sleep, and she entered the large, empty, cold rooms. She then saw Kay, recognised him at once, and running up to him, pressed him closely to her, and cried "Kay! dear little Kay! so I have found you at last!"

But he sat quite still, stiff and cold, and little Gerda cried bitter, burning tears, which fell upon his breast, and penetrating to his heart thawed the lump of ice, and dissolved the piece of broken glass. He looked at her, and she sang the hymn,—

> "The rose blooms, but its glory past,
> Christmas then approaches fast."

Kay then burst into tears, and cried till the pieces of glass were washed out of his eyes, when he recognised her, and exclaimed in delight, "Gerda! dear little Gerda! where have you been all this time? and where have I been?" He looked all around, and continued, "How cold it is here! and how vast and empty!" He pressed closely to her, and she laughed and cried in turns. There was such joy, that even the pieces of ice danced, and when they were tired and lay down again they formed the letters of the word which, when discovered, the Snow Queen said he should be his own master, and she would give him the whole world, besides a pair of beautiful new skates.

Gerda kissed his cheeks, and the colour came back into them; she kissed his eyes, and they were as bright as her own; she kissed his hands and feet, and he was himself again. The Snow Queen might now return, for his discharge was there written in sparkling ice.

They took each other by the hand, and wandered out of the palace. They spoke of their grandmother, and of the rose-trees upon the roof, and wherever they went the winds were lulled and the sun burst forth; and when they got to the bush with the red berries they found the Reindeer waiting for them, and another with it. These carried them first to the little woman, in whose hot room they warmed themselves, and got information about their homeward journey, and then to the old Lapland-woman, who made new clothes for them and got a sledge ready.

The two Reindeers took them quickly to the borders of the country, and there the first green was springing up. Here they parted from the Reindeer and the old Lapland-woman, and all cried, "Farewell!" The little birds began to twitter, the buds were green on the trees in the forest, and out of it came riding a young girl on a beautiful horse which Gerda knew, for it was one that had been harnessed to the golden carriage. This was the robber-girl with a red cap on her head, and pistols in her belt. She had had enough of home, and was now travelling towards the north, to take another direction later, if that did not please her. She and Gerda immediately recognised each other, and there was great rejoicing.

"You are a pretty fellow," she said to little Kay; "I should like to know whether you deserve that one should run to the end of the world after you."

But Gerda tapped her on the cheek, and asked after the Prince and Princess.

"They have gone to a foreign country," the robber-girl said.

"And the Ravens?" Gerda asked.

"The Raven is dead," she answered, "and his wife, now a widow, goes about with a piece of black cotton round her leg, and laments dreadfully; but that is nothing but words. But now tell me how it fared with you, and how you managed to catch him."

Gerda and Kay told her all.

The robber-girl took them both by the hand, and promised that if ever she should pass through their town she would mount up to visit them, and then she rode on into the wide world.

So Gerda and Kay continued their way hand in hand. It was delightful spring, with green leaves and beautiful flowers; the church-bells rang, and they recognised the high steeples and the large city; it was that in which they lived: so they entered it and went to the grandmother's house, up the stairs, and into the room, where everything was just as it used to be, the clock going "tick, tick!" and the hands moving, but they then noticed that they were no longer children. The roses from the roof gutter, in full bloom, hung in at the open window; and there stood the two children's stools, and Gerda seated herself on hers, and Kay took his, holding each other still by the hand. The cold, empty splendour in the Snow Queen's palace was all forgotten and faded like a disagreeable dream.

The grandmother sat in the clear sunshine, and read aloud out of the Bible, "Whosoever shall not receive the kingdom of God as a little child, shall in no wise enter heaven."

Kay and Gerda looked at each other, and both thought of the old hymn,—

> "The rose blooms, but its glory past,
> Christmas then approaches fast."

There they sat, grown up, and yet children; for in their hearts they were children and it was summer—warm, delightful summer.

THE SHEPHERDESS AND THE SWEEP

HAVE you ever seen a very old wooden cabinet, quite black with age and carved all over with leaves and filigree-work? Such an one stood in a sitting-room, and had been in the family from the great-grandmother's time. It was covered from top to bottom with carved roses and tulips, amongst which there were the most extra-ordinary flourishes, and from these sprang the antlered heads of stags, whilst on the top, in the middle, stood a whole figure. He was ridiculous enough to look at, with goat's legs, short horns on his head, and a long beard, besides which he was constantly grinning, for it could not be called a laugh. The children christened him the GoatslegHighadjutantgeneralmilitarycommandant, for that was a difficult name to pronounce, and a title not conferred upon many. To carve him cannot have been easy work, but there he stood, constantly looking at the table under the looking-glass, for there was the loveliest little china Shepherdess. Her shoes were gilt, and her dress neatly fastened up with a red rose, and then she had a gilt hat and a shepherdess's crook. She was, indeed, lovely. Close to her stood a little Sweep as black as any coal, but he, too, was entirely made of china; he was quite as neat and clean as any one else, for that he was a Sweep was, of course, only to represent something, and the potter could just as well have made a prince of him.

There he stood, with his face red and white, just like a girl and that was a mistake, for it might have been blackened a little. He was close to the Shepherdess, and they had both been placed where they stood, which, being the case, they were naturally engaged to each other, and well suited they were, for they were made of the same china, and were both little.

Not far from them there was another figure, but three times as big, a Chinese, who could nod his head. He was also made of china, and pretended to be the Shepherdess's grandfather, though he could not prove it, so claimed authority over her, and had promised her to the GoatslegHighadjutantgeneralmilitarycommandant.

"You will have a husband," the old Chinese said, "who I almost believe is made of mahogany, and he has the whole cabinet full of plate, besides the valuables that are in the hidden drawers."

"I will not go into the dark cabinet," the little Shepherdess said, "for I have heard that he has eleven china wives in there."

"Then you will make the twelfth," the old Chinese said, "for this very night your marriage shall take place." He then nodded his head and fell asleep.

The little Shepherdess cried and looked at her dearly beloved china Sweep.

"I must ask you," she said, "to go with me out into the wide world, for here we cannot stay."

and I have no doubt that by my calling I shall gain sufficient to and I have no doubt that by my calling I shall gain sufficient to keep you."

"Were we but safely down from the table," she cried, "for I shall never be happy till we are out in the wide world."

He consoled her, and showed her where to put her little feet, on the projections and ornaments, within their reach, and they got safely on to the floor, but when they looked towards the old cabinet all was confusion there. The stags stretched their heads further out, raising their antlers, and turned their necks from side to side. The GoatslegHighadjutantgeneralmilitarycommandant jumped high up into the air, and cried as loud as he could to the Chinese, "They are now running away! they are now running away!"

At this they were frightened, and they jumped into the cupboard under the window-seat.

Here lay three or four packs of cards, which were not complete, and a little doll's theatre, in which a play was being acted, and the Queen of hearts, diamonds, clubs and spades, sat in the front row fanning themselves with their tulips, whilst behind them stood the Knaves, who seemed to be their pages. The plot of the play was the difficulties thrown in the way of two persons who wished to be married, and the little Shepherdess cried, for it was her own story.

"I cannot bear this," she said, "I must get out of the cupboard." But when they were out and looked up at the table, they saw that the old Chinese was awake and his whole body shaking.

"Now the old Chinese is coming," the little Shepherdess cried, and fell down upon her china knees, she was in such a fright.

"I have an idea," the Sweep said. "Let us get into the pot-pourri-jar which stands there in the corner, where we can lie on rose-leaves and lavender, and throw salt in his eyes if he comes."

"That cannot help us," she said; "besides, I know that the old Chinese and the potpourri-jar were once engaged to each other, and there always remains some sort of tie between people with whom such a connection has existed. No, there is nothing left for us but to go out into the wide world."

"Have you really courage to go out with me into the wide world?" the Sweep asked. "Have you considered how large it is, and that we can never come back here?"

"Yes, I have," she answered.

The Sweep looked at her intently, and then said, "My way lies up the chimney, and that way I know well enough, and if you really have courage to go with me, we shall soon mount up so high that they will never be able to reach us."

And he led her to the grate.

"How black it looks up there!" she said, but still she went with him, and they had not gone far when he exclaimed, "Look, what a beautiful star is shining there above!"

It was a real star in the heavens shining down upon them, as if to show them the way. They crept on and climbed, and a dreadful way it was—so high, so high, but he held and lifted her, and showed her where to place her little china feet, till at last they reached the edge of the chimney, where they seated themselves, for they were very tired, as well they might be.

The sky, with all its stars, was above them, and below them lay all the roofs of the city, and they could see far around, so far out into the world. The poor Shepherdess had never imagined any-thing like it, and laying her little head on her Sweep's breast, she cried so that the gold was washed off her girdle.

"That is too much," she sobbed. "That I can never bear. The world is too large; oh, were I but back again on the table under the looking-glass! I shall never know happiness till I am back

F

there. I have followed you into the world, and if you care for me you must now go back with me."

The Sweep spoke most reasonably and sensibly to her, spoke of the old Chinese, and of the GoatslegHighadjutantgeneralmilitary-commandant, but she sobbed so violently that he was obliged to do as she wished, though it was foolish.

They therefore climbed down again with much trouble and difficulty, and when they got near the bottom they stopped to listen, but all being quiet they stepped into the room. There lay the old Chinese on the floor; he had fallen off the table when he attempted to follow them, and there he lay broken into three pieces. His whole back had come off in one piece, and his head had rolled far off into a corner of the room.

"That is horrible!" the little Shepherdess said. "My old grand-father is broken to pieces, and it is our fault. Oh, I shall never survive it!" And she wrung her little hands.

"He can be riveted," the Sweep said. "He can very well be riveted. Do not you give way so, for if they put a good strong rivet in his back and neck he will be as good as new again, and will be able to say many unpleasant things to us yet."

"Do you think so?" she said, and they then got on to the table again where they had always stood.

"It was of much use going all the way we did," the Sweep said; "we might just as well have saved ourselves that trouble."

"Oh, if my poor old grandfather were but riveted," the Shep-herdess said. "Will it cost very much?"

The family had him riveted, and he was in every way as good as new again, excepting that, owing to the rivet in his neck, he could no longer nod his head.

"You have grown proud since you were broken to pieces," the GoatslegHighadjutantgeneralmilitarycommandant said, "but I do not see any good reason for it. Now, am I to have her, or am I not?"

The Sweep and the little Shepherdess looked so beseechingly at the old Chinese, fearing that he would nod, but he could not. He did not choose to tell a stranger that he had a rivet in the back of his neck, so he was quiet, and the Shepherdess and Sweep re-mained together, loving each other till they got broken.

THE ELFIN-HILLOCK

SEVERAL large lizards were running about in the clefts of an old tree, and they understood each other well enough, for they all spoke the Lizard language.

"What a rumpus and confusion there is in the old Elfin-hillock!" one of the Lizards said. "I have not been able to close my eyes for two nights with the noise, so that I might just as well have had the toothache, for then I cannot sleep either."

"There is evidently something afoot there," another Lizard said, "for the hillock stands raised up on four red poles all night till the cock crows. It is being thoroughly aired, and the Elfin-maidens have been learning new dances. There is something in the wind."

"Yes; I was speaking with a Worm, who is an acquaintance of mine," a third Lizard said, "just after it had come out of the hillock, where it had been burrowing day and night. It had heard a good deal—see it can't, the miserable creature! but feeling and hearing it is up to. Strangers are expected in the Elfin-hillock—grand strangers—but who they are the Worm would not tell."

Just then the Elfin-hillock opened, and an old Elfin-maiden came tripping out. She was the old Elfin-king's housekeeper, and was distantly related to the family, on which account she wore an amber heart on her forehead. How quickly her legs moved! Trip! trip! Good gracious! how she trips along, and straight to the Carrion Crow!

"You are invited to the Elfin-hillock for to-night," she said; "but will you not first do us a great service, and undertake the invitations? You know that you ought to do something, as you do not give parties yourself. We expect some grand people, magicians, who are of great importance, and on that account the Elfin-king intends to show himself."

"Who is to be invited?" the Crow asked.

"Why, to the ball all the world may come, even human beings, if they do but talk in their sleep, or can do something of that sort; but the dinner is to be very select, to consist only of the very highest. I have had a dispute with the King about it, for it is my opinion that we cannot even admit ghosts. The Water-nix and his daughters must be the first, and, though they will not much like coming on dry land, they shall have a wet stone to sit upon, or, perhaps, something better, and so I think they will not refuse for this once. We must have all the old Demons of the first class with tails, Cobolds and Witches; and I think we can scarcely leave out the Hill-man, the Skeleton-horse, the Kelpies, and the Pixies."

"All right," the Crow said, and flew off to give the invitations.

The Elfin-maidens were already dancing on the hillock, and they wore shawls made of mist and moonshine, which look very pretty to those who like them. The great hall in the middle of the hillock was beautifully got up, the floors had been washed with moonshine, and the walls rubbed down with witches' fat, so that in the light they shone like tulip-leaves. In the kitchen there were plenty of frogs on the spits, there were snails' skins, with children's fingers inside, and salads of mushroom, the snouts of mice, and hemlock, and to drink, sparkling saltpetre wine; everything of the best. The dessert consisted of rusty nails and broken church-window glass.

The old Elfin-king had his golden crown fresh polished and in the bed-room clean curtains were put up, fastened with snails' horns. What a noise and confusion there was!

"Now the whole place must be fumigated with burnt horse-hair and hog's bristles, and then I think I shall have done my part," the old Elfin-maiden said.

"My own sweet father!" the youngest daughter said, coaxingly, "may I not now know who the noble strangers are?"

"Well, I suppose I must tell," he said. "Two of my daughters must be prepared to marry, for certainly two will be married. The old Cobold from Norway, he who lives in the Dovre-rock, and possesses many stone-quarries and a gold-mine, which is worth more than is generally supposed, is coming with his two sons, who are to choose themselves wives. He is a right-down honest northern old Cobold, merry and straightforward; and I know him from olden times, when he was down here, seeking himself a wife; she was a daughter of the Rock-king of Moen, but she is now dead. Oh, how I long to see the old Cobold again! His sons are said to be pert, forward boys, but, perhaps, it is not true, and no doubt they will improve as they grow older. Let me see you girls teach them manners."

"And when are they coming?" another of the daughters asked.

"That depends upon wind and weather," the Elfin-king said, "for they travel economically, and come by water. I wished them to come through Sweden, but my old friend does not fancy that. He does not advance with the age, and that I do not like."

Just then two Will-o'-the-wisps came hopping along, the one faster than the other, and it therefore arrived first.

"They are coming! they are coming!" they cried.

"Give me my crown, and let me stand in the moonshine," the King said.

His daughters raised their shawls, and bowed down to the ground.

There stood the old Cobold of Dovre, with his crown of hardened ice and fir-cones, dressed in a bear-skin and snow-boots. His sons, on the contrary, had bare necks, without any handkerchief, for they were hard young men.

"Is that a mound?" the youngest of them asked, pointing to the Elfin-hillock. "In Norway, we call that a hole."

"Boys!" the old man said, "a hole goes inwards, a mound upwards. Have you no eyes in your head?"

The only thing they wondered at, they said, was, that they could understand the language down there without any trouble.

"Mind what you are about," their father said, "or people will think you half fools."

They then went into the Elfin-hillock, where the high and polite company were assembled, and that in such haste that one might almost have thought they had been blown together. All the arrangements were perfect; the Water-nixes sat at table in large water tanks, and they said it was exactly as if they were at home. All behaved with the most perfect refinement of manners, with the exception of the two young northern Cobolds, who stretched their legs upon the table; but they thought everything became them.

"Feet off the table!" the old Cobold said, and they obeyed; but they did not do so at once. They made the ladies, who sat by their sides, tickle them with fir-cones, which they carried in their pockets, and gave them their boots to hold, which they took off to be more at their ease. But their father was very different; he talked so well of the proud northern rocks, and of the waterfalls rushing down with a white foam, and a noise like thunder and the notes of an organ. He talked of the salmon that leap up into the falling waters when the Nix plays on her golden harp. He told of the bright winter-nights, when the bells on the sledges tinkle, and the young men with burning torches skate across the ice, which is so clear that they can see how they frighten the fish beneath their feet. Yes, he talked so well, that one seemed to see what he described; it was just like the clapper of a sawmill.

The Elfin-maidens then danced together, and that showed them off to great advantage; then singly, or the *pas seul*, as it is called. Oh, dear! how quickly they moved their legs; there was no telling where the beginning or end was, nor seeing which were the arms and which the legs; and then they whirled round like tops, so that the Skeleton-horse turned quite giddy and had to leave the table.

"Prrrrr!" the old Cobold cried. "What a commotion there is amongst the legs; but what else can they do besides dance, stick out their legs and raise a whirlwind?"

"You shall soon see," the Elfin-king said, and he called his youngest daughter. She was very active, and transparent as moon-shine; she was the most delicate of all the sisters, and when she took a white chip in her mouth she disappeared altogether. That was her art.

But the old Cobold said it was an art he would not like in a wife, and he did not think that his sons cared about it.

The next could walk by her own side, just as if she had a shadow, which the Elves have not.

The third was of quite a different stamp, for she had learnt to brew, bake, and cook, and knew how to lard the Elfin-dumplings with glow-worms.

"She will make a good housewife," the old Cobold said, and he drank to her, but with his eyes only, for he wished to remain sober.

Then the fourth came, and she had a large harp, on which she played, and when she struck the first string all lifted up their legs, for the Cobolds are left-legged; and when she struck the second string they were obliged to do whatever she wished.

"That is a dangerous woman," the old Cobold said, whilst both the sons went out, for they found the amusements tedious.

"And what can the next do?" the old Cobold asked.

"I have learnt to like the north, and I shall never marry unless it is to go to Norway."

But the youngest of the girls whispered to the old man, "That is only because she has heard from a northern song that when the world is destroyed, the rocks of the north will still remain, and therefore she wishes to go there, for she is so dreadfully afraid of death!"

"Ho, ho! is that her meaning?" he answered. "And what can the seventh and last do?"

"The sixth comes before the seventh," the Elfin-king said, for he could count, but the sixth kept herself in the background.

"I can only tell people the truth," she said, "and therefore no one cares for me, so the best thing I can do is to prepare my shroud."

Then came the seventh, and what could she do? Why, she could tell stories, as many as any one would listen to.

"Here are all my five fingers; tell me a story of each," the old Cobold said.

She laid hold of his wrist, and he laughed till he almost choked, but when she came to the ring-finger, which had a gold ring on, as if it knew there was to be a betrothal, he said, "Keep tight hold of what you have; the hand is yours, for you shall be my wife."

The maiden said that the story of the ring-finger and of the little finger still remained to be told.

"We will have those in winter," the old Cobold said, "and have stories of the Fir-tree, and the Birch-tree, of the Fairy-gifts, and of the Frost. You shall tell stories enough, for there no one understands that properly. We will sit in the warm room, where the pine-logs are burning, and drink mead out of the golden cups of the old northern Kings, and the Echo will visit us and sing you all the songs of the Shepherdesses in the mountains. That will be glorious, and the salmon will leap in the water-fall and beat against our stone-walls, but he shan't come in. Oh, it is delightful in dear old Norway, but what has become of the boys?"

Ah, where were they? They were running about the fields, blowing out the Will-o'-the-wisps, who had been so good-natured to come and serve as torches.

"What are you up to here?" the old Cobold said. "I have chosen a mother for you, and you may choose yourselves an aunt."

But the boys said they would rather make a speech and then drink healths, for they had no fancy for marriage, so they made speeches and drank healths, turning their glasses upside down to show that they left no heel-taps. They then took off their coats and laid themselves on the table to sleep, for they did not stand much upon ceremony. But the old Cobold danced about the room with his future wife, and changed boots with her, which is better manners than changing rings.

"The cock is crowing," the old Elfin-maiden, who attended to the house duties, said. "We must now shut the shutters, so that the sun may not scorch us up."

The hillock then closed up.

But outside the lizards ran about in the split tree, and the one said, "Oh, how much I did like the old Cobold!"

"I like the boys better," the Worm said, but then it could not see, the miserable creature!

HOLGER DANSKE

IN Denmark there stands an old castle, which is called Kronburg; it stands in the Sound, where the large vessels pass daily by hundreds, English as well as Russian and Prussian, and they salute the old castle with cannon that say, "Boom!" and the old castle answers with cannon: "Boom!" for that is the way the cannon say, "Good day!" "Many thanks!" In winter no vessels sail past there, for it is all ice, right across to the Swedish coast; but it is like a regular road, where the Danish and Swedish flags are displayed, and the Danish and Swedish people say to each other: "Good day!" "Many thanks!" not with cannon, however, but with a friendly shake of the hand; and they buy cakes and biscuits from each other, fancying they taste better than their own. But the most remarkable of all is old Kronburg, and beneath it, in a deep, dark cellar, which no one ever enters, sits Holger Danske. He is clad in iron and steel, and rests his head on his strong hands, whilst his long beard hangs down upon the marble table, into which it has grown fast; he sleeps and dreams, but in his dreams he sees all that goes on in Denmark. Every Christmas-eve an angel comes down from heaven and tells him that all he has been dreaming is perfectly right, so that he may go to sleep again in peace, as Denmark is in no actual danger. But should it be in danger, then old Holger Danske will arise, breaking the table as he draws out his beard, and he will lay about him with his sword, so that it shall be heard in all parts of the world.

An old grandfather was telling all this about Holger Danske to his little grandson, and the little boy knew that all his grandfather told him was true. And whilst the old man sat talking he was carving at a large wooden image, representing Holger Danske, intending to serve as figure-head to a ship, for the old grandfather was a wood-carver, that is, a man who carves the figures after which the vessels are named. He had now carved Holger Danske, who stood so proudly with his long beard, holding a battle-axe in one hand, whilst the other rested on the Danish coat-of-arms.

And the old grandfather told so many stories of celebrated Danish men and women, that at last it appeared to the little grandson as if he knew as much as Holger Danske himself, who, after all, only dreamed it; and when the little fellow was in bed, he thought so much of it that he pressed his chin against the bed-covering and imagined he had a long beard, which had grown fast to it.

But the old man went on with his work which he was just finishing, for he was carving at the Danish coat-of-arms; and when he had done, he examined the whole, thinking of all he had read and heard, and had himself been telling his little grandson. He then nodded his head, wiped his spectacles, and putting them on again, said, "During my lifetime Holger Danske will probably not come again, but that boy in bed may perhaps see him, and be present when there is really something to do"; and he nodded his head again; and the more he looked at his work, the more evident it appeared to him that what he had done was good. It seemed to him as if it actually had colour, and that the armour glittered like iron and steel. The hearts in the Danish coat-of-arms grew redder and redder, and the lions sprang forward with the golden crowns on their heads.

"That is certainly the most beautiful coat-of-arms in the whole world," the old man said. "The lions represent strength, and the hearts mildness and love." He looked at the top lion, and thought of King Canute, who joined mighty England to the Danish throne. He looked at the second lion, and thought of Waldemar, who united the whole of Denmark and subdued Sclavonia; and as he looked at the third lion, he thought of Margaret, who joined Sweden and Norway to Denmark. But when he looked at the red hearts, they shone stronger than before; they became moving flames, and his mind followed each.

The first flame led him into a narrow, dark prison; there sat a prisoner, a beautiful woman, Elenor Ulfeld, the daughter of Christian the Fourth, and the flame settled like a rose upon her bosom, becoming one with the heart of the best and noblest of Danish women.

"Yes, that is a heart worthy of the Danish coat-of-arms," the old man said.

And his mind followed the second flame, which led him out on to the sea, where the cannon thundered and the ships lay veiled in smoke, and the flame settled as a cross of honour on the breast of Hvitfeldt, when to save the fleet he blew up his ship and himself.

And the third flame led him to Greenland's miserable huts, where the preacher, Hans Egede, by word and act performed a duty of love, and the flame was a star on his breast, a heart for the Danish coat-of-arms.

The old man's mind now went before the flitting flame, for he knew its destination. In the midst of poverty, in the room of the peasantess, stood Frederick the Sixth, and wrote his name with chalk on a beam. The flame flickered on his breast, flickered in his heart, and in the peasant's room became a heart for the Danish coat-of-arms. And the old man dried his eyes, for he had known King Frederick, with his silvery hair and his honest blue eyes, and folding his hands he sat in thought. His daughter-in-law then came and said it was time to rest, as it was late, and the table laid for supper.

"What you have done is beautiful, my dear grandfather," she said; "Holger Danske and the whole coat-of-arms. It seems to me as if I have seen that face."

"No, you have scarcely seen it," he said, "but I have, and have striven to carve it in wood, just as I bear it in memory. It was when the English ships lay in our roads, on the Danish second of April, when we showed that we were the Danes of old. When I was in Steen Bille's company, a man stood by my side. It was as if the balls were afraid of him. Merrily he sang old songs, and fired and fought as if he were more than man. I remember his face well, but where he came from, and whither he went, I do not know, and no one knows. I have often thought that was, perhaps, old Holger Danske himself, who had swum down from Kronburg to help us in our danger. That was an idea of mine, and there is his likeness."

The figure threw its large shadow on the wall, and on part of the ceiling, and it seemed as if it were the shadow of Holger Danske himself, for it moved; but that might have been in consequence of the flame of the candle not burning steadily. The young woman kissed her old father-in-law, and led him to a large arm-chair standing at the table, and she and her husband, who was the old man's son, and father of the little boy, then in bed, sat down to supper. The old man spoke of the Danish lions and of the Danish hearts, of strength and mildness, and he explained quite clearly that there was other strength besides that which lay in the sword. He pointed to a shelf on which stood some old books, and amongst them Holberg's Plays, which have been so often read because they are so interesting; and it seems as if one can recognise all the people of past days.

"He knew how to strike, too," the old man said, "and did not spare the follies and vices of the world." He then pointed to the almanack, on which was a picture of the Copenhagen Observatory, and said, "Tycho Brahe was also one who wanted the sword, not to cut into flesh and bone, but to cut out a clear way amongst the stars of heaven. And then there is he, whose father belonged to my calling, the old wood-carver's son, whom we have seen with his white hair and broad shoulders, he whose name is celebrated all over the world, Bertel Thorwaldsen. Yes, Holger Danske may come in many shapes, so that Denmark's strength is heard of in all countries of the world. Let us now drink Bertel's health."

In the meanwhile the little boy in bed saw old Kronburg quite plainly, and the real Holger Danske, who sat below with his beard grown fast in the marble table, dreaming of all that happened above. Holger Danske dreamed also of the little room where the wood-carver was at work; he heard all that was spoken there, and nodding in his dream said,—

"Yes, think of me, you Danish people, keep me in your memories! I shall come in the hour of need!"

Above Kronburg the sky was clear and the wind carried the sound of the huntsman's horn from the neighbouring land, and the ships saluted as they passed, "Boom! boom!" and from Kronburg was answered, "Boom! boom!" but Holger Danske did not wake up, as loud as they fired, for it was no more than "Good day!" "Many thanks!" The firing must be different before he awakes, but awake he will, for there is faith in Holger Danske.

MOTHER ELDER

THERE was once a little boy who had caught cold, for he had gone out and got his feet wet, though no one could imagine how, as the weather was perfectly dry. His mother having undressed him, put him to bed, and had the tea-pot brought in to make him a good cup of elder-tea, for that warms one. At the same time the good-natured old man, who lived right at the top of the house, came into the room. He lived quite alone, for he had neither wife nor children; but of children he was very fond, and knew so many stories that it was quite a treat to listen to him.

"Now, if you drink your tea," the little boy's mother said, "you may, perhaps, have a story told you."

"Yes, if I did but know anything new," the old man said, nodding kindly. "But how did the little fellow get his feet wet?" he asked.

"How that happened," the mother said, "no one can guess."

"Am I to have a story told me?" the boy asked.

"Yes, if you can tell me, pretty correctly, how deep the gutter is in the little street where you go to school, for I must know that first."

"Exactly half way up the leg of my boot," the little boy answered; "but then I have to go into the deep hole."

"Now we know how we got our feet wet," the old man said. "I suppose I must tell a story, but I do not know one."

"You can easily invent one," the little fellow said; "for mother says that you can turn all you see into a story, and can make up a tale out of everything you touch."

"Yes, but those sort of stories are good for nothing. The good ones come of their own accord. They knock here at my forehead and say, 'Here we are!'"

"Will they not knock soon?" the little boy said, and his mother laughed, put some elder-flowers in the tea-pot, and poured boiling water upon them.

"The story! the story!"

"If my story would but come of its own accord; but they are very grand in their way, and will only come when it suits them. Wait!" he suddenly exclaimed. "Now I have one! Pay attention, for it is now in the tea-pot."

The little boy looked, and the lid of the tea-pot opened more and more, when the elder-flowers came out so fresh and white, and they shot forth long, thick branches. They even came out at the spout, and spread to all sides, becoming larger and larger. It was the most beautiful elder-bush imaginable—quite a tree, stretching right up to the bed and pushing the curtains on one side. How full it was of blossom, and how it scented the air! and in the midst of the tree sat a friendly old woman with a very peculiar dress; it was green, like the elder-leaves, and figured all over with elder-flowers, so that at first sight it was difficult to make out whether it was really stuff, or the living green and flowers of the tree.

"What is the woman's name?" the little boy asked.

"Well, the Romans and Greeks called her Dryad, but that is a name we do not understand," the old man said. "We have a better name for her. We call her Mother-elder. But now attend, and look at the beautiful elder-tree.

"Just such a tree stood in the corner of a little yard, and under that tree, on one beautiful summer's afternoon, sat two old people, a very old sailor and his very old wife. They were great-grandparents, and were soon to celebrate their fiftieth wedding-day, though they could not recollect the exact date; but Mother-elder sat in the tree looking so pleased, just as she does now, and said, 'I know when it is!' They, however, did not hear her, for they were talking of old times.

"'Do you remember,' the old sailor said, 'when we were quite little and ran about and played, that we set up a railing of twigs and made a garden in this very yard where we are sitting?'

"'Yes,' the old woman answered, 'I remember it perfectly well; and we watered the twigs, one of which was an elder-twig, and it took root, and grew into the big tree, under which we are now sitting.'

"'Just so,' he said; 'and in yonder corner was a water-tub where I used to swim my boat, which I had made myself. How it sailed! but I had soon very different sailing.'

"'Yes, but before that we went to school to learn something; but in the afternoon we went to the Round Tower and looked down upon Copenhagen and the water; after which we went to Friedrichsberg, where we saw the King and Queen in their beautiful boat, driven by the breeze along the canal.'

"'But I was, for years, driven about the world very differently.'

"'Yes, and often I cried on account of you,' she said; 'for I thought you were dead and gone, lying at the bottom of the sea. Many a night have I got up to see if the weather-cock were turning. Yes, it was turning fast enough, but you did not come. I remember quite distinctly how one day the rain came pouring down from heaven, when the postman stopped at the door of the house where I was in service, and gave me a letter. It was from you. Oh, how it had travelled about! I tore it open immediately, and laughed and cried by turns, I was so happy. In it you said that you were in the warm country where coffee grows. What a delightful country that must be! You told so much, and I stood there at the door reading it, whilst the rain came pouring down, when suddenly some one seized me round the waist——'

" 'Yes, and a good box of the ear you gave me!'

" 'How could I guess it was you? you had arrived as soon as your letter, and you were so handsome—so you are still! You wore a glazy hat, and you had a large yellow silk handkerchief in your pocket. You were so smart! and, oh, goodness, how weti t was!'

" 'Then we were married!' he said, 'do you remember? And then came our first little boy; then Marianne, and Niels, and Peter, and Hans Christian.'

" 'Yes; and how they all grew up, and every one liked them.'

" 'And now their children have children,' the old sailor said. 'They are childrenschildschildren; and, if I am not mistaken, it was about this time of the year that we were married.'

" 'Yes, this very day is your fiftieth wedding-day!' Mother-elder said, thrusting her head immediately between the old couple; but they thought it was a neighbour, and looking at each other, they laid hold of hands. Then came the children, and children's children, who knew well that it was the fiftieth wedding-day, and had already that morning wished them joy; but the old people had forgotten it, though they so well remembered what had happened years before; and the elder-tree gave forth such a strong scent; and the sun, which was just going down, shone right in the old couple's faces. They had both such a colour in their cheeks; and the smallest child of the children's children danced round them, crying out joyfully that there was to be a great treat that night— that they were to have baked potatoes. And Mother-elder nodded from her tree, and cried with the others, 'Hurrah!' "

"But that is no story at all," the little boy said, who had been listening attentively.

"Do you think not?" the kind old story-teller answered; "but let us ask Mother-elder about it."

"No, it was no story," she said; "but now comes one. It is just from reality that the most wonderful tales take their beginning, or how could my beautiful elder-tree have grown out of the tea-pot?"

She then took the little boy out of his bed, and as she held him in her arms, the elder-branches covered with blossom closed round them, so that they sat in a thick bower, which flew away with them through the air. How beautiful it was! Mother-elder all at once changed into a pretty young girl; but her dress was still the same green one, covered with white flowers, as worn by Mother-elder. At her breast she wore a real elder-flower, and round her curly, yellow hair a whole wreath of the same. Her eyes were so large and so blue; she was, indeed, lovely, and she and the boy kissed each other, for they were of the same age, and experienced the same feelings.

Hand in hand they now went out of the bower, and were at home in the beautiful flower-garden, where on the green grass-plot lay their father's stick. There was life in the stick as soon as they seated themselves across it; the bright knob changed into a magnificent neighing head; the long black mane fluttered in the wind; four slender legs shot forth; the animal was spirited and strong, and in a gallop they went round the grass-plot.

"Hurrah! now we'll ride many miles away," the boy said. "We'll go to the castle where we were last year," so they rode round and round the grass-plot; and the little girl, who we know was no other than Mother-elder, kept calling out, "Now we are in the country! Do you see that farmhouse with the large oven, projecting from the wall like a monstrous egg? The elder-tree spreads out its branches over it, and there, below, the cock is scratching up the earth for the chickens. See how consequential he looks! Now we are near the church; it stands up there on the hillock, under the huge oak-trees, one of which is half withered. Now we are by the side of the smithy. How the fire burns, and the half-naked men strike the red-hot iron, that the sparks fly far around! On, on to the beautiful castle!" and all that the little girl mentioned, as she sat behind him on the stick, passed by them, and the boy saw it, though they did not move from the grass-plot. They then played in one of the side-walks, scratching up the earth to make a garden; and she took some of the elder-flowers out of her hair and planted them, and they grew, just as with the old people when they were little, and as has already been told. They walked hand in hand, as the old people did when children, but not to the Round Tower nor the Friedrich's garden; no, the little girl took him round the body, and they flew far about the country. It was now spring, then summer and harvest-time, and then winter; and thousands of pictures appeared before the little boy's eyes and were impressed upon his heart, the little girl singing to him all the time, "That you will never forget!" During their whole flight the elder-tree sent forth such a sweet and delicious perfume, stronger than the roses which he saw, for the elder-flowers were at the little girl's bosom, on which he often rested his head.

"It is beautiful here in spring," the young girl said, and they stood in a beech-forest, where the fresh leaves had just burst from the buds, and amongst the green clover at their feet they saw the pale red anemones, looking so lovely. "Oh, were it always spring in the Danish beech-forests!"

"It is delightful here in summer," she said, as they passed by the old castles of former days, the red walls and pointed gables of which were reflected in the rivers, where the swans swam, and looked up the cool shady walks. The corn was waving in the fields like a lake, in the ditches grew red and yellow flowers, and in the hedges wild hops and blowing convolvuli. In the evening the moon rose, large and round, and the haycocks in the meadows perfumed the air. "That is never to be forgotten."

"It is delightful here in autumn," the little girl said, and the sky seemed twice as lofty and blue, whilst the forest assumed the most beautiful colours of red, green, and yellow. From the copses, thick with brambles, overgrowing the old stones, rose whole flights of birds as the dogs broke in, and the sea was dark blue, spotted with white sails. In the barn sat old women, girls, and children, plucking hops, whilst the young ones sang songs, and the old ones told stories of ghosts and goblins. Nowhere could it be better.

"It is beautiful here in winter," the little girl said, and all the trees were covered with frost, so that they looked like white coral. The snow creaked under the feet, as if everyone had new shoes on, and one shooting-star fell after the other. In the rooms, Christmas-trees were lighted, and there were presents and merriment; and in the peasants' houses, in the country, there was dancing to the sound of the violin. Even the poorest child said, "It is beautiful in winter."

Yes, it was beautiful; and the little girl showed the boy everything, and the elder-tree continued to scent the air, and the red flag with the white cross waved—the flag under which the old sailor had gone to sea. The boy became a young man, and he was to go out in the world, far away to the warm countries where the coffee-plant grows. At parting, the little girl took one of the elder-flowers from her bosom and gave it him, and it was put into his Prayer-book; and in foreign countries, when he opened the book, it was always at the place where the flower was, and the more he looked at it, the fresher it became; so that it was almost as if he inhaled the air of the Danish forests; and plainly he saw the little girl, as with her clear blue eyes she looked out from amongst the flower-leaves, and whispered, "It is beautiful here in spring, in summer, autumn, and in winter," and hundreds of pictures glided through his thoughts.

Many years passed thus; and he was now an old man, and sat with his old wife beneath an elder-tree full of blossom.

They held each other by the hand, exactly as the great-grand-father and the great-grandmother had done before them, and they spoke exactly like them of old times, and of their fiftieth wedding-day. The little girl with the blue eyes, and the elder-flowers in her hair, sat in the tree, and, nodding to them both, said, "To-day is your fiftieth wedding-day"; and then she took two flowers out of her wreath, kissed them, and they shone, first like silver, and then like gold, and as she placed them upon the old people's heads, the flowers turned to golden crowns: so there they sat like a king and queen under the tree, which looked exactly like an elder-tree. He then told his old wife the story of Mother-elder, as it had been told him when he was still a little boy, and it seemed to them that it contained so much that was like their own story; and just those parts that were like pleased them most.

"Yes, so it is," the little girl in the tree said; "some call me Mother-elder, whilst others call me Dryad; but my name in reality is Recollection. It is I, sitting in the tree, who grow and grow. I can recall the past, and I can tell stories. Now let me see whether you have your flower still."

And the old man opened his Prayer-book, and there was the elder-flower, as fresh as if it had just been put there. Recollection nodded her head. And the old couple, with the golden crowns on their heads, sat in the red evening sun; they closed their eyes, and—and—well, that was the end of the story.

The little boy lay in his bed; he did not know whether he had dreamed or heard the story. The tea-pot stood on the table, but no elder-tree was growing out of it, and the old man, who had been telling the story, was just on the point of going out of the room, which he did.

"How pretty that was!" the little boy said. "Mother, I have been in the warm countries."

"I should think you have!" his mother said, "for any one who has swallowed two cups of elder-tea may well be in a warm country"; and she covered him up well, that he might not catch cold. "I suppose you have slept whilst I was disputing with him whether it was a history or a tale."

"And where is Mother-elder?" the boy asked.

"She is in the tea-pot," his mother said, "and there let her remain."

THE BELL

OF an evening, in the narrow streets of the large town, when the sun was going down and the clouds shone like gold between the chimney-pots, there was frequently heard, first by one and then by another, a strange sound, like the ringing of a church-bell; but it was only heard for a moment, for there was too great a rattling of carts and noise of voices. "That evening-bell is ringing," it was then said; "the sun is setting."

Those who were outside of the town, where the houses are further apart, with gardens and little fields, saw the beauty of the sky more clearly, and more plainly heard the sound of the bell, and to them it appeared to proceed from a church in the depth of the large forest.

When this had continued some time, one said to another, "I wonder whether there is really a church in the forest? The bell has a peculiarly beautiful tone, suppose we go and try to find out where it comes from." So the rich people drove out of the town, and the poor walked; and when they came to a number of willow-trees, which grew on the borders of the forest, they rested there, and looking up amongst the long, thick branches, thought they had gone far enough. A confectioner from the town came and erected himself a tent there; and then came another confectioner, who hung up a bell over his tent, which he had tarred to keep it dry; but it had no clapper. When the people got home again, they said it had been very romantic out there—much better than a tea-party. Three people pretended that they had been in the forest, right to the end of it, and that they had still heard the peculiar tones of the bell, but that the sound seemed to come from the town. One of them wrote a whole poem about it, saying that the bell sounded like the voice of a mother to her dear child, and that no melody could be more delightful.

Thus the Emperor's attention was called to it, and he promised that whoever discovered whence the sound came should have the title of "The World's Bell-ringer," if even it were no bell at all.

For the sake of so good an appointment, many now went to the forest, but only one returned with anything like an explanation of the mystery. No one had penetrated far enough, and he no

further than the others, but he said that the bell-like sound
proceeded from a very large owl knocking its head against a
hollow tree in which it dwelt; but whether the sound came from
the head or the tree he could not with certainty determine, and he
received the appointment of the World's Bell-ringer, and wrote a
short pamphlet about the owl every year, in spite of which people
were no wiser than before.

It was now Sunday, and the clergyman spoke so beautifully and
impressively that all were very much affected. The sun shone
beautifully as they went out of the town, and just then the
mysterious bell from the forest sounded particularly loud. They
were all immediately seized with a desire to be there, with the
exception of three of them; one of these wanted to get home, in
order to try on her ball-dress; the second was a poor boy, who had
borrowed the coat and boots which he wore from a young friend,
and had to return them at a certain time; and the third said that
he never went to strange places without his parents; that he had
always been a good boy, and intended to remain so; and that they
need not laugh at him on that account, which they did, however.

Three of them, therefore, did not go with the rest, but the
others ran off. The sun was shining and the birds singing, and the
young party sang with them, for they had no appointments as yet,
and had therefore nothing else to do.

But two of the smallest soon grew tired, and they returned to
the town, and two young girls seated themselves in the grass to
make wreaths of the flowers they had gathered, so they did not go
either; and when the others reached the willow trees where the
confectioners had their tents, they said, "We have now come far
enough to find out that the bell really does not exist; it is only a
thing of the imagination."

Then suddenly the bell sounded from the depth of the forest, so
beautifully and solemnly, that four or five determined to go
further in; but the trees and bushes were so thick, the hyacinths
and anemones grew so high, and brambles and convolvuli hung in
festoons from tree to tree, that, however beautiful, it was really
difficult to get on, and for girls quite impossible, for they would
have torn their clothes. Large pieces of rock lay there covered with
different-coloured mosses, and clear spring water oozed from between them. "Bubble, bubble, bubble!"

"Can that be the bell, I wonder?" one of the party said, and he
lay down to listen. "That is worth examining into!" so he remained and let the others go on.

They came to a house built of branches and the bark of trees, and the roof was covered with roses. A large wild apple-tree bent over it, and on one of the branches hung a small bell. Could that be the bell that was heard? All agreed that it was so, with the exception of one, who maintained that the bell was much too small to be heard at such a distance. This one was the son of a King, and the rest said, "The like of him must always be wiser than others."

So they let him go on alone, and as he pursued his way his breast was more and more filled with the solemnity of the forest. He still heard the little bell, over which the others were rejoicing, and occasionally, when the wind blew that way, the sounds of singing were carried over from the confectioner's tent; but there were the deep tones as of a large bell above all, and with them the notes of an organ, which sounds came from the left side, the side of the heart.

There was a rustling in the bushes, and a little boy stood before the King's son, a boy in wooden shoes, and with the sleeves of his jacket so short that they did not nearly reach to his wrists. They knew each other, for the boy was that one who had not been able to come with the rest, as he had to go home to return the borrowed clothes, which he had done, and was now in wooden shoes and shabby clothes, but the bell sounded so loud that he could not remain at home.

"Now we can go together," the King's son said, but the poor boy was quite ashamed; he tried to pull down his short sleeves, and said he was afraid he could not get on fast enough; besides that, he thought the bell must be sought to the right, as that was the place for all that is great and glorious.

"Then we shall not meet at all!" the King's son said, and nodded to the poor boy, who pressed on into the thickest part of the forest, where the thorns tore his clothes to pieces and scratched his face, hands, and feet. Neither did the King's son escape some good scratches, but the sun shone on his path, and him we shall follow, for he was a brisk lad.

"I must and will find the bell," he said, "if even I have to go to the end of the world!"

Ugly monkeys sat in the tops of the trees chattering. "Let us give it him well; let us thrash him, for he is a King's son."

But, undaunted, he went deeper and deeper into the forest, where the most wonderful flowers grew—asters with blood-red stamens, sky-blue tulips, and apple-trees the fruit of which was exactly like large shining soap-bladders; so you may imagine how they glittered in the sun. There were beautiful green meadows with deer playing in the grass, and there were large lakes with white swans swimming about on them. The King's son often stood still and listened, for every now and then he thought that the sound of the bell came up from one of these lakes; but then, again, it was clear to him that it did not come from there, and that the bell sounded from still deeper in the forest.

The sun was fast going down, the whole air looked red, as if from fire, the forest was still, and sinking down upon his knees, he sang the evening hymn, and then said, "I shall never find what I am looking for. The sun is going down, and now comes night, dark night; but once more, perhaps, I shall be able to see the sun before it sinks entirely behind the earth. I will climb up on to the rocks which are about the height of the highest trees."

He laid hold of tendrils and roots and climbed up the wet stones, where the water-snakes were gliding about, and the toads seemed to bark at him, but he reached the top before the sun, seen from this height, had quite disappeared. Oh, what magnificence! The sea, the vast, beautiful sea, rolling its high waves towards the shore, lay stretched out before him, and the sun stood there, like a large glittering altar where the sea and sky met. All melted in glowing colours into one. The forest sang, and the sea sang, and his heart sang too. Nature was a vast, glorious church, trees and clouds forming the pillars, grass and flowers the embroidered altar-cloth, and heaven itself the large dome. The red colours faded from the sky as the sun disappeared, but millions of stars were lighted, there shone millions of diamond-lamps, and the King's son spread out his arms towards the sky, towards the sea and the forest, when suddenly the poor boy with the short sleeves and the wooden shoes appeared from the right side. By the way he had chosen he arrived at the same point, and taking each other by the hand they stood in the vast church of Nature and of Poetry, and from above them sounded the invisible, holy bell, whilst the spirits of the blessed hovered around them, dancing to the music with a universal Hallelujah.

THE ROSE-ELF

Many, many years ago, in a large garden, there grew an enormous rose-tree, which was literally covered with roses, and in one of these, the most beautiful of them all, lived an Elf. He was so very small that he was not perceptible to any human eye, but, at the same time, so delightfully and so beautifully made—as one can only imagine an angel to be; and two transparent wings, which reached from his shoulders to the soles of his feet, made him still more like an angel. Beneath each rose-petal he had a soft chamber, and oh! what a delicious scent filled all his apartments, and how beautifully clear and bright were the walls, for they were the delicate, pale red rose-leaves themselves.

The whole day long he luxuriated in the warm sunshine, and danced on the wings of the roving butterflies, and sometimes in the dreamy hours of idleness he would sportively calculate the number of steps he would have to take to walk along all the high-roads, bye-roads, and footpaths, on a single lime or horse-chestnut leaf. The so-called veins in a leaf he looked upon as roads; and, indeed, they were interminable roads to him, for one day, before he had accomplished that long-meditated journey, the sun unfor-tunately went down. He should have begun earlier, but the first dawn of morning had failed to wake him.

It was growing cold, the dew fell and the wind blew, and the most prudent thing for the delicate little gentleman to do was to get home as fast as possible. He hurried as much as he could, but before he reached the tree the roses were closed, so that he could not get in, and, alas! there was not a single rose within his reach open for his reception. The poor Elfin-prince was dreadfully frightened, for he had never been out so late before, but at that hour had always been safely slumbering behind the sweet roseleaf walls. Passing a night in the open air would, no doubt, cause his death in the bloom of youth, and the very thought of it gave him a shivering fit.

At the other end of the garden he knew there was a bower of splendid honeysuckle, and here he determined to pass the night.

Quickly he flew thither—but softly! In the bower were two beings anxious to hide from every obtrusive eye; the one, a hand-some young man, and the other, the most charming girl. They

were sitting side by side, and their sincerest wish was never to be
parted, for they loved each other very much; but the young man
said, with a heavy sigh—

"We must part, for your brother is not well-disposed towards
me, and, therefore, he now sends me on a disagreeable commission, far from here, across mountains and rivers. Farewell, my
dearest, my own beloved!"

They kissed each other again and again, the young girl crying
bitterly, and, at parting, she gave him a rose; but, before doing so,
she pressed a kiss upon it, so fervently that the flower opened. The
little Elf immediately slipped in amongst the leaves and, exhausted, rested his head against the soft, sweet-smelling walls; but
he could hear that "Farewell! farewell!" and he felt that the rose
had its place on the young man's heart. Oh, how that heart beat!
so violently, indeed, that the little Elf could not sleep.

The rose did not long remain quiet in its resting-place, for the
young man drew it forth, and as he walked alone through the
dark forest he kissed it so often and so passionately that the Elfin-
prince was near being squeezed to death. But too sensibly could he
feel, through the, at least, ten-leaf-thick covering, how the youth's
lips burned, and the rose had completely unfolded itself as in the
heat of the midday sun.

Another man then appeared, with a fierce, sinister-looking
countenance, and this was the wicked brother of the beautiful girl.
He held a large, sharp knife in his hand, and whilst the other was
kissing the rose, treacherously stabbed him in the back. He then
cut off his victim's head, which, together with the body, he buried
under a large lime-tree, where the ground was soft.

"Now he is gone, and will be forgotten," the villain said. "He
was to go a long journey, across rivers and mountains, and, travelling, one may easily lose one's life. He will never return, and never
will my sister dare to ask me about him."

With his foot he then drew some dead leaves together over the
newly-dug grave, and in the dark night returned home, but not
alone, as he thought. The little Elf accompanied him, seated in a
withered, curled-up lime leaf, which had fallen into the murderer's
hair whilst he was digging the grave, for he had taken off his hat,
and when he resumed it the leaf was underneath. The Elf was
now in the most terrifying darkness, which made him tremble
doubly with fear and anger at the horrible crime.

The wicked man reached home early in the morning, and
having taken off his hat, went at once into his sister's bedroom.

The beautiful girl was asleep, dreaming of him she loved so inexpressibly, and who, she thought, was then wandering over the mountains; but her unnatural brother, guessing her thoughts as he bent over her, laughed as one would imagine a fiend only could laugh, and, as he did so, the withered leaf fell out of his hair upon the bed. He did not notice it, but left the room to seek a few hours' rest in his own. The little Elf now left the leaf, and cautiously creeping into the sleeping girl's ear told her, as if it were a dream, of the horrible murder, minutely describing the place where her lover was buried, and finally said, "That you may not think what I tell you is a mere dream, you will, on awaking, find a withered leaf upon your bed." She awoke immediately and found it there.

Oh, what bitter tears she shed! And to no one dared she discover the cause of her sorrow and despair, which bordered upon insanity. The whole day her window stood open, and easily could the tender-hearted Elfin-prince have flown out to the roses and other flowers, but he would not leave the poor girl in her sorrow, so he seated himself in a rose that stood in the window and watched her. Her brother came into the room several times during the day, and the poor girl was obliged to hide the grief which was consuming her heart, but as soon as night approached she stole quietly out of the house and hurried into the forest, which was familiar to her, where she sought the lime-tree under which the darling of her heart lay buried. With her tender hands she dug up the earth, and soon found the lifeless body of her lover. How she cried and prayed to God that she, too, might soon die!

Gladly would she have carried the body home, but, unable to do that, she raised the head, kissed its cold lips, and, having filled up the grave again, took it with her, as well as a twig of jasmine which grew near the spot where the murder had been committed.

Having reached her quiet little room she took a large empty flower-pot, put the head in, and, having covered it with mould, planted the jasmine-twig.

"Farewell, farewell!" the little Elf whispered, and, finding it impossible to witness so much sorrow, he flew into the garden to his rose-tree, but the roses had withered; and as he sought another dwelling he sighed, "Oh, how quickly all that is beautiful and great passes away!"

Every morning, early, he flew to the poor girl's window, and there he always found her crying by the side of the flower-pot in which, watered incessantly by her tears, the jasmine-twig took root; and as, day after day, she grew paler, it sent forth shoots, and at length the little white buds became flowers. But her wicked brother could not imagine why she was always crying over the "foolish flower-pot," and he scolded, asking, since when had she lost her senses, for he did not know what treasure it contained. One day, when the little Elfin-prince came from his rose to pay her a visit he found her dozing, and creeping into her ear, he told her of the night in the bower, of the scent of the rose, and the love of the Elves. She dreamed so delightfully, and during the dream her life passed away; she had died an easy death, and was now in heaven with him whom she loved beyond everything.

The jasmine-flowers opened their white bells and sent forth such a delightfully sweet perfume, for that was the only way they could cry over her who was dead.

The wicked brother thoughtfully examined the beautiful tree, now in full blossom, which he had placed in his bedroom close to the bed, for it was so very pretty, and the scent so delightful; but the little Elf went with it, fluttering from flower to flower, for in each flower dwelt a spirit, and he told of the young man whose head was now earth under the earth; he told of the wicked brother and his poor sister.

"We know it already," the spirit answered from each of the flowers; "we know it, for have we not sprung up from between the lips and out of the eyes of the dead man? We know it! we know it." And as they said this they nodded their heads in a peculiar manner.

The Rose-elf could not imagine how it was they remained so quiet, and he flew away to the bees, who were gathering honey. He told them the story of the wicked brother, and the bees told their Queen, who immediately ordered that they should kill the hateful murderer the next morning.

But that very night—it was the first night after the sister's death—whilst the brother was lying in bed asleep, close to the jasmine-tree, every flower opened suddenly, and from each issued the spirit of the flower, invisible, but armed with a poisoned spear. They first whispered horrible dreams into his ear, and then, flying across his lips, pricked the sleeper's tongue with their spears. "Now we have avenged the murdered man," they said, and returned to their flowers.

As soon as it was morning, the window was violently thrown

open from the inside, and the Rose-elf with the Queen-bee and the whole swarm flew in to hold judgment on the murderer.

But he was already dead, and by his bed-side people were standing who said, "The strong scent from the jasmine has killed him."

The Rose-elf then understood the revenge of the flowers, and he told it to the Queen-bee, who with her whole swarm surrounded the mysterious flower-pot. They could not be driven off, and when one of the bystanders took it up to carry it away, the bees stung him so severely in the hand that he let it fall, and the broken pieces rolled about the floor.

With astonishment and horror the people saw the white skull, and they now knew that he who was lying dead in his bed was a murderer.

And the Queen of the bees flew out into the open air, humming the revenge of the flowers, the praise of the Rose-elf, and how beneath the smallest leaf dwells one who can expose and avenge crime.

THE WILD SWANS

FAR from here, in the favoured country whither the swallows fly, when with us all is covered with snow, there lived a King, who had eleven sons and one daughter named Elsie. The eleven brothers, all born princes, went to school with stars on their breasts and swords at their sides, and wrote with diamond pens on gold tablets. It could be seen at once that they were of royal blood. The sister, Elsie, sat in the meanwhile on a little stool of looking-glass, turning over the leaves of a picture-book which had cost half a kingdom.

Oh! those children were very happy, although their good mother was no longer living; but that was not to last.

Their father, who reigned over the whole land, married a wicked Queen, who could not bear the dear little children. Already, on her wedding-day, she plainly showed her unnatural feelings towards them, for although there was great feasting and rejoicing going on in the palace, she gave the children only a little sand in a tea-cup, telling them to imagine that was something nice, whereas they had been accustomed to have as much sweet cake and as many roasted apples as they could eat.

The very next week the wicked step-mother sent little Elsie into the country to rough peasants, and before long she had told the weak King so much that was bad of the hated princes that he no longer troubled himself about them.

"Fly out into the wide world," the wicked Queen said, "and take care of yourselves. Fly away as large birds without voices." However, it did not happen quite as she wished, for they were changed into eleven beautiful wild swans, and with a peculiar scream they flew out of the palace across the park and the forest.

It was still quite early in the morning when they came to the peasant's hut where their sister Elsie was lying fast asleep. They flew repeatedly round the roof, turning their long necks first to one side and then to the other, looking for their sister, and flapped with their wings; but no one heard them nor saw them, and they had to continue their flight, high up towards the clouds, and far, far into the vast, boundless world.

Poor little Elsie, in the meantime, sat in the peasant's room playing with a green leaf, for she had no other plaything. She pricked a hole in the leaf with a pin, and looked through it up at the sun, when it seemed to her as if she saw her brothers' clear, bright eyes, and whenever the warm rays of the sun fell upon her cheeks she thought of all their affectionate kisses.

One day passed exactly like the others, and when the wind blew through the rose-bush hedge, by the side of the hut, it whispered to the Roses, "Who can possibly be more beautiful than you?" and the Roses answered, "Oh, Elsie is more beautiful." And when on Sundays the old woman sat at her door reading the Psalm-book, the wind turned over the leaves and said, "Who can be better than you?" "Oh, Elsie is better!" the Psalm-book answered. And what the Roses and the Book said was true.

At the age of fifteen she was fetched home, but when the Queen saw how beautiful she had grown, she was inflamed with envy and anger, and hated her lovely step-daughter twice as much as before. She would gladly have changed her into a wild swan, like her brothers, but she dared not, for the King wished to see his daughter.

Early in the morning the Queen took three hideous toads into the bath-room with her, which was built of marble, and most extravagantly furnished and decorated, and affectionately kissing the nasty creatures, she said to the one, "Seat yourself on Elsie's head when she gets into the bath, so that she may be as stupid and sleepy as you are." "Take your seat," she said to the second, "on her forehead, that she may be as ugly as yourself, and that her father may not recognise her." And to the third she said, "Seat yourself upon her heart, so that she may have a bad, spiteful disposition, which will consume her like slow poison." She then threw the toads into the clear water, which immediately assumed a green tinge, and having called Elsie to her, with cruel delight helped her to undress and get into the water. No sooner did the unsuspecting princess dip under the water than the three toads took their appointed places, the first in her hair, the second on her forehead, and the third on her breast; but she did not seem to notice it. When she rose from the water, three red poppies floated on its surface. If the creatures had not been poisonous and kissed by the witch, they would have been changed into red roses, but flowers they still became, because they had rested upon Elsie's head and heart. She was much too good and innocent for the charm to take any effect upon her.

When the wicked step-mother saw this, she rubbed Elsie all over with walnut-juice, so that her skin, formerly as white as snow, became a dark brown colour. She then smeared her lovely face over with an offensive salve, and rubbed it into her beautiful soft hair till it was inextricably entangled, so that it was utterly impossible to recognise the charming Elsie.

Her father was horrified, when the Queen, with ill-concealed delight, led her to him, and the deceived monarch disowned her as his daughter; nor was there any one found who would acknowledge knowing her. Only the house-dog and the swallows, in their own particular ways, greeted the discarded Princess as an old and loved acquaintance; but what good could they do, poor creatures?

Poor Elsie wept, and thinking of her eleven lost brothers with a heavy heart stole out through the castle-gate, and after wandering the whole day over fields and through swamps, entered a large, dark forest. She had not the slightest idea which way to turn her steps, but she was so dejected, and felt such an inexpressible longing after her brothers, who, no doubt, like herself, were now wandering about the world, that to seek and find them must henceforth be the task of her whole life.

She had been only a short time in the forest when it became night, and having lost all trace of a path, despondingly she stretched herself upon the soft moss, and having said her evening prayer, leant her head against the stump of a tree, which had in all probability been destroyed by lightning. A soft, melancholy stillness reigned through the whole of nature; the air was so mild, and all around shone hundreds of glow-worms, which fell down upon her like shooting-stars when she touched one of the branches which formed a covering to her.

The whole night she dreamed of her brothers; they were again playing joyfully together like children, wrote with their diamond pencils on the gold tablets, and turned over the leaves of the splendid picture-book which had cost half a kingdom. But her grown-up brothers no longer scribbled mere noughts and strokes, but wrote down, in intelligible words, all their deeds, and all that they had experienced and seen. The tablets assumed a new and far greater importance, and in the picture-book all was alive. The different figures stepped out from the book, kindly speaking to Elsie and her brothers, but as each leaf was turned over they went back to their places, so that the order and the story of the pictures might not be interfered with. For order rules the world.

When she awoke from her refreshing sleep the sun was already high up in the heavens. She could not see it, indeed, for the branches of the trees formed so close a covering over her head, but here and there a ray broke through like burnished gold. A balmy scent filled the air, and the birds seated themselves upon her shoulders. She heard the splashing of water, for several running streams emptied themselves together into a lake, the bottom of which was strewed with the most inviting sand. The luxuriant creepers and bushes here formed an impenetrable barrier; but in one place the deer had made an opening, and through this Elsie crept to reach the water, which was so clear that if the wind had not moved the branches and leaves, she would have almost thought the reflection of them a skilful imitation, painted at the bottom, so clearly was each leaf reflected, that on which the bright sun shone being no clearer than that which was in the shade.

When she saw her own face in the clear water, she started back in surprise and horror, she was so brown and ugly; but when she wetted her little hands and rubbed her eyes and forehead, her snow-white skin shone gradually brighter and brighter through the nasty coating. Elsie was so delighted at this that she did not hesitate to throw off her clothes and entrust herself to the clear, refreshing water. And a more beautiful daughter of royalty than she was never seen in the world.

No sooner was she dressed again, and had simply but prettily plaited her hair, than she went to one of the bubbling springs, and having drunk out of the hollow of her hand, wandered joyously deeper and deeper into the forest, without knowing where she was going. She thought of her brothers, and of her heavenly Father, who would certainly not forsake her, for He made the wild-fruits grow to feed the hungry. She soon found a tree of beautiful apples, which hung nearly down to the ground, and of these she made her morning meal. When she was satisfied, she gratefully put props under the heavy, hanging branches, and pursued her way through the darkest part of the forest. All was so still that she plainly heard her own footsteps and the rustling of each leaf as she lightly trod upon it; not a single bird was to be seen, and no ray of the sun could penetrate the thick, leafy covering. The high trunks of the trees stood so close together that they looked like the bars of a railing, and here reigned a solitude such as she had never before known.

It grew darker and darker, till it was quite night; not a single glow-worm was to be seen, and quite sad Elsie laid herself down to sleep. Then it seemed to her as if the branches above her head were suddenly drawn back, and she saw an angel looking kindly down upon her from heaven. When she awoke the next morning she did not know whether she had merely dreamed this, or whether it was really true.

She went on a few steps, when she met an old woman with all sorts of wild berries in a basket. She gave Elsie some of them; and to her question, whether she had happened to see eleven Princes ride through the forest, she answered,—

"No; but yesterday I saw eleven swans, with golden crowns upon their heads, swim down the brook that runs close by here."

She led Elsie a short distance towards some sloping ground which was a little less thickly wooded; and there, indeed, she saw a stream below. The trees on the banks of this stream stretched forth their branches as if lovingly striving to meet; and where the natural growth of the trees would not allow this, their roots had torn themselves from the earth, and spread over the quiet surface of the water.

Elsie wished the old woman a friendly farewell, and followed the windings of the stream till it flowed into the sea.

The grand expanse of sea was majestically spread out before the young girl's eyes, but no sail was to be seen, and how should she now go further? She examined the innumerable stones on the shore, and all had been polished smooth and round by the water. Glass, iron, stones, and all that had been thrown up there was ground to one form by the waves, although the water was much softer than her tender hands.

"It rolls incessantly backwards and forwards, and thus the hard edges are gradually ground off," she uttered, involuntarily. "I also will have untiring perseverance, and my heart tells me that some day I shall find my dearly beloved brothers. Many thanks, you clear, rolling waves, for the lesson!"

On the seaweed that had been washed on to shore lay eleven white swans' feathers, which she quickly picked up and tied together. Single, clear drops of water hung upon them like pearls, as if, by their purity, to heighten the charm of the beautiful feathers; but whether those drops were the morning dew or tears, no one could distinguish. It was solitary there on the shore, but Elsie scarcely felt it, for the sea offered constant variety; yes, more in a few hours than a dozen of the most picturesque lakes can show in a year. When a large, dark cloud came floating along in the air, it seemed as if the sea said, "I can look black too." And then the wind blew, and the waves threw up their white foam. If, on the contrary, the clouds were red and transparent, the sea looked like a gigantic rose-leaf; but soon it changed colour, as if it were fading, for at one time it was green, then blue and then white; and, however calm and quiet the water was, there was a constant noise, like breathing, on the shore, and the waves rose gently, like the breast of a sleeping child.

When the sun was going down, Elsie saw eleven wild swans, with gold crowns upon their heads, flying towards her. They floated high up in the air, once behind the other, forming in appearance a fluttering silver ribbon. Elsie then mounted an eminence that was near, and hid herself behind a bush, and soon the swans alighted by her side, flapping their large white wings.

The very instant that the sun had entirely disappeared behind the water the swans' feathers fell off, and, behold! there stood eleven handsome Princes by Elsie's side. These were her brothers. She uttered a loud cry; for although they had altered much, she knew them, and felt that it must be they. She threw herself into their arms, calling each by his name, and they were no less filled with delight to see their little sister, who had grown so tall and so wonderfully beautiful. They laughed and cried by turns at this unexpected meeting, and soon they had related to each other how cruel their step-mother had been to them all.

"We eleven," the eldest said, "fly about as wild swans as long as the sun is up in the heavens; but when it has gone down, we regain our human form; and, therefore, we must be careful to find a resting-place for our feet towards evening; for should the sun set whilst we were high up in the clouds, we should, as human beings, fall down to our destruction. We do not live here, but on the other side of the sea, where there is a country as beautiful as this, which is, however, very far, and there is not a single island where we can pass the night, only a small rock rises from amidst the rolling waves. This rock is merely just large enough for us to lie upon, close, side by side; and when the sea is rough, the water is thrown up over us; but yet we are thankful for that dangerous resting-place. There we pass the night in our human forms; and without that place of refuge we should never be able to visit our own dear country, for it requires two of the longest days in the year to accomplish the distance. Only once a year are we allowed to visit the land of our birth; and then we can remain eleven days and fly over this vast forest, from whence we can see the proud palace where we were born, and where our father lives, and the high steeple of the church where our dear mother lies buried. Here it seems as if the trees and bushes were related to us; here the wild horses race with joyous leaps across the grassy plains, just like during the days of our happy youth; and here the charcoal-burners sing their old songs, to which, as boys, we delighted to dance. This is our country, to which we are irresistibly drawn, and here we have at last found you, our own dear, beautiful sister! We have still two days to remain; but then we must fly across the sea to a country which, though beautiful, is unfortunately not our home. How can we take you with us, for we have neither ship nor boat?"

"Oh, how can I save you?" the Princess said, sighing.

They passed nearly the whole night talking to each other, and only a couple of hours before daybreak were devoted to sleep.

Elsie was waked by the noise of the swans' wings, and, already high above her, she saw her brothers, who had been again changed, flying in wide circles, till they were lost in the distance. But one, the youngest of them, remained behind; and the swan laid its head in her lap, whilst she stroked his white plumage, and the whole day the brother and sister were side by side. Towards evening the others returned; and when the sun had fully gone down, they all appeared again in their natural forms.

"Tomorrow we fly away from here," the eldest said; and the other ten confirmed these words, spoken with evident emotion; "but we cannot thus forsake you. If you have the inclination and courage to go with us, we certainly shall have strength enough in our wings to carry you across the sea."

"Yes, take me with you!" Elsie said, beseechingly.

That whole night, without once closing their eyes, the eleven brothers spent in unremitting industry over the difficult task of making a net sufficiently large and strong, of the peel of the young willow-branches and of tough reeds. On this they laid Elsie; and when the sun rose, and they had been changed into swans, they laid hold of the net with their beaks and flew high up towards the clouds with their dear sister, who was still asleep. One of the swans constantly flew over her head, in order to shade her with his large wings from the rays of the sun.

They were already far from land when Elsie awoke, and it seemed to her as if she must still be dreaming, so strange it was to be floating in the air above the sea. By her side, on the net, lay a branch covered with delicious berries, and a handful of sweet-tasting roots, which her youngest brother had gathered for her; and she smiled him her thanks, for she guessed it was he who was flying above, shading her with his wings.

They were up so high that the first ship which they saw under them looked only like a white gull floating on the water. A huge cloud, like a mountain, hung in the air behind them, and on this magic background she saw the shadow of herself and the eleven swans of a gigantic size. She thought she had never seen so beautiful a painting; but, as the sun rose higher and they left the cloud further behind them, the picture gradually faded.

With untiring exertion they sped through the air during the whole day, like the whizzing of the swiftest arrow; but yet, having their sister to carry, their flight was not so fast as usual. A storm was blowing up towards evening, and with fear Elsie saw the sun sinking, when there was yet no rock to be seen. She thought the swans' wings moved quicker; that they could not get on faster she knew was her fault. When the sun had disappeared, they would be changed to human beings, and falling into the sea, be drowned. The thought of this almost killed her, and then she prayed most fervently to God, but still her strained eyes could not discover the saving rock. The dark clouds came lower and lower till at last they seemed to form one black mass with the element below, which rolled on like a sea of lead. One flash of lightning followed rapidly upon the other.

The sun was now close upon the edge of the water. Oh, how Elsie's heart beat! Then the swans shot down with such velocity that she thought they were falling; but they floated in the air again, and, now that the sun had half disappeared, she saw the point of the rock below, no larger than the head of a porpoise, rising above the sea. The sun sank so swiftly, and now it only

appeared as a star when Elsie felt her foot touch the firm rock.
Then the sun disappeared like the last spark in smouldering paper,
and the terrified Princess saw her eleven brothers, arm-in-arm,
standing in a close circle around her; but there was only just room
for the twelve. The sea broke furiously against the rising rock,
throwing its spray over the half-fearing and half-hoping sister and
brothers. The thunder continued to roll, and the sky seemed as if
on fire; but the twelve stood hand-in-hand, joined in the bond of
truest love and affection, and they fervently sang some hymns in
praise of their heavenly Father, which filled them with renewed
hope and courage. With the break of day the sky became clear,
and as soon as the sun rose the swans flew away with Elsie from
their little resting-place. The sea was still rough; and, from the
height they were flying, the white foam on the dark green water
looked like a number of swans floating along its surface.

When the sun had risen high up in the heavens, Elsie saw
beneath her, floating in the air, a mass of mountains with ice-
covered rocks, and in the midst of them a place miles in length,
with one row of columns rising above another. There were also
forests of palm-trees, and the most wonderful flowers, as large as
the wheels of a water-mill. She asked if that were the country to
which they were going; but the swans shook their heads, for what
she saw was the splendid, constantly-changing Palace of the Fairy
"Morgana," which no human being might enter. Elsie kept her
eyes immovably fixed on the splendour below her, when mountains, palaces and forests fell together in one chaotic mass,
and in their places stood twenty proud churches, exactly like
each other, with pointed windows and high steeples. She thought
she heard organs, but it was the melodious murmuring of the sea.
They were now close upon the churches, which, however, changed
into a fleet of stately ships, and when she looked down upon them
these were again changed into a sea-mist, which, like swelling sails,
swept along the surface of the water. A constant change was going
on before her eyes, one picture taking the place of the other; and
now she at length saw the real land, which for a time was to be
her and her brothers' abode. There arose, in soft outlines, the most
wonderful blue mountains, cedar forests, cities, and palaces; and
long before the sun had gone down, Elsie sat before a cave covered
inside and out with luxuriant green creepers, as if decorated by
the hand of Nature with the most costly tapestry.

"Now we shall see what you dream here to-night," her youngest
brother said, as he showed her her sleeping apartment.

"Oh, may I but dream how I can disenchant you!" she said, and this thought occupied her incessantly till she retired to rest. She then prayed fervently for assistance, and even in sleep her prayer continued, till it seemed to her as if she were floating high up in the air, towards the cloud palace of the Fairy "Morgana," when the Fairy herself came towards her, so beautiful and luminous, and yet resembling the old woman who had given her the berries in the forest, and told her of the eleven swans with the golden crowns.

"Your brothers can be saved," the Fairy said; "but will you have sufficient courage and perseverance to accomplish the difficult task? Certainly the sea is softer than your delicate hands, and yet it polishes the hard stones; but then it does not feel the pain your tender fingers will have to experience; it has no heart and therefore cannot suffer from the anxiety and agony you must necessarily endure. Do you see these stinging-nettles in my left hand? Of these there are quantities growing round the cave in which you sleep; such only and those which are sometimes seen on the graves in the churchyard serve the purpose for which they are required—remember this. You must gather them yourself, if even they raise blisters on your skin. These you must crush with your naked feet, and you will obtain yarn, with which you must make eleven shirts with long sleeves, and throw them over the wild swans. If you succeed in this, as I trust you will, the charm will be immediately broken; but, of all things, do not forget what I am about to say. From the moment that you begin your work up to the hour—the very minute—that the task is accomplished, you must not speak a single word, if even years should pass by, for the first syllable your lips should utter would penetrate your brothers' hearts like a dagger. On your tongue hang their lives. Remember all this!"

The Fairy then touched the sleeping girl's hand with the nettles, and she was awakened by the burning pain. It was broad daylight, and close by her side lay a nettle, just like those she had seen in her dream. She fell upon her knees, thanked her heavenly Father for His mercy, and left the cave, in order to begin her work.

She thrust her tender hands amongst the nasty nettles, which burned like red-hot coals, so that her hands and arms were covered with blisters; but that she would cheerfully bear, if she could but save her dear brothers. She crushed each nettle with her naked feet, and with her blistered fingers wound the yarn.

Immediately after sunset her brothers came, and they were greatly frightened to find her apparently dumb. They thought, at first, it was a new charm of their wicked step-mother's; but when they saw the dreadful state of their noble sister's hands, and the nettles by her side, they understood what she was doing for their sakes, and the youngest cried bitterly over her. Wherever his tears fell she felt no pain, and the burning blisters disappeared.

The whole night she continued her work without ceasing, for she could have no rest till she had saved her dear brothers; and the whole of the following day, whilst the swans were absent, she sat at work in her solitude, and never had the time flown so quickly. One shirt was finished, and instantly she began another.

All of a sudden she heard the merry sound and echo of huntsmen's horns amongst the mountains, and the young Princess was filled with fear and dread. The noise came nearer and nearer, till she plainly heard the barking of the dogs, and, trembling with anxiety, she withdrew into the cave, and, having tied the nettles, which she had gathered and crushed, into a bundle, she seated herself upon it, as if to protect this her most valuable treasure from all danger.

The next moment a large, fierce-looking dog broke through the bushes, and immediately after a second, and then a third. They barked furiously, ran back, and then appeared again, and in a few minutes all the huntsmen stood before the cave, of whom the handsomest was King of the land. Quickly he advanced towards Elsie. Never had he seen so beautiful a girl.

"How did you get here, you lovely child?" he asked; but Elsie shook her head sadly, for she dared not speak, as her brothers' lives depended upon it, at the same time hiding her hands under her apron, that the King might not see what she was suffering.

"Follow me," he said; "for here you must not remain; and if you are as good as you are beautiful, I will clothe you in silk and satin, place the golden crown upon your head, and you shall dwell in my splendid palace." With these words he lifted the fainting and struggling Princess upon his horse; and as she continued to cry and wring her hands, he said, "Calm yourself, you lovely girl! for it is only your good I wish, and some day you will thank me with all your heart." He galloped off over the beautiful mountains, carrying his lovely burden before him on his horse, and the huntsmen followed.

Towards sunset the magnificent, regal city, with its churches and domes, rose from the valley, forming an inimitable panorama; and the King hastened to conduct his charming companion to the palace, where sparkling fountains played in the lofty marble halls, decorated with paintings and curiosities; but she had no eyes for all the splendour, as, buried in grief, she continued to cry. Unresistingly she allowed the ladies' maids to array her in princely garments, put pearls in her hair, and draw silk gloves on her blistered hands.

As she now appeared, her beauty was so dazzling that the whole court bowed down before her, and the King at once declared her his future bride, although the archbishop shook his head, whispering to his friends that the beautiful forest maiden was no doubt a witch, who fascinated and deceived the King.

But the King shut his ears to such suspicions, the music sounded louder, the most delicious refreshments were provided, and he hastened the preparations for more splendid festivities. Through the most delightful gardens Elsie was conducted to splendid apartments, where the loveliest girls surrounded her with joyous dances; but no smile parted her lips, nor ray of merriment lighted up her eyes; no, every feature, and her whole expression, denoted the deepest, all-consuming sadness. The King then opened a small room, by the side of her sleeping apartment, which was painted and fitted up in exact imitation of the cave in the forest where he had found her. On the floor lay the yarn which she had made from the nettles, and which in spite of her surprise and fear, she had so carefully made up into a bundle, and from the ceiling hung the one shirt she had already finished.

"Here you can, in imagination, return to your former home," the King said. "Here is the work at which you were occupied, and it may, perhaps, in the midst of all the present splendour, afford you pleasure to think sometimes of the past."

When Elsie saw these things, which were of such inestimable value to her, a happy smile played around her lovely mouth, and the blood returned to her cheeks. She thought of the time when she could save her brothers, and in the overflowing of her gratitude she kissed the King's hand. He pressed her to his beating heart, and ordered all the church-bells to proclaim their speedy marriage. The charming dumb girl of the forest was Queen of the country.

The suspicious archbishop whispered evil words into the King's ear, but they did not sink as deep as his heart. The marriage took place, and the archbishop himself had to place the crown upon the bride's head, which he pressed down so heavily that it hurt her forehead; but grief and anxiety for her brothers caused her heart much more intense suffering. What was bodily pain? Her mouth remained dumb, for a single word would have destroyed her brothers' lives, but her eyes expressed the deepest love for the good, handsome King, who left nothing untried to cheer her. Daily she became more devoted to him; oh, could she but have confided in him all her grief! But she must remain dumb till her task should be completed. For this she stole away from his side at nights, and hurried to the little room, like the cave in the forest, of which she always carried the key with her. Here she worked, finishing one shirt after the other, but when she wanted to begin the seventh she had no more yarn.

She knew that in the churchyard the same sort of nettles grew, which she might use, but she must gather them herself, and how could she do that unnoticed?

"Oh! what is the pain in my fingers," she thought, "compared to the agitation of my heart? It must be ventured, and my heavenly Father will not withdraw His protection from me in this hour of trial." With fear and trembling, as if she were about to commit a bad action, she stole down into the garden, through the avenue and along the deserted streets to the churchyard. With horror, she there beheld a circle of the most revolting witches, who threw off their disgusting rags, and began digging with their long, bony fingers down into the newly-made graves. She had to pass close by the side of them, and they fixed their evil eyes upon her, but, praying to herself, she hastily gathered the burning nettles and carried them home to the palace.

Only one human being had seen her during her night expedition, and that was the archbishop, who was up and awake whilst the others were sleeping. There could be no doubt now that his suspicions were well founded, that all was not right with the Queen. She was evidently a wicked sorceress, who had bewitched the King and all the people.

He told the King his suspicions, and all that he had seen; and as his venomous tongue, with cruel eloquence, uttered the words, the carved images of the saints shook their heads, as if to say, "It is not so, Elsie is innocent." But the archbishop explained it otherwise, maintaining that they confirmed his words. Two large tears rolled down the King's cheeks, and with the first seeds of suspicion sowed in his breast he returned to the palace. At night he pretended to be asleep, but watched Elsie as she got up. Every night she repeated this, and each time he followed her noiselessly and saw her enter the little room, the door of which she immediately locked after her.

Day after day the King's countenance became more sombre, and

Elsie, in secret, fretted at this change, the reason for which she could not guess; and her heart was, besides, torn by the most acute suffering on account of her unfortunate brothers, who, as wild swans, were still wandering about far from her. Bitter tears fell upon the satin and velvet of her attire, where they lay like glittering diamonds; but all the people, seeing such splendour, only envied her. Her task was at length nearly accomplished; only one shirt still remained to be done; but she had no more yarn, and not a single nettle of which to make any. Once more, therefore, and now for the last time, she must go to the churchyard to gather a few handfuls. She shuddered at the thought of that lonely walk and the hateful witches, but her will was as firm as her trust in the Ruler of the destiny of man.

Elsie went, but followed at a distance by the King and the archbishop, who lost sight of her as she disappeared through the churchyard-gate, which they no sooner reached than they saw the witches as Elsie had seen them. Shuddering, the King averted his face from the scene of horror, for in the midst of the group he imagined her whose head but a short time back had rested on his breast.

"The people shall judge her," he said, in a scarcely audible voice; and the people condemned her to be burned.

She was dragged from her magnificent rooms to a damp hole, where the wind whistled incessantly through the window, but ill secured by the rusty iron bars. Instead of velvet and satin, they gave her the bundle of nettles she herself had gathered in the churchyard, for her to lay her head upon; and for a covering they gave her the harsh burning shirts she had made. Nothing could have been so welcome to her, and immediately she resumed her painful work, praying at the same time with increased fervour. The rabble sang songs in derision of her, and there was not one being to console her with a single word of pity.

Towards evening she heard the "whirring" of a swan's wings close to the grating of her window. It was her youngest brother who at length had found her, and she smiled with delight and happiness, though there was scarcely a doubt but that this would be her last night. But now her work was nearly finished, and her brothers were at hand.

The archbishop came to pass the last hours with her, as he had promised the King; but she shook her head, and by signs gave him to understand that she wished to be left alone. In this the most important night of her life, her work must be finished, or all would have been in vain—all—her sufferings, tears, silence, and sleepless nights. The archbishop went away uttering angry words, but poor Elsie knew that she was innocent, and without ceasing she continued her work.

The little mice ran about the floor quite tame and fearlessly; they dragged the nettles and laid them at her feet, that they might be of some use to her, and a thrush sat on one of the iron bars of her window, singing as merrily as it possibly could during the whole night, that the prisoner might not lose her courage.

It was just break of day, an hour before the rising of the sun, when the eleven brothers appeared at the palace gate and desired earnestly to be conducted to the King, but they were answered that it was impossible, as it was still night, and they dared not wake the King from his sleep. They begged, they threatened, when the guards came, and at length the King himself. Just then the sun rose, and no longer were any brothers to be seen, but eleven wild swans flew over the palace.

An innumerable concourse of people crowded together to witness the burning of the witch. A miserable horse, a walking skeleton, dragged the cart in which she sat. A loose smock of sackcloth had been thrown over her, and her beautiful long hair hung down upon her shoulders, surrounding her noble face, childishly pious, like that of an angel. She was made as pale as death, and there was a scarcely perceptible movement of her lips, whilst her fingers with strained velocity strove to finish the almost-accomplished task, which she would not give up, even on her way to death. At her feet lay the ten finished shirts.

"Look at the witch!" the rabble cried, "how she presses her lips together. There is no hymn-book in her hands—no, she is going on with her horrid sorcery. Let us tear her work into a thousand shreds."

They began to press upon her, intending to deprive her of the fruits of the noblest sisterly sacrifice and love, when eleven white swans surrounded her, and the crowd fell back in terror.

"That is a sign from heaven of her innocence," many whispered, but they dared not say it out loud.

The executioner now laid hold of the unfortunate Princess's hand, when hastily she threw the eleven shirts over the swans, and in their places there suddenly stood eleven handsome princes; but the youngest of them had a swan's wing instead of one of his arms, for one sleeve was wanting to his shirt, though his good sister Elsie had striven with unexampled industry to finish it.

"Now I may speak," she said. "I am innocent!"

And the people, who saw what had happened, bowed down before her, whilst she sank lifeless into her brothers' arms, so violently had anxiety, fear, and pain affected her.

"Yes, she is innocent!" her eldest brother exclaimed, and whilst he was relating all the events that had occurred, a sweet scent, as of thousands of roses, filled the air, for each stick of a pile that was to consume the Princess had taken root, and they formed a high, thick hedge of dark red roses. But higher than the rest was one flower of dazzling whiteness, which shone as a silver star, crowning the red tint of a fine sunrise. This flower the King plucked and laid upon Elsie's breast, when animation, for a short time suspended, returned, and peace and happiness filled her heart.

All the bells rang of their own accord, whilst innumerable flights of birds gathered around, and there was a bridal procession back to the palace such as had never before been witnessed.

THE GOLOSHES OF FORTUNE

I

A Beginning

IN one of the houses in Copenhagen, not far from King's Newmarket, company had been invited—a very numerous company—in order, as is frequently done, to secure an invitation in return from the others. One half were already seated at the cardtables, whilst the other half were awaiting the result of the stereotyped introductory speech of the lady of the house, "Well, we must now really begin to think of what can be found for our amusement this evening." So far the conversation had advanced, when it began to crystallise on account of the scarcity of helping springs in this every-day world. Amongst other things, the conversation turned upon the middle ages, which some praised as more interesting and poetical than the over-steady present. The Minister of Justice, Knapp, supported his opinion so warmly that Madame attached herself to that party; and there was rivalry of eloquence between the two, the Minister of Justice declaring the times of King Hans to be the noblest and happiest.

Whilst this discussion was being carried on, only momentarily interrupted by the production of a worthless pamphlet, we will step into the ante-room, where the cloaks, mackintoshes, sticks, and goloshes, were kept. Here two women were seated, one young and the other old. At first they might have been taken for servants, come to accompany their mistress home; but, if examined more attentively, they would scarcely appear to be common servants, for their forms were too noble, and their skins too delicate; besides, there was something superior in their dress. They were two fairies; the younger not exactly Dame *Fortune* herself, but one of her lady's maids, who distribute the inferior gifts of fortune; whilst the elder, who looked particularly sombre, was *Care*. This high personage always attends to her business herself, for she is then sure that it is properly done.

They told each other, in confidential discourse, how they had been occupied during the day. *Fortune's* envoy had only executed some few unimportant commissions, such as saving a new hat from a shower of rain, and procuring for an honest man a nod from a noble nullity, and such like; but what still remained for her to do was something quite out of the common.

"I must tell you," she said, "that this is my birthday, and in honour of that a pair of goloshes have been entrusted to me to present to the human race. These goloshes possess this virtue, that whoever has them on is immediately transported to the time or place in which he would like to be. Every wish in respect of place, time or being is fulfilled on the instant, and the man made happy for once in his life."

"Do you believe that in earnest?" *Care* asked, in a tone of reproach. "On the contrary, he will be very unhappy, and will bless the moment when he is rid of the fatal goloshes again."

"Nonsense!" the other said, in anger. "Some one will make a mistake, and take the wrong over-shoes, and that will be the happy one."

Such was the conversation that took place between the two.

II

What happened to the Minister of Justice

IT was late when the Minister Knapp, deeply interested in the times of King Hans, thought of going home; and malicious fate brought it about that his feet slipped into the goloshes of Fortune instead of his own. Thus shod, he stepped out of the house, blazing with light, into Oster Street. Now, through the magic power of the goloshes, he was transported back to the times of King Hans, and, as a matter of course, his feet sank deeper into mud and puddles, for in those times the streets of Copenhagen were not paved.

"Why, this is too abominable!" he sighed. "How dirty it is here, and the lamps have all said good-night!"

The moon had not yet risen, and the air was, besides, not very clear, so that all was a dark chaos. At the first corner hung an old-fashioned lamp in front of a picture of the Virgin, but the light it gave was next to nothing. Indeed, he only noticed it when standing immediately under it; and his eye was attracted by the strange painting representing the Virgin with the infant Christ in the conventional style of old compositions.

"That is, no doubt," he thought, "some repository of art, where, in the vain hope of a late purchaser, they have delayed taking in the sign-board."

A couple of people in the costume of the time of King Hans passed quickly by.

"What strange figures! The good people come apparently from some masquerade."

Suddenly there was a loud sound of drums and fifes, and every now and then a bright red light shot up in the air, in strong contrast to the modest light of the torches.

The Minister of Justice stopped, and there passed a most extraordinary procession. In front were about a dozen drummers, who played by no means badly, followed by soldiers carrying cross-bows. Seeing that the principal person was clerical, the Minister of Justice asked in astonishment what this meant, and who that person was.

"It is the Bishop of Zealand," he was answered.

"Good gracious! what has come to the bishop?" the Minister of Justice said, shaking his head. It could not possibly be the bishop though he was considered, and that with justice, the most eccentric man in the whole kingdom, and the strangest anecdotes were told of him in the town. Meditating on all this, without looking to the right or to the left, the Minister walked along Oster Street and crossed Haebro Place. The bridge leading to Castle Place was nowhere to be found, and the night wanderer scarcely trusted his eyes when he discovered some dirty water and two men lazily lounging in a boat.

"Does the gentleman wish to cross over to Holme?" they asked.

"Cross over to Holme?" the Minister of Justice repeated, not having the slightest knowledge to what age he had for the time being transported. "No, I wish to go to Christianshaven, to Little Market Street."

The men only stared at him in surprise.

"Just tell me, if you please, where the bridge is?" he begged. "It is really disgraceful that the lamps are not lighted here; and as for the mud, it is exactly as if one were wading through a bog."

The longer he talked to the boatmen the less he understood them, and at length he turned his back upon them in a considerably bad humour. The bridge he could not find, nor was there a railing of any sort. "It is most scandalous what a state the whole place is in!" he grumbled, and never had he been so dissatisfied with the age he lived in, much as he railed at it. "I think I'll take a coach," he said, but where were the coaches? Not one was to be seen.

"I suppose I must go back to King's Newmarket, where it is to be hoped there will still be coaches, or I shall never reach Christianshaven."

So he returned along Oster Street, and had nearly reached the end of it when the moon burst forth.

"Good heavens!" he exclaimed, as he saw the Oster Gate, which in those times stood at the end of Oster Street, "what scaffolding and wood-work have they been raising here!"

He, however, found a little side-door open, and through this he stepped out into what is now Newmarket. It was a large waste common, with here and there a stunted, miserable bush, and right across the common ran a broad canal or stream. On the opposite bank lay scattered a few box-like booths for the Dutch sailors, on which account the place was called "the Dutch swamp."

"Either I behold *fata morgana,* or I am certainly tipsy," the Minister of Justice said, despondingly. "What can all this be?"

He turned again, in the firm belief that he was seriously ill. The street formerly so familiar to him was all strange now, for when he examined the houses, he saw that for the most part they were slightly built of wood, and many only had thatched roofs.

"I do not feel at all well," he sighed, "and yet I only drank one glass of punch, but then it never did agree with me; it was very wrong, too, to give us punch on hot salmon. I will speak to the Commissioner's lady about it the first opportunity. Shall I go back now and tell them my distress? No, that would look too foolish; besides, who knows whether they are still up?"

He looked for the house, however, but it had entirely disappeared.

"This is really dreadful!" he said, now seriously alarmed. "I no longer recognise Oster Street; there is not one decent shop remaining; nothing but the most miserable holes, as if it were the lowest part of the town. Oh, I am indeed ill, and must go back to the Commissioner's; but where is the house? It ought to stand on this very spot, but there is not the most distant resemblance. How everything is changed during this night! There must be someone up somewhere. Oh, dear, how ill I am!"

He found a door half open, and saw a faint light within. It was one of the inns of those times, a sort of beer-house; and on entering a good-sized room he saw numerous company, consisting of sailors, Copenhagen tradesmen, and a couple of men who seemed to belong to some learned profession, all being so engaged in conversation over their tin drinking mugs that the stranger's entrance was scarcely noticed.

"May I beg of you," the Minister of Justice said, to the bustling landlady, "to procure a coach for me to go to Christianshaven, for I have turned suddenly very unwell?"

The woman stared at him in astonishment, shaking her head, and then addressed him in German. The Minister of Justice, thinking that she did not understand the Danish language, repeated his request in German, and this, added to his costume, confirmed her in the belief that he was a foreigner. Perceiving, however, that he was unwell, she brought him a jug of water, which tasted rather strong of the sea, though it had been fetched from the pump outside.

The Minister of Justice rested his head on both hands, and, drawing a deep breath, meditated on all the strange events that had occurred, and on all he saw around him.

"Does that happen to be the 'Dagen' of this evening?" (a Copenhagen daily paper), he asked mechanically, seeing the landlady push a sheet of paper on one side.

The meaning of his question was, of course, utterly unintelligible to her, and instead of any answer she handed him the paper, which turned out to be a coarse wood-cut, representing an extraordinary appearance in the sky, "seen in the town of Cologne," as was printed below in illuminated characters.

"That is very old," the Minister said, considerably cheered by this piece of antiquity. "May I ask how you became possessed of this curious print? It is highly interesting, though it is nothing more than a fable. Such appearances are explained as being re-flections of the aurora borealis, caused, no doubt, principally by electricity."

Those who were sitting near, and heard what he said, looked at him now in astonishment, and one of them rising, respectfully took off his hat, and said, in a serious tone, "Monsieur is no doubt a very learned man."

"Oh no," the Minister of Justice answered, "I can only talk a little on general topics, as in the present age one is obliged to be able."

"*Modestia* is a becoming virtue," the gentleman resumed, "but I must say to your address *mihi secus videtur*, though I will not offer an opinion."

"May I ask with whom I have the honour of speaking?" the Minister of Justice said.

"I am a bachelor of Theology," the other answered, with a stiff bow.

This answer was highly satisfactory, for the title suited the costume, and the Minister of Justice thought, "He is, no doubt, some old village schoolmaster, an old original, such as may still be found in Jutland."

"It is true this is no *locus docendi,*" the reverend gentleman continued, "but I must still beg you will deem us worthy of your instruction. You are *sine dubio*, deeply read in the ancients."

"Oh, I am very fond of useful old writings, but I do not on that account despise the more modern," the Minister of Justice replied: "It is only the miserable stories of the day that I cannot bear."

"Stories of the day?" our bachelor asked.

"I mean those tame, stupid romances which are thrust upon the reading public."

"Oh," the theologian said smiling, "there is a good deal of wit in them too, and they are much read at court. The King is particu-larly fond of the story of Iffven and Gandian, which treats of King Arthur and his knights of the Round Table. He has frequently joked about it with his high vassals."

"I have not yet read that romance," the Minister of Justice said. "It must be quite a new one, published by Heiberg."

"No," the reverend gentleman of King Hans' time answered, "the book is printed by Godfried of Gehmen."

"Oh, that is a very old name," the Minister of Justice said. "If I recollect right, he was the first printer in Denmark."

"Yes, he is our first printer," the reverend gentleman replied.

So far all went well, and then one of the tradesmen spoke of the dreadful pestilence which had raged in the neighbourhood a few years past, meaning that in the year 1484; but the Minister of Justice supposed he meant the cholera of which there had been so much talk, and that passed off well. The war of 1490 was so recent that it was naturally touched upon, all agreeing that the English privateers had acted shamefully, and the Minister of Justice, who held very strong opinions respecting the occurrence of 1801, joined in most heartily against the English. The rest of the conversation, however, did not go on so smoothly, for it got into a confusion which threatened almost to become inextricable. The worthy bachelor was really too ignorant, whereas the simplest observations of the Minister of Justice appeared too bold and fantastic. They measured each other from head to foot, and when it got too bad, the bachelor spoke Latin, in the hope of making himself better understood, but that was of no use.

"How are you now?" the landlady asked, giving the Minister of Justice a gentle pull by the sleeve, and this brought him back to his senses, for in the heat of conversation he had clean forgotten all that had happened.

"Merciful heaven! where am I?" he exclaimed, in utter despair, and at this thought a momentarily increasing giddiness came over him, which all his energy could not resist.

"Let us have some claret and Bremen beer," one of the company cried out, "and you shall drink with us."

Two girls, in very strange costumes, now entered, and with a most familiar smile and nod filled the glasses. A cold perspiration trickled down the Minister of Justice's back, and he sighed, "What will happen next and what will become of me!" In spite of all his resistance he was forced to drink with them; and when he heard it said on all sides that he was drunk, he did not in the least doubt the truth of this not over-polite observation, but begged that the ladies and gentlemen would be good enough to procure him a coach. What he said, however, was no more intelligible to them than Hebrew.

He had never before been in such rough, uncivilised company, so that it almost seemed to him as if the heathenish times had come back again, and he thought, "This is the most dreadful moment of my life, for the whole world is leagued against me." It then suddenly occurred to him that he might get under the table, unobserved, and so creep to the door. He did so, but just at the moment he reached the entrance the others saw what his intention was, and they seized him by the legs. The fatal goloshes now fortunately fell off, and thus the spell was dissolved.

The Minister of Justice quite plainly saw a bright lamp burning before him, and behind this there stood a beautiful large house. All seemed in proper order, as of old; it was Oster Street exactly as we know it. He was lying with his feet on the step of a door, and just opposite to him sat the watchman asleep.

"Can it be possible," he exclaimed, "that I have been lying here and dreaming? Yes, it is Oster Street, and how beautifully light and clean! It is most extraordinary that one single glass of punch should have had such an effect upon me!"

Two minutes later he was seated in a coach being driven towards Christianshaven; and as he thought of his past anxiety and distress, he felt heartily thankful to the happy reality of the present time, for, with all its imperfections, how infinitely better it was than that to which he had just been transported!

III

The Watchman's Adventures

"Why, there are a pair of goloshes!" the watchman said, waking up from a sound sleep. "They, no doubt, belong to the lieutenant, who lives up there, for they are lying close to his door."

The honest man first thought of ringing and restoring them, for there was still light in the room; but on consideration, he did not do so, for fear of waking the other inmates of the house.

"It must be comfortable and warm to have such machines as those on," he said. "Oh, how elastic and soft they are!" They fitted him as if they had been moulded on his feet. "How curiously this world goes on!" he philosophised. "Now, there's the lieutenant might have been snug in bed long ago, where one can, no doubt, stretch out one's legs most comfortably, and yet there he is wandering up and down his room, because he possibly had too many good things at dinner. He is a happy man, for he has neither a needy mother nor a host of eternally hungry children. Every night he goes out into company, where he gets a good supper for nothing. Oh, could I but for once exchange with him, how happy I should be!"

As he uttered the wish the magic power of the goloshes began to operate, and the watchman's very being passed into that of the lieutenant. There he stood in the handsomely-furnished room, and held between his fingers a sheet of pink note paper, on which a poem was written, the officer himself being the author; for who has not, at least once in his life, had a moment of lyric inspiration? and if one writes down one's thoughts, that is poetry. Now here was written—

"OH, WERE I RICH!

"Oh, were I rich! that fervent wish, in truth,
Was very often mine in early youth.
Oh, were I rich! an officer I'd be,
With sword and uniform so gay and free!
As time passed on this gift was granted me,
An officer I was, but riches never
Were mine, for still I am poor as ever.

"Yes, rich I was in one thing—poetry,
And loved a girl, who fondly clung to me.
Charmed by the fund of rich, poetic lore,
Of which I had a never-ending store.
For this she craved, and wished for nothing more.
Then did I pray that nothing might us sever;
But no, alas! that could not last for ever.

"Oh, were I rich! so sounds to heaven my prayer:
I've watched that girl grow up so tall and fair,—
She is so good, so pretty, and so wise,—
Could she but read my heart with those dear eyes—
Did she but share those throbbings——No, hope dies,
For still to silence I am doomed as ever,
Let her not feel my torture now and never!"

Such poetry a man may write when he is in love, but a man of sense will not let it be printed. Here is depicted one of the sufferings of life, in which there is really poetry, and the higher the position in society, the greater the pain. Daily want is the stagnant pool of life without one of its pleasant pictures reflected in it. A lieutenant, love, and poverty, fit very well together; but who would not feel it even more distressing than appropriate? This the lieutenant felt most keenly, and therefore he leant his head against the side of the window, and sighed deeply.

"The poor watchman outside in the street is far happier than I, for he does not know the feeling of the distress I suffer. He has a home, a wife and children, who cry at his sorrows and rejoice in his happiness. Oh, I should be much more happy if I could change with him, and wander through this life with his requirements and his hopes! Yes, he is a hundred times more happy than I. Oh, were I but he!"

The watchman was, all of a sudden, a watchman again. Through the agency of the goloshes of Fortune, unbeknown to himself, his identity had passed over into that of the lieutenant; but, as we have just seen, he then felt much less contented, and preferred that state he had just before bewailed. So the watchman was again a watchman.

"That was an ugly dream," he said, "though funny enough, too. It seemed to me as if I were the lieutenant there above, and yet somehow I could not quite like it. I missed my good old mother and those dear little ones, who, from sheer love, almost smother me with kisses."

He could not get the dream out of his head; and he sat staring before him, up in the darkness, when he saw a shooting-star. "There! another star has fallen," he said; "but what does that matter, for there are plenty of them left? I should like to examine those sparkling little things nearer; but more particularly the moon, which is more steady. The student for whom my wife used to wash said that when we die we fly, as light as a feather, from one star to another. Now, of course, that is all nonsense; but it would be very pleasant could I but for once take a jump up there, and my body might, for aught I care, remain here on the door-step."

There are certain things in this world to which one should only give utterance after the most mature consideration; and one must be doubly careful when one has Fortune's goloshes on. You shall hear what happened to the watchman.

Now, we know what speed has been obtained by means of steam; we have experience of it, either on the railway or on board a steamer; but this is like a snail's progress compared to the swiftness with which light travels. It flies twelve million times quicker than the fastest race-horse, and yet electricity is still swifter. Death is an electric shock received in the heart; and on the wings of electricity the soul takes its flight. The light of the sun requires eight minutes and a few seconds to travel a distance of ninety-five millions of miles, and the soul travelling by electricity would accomplish the same distance in a few minutes less. The distance between the different heavenly bodies is, therefore, no greater for it than to us the distance between the houses of our friends in the same town. However, after the electric shock in the heart, just mentioned, the soul has done with the body here on earth for once and all, unless, like the watchman of Oster Street, we have the goloshes of Fortune on.

In some few seconds the watchman had accomplished the 240,000 miles to the moon, which, as we all know, is of a much lighter material than our earth, or, as we should say, like newly-fallen snow. He found himself on one of the innumerable mountain-ridges which we are acquainted with from maps of the moon. In the inside it went down perpendicularly, like the inside of a caldron, to the depth of two or three miles; and at the bottom there stood a city, which we can only imperfectly imagine if we beat up the white of an egg in a glass of water. The material was quite as soft, and formed just such towers and domes, transparent and wavering in the thin air. Our earth hung above his head like a large fiery ball.

He at once discovered a quantity of beings, which were, no doubt, what we call human beings; but they looked very different from what we do. If they were accurately copied by an experienced artist's hand, we should no doubt exclaim, "What a wonderfully beautiful arabesque!" They also had a language; but no one can expect that the watchman's soul could understand it. It could, however, for in our souls lie far greater powers than we earth-worms have any notion of, for all our fancied wisdom. Does not the mighty queen, in the land of magic, show us her wonderful dramatic talent in our dreams? Our acquaintances appear so characteristic in word and action that none of us whilst awake could so faithfully imitate them. Are not persons suddenly recalled of whom we have not even thought for years, and portrayed as accurately as by the most faithful daguerreo-type? There is something troublesome in this memory of the soul, for it can repeat every sin and every bad thought, quite independent of our will; and it depends whether we are prepared to give an account of every expression of levity that has come from our hearts and lips.

The watchman's soul understood the language of the inhabitants of the moon pretty well. The Moonites were disputing about our earth, and doubted that it could be inhabited; for certainly, they said, the air must be too thick there to allow a rational creature to breathe at all. They considered the moon alone to be inhabited, and that it was the heart of the whole planetary system, on which the real cosmopolites lived. What strange ideas men, or rather Moonites, have! There was a good deal of talk about politics as well; but we must be on our guard what we say, and not tell stories out of school, for if we were to offend that formidable power we might, perhaps, receive a shower of stones upon our heads, or possibly the German Ocean would overflow its gigantic bowl; so we will not betray a single word, but return to Oster Street, to witness what happened to the watchman's body.

Lifeless it sat upon the step; the watchman's staff had fallen out of its hands, and its eyes were fixed upon the moon, looking after its soul taking a holiday up there.

"What o'clock is it, watchman?" a passer-by asked; and not receiving any answer, the young gentleman, who was returning home in rather a merry humour, with several companions, thought he would try the effect of a fillip on the nose, which made the watchman's body lose its equilibrium, and it rolled over upon the ground. Surprise and terror seized upon the whole company, for it was evident that the man was dead; and it being reported to the police, the body was carried to the hospital in the dawn of the morning.

It might be now rather puzzling for the soul if it returned and looked in vain for its body in the street where it had left it; but, as the soul is brighter when independent of the body, it would, no doubt, run at once to the police-officer, then to the office for lost goods, and finally to the hospital.

Here, as already said, the body had been carried, and, as the first thing to be done was to undress it, the goloshes were naturally taken off first, whereupon the soul, which had only gone out on an adventure, had to return as quick as lightning to its worldly habitation. It took its course in a straight line towards the body, and in a few seconds life returned to the man in its full vigour. He stated that it had been the most dreadful night he had ever passed, and that he would not for five shillings again experience those indescribable feelings and wanderings of lunacy but that he was all right again.

That same day he was discharged from the hospital as perfectly well; but the goloshes remained there.

IV

A Critical Moment. A Most Extraordinary Journey

EVERY inhabitant of Copenhagen knows what the entrance to Frederick's Hospital is like; but, as possibly some strangers to the city may also read this little story, we must give a short description of it.

The hospital is separated from the street by a rather high railing, the thick iron bars of which stand so far apart that, as is said, a very thin chaplain managed to squeeze himself through them, and pay his private visits outside. The part of the body most difficult to get through is the head, so here, as often in the world, small heads are most favoured. This will be enough of an introduction.

One of the young volunteers, of whom it might be said that he had a large, thick head, happened to be on duty there that evening. The rain poured down in torrents, but in spite of that he must go out for a quarter of an hour, and he thought it quite unnecessary to let the porter know anything about it, if he could but slip through the bars. There lay the goloshes, which the watchman had left behind him, and, having no notion they were those of *Fortune*, he thought that in such weather they were most desirable; so he put them on. And now the only question was whether he could squeeze through the railings, for he had never yet tried it.

As he stood there, he said, "Would to goodness my head were only through!" and on the instant, big and thick as it was, it slipped through without the slightest difficulty. That was the goloshes' doing, but now the body was to follow.

"Oh, dear!" he exclaimed, "I am too fat. I thought the greatest difficulty would be with the head. I shall never get through."

He now tried to draw his head back; but it would not do. He could move his neck easily enough; but that was all. His first feeling was vexation and anger; then his spirits began to sink below zero. The goloshes of Fortune had brought him into this dreadful fix; and, unfortunately, it never entered into his head to wish it back again. He acted, and could not move from the spot. The rain came down in torrents, and not a human being was to be seen in the streets. He could not reach the bell; so he foresaw that he might have to remain there till morning, when a smith would have to be sent for to file the bars through; but all that would take time, and the whole school of boys, just opposite, would be on their legs; and, worse still, the whole quarter inhabited by the sailors would be alive—a nice concourse to see him in the stocks, as it were! "All the blood will rush to my head, and I shall lose my senses; yes, I shall go mad. Oh, were I but free again, it would pass over!"

He should have said that sooner; for the instant the wish was uttered his head was free, and he rushed to his room, quite bewildered by the fright Fortune's goloshes had caused him.

We must not think that this was the end of his troubles; no, there is worse to follow.

The night passed, and the following day, too, but the goloshes were not sent for.

That evening there was to be a declamatory representation in the little theatre in Kanniken Street. The house was crammed full, and amongst the audience was our volunteer from the hospital, who seemed to have forgotten his adventure of the night before; and, as it was dirty in the streets, he had put on the goloshes, they not having been claimed. A new poem, entitled *My Grandmother's Spectacles*, was recited. These were spectacles of no ordinary description, for to any one who had them on, if before a large assembly, the people appeared as cards, from which all that would happen to them in the coming year could be foretold.

The thought occupied him that he would like to have such a pair of spectacles, for, if properly used, one might, perhaps, be able to see right into people's hearts, which, it seemed to him, would be far more interesting than merely seeing what their fortunes would be the next year, for that one would know anyhow when the time came, but the other never. "I can imagine now the whole row of ladies and gentlemen on the first seat; if I could see into their hearts, it would be like so many shops; and how my eyes should wander about in them! That lady's shop there would be a milliner's, and the shop of this one would be empty; but still I think it would not hurt to have it cleaned out a little. Some of the shops, however, would be well filled with useful articles. I know such an one; but there is already a shopman in it, which is the only fault in the whole shop. From this and that one it would sound, 'Walk in! please to walk in.' Yes; could I but enter as a thought, and wander at will through the hearts!"

Well, this was the cue for the goloshes, the volunteer shrunk up into nothing, and an unprecedented journey began right through the hearts of the audience of the first row. The first heart through which he passed was that of a lady, but his impression was, that he had entered the Orthopædic Institution, into the room where the casts of the various deformed limbs hang up against the wall; though there was this difference, that in the institution the casts are taken on the entry of the patient, whereas here, in the heart, they were taken at the time the good people went out. They were casts of various deformities, both bodily and mental, of different friends that were here preserved. His next visit was to another female heart, and this seemed a large solemn church. The white dove of innocence fluttered above. How gladly would he have fallen upon his knees, but he was obliged to move on into the next heart, though he still heard the notes of the organ, and he felt as if he were a new and better man, and not unworthy to enter the next sanctuary, which showed him a poor garret and a sick mother. The warm sun shone through the open window, beautiful roses nodded from the little wooden box on the roof, and two lovely birds sang of the joys of youth, whilst the sick mother prayed for a blessing on her daughter.

He now crept on hands and feet through an over-filled butcher's shop; here was meat, and nothing but meat. This, however, was the heart of a rich, highly respectable man, whose name is, no doubt, in the directory.

Then he passed into the heart of this man's wife, which was an old tumble-down pigeon-house; her husband's portrait served as weathercock, and was in connexion with the doors, so that these opened and shut as the man turned.

After this he thought himself transported into a narrow needle-case, full of sharp-pointed needles, and imagined that must surely be the heart of an old maid; but such was not the case, for it belonged to a quite young officer with several orders, of whom it was said he was a man of heart and talent.

Quite bewildered, the poor volunteer left the heart of the last person in the row, and could not bring his thoughts into anything like order, settling in his own mind that he must have been carried away by too quick an imagination.

"Good heavens!" he sighed, "I certainly must have a disposition to go mad. It is abominably hot here, so that the blood rushes to my head." He then remembered his adventures of the night before, how his head had got fixed between the iron bars of the hospital. "That must be the cause of all this," he said, "and I must see to it in time. A vapour-bath would be the thing. Oh, were I in one now!"

And there he lay in the vapour-bath, but with his clothes, boots, and goloshes on, the drops of hot water falling down from the ceiling on to his face.

"Whew!" he exclaimed, and rushed to the door. The attendant uttered an exclamation too, when he saw a man in that state, but the volunteer had the presence of mind to say, "It is for a wager."

The first thing he did when he reached his own room was to put a blister on the back of his neck, to draw out the madness.

The next morning he had a sore back, and that was all he gained by Fortune's goloshes.

V

The Clerk's Transformations

THE watchman, who, no doubt, you have not yet forgotten, thought of the goloshes he had found, so he fetched them from the hospital, but as neither the lieutenant nor any one else in the street owned them, he delivered them over to the police.

"They are exactly like my goloshes," one of the clerks said as he placed them by the side of his own. "Even a shoemaker's eye could scarcely distinguish one pair from the other."

At that moment a servant came in with some papers.

The clerk turned round to speak to the man, but after that, when he again looked at the goloshes, he was puzzled to tell whether those to the right or the left were his own.

"It must be those that are wet," he thought; but he just thought wrong; and why should not even the police be wrong sometimes? He therefore put on Fortune's goloshes instead of his own, and taking the papers under his arm, for he intended to read them over and make notes of them at home, he left the office; but as it was then fine, he thought a walk to Friedrichsberg would do him good, so he took that road, safely depositing his papers in his pocket.

No one could be more quiet and steady than this young man, and we will therefore not begrudge him this little walk, which, after so much sitting, will be most beneficial to him. At first he walked along, as it were, in a state of vegetation, so the goloshes had no opportunity to exercise their magic power.

When he had got a short way out of the town, he met an acquaintance, a young poet, who told him that on the following day he was going to start on his summer excursion.

"What! going off again?" the clerk exclaimed. "Well, you are a happy fellow! You can fly in whatever direction you like, whereas we others have a chain round the leg."

"But the chain is fastened to the tree of life," the poet answered. "You need feel no anxiety for the morrow, and when you grow old you will receive a pension."

"Still, you are the best off," the clerk continued. "Why, there is a pleasure in sitting and composing. Every one has something agreeable to say to you, and then you are your own master. You should just try it for once to sit shut up in an office over uninteresting work."

The poet shook his head, the clerk shook his head, and they parted, each holding to his opinion.

"Strange people, these poets are," the clerk said. "I should like to enter into their feelings, and to be a poet myself. I am quite sure that I should not write such doleful verses as many do. Now, this is a delightful day for a poet! The air is unusually clear, the clouds so beautiful, and there is such a sweet scent from all the vegetation. For many years I have not felt it so delightful as at this moment."

We perceive already that he has become a poet. This remark would, in most cases, be a folly, for it is nonsense to suppose that poets are different from other men, there being amongst these, occasionally, far more poetical natures than many amongst the authors of acknowledged talent. The only difference is, that the poet has a better spiritual memory, that he can retain the thought and the feeling till they are clearly and intelligibly embodied in words, which others cannot. But the transition from a commonplace to a gifted nature remains a transition, and can, therefore, not fail to be noticed in the clerk.

"The delicious perfume!" he said. "How it reminds me of the violets at Aunt Lone's. That was when I was still a little boy. Good gracious! how long it is since I have thought of that. The good old girl, she lived out there, behind the bank. She always had a twig, or a couple of green cuttings, in water, let the winter be ever so severe. Violets scented the room at the time when I placed the warm halfpence against the frozen windows to make peepholes. It was pretty to see the ships lying frozen in, on the canal below, deserted by their crews, a screeching raven forming the garrison. Then later, the spring breezes brought life everywhere. Amidst singing and hurrahing the ice was sawed, the ships were tarred and rigged, preparatory to sailing off to foreign countries. But I have remained here, and must still remain; and, seated at my desk, see others fetch passports for their journeys. Such is my fate. Oh, yes!" he sighed, then suddenly stopped. "Good heavens!" he exclaimed, "what can be the matter with me? Never before had I such thoughts or feelings; the spring air must be the cause, and there is as much anxiety as pleasure in the feeling." He took his papers out of his pocket, saying as he did so, "These will give me something else to think of." He ran his eyes over the first leaf and read, "*Dame Sigbrith*, an original tragedy, in five acts. What is this? and it is my writing too. Can I really have written the tragedy? *The Intrigue in the Park, or the Day of Repentance*, a vaudeville. Where can I possibly have got these? Some one must have put them into my pocket. But here is a letter." It was, indeed, a letter from the director of the theatre rejecting the pieces, and was by no means polite. "Hem! hem!" the clerk mumbled, and seated himself upon a bench. His thoughts were so elastic, and his heart so soft, and unintentionally he laid hold of one of the flowers nearest to him, which happened to be an ordinary little daisy. In one minute it related what botanists would only teach us in several lectures; it told of its birth, of the power of the sun's light, which expands the little leaves, and forces them to exhale their fragrance. Air and light are the flower's lovers, but light is the favoured one, for towards the light it turns, and when this disappears it folds up its leaves and sleeps. "It is the light that gives me beauty," the flower said; "but air gives you breath," the poet's voice whispered.

Close by stood a boy striking into a marshy ditch with a stick, so that the drops of water flew high up into the air, and the clerk thought of the millions of invisible insects thus hurled aloft, as high for them, according to their size, as it would be for us to be sent whirling above the clouds. As the clerk thought of this, and of the change that had taken place in himself, he could not help smiling, and said, "It is evident I am asleep and dreaming; but how strange it is that a dream should seem so natural, and that one should know at the same time that it is only a dream? Could I but remember it all when I awake tomorrow morning! I seem to be particularly bright now, and to take a clear view of all things, and yet I am quite sure that if I recollect anything of it tomorrow, it will be all nonsense, for that has happened to me before. All that is clever and to the purpose which one hears and says in a dream is like fairy money, which is all pure gold when one receives it, but when looked at by daylight, is only stones or dry leaves." As he now watched the birds hopping joyously from branch to branch, he sighed and said quite plaintively, "They are better off than I, for to be able to fly is a delightful thing, and happy must the being be that is born with wings. Now, if I could change, it should be into a lark."

That very instant his arms and coat-tails became wings, his clothes turned into feathers, and the goloshes into claws. He saw it well enough, and laughed inwardly. "There can be no doubt whatever now that I am dreaming, but it is exactly like reality"; and he flew up amongst the green leaves and began to sing; but there was no poetry in his song, for he had ceased to be a poet; the goloshes, like every one who does a thing well, could only do one thing at a time. He had wished to become a poet, and was one; then he wished to be a little bird, and on becoming that had given up his former nature.

"This is charming!" he said. "The whole day I am at the police-office engaged in the steadiest possible work, and at night dream that I am a lark flying about the garden of Friedrichsberg. A farce might be written about it."

He then flew down into the grass, turned his head first to one side and then to the other, pecking at the blades of grass, which in comparison to his present size seemed to him like the palm-trees of North Africa.

This only lasted for a minute, and then it became pitch-dark all at once, seeming to him as if some enormous object had been thrown over him. This was a large cap, and immediately a boy's hand, thrust under it, caught the clerk round the back and wings, and in his fright he exclaimed, "You impudent fellow! I am a clerk at the police-office"; but to the boy that only sounded like the "Pipipip" of a bird, so he gave it a tap on its beak and went on.

In a few minutes he met two school-boys of the higher class, that is as to the family, for as to behaviour they were of the very lowest. They bought the bird for sixpence, and the clerk was carried to Copenhagen to a house in Gother Street.

"It is well that I am only dreaming," the clerk said, "or I should really be in a rage, for at first I was a poet and now a lark. I suppose it must be a poet's fancy has changed me into this little creature. It is a miserable story, particularly the falling into a boy's clutches. I wonder how it will all end?"

The boys took him into a very elegant room, where they were received by a fat, smiling lady, but she was not at all pleased to see the common field-bird, as she called the lark, brought there; however, for that day she would allow it, and it was put into an empty cage that stood at the window. "It may amuse Poppy," she said, nodding smilingly to a large green parrot, which was proudly swinging itself in its ring in a splendid brass cage. "It is Poppy's birthday," she added, with stupid simplicity, "and the little field-bird has come to wish him joy."

Poppy did not answer a single word, but went on swinging himself backwards and forwards; but a beautiful canary, which had been brought from its warm, balmy country the previous summer, began to sing with all its might.

"Screecher," the lady said, and threw a white pocket-handker-chief over the cage.

"Pipip!" he sighed, "what a dreadful snow-storm!" and with this he was silent.

The clerk, or field-bird, as the lady called him, was placed close by the side of the canary, in a small cage, and not far from the parrot. The only words Poppy could chatter, and which often sounded oddly enough, were, "But let us be men!" The rest of his talk was quite as incomprehensible as the twittering of the canary; but not to the clerk, as he was now a bird himself, for he could understand his companions well enough.

"I flew under the green palm-trees and the blooming almond trees," the Canary sang; "I flew with my brothers and sisters over the beautiful flowers and the clear lake, the bottom of which was covered with plants. And I saw many beautiful parrots, who told the funniest stories—so many, and such long ones!"

"Those were wild birds," the Parrot put in, "and had no sort of education. But let us be men. Why do you not laugh? As the lady and all her friends laugh, you might too. It is a great misfortune not to be able to enjoy what is funny."

"Oh, do you remember the beautiful girls that used to dance under the tents? Do you remember the sweet fruits, and the cooling juice of the wild-growing plants?"

"Oh yes!" the Parrot answered; "but I am much better off here, for I get good food, and am treated with familiarity; I know that I am clever, and with that I am satisfied. Let us be men. You have a poetical turn, as it is called, whereas I have solid sense and wit. You have genius, but no prudence, and thus you take your high flights of fancy and get covered up. They do not treat me in that way. No, I have cost them too much, and then I can make myself respected with my beak. But let us be men."

"Oh, my warm, beautiful country!" the Canary sang; "I will sing of your dark green trees and calm bays, where the drooping branches kiss the clear water; I will sing the joys of my glittering brothers and sisters."

"Have done with your elegiac strains!" the Parrot said. "Tell us something to make us laugh. Laughter is a sign of the highest mental powers. See whether a dog or a horse can laugh—no, they can cry, but to laugh is human. Ha, ha, ha!" the Parrot laughed, adding his piece of wit, "Let us be men."

"You little brown Danish bird," the Canary said, "you, too, have been taken prisoner. No doubt it is cold in your forests; but there is freedom, at any rate. They have forgotten to shut your cage, and the upper part of the window is open, so fly away. Fly away whilst you can."

Instinctively the clerk did as he was told, but at the very moment he left the cage, the door leading into another room creaked, and with green flashing eyes stealthily the cat came in and hunted him. The Canary fluttered in its cage, the Parrot flapped its wings and cried, "Let us be men!" The clerk was almost dead with fright, and flew out at the open window, away over the houses and streets, till at last he was obliged to rest.

He reached a house which had something familiar in its appearance; the window was open, so he flew in. It was his own room, and he alighted on the table.

"Let us be men!" he said, quite unintentionally, imitating the parrot, and that instant he was the clerk again, but was sitting on the table.

"Good gracious!" he exclaimed, "how did I get up here and fall asleep? That was a troubled, uncomfortable dream. What nonsense it all was!"

VI

The best thing that the Goloshes brought

THE next day, early in the morning, whilst the clerk was still in bed, there was a knock at his door. It was a neighbour living on the same floor, a young clergyman, who entered.

"Lend me your goloshes," he said, "for it is dreadfully wet in the garden, but the sun shines so beautifully that I should like to go and smoke a pipe down there."

He put on the goloshes, and was soon below in the garden, which contained one plum and one apple-tree; but a garden as small even as that, in Copenhagen, is considered a great treat.

The clergyman wandered up and down the walk. It was just six o'clock, and the stage-coach horn sounded from the street.

"Oh, travelling, travelling!" he cried. "That is the greatest happiness in the world, and the fondest of my wishes. It would cure this restlessness that I feel, but it must be far. I should like to see delightful Switzerland, and to travel through Italy, and——"

It was well that the goloshes acted at once, or he would have gone too far, as well for himself as for us. He did travel. He was in the heart of Switzerland, but with eight others, packed together in a diligence. His head ached, he had a pain in the back, and the blood had run down into his feet, which were swelled in consequence, and his boot hurt him. He was in a state between sleeping and waking. In his right-hand pocket he had a letter of credit, in the left his passport, and in the breast-pocket a little leather purse full of gold. Each dream announced the loss of one or the other of these treasures, so that he was constantly starting up in feverish excitement, and the first movement of his hand was in a triangle, from the right to the left, and then to the breast, to find out whether he had his property still. Umbrellas, sticks, and hats dangled from the top in the net, considerably hiding the view, which was very imposing.

Grand, solemn, and dark was the face of nature all around. The pine-forests looked only like heather on the high rocks, the tops of which were lost in the clouds; and now it began to snow, a cold wind blowing.

"Oh, were we but on the other side of the Alps!" he said, "for then it would be summer, and I should have got money on my letter of credit, the anxiety respecting which destroys all my enjoyment of Switzerland. Oh, were I but on the other side!"

And there he was on the other side, right in Italy, between Florence and Rome. The lake Trasimene lay there in the light of the setting sun, like burnished gold, between the dark blue mountains. Here, where Hannibal vanquished Flaminius, the vines hold each other in a friendly embrace. Lovely, half-naked children were tending a herd of coal-black pigs under a group of sweet laurel-trees by the roadside. Could we but do justice to this delightful scene, every one would exclaim, "Delightful Italy!" but our young clergyman did not say this by any means, nor a single one of his travelling companions in the veturino.

Poisonous flies and gnats came flying by thousands into the carriage, and in vain they tried to beat them off with myrtle-twigs. The flies stung them in spite of all, and there was not a being in the carriage whose face was not swelled with the bites of these venemous insects. The poor horses were literally covered with them, and it was only a momentary relief when the coachman got down and scraped them off. The sun now went down, and an icy coldness, though of short duration, followed, like the cold air from a tomb on a hot summer's day; but all around, the mountains and the clouds assumed that peculiar green tint which we see in some old paintings, and which we think unnatural, if we had not witnessed the changes of colour in southern climes. It was a delightful sight, but the stomach was empty, the body fatigued, and the longing of the heart fixed upon comfortable night-quarters; but where were such to be found? The eye sought this much more anxiously than the beauties of nature.

The road led through an olive-grove, something like our knotty willow-trees, and here stood the solitary inn. A dozen crippled beggars were collected before the door, the most brisk of whom, to use an expression of Marryat's, looked like "the eldest son of Hunger, who had just come to age," and the others were either blind or had paralyzed legs, and crawled on their hands, or had withered arms with fingerless hands. That was, indeed, Misery in rags. "Eccellenza, miserabili!" they groaned, stretching forth their diseased limbs. The hostess, with bare feet, uncombed hair, and covered only with a dirty blouse, received the guests herself. The doors were fastened with string, and the flooring of the rooms was broken plaster and rough stones; bats were flying about, and the smell was dreadful.

"For goodness' sake, let the cloth be laid below in the stable!" one of the travellers said, "for there, at least, we shall know what we breathe."

The windows were open to let in a little fresh air, but quicker than this in came the withered arms, and the perpetual wailing, "Miserabili, eccellenza." On the walls were numbers of inscriptions, more than the half being anything but in praise of la bella Italia.

Supper was brought up, consisting of water-soup, seasoned with pepper and bad oil, the latter of which played the principal *rôle* in the salad. Bad eggs and roasted cocks' combs were the delicacies of the repast: even the wine had an after-taste, it was a most decided mixture.

At night all the trunks were heaped up against the door, and one of the travellers was to keep watch whilst the others slept. The watching fell to our young clergyman;—oh, how oppressively hot

and suffocating it was! the gnats whirred and stung, and the
miserabili outside groaned in their sleep.

"Travelling would be all very well," the young clergyman said,
"if one had no body. It would be delightful if that could remain
at rest whilst the spirit took its flight. I always find some want that
oppresses my heart, a longing after something better than the
present affords. Something better—yes, the best, but where, and
what is it? It is a final happy resting-place I wish for."

As soon as the wish was expressed he was at home. The long
white curtains hung before the windows, and in the middle of the
room stood the black coffin, in which his body had found a resting-
place. His wish was fulfilled, his body was at rest, and his spirit
had taken its flight. No one is happy before he is in his grave,
were the words of Solomon; and they were now verified.

Two figures were present in the room; we know them both: the
one was *Care*, and the other *Fortune's* envoy. They bent down
over the dead body.

"Now, you see," *Care* said, "what happiness your goloshes have
brought mankind."

"To him, at least, who slumbers here, they have brought a
lasting good," the other answered.

"Oh, no!" *Care* continued, "he went of his own accord, he was
not called, and has not accomplished what was set him in this
world. I will do him a favour."

She took the goloshes off his feet, the sleep of death was ended,
and he arose: *Care* disappeared, and with her the goloshes, which
she, no doubt, looked upon as her own.

THE UGLY DUCKLING

It was so delightful in the country, for summer was at the height
of its splendour. The corn was yellow, the oats green, the hay,
heaped into cocks in the meadow below, looked like little grass
hillocks, and the stork strutted about on its long, red legs, chattering Egyptian, for that was the language it had learnt from its
mother.

The fields and meadows were surrounded by more or less thickly-
wooded forests, which also enclosed deep lakes, the smooth waters
of which were sometimes ruffled by a gentle breeze. It was, indeed,

delightful in the country. In the bright sunshine stood an old mansion surrounded by a moat and wall, strong and proud almost as in the feudal times. From the wall all the way down to the water grew a complete forest of burdock-leaves, which were so high that a little child could stand upright under them; it was a real wilderness, so quiet and sombre, and here sat a Duck upon her nest hatching a quantity of eggs; but she was tired of her tedious, though important, occupation, for it lasted so very long, and she seldom had any visitors. The other ducks preferred swimming about on the moat and the canals that ran through the garden, to visiting her in her solitude.

At length, however, there was a crackling in one of the eggs, then in a second, third, fourth, fifth, and sixth. "Peep! Peep!" sounded from here; "Peep! peep!" sounded from there, at least a dozen times. There was, all of a sudden, life in the eggs, and the little half naked creatures, their dwellings having become too confined for them, thrust out their heads as out of a window, looking quite confused.

"Quick! quick!" their mother cried, so the little ones made as much haste as they possibly could. They stared about them, as if examining the green leaves, and their mother let them look as long as they liked, for green is good for the eyes.

"How large the world is!" they said; and certainly there lay before them a much more extensive space than their eggs.

"Do you imagine this is the whole world?" their mother answered. "Oh, no, it stretches far beyond the garden, and on the other side the meadow, where the parson's cows are grazing, though I have never been there. But you are all here, I suppose?" she added, with true maternal solicitude, and she stood up, whereby, in spite of all her care, there was a great overthrow and confusion amongst the little ones. "No, I have not them all yet," she said, sighing. "The largest of the eggs lies there still. How much longer is it to last? It is becoming really too wearing." She mastered, however, all her patience, and sat down again.

"How are you getting on?" an old Duck inquired, coming to pay her friend a formal visit.

"With one of the eggs there seems no end of trouble," the over-tired mother complained. "The shell must be too thick, so that the poor little thing cannot break through; but you see the others, which are the prettiest little creatures that a mother could ever wish for. And what an extraordinary resemblance they bear to

H

their father, who is certainly the handsomest drake in the whole yard, but he has not visited me once here in my solitude."

"Show me the egg which will not break," the old Duck said, interrupting her. "Take my word for it, it is a turkey's egg. I was once played the same trick, and precious trouble I had with the little ones, for they were afraid of the water. How I coaxed, scolded, and fumed, but all of no use, they would not be induced to go in. Now let me examine the obstinate egg. Yes, it is just as I suspected, it is a turkey's egg. Take my advice, leave the nest and go and exercise the other little ones in swimming, for you are not bound by any duties towards this cheat."

"I would rather sit a little longer on it," the other said, shaking her head. "I have already had so much trouble that it does not matter whether I am kept to it a day or two longer or not."

"Oh, if you like it, I have no objection," the old one answered, and with a stiff courtesy took her leave, saying as she went on her way, "She'll have trouble enough with it."

At length the large egg broke. "Peep, peep!" cried the tardy comer, and he fell head-foremost out of the shell. He was so big and ugly that his mother scarcely dared look at him, and the more she did so the less she knew what to say. At last she exclaimed, involuntarily, "That is certainly the most frightfully curious young drake: can it possibly be a turkey? But wait, we will soon see, for into the water he shall go. I will push him in myself, without further to-do; and then, if he cannot dive and swim, he may drown, and serve him right too!"

The following day it was splendid weather, the sun shining brightly upon the burdock-leaves, and the duck mamma with her whole family waddled down to the moat. "Splash!" and she was in the water. "Quick, quick!" she cried, and one duckling after another followed her example; not one would remain behind. The water closed over their heads, but they immediately came to the top again and swam most beautifully. Their legs moved of their own accord, and even the ugly, grey late-comer swam merrily with them.

"He is no turkey," the mother duck said; "only see how quickly he moves his legs, and how straight he holds himself! Yes, he is my own flesh and blood; and, after all, on more careful examination, he is a good-looking fellow enough. Now follow me quickly, and I will introduce you into the world, and present you in the poultry-yard. But mind you keep close to me, that no one may tread on you. Of all things, take care of the cat."

They reached the yard, where there was a dreadfully noisy commotion, for two worthy families were disputing about the head of an eel, which the cat took from both of them.

"That's the way of the world," the mother-duck said, and her mouth watered, as she, too, would have gladly had the eel's head, for which she had a particular weakness. "Now move your legs," she said, "and bow prettily, slightly bending your necks, before the old duck you see there, for she is considered the highest of all. She is of pure Spanish blood, and therefore she is so solemn and proud. Do you see she has a piece of red cloth round her left leg, which is something extraordinarily splendid, and the greatest mark of distinction that can be conferred upon a duck? It means, that she shall be known to all beasts and men, and that she is to enjoy the most unusual piece of good fortune—to end her days in peace. Make haste, my children, but for goodness' sake don't turn your legs in so, for a well-bred duck must keep its legs far apart, just like papa and mamma. Imitate me in all things, and pay attention to the word of command. When you bow do not neglect to bend your neck gracefully, and then boldly say, 'Quack, quack!' Nothing more!"

So they did, but the other ducks round about looked upon them with contempt, and said, quite out loud, "Well, well, now all this stupid pack is to be foisted upon us, as if we were not numerous enough without them; indeed, we do not require any increase of that sort,—and, oh, dear, just look at that big thing! such a deformity, at least, we will not allow amongst us!" Hereupon an upstart Drake made a rush at the poor, green-grey youngster, and bit him in the neck.

"Leave him alone!" cried the highly-incensed mother, "for he is not doing anything to offend you; and I will not allow him to be ill-used."

"That may be; but for his age he is much too big and peculiar," the snappish Drake answered; "and naturally, therefore, he must be put down."

"They are very pretty children, indeed, that mamma has there," the old Duck with the red cloth round her leg said, "all of them, with the exception of one only, and he has certainly not succeeded."

"I am very sorry, gracious madam!" the mother answered, with difficulty swallowing her mortification. "He is certainly not a pattern of beauty, but he has a charming disposition, and swims as well as any of them; indeed, I may say a little better; and I am of opinion that he will grow up handsome enough, when, instead of growing taller, he spreads out, and gains roundness of form. He lay too long in the egg, and therefore has not his proper shape." Whilst she spoke thus in the youngster's favour, she did her best to smooth down her grey-green uniform where it had been ruffled. "Besides," the good mother continued warmly, "the same fulness and elegance of form is not expected from a drake as from a duck. I have an idea that he will make his way."

"The other little ones are charming," the old Spanish Duck repeated. "Now make yourselves at home, and if you should happen to find an eel's head, you may bring it me without hesitation. You understand me!"

And now they were at home.

But the poor, ugly green-grey youngster, who had come last out of the egg, was bitten, jostled, and made game of by the Ducks as well as by the chickens. "He is much too big!" they all said, with one accord. And the stuck-up Turkey, because he was born with spurs, fancied himself almost an emperor, gave himself airs, and strutted about like a ship in full sail, whilst his fiery head grew redder and redder. The poor, persecuted young thing neither knew where to stand nor where to go, and his heart was saddened by all that he had to suffer on account of his ugliness.

Thus it was the first day, and day after day it only grew worse. The ugly, green-grey youngster was worried and hunted by all; even his own brothers and sisters were against him, and were constantly saying, "If the cat would take you, you horror!" His mother, weighed down by sorrow, sighed, "Oh, I wish you had never been born, or were you but far away from here!" The ducks bit him, the chickens pecked him, and the girl that brought them their food kicked him.

Driven by fear and despair, he now ran and flew as far as his tired legs and weak wings would carry him, till, with a great effort, he got over the hedge, which, no doubt, was not very low. The little singing birds in the bushes flew up in a fright, and the young fugitive thought, "That is because I am so ugly." He, however, hurried forward, led by instinct, towards an unknown goal. This was a swamp, surrounded by a wood, and was the dwelling-place of shoals of wild ducks. Sad and tired to death, he remained here the whole night, almost in a state of unconsciousness, whilst the full moon above bore such a friendly countenance, as if laughing at the foolish frogs, which kept jumping from the water on to the grass, and back again into the water, as if imitating the dance of merry elves.

Early the next morning, aroused by the first glimmer of the sun, the wild ducks rose from their watery beds to take a turn in the warm summer air, when with surprise they saw the stranger. "What funny guy is this?" they exclaimed. "Where can he have come from?" they inquired of each other; whilst the stranger, with all possible politeness, turned from side to side, first bowing to the right and then to the left, as no ballet-mistress, much less a ballet-master, could do.

"You are right-down ugly," the wild ducks said; "but that does not make much difference to us, as long as you do not marry into our family."

The poor outcast thought of nothing less than marrying. All he wished for was to remain undisturbed among the rushes, and drink a little water of the swamp. Here he lay two whole days, when two wild geese arrived, or rather goslings, for they had not long come out of the egg, and therefore were they so merry.

"Well met, comrade!" one of them said; "you are so ugly that I like you. Come with us, for close by there is another swamp, where there are some very fine geese, the sweetest of young damsels, who did not get married last autumn. You are just the fellow to pick up a wife amongst them, you are so ugly."

"Bang, bang!" it sounded at that very moment, and the two wild goslings fell down dead, the water being discoloured with their blood. "Bang, bang!" it went again, and a quantity of geese flew up from the rushes. There was more firing, for the sportsmen lay all around the marsh, some of them sitting in the branches of the trees that overhung the masses of rushes. The blue smoke from the powder rose like clouds amongst the dark foliage, and "splash" the dogs sprang into the water, little heeding the fresh breeze which whistled among the waving reeds. A nice fright the poor green-grey youngster had, and he was about to hide his head under one of his wings, that, at least, he might see no more of the horrors, when, close by him, appeared an enormous dog, its tongue hanging far out of its throat, and blood-thirsty rage sparkling in its eyes. With wide-open jaws, showing two formidable rows of murderous teeth, the water spaniel advanced towards the poor bird, which now gave itself up as utterly lost, but, generously disdaining to seize upon its easy prey, the noble creature went on.

"Thank goodness!" the poor outcast said. "I am so ugly that the dog does not like to touch me"; and he lay perfectly quiet, whilst the shot whizzed over his head amongst the rushes.

Not till late in the afternoon did the firing cease, but even then the poor youngster, whose life had been saved as if by a miracle, did not venture to move. He waited several hours before he drew his head from under his wing, and cautiously looked about him; but then he hastened, with all possible speed, to get away from the scene of horror. As before he had flown from the poultry-yard, so now, but with redoubled exertion, he fled, he knew not whither. A boisterous wind, which followed upon the setting of the sun, was ungracious enough to have no consideration for the scantily-covered traveller, and considerably impeded his progress, exhausting his strength.

Late in the evening our fugitive reached a miserable cottage, which was in such a wretched state that it did not know on which side to fall, and on that account it remained standing for the time being. The wind blew around him and shook the poor bird so violently that he had to seat himself upon his tail to be able to offer the necessary resistance. He then, with no small delight, discovered that the rickety door of the cottage, which, though it did not promise much comfort, yet offered a shelter against the now doubly-raging storm, had broken loose from the lower hinge, and that there was thus a slanting opening, through which he could slip into the room; and this he did without loss of time.

Here lived an old woman with her Tom-cat and her Hen.

The cat was a perfect master in "purring" and in "washing," and he could turn head over heels—no one in the neighbourhood could equal him, and one only needed to rub his hair repeatedly the contrary way to bring bright sparks from his back. The old woman called him her little son. The Hen, for her part, had very thin, short legs, on which account she was called "Clucky Short-legs." She most industriously laid the very best eggs, and her mistress loved her as if she were her own child.

Peace, concord, and happiness evidently reigned in this miserable hut, as they do in many others of a like sort.

In the morning, the strange, unbidden guest was immediately discovered, when the Cat began to purr, and the Hen to cluck.

"What is this?" the old woman said, and began a close examination; but, as she could not see well, she took the young, meagre bird for a fat duck, which had got into her room by mistake. "Here is an unusual piece of good fortune!" she exclaimed, in joyous surprise. "Now I shall have duck's eggs—that is, if the stupid thing should not at last prove to be a drake," she added, thoughtfully. "We will give it a trial."

So the green-grey youngster remained there three weeks on trial, but no egg made its appearance. Now, the Cat was master in the house, and the Hen mistress, and they used to say, "We, and the world," for they thought they constituted the half, and by far the better half, of the world. It appeared to the young stranger that others might have another opinion, which the Hen would by no means allow.

"Can you lay eggs?" she asked.

"No."

"Then please to hold your tongue."

And the Cat asked, "Can you purr, or arch your back?"

"No."

"Then you have no right to offer an opinion when sensible people talk."

And the poor, ugly outcast sat in the corner quite melancholy, in vain fighting against the low spirits which his self-satisfied companions certainly did not share. Involuntarily he thought of the fresh air and the bright sunshine out of doors, and felt himself agitated by so violent a desire once more to be swimming on the clear water, and to sport about in the liquid element, that he could not resist one morning, after a sleepless night, opening his heart to the Hen.

"What mad fancies are turning that poor, shallow brain of yours again?" the Hen cried, almost in a rage, in spite of her natural quiet indifference. "You have nothing to do, and it is sheer idleness that torments you and puts such foolish fancies into your head. Lay eggs, or purr, and you will be all right."

"But it is so pleasant to swim," the poor child answered; "so delightful to dive to the bottom and look up at the moon through the clear water!"

"Yes, that must be a great treat," the Hen said, contemptuously. "You must have gone stark staring mad. Ask the Cat, and I know no one more sensible, whether he likes swimming about in the water and diving to the bottom. I will not speak of myself, but just ask our mistress; and there is no one wiser than she in the whole world. Do you think she has a fancy for diving and swimming?"

"You do not understand me," the poor Duckling sighed.

"And if we do not understand you, pray, who can, you conceited, impertinent creature!" the Hen replied, warmly. "You will not, surely, set yourself up as cleverer than the Cat and our mistress, not to mention myself. Pray think a little less of yourself, and thank your stars for all the kindness that has been shown you.

Have you not got into a warm room here, and amongst company from whom you may learn some good? But you are a shallow prattler and a long-necked dreamer, whose society is anything but amusing. You may believe me, for I mean really well with you, and therefore tell you things you do not like to hear, which is a proof that I am your true friend. Now, of all things, mind that you lay eggs and learn how to purr."

"I think I shall wander out into the world," the young Duck said, mustering up courage.

"Do so, by all means," the Hen answered, with contempt. "One comfort, we shall lose nothing by your absence."

And now the green-grey youngster, without many parting thanks, began his wanderings again, leaving the inhospitable hut without regret, and he hurried towards the so-much-longed-for water. He swam about joyously, and boldly dived down right to the bottom, from whence he saw the pale moon like a rolling ball; but at length the loneliness and death-like silence became oppressive, and when another creature did appear, it was sure to be with the same greeting as of old, namely, "Oh, how frightful you are!"

It was now late in autumn, with frequent storms of snow and hail, and the brown and yellow leaves from the forest danced about, whipped by the winds, whilst above all was a cold leaden colour. The crows sat in the hedge and cried, "Caw! caw!" with sheer cold. It makes one shiver to think of it. The poor outcast was anything but happy.

One frosty evening, when the sun began to set, a quantity of magnificent large birds swept past, and the ugly, green-grey youngster thought he had never seen anything so beautiful. Their spotless plumage shone like driven snow, and they uttered a cry, half singing, half whistling, as they rose higher and higher in their flight towards more extensive lakes. A strange sensation came over the poor young Duck, and he turned round and round like a top, and stretching out his neck after the departing birds, gave a cry, for the first time in his life, so loud and shrill that he was frightened at it himself. When they quite disappeared from his sight, he suddenly dived down to the bottom of the water, and when he rose again was as if beside himself. From that moment, never could he forget those beautiful, happy birds; he did not know that they were called swans, nor where they were flying to, but he loved them as he had never loved anything before. He did not envy them in the least, for how could it ever enter his head to wish himself so splendid and beautiful? He would have been contented to live among the stupid ducks, if they would but have left him in peace, a neglected, ugly thing.

The winter grew so bitterly cold that the poor creature had to swim about incessantly to prevent the water freezing quite over. Night after night the hole became less, till at last, exhausted by constant exertions, he got frozen tight into the ice.

Early in the morning a peasant came that way, and seeing the poor bird in so wretched a plight he had compassion on it, and ventured boldly on to the ice, for he was a good Christian, and not one of those who first see that no inconvenience will attend an act of kindness. With his wooden shoes he broke the ice, extricated the to all appearance dead bird, and carried him home to his wife, where, in a warm room, the green-grey youngster soon recovered animation and strength.

The children wished to play with him, but the young Drake thought they were bent on ill-using him, so in his fright he flew into an earthenware milk-pan, which he turned over, and the milk ran about the floor. The woman uttered a loud cry and raised her hands in consternation, which thoroughly bewildered the poor bird, and he flew into the freshly-made butter, and then into the flour-tub, and out again. Oh, what a figure he was now! Bewailing her losses, the woman pursued him with the tongs, and the children, laughing and shouting, rolled over each other as they tried to catch him.

Fortunately for our youngster, who was no longer green-grey, but of a delicate paste colour, the door was open, and, taking advantage of the general confusion, he rushed out into the open air, and with difficulty fluttered to some bushes, not far off, where he sank down, exhausted, into the deep snow. Here he lay unconscious.

But it would be too painful to follow the poor outcast through all his misfortunes, and to witness the misery and privation he suffered during that severe winter; we will therefore only say that he lay in a dreamy state amongst the rushes in the marsh, when the sun again began to shine warmly upon the earth, and the larks began to sing, for it was early spring.

Then the young Drake spread out his wings, which had grown much stronger, and with ease they carried him away, so that almost before he knew it, he found himself in a large garden, where the fruit-trees were in all the splendour of full blossom, and the lilac scented the air, whilst the green branches hung down to the stream which wound picturesquely through the soft lawn. Oh, it was so spring-like and enchanting! a short distance before him three beautiful white swans came sailing along the water from behind some bushes. The poor, hitherto-despised outcast knew the magnificent birds, and suddenly a feeling of deep sadness came over him.

"I will fly to them, the beautiful birds! and they will take my life, because I, ugly as I am, have ventured to go near them. But it does not matter, for it will be better to be killed by them than being bitten by the ducks, pecked by the chickens, and kicked by the girl in the poultry-yard, or suffering all the hardships of this winter." Agitated by these feelings, without further consideration, but with assumed confidence, he swam towards the three swans, which, as soon as they perceived the stranger, shot through the water with rounded wings and ruffled feathers to meet him.

"Kill me!" the poor thing said, and with bent-down head awaited his death in quiet resignation. But what did he now see in the clear water? He saw his own reflection; but it was no longer the ugly, dirty, green-grey bird,—no, it was a proud, princely swan!

True, he was hatched by a duck, but why should that not happen to a swan's egg?

The now snow-white youngster, with the lovely form, heartily rejoiced in the misery and hardships of his early youth, for he could the better appreciate all his happiness, and the heavenly beauty by which he was surrounded. And the large swans surrounded him with a friendly welcome, and lovingly stroked his neck with their bills.

Just then some young children appeared in the garden, running merrily down to the water, into which they threw bread for the swans.

"Look, look!" the youngest cried, "here is a new one!" and they clapped their hands and danced about, shouting with delight, and then ran off to call papa and mama. Now fresh bread and cake were thrown into the water, and all said, "The new one is the most beautiful of all, so young and so graceful!" And the old swans showed no envy, but treated him as friendly as before.

But the young stranger felt quite ashamed, and hid his head under his wing. He scarcely understood his own feelings; he was too happy, but not at all proud, for a good heart is never proud. He thought, without bitterness, of how he was formerly persecuted and mocked, whereas now all said that he was the most beautiful of these magnificent birds; and the lilac, with its long green branches and sweetly-smelling blossom, bent down to him in the water. The sun shone brightly, and from the depth of his heart he said, "Such great happiness I never dreamed of when I was the Ugly Duckling."

THE NEIGHBOURS

IT might have been thought that there was something out of the way going on in the village-pond, but there was not. All the ducks, whether lying on the water or standing on their heads—for they could do that too—swam with one accord to land, where the marks of their feet could be seen in the wet clay, and they could be heard from afar off. The water was in a regular commotion, whereas before it had been like a looking-glass, in which could be seen every tree and every bush that was near, as well as the old house with the holes in the gable and the swallow's nest, not forgetting the large Rose-tree, covered with flowers, which hung down from the wall almost across the water. All stood reflected there just like a painting, only everything was upside down, and when the water was ruffled one thing ran into another, and the picture was gone. Two feathers, which had fallen from the ducks as they flew away, were rocking up and down, when all at once they sailed along, exactly as if it were windy; but there was no wind. Then they lay quiet, and the water again became as smooth as a looking-glass, and again the gable was plainly reflected, with the swallow's nest and the Rose-tree. Each Rose appeared there, and they were so beautiful; but they themselves did not know it, for no one had told them so. The sun shone between the delicate, fragrant petals; and it was with the Roses just as it is with us, when we are buried in thought and feel particularly happy.

"How delightful life is!" each Rose said; "the only thing I could wish is, that I might kiss the sun, because it is so warm and bright; and then I should like to kiss the Roses that are down there in the water, they are so exactly like us; and the dear little birds in their nests I should like to kiss. There are some others above us, too; they stretch out their little heads and 'Peep' quite softly; but they have no feathers, like their father and mother. Those are good neighbours of ours, those above as well as below. Oh, how delightful life is!"

The little young ones above and below, for those below were only reflections in the water, were Sparrows, and the father and mother were Sparrows. They had taken possession of the swallow's nest of the year before, and there they lay, quite at home.

"Are those young ducks?" the little Sparrows asked, when they saw the feathers sailing along.

"When you ask a question, let it be a sensible one," the Sparrow-mother said. "Do you not see that they are feathers—a living covering for the body, the same as I have, and you will have some day, only ours are finer? I wish, however, that we had them up here in our nest, for they keep one warm. I should like to know what frightened the ducks so. It must have been something in the water; for surely it was not I, though I did say 'Peep' rather loudly to you. Those thick-headed Roses ought to know, but they know nothing; they can only look at themselves and scent the air. They are stupid neighbours!"

"Listen to the dear little birds above!" the Roses said; "they begin to make an attempt at singing. They don't quite know how as yet, but it will come. What happiness that must be! It is really delightful to have such merry neighbours!"

Just then two horses came galloping up to be watered, a boy with a broad-brimmed black hat sitting on the back of one of them, and he whistled just like a bird, as they rode into the deepest part of the pond. When he got to the Rose-tree he tore off one of the Roses and stuck it in his hat and rode away again, thinking himself very smart. The other Roses looked after their sister, and asked each other, "Where is she going to?" but none could tell.

"I should like to go out in the world," one said to the other; "but here, in our own green home, it is beautiful too. During the day the sun shines so warm, and at night the sky is still brighter, as we see through the innumerable holes that are in it."

Those were the stars which the Roses called holes, for they knew no better.

"We give life to the house," the Sparrow-mother said; "and swallows' nests bring luck, people say, wherefore they are glad to have us; but our neighbour there, the large Rose-tree by the side of the wall, causes dampness, and I hope will be removed, when corn can grow in its place. Roses are only good to look at and to smell, or perhaps to stick in a hat. I know, from my mother, that they fall off every year, when they are put by and receive a French name, which I cannot pronounce, and about which I do not trouble myself either. They are then strewn on the fire, and are said to smell nice. That is the whole of their life, so you see that it's only for eyes and noses they serve any purpose. You now know all about them!"

In the evening, when the gnats danced about in the warm air, and the clouds were so beautifully tinged with red, the Nightingale came and sang to the Roses; it sang that the beautiful in this world was like sunshine, and that beauty lived for ever. But the Roses thought the Nightingale was singing of itself, and so might any one have thought. It never occurred to them that the song referred to them; but they were pleased, and meditated whether all the young Sparrows might not turn to nightingales.

"I understand perfectly well what the bird sang," the young Sparrows said; "there was only one word I could not make out. What is beauty?"

"That is nothing," their mother said. "It is only show. Down there, at the manor-house, where the Pigeons have a house of their own, and peas and barley are thrown into the yard for them every day—I have eaten with them, and so shall you some day (tell me with whom you associate, and I will tell you what you are)—well, down there, at the manor-house, they have two birds with green necks and tufts on their heads, and tails which they can spread out till they are like wheels, with so many colours that it makes one's eyes ache to look at them. They are called Peacocks, and they are beauty. They should be plucked a little, and then they would not be different from us. I would have plucked them, if they had not been so large!"

"I will pluck them!" the least of the Sparrows cried, and he had no feathers himself.

In the old house there lived two young people who loved each other very much; they were very industrious and neat, so it always looked nice in their room, and every Sunday morning the young woman came out, gathered a handful of the finest Roses, which she put into a tumbler and stood it on the chest of drawers.

"I can see that it is Sunday," the man said, kissing his dear little wife, and they then seated themselves and read a Psalm, the sun shining in at the window upon the fresh Roses and upon the young couple.

"This sight annoys me!" the Sparrow-mother said, looking straight out of the nest into the room, and she flew away.

She did the same the following Sunday, for, as usual, fresh Roses had been put in the tumbler; and the young Sparrows, being now fledged, wished to go with her; but their mother said, "You will stop here," and they did stay accordingly. She flew away; but it so happened that she was caught in a snare made of horse-hair, which some boys had fastened to a branch. The horse-hair cut into her leg as if it would cut it off. Oh, what pain it was! and the boys, who rushed forward, seized the bird, and squeezed the poor thing terribly! "It is only a Sparrow!" they said, but still did not let it go. They carried it home; and whenever it made a noise, it received a tap on the beak.

There was an old man who sold soap for shaving and for washing; soap in balls and in squares. He was a merry old pedlar, and when he met the boys coming along with the Sparrow, which they said they did not at all care about, he asked them, "Shall we make it beautiful?" The Sparrow shuddered as it heard the word; and the old man took some gold-foil out of his box, in which he had all manner of beautiful colours, and, the boys having got him an egg, he smeared the Sparrow over with the white of it, and laid the gold-foil on, so that the bird was now gilt; but the Sparrow trembled in all its limbs, not thinking of its splendour. The pedlar then tore a piece of red cloth out of the lining of his coat-collar, cut it into the shape of a cock's-comb and stuck it on to the Sparrow's head.

"Now you shall see the golden bird fly!" he said, letting the Sparrow go, which, in the most dreadful fright, flew off in the bright sunshine. How it did glitter! All the Sparrows, and even a Crow—not a young one either—were quite frightened at the apparition, but flew after it nevertheless, for they wanted to know what foreign bird that might be.

"Where from? Where do you come from?" the Crow cried.

"Wait a bit! wait a bit!" the Sparrow said; but she would not wait. Driven by fear, she flew towards home; but the number of birds in pursuit was constantly increasing, some trying to peck her, and all cried, "Look at this one! look at this one!"

"Look at this one! look at this one!" her children cried, when she reached the nest. "It is, no doubt, a young Peacock, for it has all the colours that dazzle the eyes, as mother said. Peep! that is beauty!" and they pecked at her with their little beaks so that she could not possibly slip into the nest, and she was so exhausted, that she could not cry "Peep!" much less, "I am your mother!" The other birds now pecked at her too, and tore her feathers out, till she fell, nearly dead, down into the Rose-tree.

"Poor thing!" the Roses said. "Come, we will hide you. Lean your little head upon us!"

The Sparrow-mother spread out her wings once more, then pressed them closely to her side again, and died amidst her neighbours, the beautiful fresh Roses.

"Peep!" the young Sparrows cried in their nest. "I wonder why mother does not come home? I cannot understand it. Can it be that she is playing us this trick to oblige us to provide for ourselves? She has left us the house as an inheritance, but who is to be the sole possessor when we have families?"

"I cannot keep you here, when I have a wife and family!" the smallest of them said.

"I shall have more wives and children than you!" another broke in.

"But I am the eldest!" a third cried. They now began to quarrel and fight, and plump, one after another was pushed out of the nest. There they lay as angry as possible, with their heads turned on one side and with sparkling eyes, which were turned up towards the nest. That was their way of sulking.

They could fly a little, and it was settled between them that, in order to know each other, when they should meet later in the world, they should cry, "Peep!" and scratch three times with the left foot.

The little one that had remained in the nest made himself as big as possible, for he was now a house-proprietor; but that did not last long. In the night flames burst from the windows and from under the roof, the dry thatch soon caught, the whole house was speedily burnt, and the little Sparrow with it, but the young people escaped uninjured.

The next morning, when the sun had risen, and the whole of nature seemed refreshed, as after a soft night's rest, there remained nothing of the old house but a few black beams, which leant against the chimney, now its own master. A thick smoke still rose from the ruins, but before them stood the Rose-tree, quite fresh and blooming, every branch and every flower reflected in the calm water.

"How beautiful the Roses look, before that black, smoking ruin!" a man exclaimed, as he came in sight of them. "I must have that, for it is a charming little picture!" and the man took a small book and a pencil from his pocket and sketched the smoking ruin and the blooming Rose-tree, for he was an artist.

Later in the day, two of the Sparrows that had been born there flew past. "Where is the house?" they cried. "Where is the nest? Peep! all is burnt, and our strong brother has perished; that is all he gained by keeping the nest. The Roses have escaped well; there they are, their cheeks as red as ever; so it seems they do not fret about their neighbour's misfortune. I shall certainly not speak to them; and it is my opinion that it is very ugly here."

They then flew away.

Late in autumn there was a bright, sunshiny day, so warm that one might imagine it was the middle of summer, and in the yard behind a gentleman's house all was so dry and clean, and black, white, and red Pigeons were walking about, whilst the mothers said to their young ones, "Stand in groups, stand in groups!" for that was how they looked best.

"Who are the little brown creatures running about amongst us?" one of the Pigeons asked.

"They are Sparrows, poor little things! and as we have always borne the name of being good-natured, we will allow them to pick up what they can. They do not presume to speak to us; and just see how prettily they scratch with their feet!"

Yes, they scratched with their left foot, and that three times, at the same time saying, "Peep!" when they recognised each other, for they were three Sparrows from the burnt house.

"There is good feeding here!" the Sparrows said, and the Pigeons strutted about, holding up their heads and talking to themselves.

"Look at that pouter!" one said to another, "see how she gobbles down the peas! She gets too many, she gets the best! Kourre, kourre! Look at the ugly, greedy thing! Kourre, kourre!" All their eyes looked red and sparkled from sheer spite, and "Kourre, kourre, kourre!" sounded from all sides.

The Sparrows ate well, and when they were satisfied went away from the Pigeons, speaking pretty freely about them amongst themselves, and then hopped through the gate into the garden; and as the door of the summer-house happened to be open, one hopped up to the threshold, for, being well fed, he was valiant.

"Peep!" he said, "I'll venture so far!" "Peep!" said the second, "I'll venture as far, and further, too!" and he hopped into the room. There was no one in the room, which the third, no doubt, saw, and he therefore flew in further than the other, saying, "All or nothing! and a most strange place it is! What have we here?"

Immediately before the Sparrows was the Rose-tree in full blossom, reflected in the water, and the black beams were leaning against the chimney; but how did all this get into the room of a gentleman's house? All three Sparrows thought of flying over the Rose-tree and the chimney, but only knocked their heads against the flat wall, for it was a large beautiful painting the artist had done from his little sketch.

"Peep!" the Sparrows cried, "that is only a deception! Peep! that is beauty! Can you understand it, for I cannot?" And they flew away, for people came into the room.

Years passed by, the Pigeons went on much as usual, and the Sparrows, after freezing in winter, enjoyed themselves in summer. They were all engaged or married, or what one chooses to call it. They had children, and, of course, each thought its own the prettiest and cleverest. One flew this way, the other that way, and if they met in the world they knew each other by the "Peep!" and the scratching three times with the left foot. The eldest was an old maid, had neither child nor nest, but had a great longing to see a large town, and therefore she flew to Copenhagen.

There stood a large house close to the palace and the water, where there were ships laden with apples and with earthenware. The windows were wider at the bottom than at the top, and when the Sparrows looked through, it appeared to them exactly as if they were looking into a tulip, for they saw all imaginable colours and curved lines. In the middle of the tulip were white figures, some of marble and some of plaster, but to the eyes of a Sparrow there was no difference between them. On the top of the house was a metal car with metal horses, driven by Victory, also of metal. This was Thorwaldsen's Museum.

"How dazzling it is!" the old Sparrow-maiden said; "surely that is beauty. Peep! that is larger than a peacock!" She thought of her youth, and of what her mother had considered beauty, and she flew down into the yard, where it was beautiful too. There were palm-trees and plants of different sorts painted on the walls, and in the middle of the yard stood a large Rose-tree, which spread out its branches full of roses over a grave, and thither she flew, for there she saw other Sparrows. "Peep!" she cried, and gave three scratches with her left leg, which salute she had frequently tried, but very seldom was it understood, for those who are once separated in this world do not meet every day. This greeting had become a habit with her, and just this day there were two old Sparrows and one young one who answered with a "Peep!" and three scratches.

"Well met; how do you do? how do you do?" These were three

of the old Sparrows from the swallow's nest, with one young one of the family. "So we meet at last," they said. "This is a grand place, but there is not much to eat. This, no doubt, is beauty! Peep!"

Then several people came from the different rooms of the building, where the beautiful marble statues stood, and went to the grave which contained the great master, the sculptor of the figures, and with beaming countenances they stood round Thorwaldsen's grave, some of them taking as a remembrance the Rose-leaves that had fallen. There were people from distant countries, from England the great, from Germany, and from France; and the handsomest of the ladies plucked one of the roses, which she stuck in her bosom. Seeing this, the Sparrows thought that the Roses ruled here, and that the whole house was built for them, which certainly seemed paying them too much respect; but as all the people showed much love for the Roses, they would not be behind-hand. "Peep!" they said, and swept the ground with their tails, fixing one eye upon the Roses, when they were convinced that they were indeed their old neighbours; and so they were. The artist who sketched the Rose-tree by the side of the burnt-down house had, towards the end of the year, got permission to dig up the tree, and had given it to the architect, for there were no more beautiful roses to be found; and he had planted it on Thorwaldsen's grave, where the flowers bloomed an emblem of beauty, and their sweet-scented leaves were carried to distant countries in remembrance of him who lay beneath them.

"Have you got an appointment here in the city?" the Sparrows asked, and the Roses nodded; they recognised their little brown neighbours, and were glad to see them again.

"How delightful it is to live and to blossom, to see old friends, and to be daily surrounded by friendly faces! It is here exactly as if every day were a fête-day."

"Peep!" the Sparrows said; "those are undoubtedly our old neighbours; we remember well how they stood by the village-pond. Peep! what honours they have come to! The same happens to some in their sleep. But what is to be seen in such a red lump is more than I can understand."

The Rose-tree, however, stood there green and fresh on Thorwaldsen's grave, joining its beauty to his immortal name!

THE OLD STREET-LAMP

HAVE you heard the story of the old Street-lamp? It is nothing so wonderfully amusing, but it will very well bear to be heard once. It was a good old Lamp, which had served for many, many years, but was about to be replaced by a new one. The last night had come that it was to sit on its post and give light in the street, and it felt exactly like an old ballet-dancer, who dances for the last time, knowing that on the morrow she will be forgotten.

The Lamp had great fear of the following day, as it knew that it would then be carried for the first time to the Town-hall, there to be judged by the honourable council, whether fit for further service or not. Then would be settled whether it was to be sent to one of the bridges, to give light there, or to a manufactory in the country, or perhaps an iron foundry. True, there was no knowing what might not be made of it there, but it grieved that it did not know whether it would then retain consciousness that it had been a Street-lamp. Whatever might happen, it would anyhow be separated from the lamplighter and his wife, whom it looked upon as its family. It had become a Lamp when he was appointed lighter. His wife was then young and pretty, and only at night, when she passed the Lamp, did she look at it, but never in the daytime; but now that all three, the lamplighter, his wife, and the Lamp, had grown old, she would occasionally trim it. They were a thoroughly honest couple, and had never cheated the Lamp out of one drop of oil. This was the last night, and on the following day it was to go to the Town-hall.

These were two sombre thoughts, so one can imagine how the Lamp burned. But other thoughts occupied it as well: it had seen so much, and had diffused so much light, perhaps as much as the "honourable town-council" itself; but that it did not say, for it was a worthy old Lamp, and would not hurt any one's feelings, more particularly those of its masters. So many recollections crowded upon it, and the flame burned up as an inward feeling said, "I shall be remembered too. There was that handsome young man—well, that is a good many years ago—he came with a letter written on such pretty pink, gilt-edged paper; it was a lady's handwriting. He read it twice, kissed it, and, looking up to me, said, 'I am the happiest of men!' Only he and I knew what his love's first letter contained. I remember two other eyes as well. It is extraordinary how thoughts can travel. There was a splendid funeral procession here in the street; a young and beautiful woman lay in her coffin, covered with rich velvet and strewed over with wreaths and flowers. The whole street was filled with people, and there were so many torches burning that I was quite eclipsed, but when the procession had passed and the torches disappeared, I saw a man who stood here at my post crying—oh, I shall never forget his sorrowing look!"

Thoughts crowded one upon another on the old Street-lamp this last night of its duty. The sentinel who is relieved knows who follows, and can exchange a word with him, but the Lamp did not know its successor; when, too, there was many a hint it could have given about the rain and snow, of how far the moon shone into the street, and which way the wind mostly blew.

Close by stood three candidates for the office about to become vacant, for they thought the appointment was in the gift of the Lamp. One of these was a herring's head, for that shines in the dark, and it pleaded the saving of oil there would be if it were placed on the lamp-post. The second was a piece of rotten wood, which also gives out light, and more, as it itself said, than a fish's head; besides which, it was the last piece of a once mighty tree in the forest. The third was a glow-worm: the Lamp could not imagine where it came from; however, there the worm was, and gave light too, but the rotten wood and the herring's head asserted that it only shone at certain times, and could not, therefore, be taken into consideration.

The old Lamp said that neither of them gave light enough, which, however, they would not believe; and when they heard that the appointment was not in the gift of the Lamp, they said that was very fortunate, as it was evidently too old and feeble to be able to choose at all.

Just then the Wind came round the corner of the street, and, blowing down the old Lamp's chimney, said, "What is this I hear—that you go to-morrow? Is this really the last night that I shall find you here? If that is the case, I must make you a present. I will brighten your understanding, so that you shall not only clearly and distinctly recollect what you have seen and heard, but, when anything is said or read in your presence, you shall actually see as well as hear it."

"My best thanks," the Lamp said, "for your great kindness. If only I am not melted down."

"That will not happen yet," the Wind said; "but now I must sharpen your memory, and if you receive many more such presents, yours will be a pleasant old age."

"But I hope I shall not be melted down; or can you perhaps then, too, secure me my memory?" the Lamp asked.

"Old Lamp," the Wind answered, "be reasonable"; and as the Moon just then appeared, it continued, "And what will you give?"

"I shall not give anything," the Moon answered. "I am on the decrease; and, besides, the lamps have never helped me to give light, but I have helped them." The Moon then disappeared behind a cloud again, so that it might not be asked any more. Then a Drop of Water fell upon the Lamp's chimney, as if it had come from the roof, but it said it came straight from the grey clouds as a present, and perhaps the best of all. "I will penetrate through you, so that you will have the power, whenever you wish it, to turn into rust in one night, and crumble into dust." But the Lamp thought that a bad present, and so thought the Wind too. "Is there nothing better? is there nothing better?" he blew as loud as he could, and just then a Star fell, leaving a long streak of light behind it.

"What was that?" the Herring's head exclaimed; "did not a Star fall? and I think it went straight into the Lamp. Well, if the office is sought by such high people we may retire!" which it did, and the others as well; but the old Lamp gave a brighter light than ever. "That was a splendid gift!" it said. "The bright Stars, which have always been my delight, and which shine so brightly that I have never been able to equal them, though it has been my constant aim, have honoured me by sending me a present, which consists in the power of making those whom I love see all that I see and remember. That is a delightful present! for there is only half pleasure in that which cannot be shared with others."

"That sentiment does you honour!" the Wind said, "but you do not know that a wax-candle is necessary to render the gift of any use; for unless a wax-candle is burning in you, no one will be able to see anything. The Stars did not think of that, for they imagine that everything that shines has, at least, one wax-candle within it. But now I am tired, so I will rest a little."

The next day—well, the next day we will pass over—but the next night the Lamp lay in the arm-chair; and where?—at the old lamplighter's. As a reward for his long and faithful services he had begged to be allowed to keep the old Lamp. The honourable council had laughed at him, but had given him the Lamp, and now it lay in an arm-chair by the side of the warm stove. The old couple were sitting at their supper, and would gladly have made room at the table for the old Lamp, at which they cast friendly glances.

They lived in a cellar, it is true, two yards underground, but it was warm there, for they had the doors well listed; it was clean and neat in their room, with curtains round the bed and at the small window, where, on the high window-ledge, stood two most peculiar flower-pots. The sailor, Christian, had brought them home with him from the East or West Indies; they were two elephants of earthenware with hollow backs, filled up with mould, and out of the one grew the finest garlic, that being the old people's kitchen-garden; whilst out of the other, which was their flower-garden, grew a beautiful geranium.

On the wall hung a large coloured print of the Congress of Vienna; so they had at once all the emperors and kings. A wooden clock, with its heavy leaden weights, went "Tick! tick!" and always too fast; but that was better, the old couple thought, than going too slow.

They were eating their supper, and the old Lamp lay, as already stated, in the arm-chair, close by the side of the warm stove. It appeared to the Lamp as if the whole world were turned upside down, but when the lamplighter looked at it and spoke of all that they had experienced together, in rain and snow, in the short summer nights, and in the cold nights of winter, when it was a treat to get back into his cellar, then all seemed restored to proper order, and it was as if the past were present again. The Wind had, indeed, refreshed its memory.

The old couple were so active and industrious, not a single hour was entirely dreamed away. On Sunday afternoons one book or another was brought forth, generally a book of travels, and the old man read out loud about Africa, of the vast forests, and the elephants which ran about wild, when the old woman would give a side-glance at the earthenware elephants, which were flower-pots. "I can almost imagine it all," she said; and then the Lamp wished most anxiously that it had a lighted wax-candle inside, so that the old woman might see all as clearly as they did—the lofty trees with the closely-intertwined branches, the naked men on horseback, and whole herds of elephants crushing the reeds and bushes beneath their broad feet.

"Of what use are all my capabilities without a wax-candle?" the

Lamp sighed; "they have only oil and tallow-candles, which are of no use."

One day the old man brought a whole quantity of wax-candle ends into the cellar, the largest pieces of which were burned, and the smaller were used by the old woman to wax her thread when she sewed. Now there were wax-candles, but it never entered their heads to put a piece in the Lamp.

"Here I stand with my extraordinary talents," the Lamp said. "I have so much within me, but cannot share it with them. They do not know that I can change the white walls into the most beautiful tapestry, into dark forests, or anything that they could wish to see. Oh, they do not know it!"

The Lamp stood, well scoured, in a corner, where it could not fail to be seen, for though every one said it was only an old piece of lumber, the old people did not care, as they loved it.

One day—it was the old man's birthday—the old woman went up to the Lamp, and smilingly said, "There shall be an illumination for him"; and the old Lamp trembled with delight, for it thought, "They shall see what they little expect!" but only oil was put in; and though it burned the whole evening, the old Lamp was now convinced that the gift of the Stars would remain a useless treasure for this life. Then it dreamed—and with such talents any one might dream—that it was taken to a foundry, in order to be melted down, and it was as much frightened as when about to be judged by the town council; but, although it had the power of turning itself into rust and dust, yet it did not do so, but was melted down; and a beautiful candlestick was made of it, in which a wax-candle was stuck. It was cast in the form of an angel, carrying a large nosegay, in the middle of which the candle was put; and the candlestick was placed upon a green writing-table in a poet's study. The room was so comfortable; there were many books and beautiful pictures, and all that the poet thought and wrote curled up the walls like smoke, and the room was turned into vast, gloomy forests, into smiling meadows, where the stork strutted about, and into the deck of a vessel on the swelling sea.

"What talents I have!" the old Lamp said, when it awoke; "I could almost wish to be melted down;—but, no, that must not be as long as the old people live. They love me, for my own sake; I am as a child to them, and they have scoured me, and given me oil. I am as well off as the 'Congress,' and that is something very grand!"

From that time the old Lamp enjoyed greater peace of mind, and that it deserved—the honest old thing!

THE RED SHOES

THERE was once a little girl who was very pretty, but in summer she had to go bare-footed, for she was poor, and in winter she wore heavy wooden shoes, which made her little feet so red that it was dreadful to see them.

In the middle of the village, the old shoemaker's wife sat sewing, as well as she could, at a pair of small shoes, made out of pieces of old red cloth; they were very clumsy, but it was well meant, for they were intended for the little girl. The little girl's name was Karen.

On the very day that her mother was buried she received the red shoes and wore them for the first time, though they were certainly not suited for mourning; but she had no others, and in them, without stockings, she followed the miserable coffin.

Just then came a large, old carriage, and in it sat a fat old lady, who, having looked at the little girl, felt pity for her, and said to the clergyman, "Give me that little girl, and I will adopt her."

Karen thought that certainly the red shoes were the cause of this, but the old lady thought them hideous, and they were burned. Karen was clothed neatly and cleanly, and people said she was pretty, but the looking-glass said, "You are more than pretty, you are beautiful!"

The Queen then passed through the land, having her little daughter with her, who was a Princess, and the people crowded to the palace, and Karen with them, where the little Princess, in fine white clothes, stood on a balcony and let herself be stared at. She had neither train nor crown, but wore magnificent red satin shoes, which were much more beautiful than those the old shoemaker's wife had made for Karen. Certainly nothing in the world could be compared with those red shoes.

Karen had now grown old enough to be confirmed, for which occasion she had new clothes, and was to have new shoes too. The rich shoemaker in the town took her measure, and that was in his own shop, where there were glass cupboards full of pretty shoes and shining boots. They looked very pretty, but the old lady could not see well, nor did she take much pleasure in looking at them. Now, amongst the shoes were a red pair, exactly like those the Princess had worn, and the shoemaker said, "They had been made for a Count's daughter, but did not fit her. They are very beautiful."

"I suppose those are patent leather, they are so shiny," the old lady said.

"Yes, they do shine," Karen answered, and as they fitted her they were bought, but the old lady knew nothing about their being red, for she would never have allowed Karen to be confirmed in red shoes, which, however, happened.

Every one looked at her feet, and as she walked across the church, it seemed to her as if even the old pictures of the bishops and the saints in the windows had their eyes fixed upon her shoes; and it was of these only she thought when the clergyman laid his hand upon her head. The organ was played so solemnly whilst the pretty voices of the children sang, and the old clergyman sang too, but Karen only thought of her red shoes.

In the afternoon the old lady learnt that the shoes were red, and she said that it was very wrong and unbecoming, and particularly told Karen that she should always wear black shoes when she went to church, even if they were old.

The next Sunday Karen was to take the sacrament, and she examined her black shoes: she looked at the red ones—and looked at them again, and put the red ones on.

It was a beautiful sunshiny day, and she and the old lady walked along the footpath across a cornfield, where it was rather dusty.

At the door of the church stood an old soldier with a crutch and a wonderfully long beard, which was more red than white, and he bowed down to the ground, asking the old lady whether he should wipe the dust off her shoes. Karen stretched out her little foot as well, and the old soldier said, "See, what beautiful dancing shoes! They will keep on when you dance," and he gave the sole a slap with his hand.

The old lady then gave the soldier some money and went into the church with Karen.

And all the people inside looked at Karen's red shoes, and all the pictures looked at them, and when she knelt to say her prayers, she could think only of her red shoes.

Now all the people left the church, and the old lady got into her carriage. Karen lifted up her foot to get in also, when the old soldier said, "See, what beautiful dancing shoes!" and Karen could not resist dancing a few steps; but, now she had begun, her feet continued to dance: it was exactly as if the shoes had power over them. She danced round the churchyard wall, and could not stop herself, so that the coachman had to run after her and lay hold of her, and he lifted her into the carriage, but her feet went on dancing so that she kicked the old lady, and her legs had no rest till the shoes were off.

When they got home the shoes were put into a cupboard, but she could not resist looking at them.

The old lady was now taken ill, and it was said she could not survive. She had to be watched and waited upon, and no one was more attentive than Karen, but there was a great ball in the town, to which Karen was invited; she looked at the old lady, who could not recover, and she looked at the red shoes, thinking there could be no sin in that; she then put them on; and in that there was no harm; but then she went to the ball and began to dance.

When she wanted to dance to the right, the shoes danced to the left, and when she wanted to dance up the room the shoes danced down, down the stairs, through the streets, and out at the city gates. She danced and could not help dancing, across the fields into the dark forest.

There was light between the trees, and she thought it was the moon, for there was a face, but it was the old soldier with the red beard, who nodded and said, "See, what beautiful dancing shoes!"

She was now frightened, and wished to throw off the red shoes, but they stuck fast. She tore off her stockings, but the shoes seemed to have grown to her feet, and she danced across the fields and meadows, in rain and sunshine, by day and by night, but at night it was the most dreadful.

She danced into the churchyard, but the dead there did not dance; they had something better to do; for her, however, there was no rest; and when she danced up to the open church-door, she saw an angel in white garments, with wings reaching from the shoulders down to the ground. His countenance was serious and severe, and in his hand he held a sword, which was broad and shining.

"Thou shalt dance," he said, "dance in thy red shoes till thou art pale and cold, till thou shrinkest away to a skeleton. Dance shalt thou from door to door, and where proud children dwell shalt thou knock, so that they may hear and fear thee. Thou shalt dance, dance——"

"Mercy!" Karen cried, but she did not hear the angel's answer, for the shoes carried her on, across the fields and roads, and incessantly she had to dance.

One morning she danced past a door which she knew well. From within sounded the singing of hymns, a coffin was carried out covered with flowers, and she then knew that the old lady was dead, and felt that she was forsaken by all and condemned by the angel of God.

She danced—could not help dancing. The shoes carried her through brambles and thorns, till the blood ran down her lacerated limbs, and she danced across the heath towards a little lonely house. She knew that the executioner lived there, and knocking at the window with her knuckle, she said—

"Come out!—come out!—I cannot come in, for I am obliged to dance!"

And the executioner said, "I suppose you do not know who I am? I cut wicked people's heads off, and I now hear my axe ring."

"Do not cut my head off," Karen said, "for then I could not repent of my sin, but cut off my feet with the red shoes."

She then confessed her whole sin, and the executioner cut off her feet with the red shoes, but the shoes danced with the little feet in them, across the fields far into the forest.

He made feet of wood for her, and a pair of crutches, teaching her the hymn which condemned criminals always sing, and she kissed the hand which had wielded the axe, and went her way across the heath.

"I have now suffered enough for the red shoes," she said, "and I will go into the church that the people may see me"; but when she got near the church the red shoes danced before her, and, frightened, she turned back.

The whole week she was sad, and shed many bitter tears, but when Sunday came she said, "Now, surely, I have striven and suffered enough, and I believe I am as good as many of those who sit in church and think so much of themselves. I will go there too." But she got no further than the churchyard, for there she saw the red shoes and was frightened, and, turning back, truly repented of her sins.

She then went to the clergyman's house, and begged that she might be taken into service, promising that she would be industrious and do all she could. Wages she did not care for, but only sought a roof to cover her, and to be with good people. The clergyman's wife had pity on her and took her into her service, and she was steady and industrious. She sat perfectly still and listened when of an evening the clergyman read the Bible out loud, and all the little ones were very fond of her, but when they spoke of dress, show, or beauty, she shook her head.

The following Sunday all went to church, and they asked her whether she would not go with them, but sadly, and with tears in her eyes, she looked towards her crutches, and then the others went there to hear the Word of God; but she went all alone to her little room, which was only large enough for her bed and one chair, and there she seated herself with her Prayer-book; and as she read in it with pious earnestness, the wind carried the sound of the organ across to her from the church, and raising her eyes filled with tears, she cried, "O Lord, have mercy upon me!"

The sun then shone in so brightly; and immediately before her stood the angel she had seen at the church-door, not holding, as then, a sharp sword, but a green branch covered with roses, and he touched the ceiling with it, which was immediately raised, a golden star glittering where he had touched it, and he touched the walls, which spread themselves out, and she saw the organ, the old windows of the saints and bishops, and the whole congregation singing out of their hymn-books, for the church had come to the poor girl into her little room, or she had been transported there. She sat among the rest of the congregation, who looked up when the hymn was ended, and nodding to her, said, "It was right of you to come, Karen."

"It is an act of grace," she said.

The notes of the organ vibrated through the church, and the voices of the children sounded so soft and beautiful. The clear, bright sunshine streamed in through the window upon Karen, and her heart was so filled with sunshine, peace, and joy, that it broke. Her soul took its flight up to heaven, and no one there asked after the red shoes.